THE BEAUTY OF THE DARKNESS

Recalling her determination to stop calling him creature or monster, Psyche said, "People have names, but you have never told me yours. I am ashamed not to have asked sooner."

"My name?" He hesitated, and then said slowly, as if he were trying to remember, "Teras. You are kind. But why not call me 'monster'? I will answer to it."

Psyche was appalled and said sharply, "Perhaps I do not wish to call you 'monster' because I do not wish to think of you as a monster any longer. You have been much kinder to me than I to you. I am beginning to think you were quite correct when you called *me* a monster. In the past few days, I have had more time than usual to think, and I have discovered some very unpleasant things about myself."

"No! You must not spend your time tearing your heart to shreds. There is nothing unpleasant about you."

The voice was that of a man who had torn his own heart to shreds and wished to spare anyone else that agony. Psyche did not even realize she had stretched out her hand. She had closed her eyes for a moment, as one does to shut out the sight of a face ravaged by pain. She felt her hand taken in a firm, warm grip. Her eyes shot open to see her body end at her shoulder. She must have gasped, because the hand let go and the darkness shrank back, but what remained with her was the feeling. She had not lost sensation, even where Teras had not touched her. She had felt her arm extended, the brush of her sleeve against her flesh as she moved. The darkness around Teras did not swallow her up any more than did the night.

Slowly Psyche put her hand out again. "May I touch your face?" she whispered.

FROM BESTSELLING AND AWARD-WINNING
AUTHOR ROBERTA GELLIS COMES A
STUNNING LOVE STORY FROM THE
LEGENDS OF TIME

Renowned for her classic romances, Roberta Gellis has
recreated the world from a long-ago era and told the
story of two exquisitely beautiful people. But the love
between Psyche and Eros is confronted with challenges
and powers that neither can control, and it is only their
enduring passion and trust which keep them together
through it all. *Rendezvous* called her last work, DAZ-
ZLING BRIGHTNESS, ". . . a scintillating master-
piece." SHIMMERING SPLENDOR is certain to
receive even more acclaim. . . .

NOW, READ ON FOR THE MYTHIC STORY
AND LEGENDARY LOVE OF PSYCHE AND
EROS . . .

Roberta Gellis

SHIMMERING SPLENDOR

PINNACLE BOOKS
KENSINGTON PUBLISHING CORP.

PINNACLE BOOKS are published by

Kensington Publishing Corp.
850 Third Avenue
New York, NY 10022

Copyright © 1995 by Roberta Gellis

The P logo Reg U.S. Pat. & TM Off. Pinnacle is a trademark of Kensington Publishing Corp.

First Printing: May, 1995

Printed in the United States of America

To Jennara, who gave me the clue that made the book work

CHAPTER 1

Aphrodite was frowning. The expression was so unusual that Eros stopped and stared at her. The cessation of movement drew her attention, and her eyes came into focus on the man with whom she had shared her home, but never her bed, for many years. She looked at him with a kind of affectionate indifference, despite the fact that his face and figure were of a beauty to stop a woman's—or a man's—heart.

Something in the arrested pose, the inquisitive cock of his head, made Aphrodite reassess her longtime companion and confidant. His hair was the color of honey, his brows and lashes a glossy chestnut. His mouth was soft and perfectly formed, the nose above it also perfect, the chin below strong enough to look firm without marring the lovely oval of the face. His walk was a pure, lithe grace as he came more directly toward her, the shoulders broad and muscular, the arms corded with muscle, too—as was natural for a master bowman—but subtly, smoothly, as if no sharp ridge could be allowed to mar the polished perfection of the whole.

His eyes should have been the best part of him. Large and almond shaped, with long, curling dark-chestnut lashes, they were a clear green, the kind that darkens almost to black with thought or sorrow and can become incandescent with joy and laughter. But Eros's eyes had shown no such changes for many years; they were flat as a painting, dull and empty. The spark that should have lit them from within had been quenched.

Even the dead eyes could not spoil the perfection of his face; they only managed to withdraw all life from it, leaving it a strangely animated marble mask—a marble mask that grew more and more quizzical, the brows rising, the lips parting to ask, "What is troubling you, Aphrodite?"

The voice almost made up for the dead eyes; it was rich and warm, soft now, but with a timbre that promised it could sound like a brazen horn across a battlefield. Involuntarily Aphrodite's frown deepened. No battlefields for Eros; even after these many years since Zeus had overthrown Kronos, the denizens of Olympus did not trust Eros. He was simply too beautiful—no, not only beautiful; she, too, was beautiful, but she did not affect others as Eros did. Some other quality, perhaps a Gift, coupled with the beauty so that one look and most—even the great mages—forgot their own purpose and desired only to please Eros.

Zeus had forced her to set a spell of revulsion on him, but Eros had his own strange power and over the years he had learned to tune that spell to his own desire and need. Aphrodite's own perfect lips tightened. She had made her contribution to the wary distaste Olympians felt for Eros. She had urged certain acts of mischief on him, and whether out of gratitude to her for giving him a home or delight—no, not delight; Eros seemed to delight in nothing—perhaps out of bitter satisfaction in generating trouble for those who would not accept him, he had performed that mischief.

The idea of doing mischief connected with Eros's question. "What troubles me?" Aphrodite repeated. "My temple has been desecrated, my priestess defiled."

One corner of Eros's mouth twitched. Considering the acts of worship performed in some of Aphrodite's temples—albeit she was called by other names in those temples—he found that statement amusing. Dear Aphrodite, she was again trying to drag him up out of the pit into which he had been sliding, he thought. But then he recalled that he had entered the inner courtyard because she had been frowning, and that was before she had seen him. So she had not assumed the expression to engage him in conversation, although she often pretended worry when he was feeling particularly . . . indifferent to life. The thought warmed him, reopened the little crack in the casing of ice that had been slowly thickening around him until all sensation was lost. Aphrodite had been kindness itself to him all these years.

"In what way defiled?" he asked, frowning in sympathy.

"Beaten! My high priestess has been beaten and the people forbidden to make sacrifice at my temple!"

"What! Why?" Eros's frown grew darker.

"Because Hyppodamia—you remember, do you not, that she is the high priestess in Iolkas?—would not accept into the temple the youngest daughter of the king."

"Was the girl *that* ugly?" Eros asked, amused again.

"Not at all. She is said to be the most beautiful woman in the world."

"You are the most beautiful woman in the world," Eros said, his voice flat and angry.

"Oh, don't be a fool, Eros," Aphrodite snapped. "I am what I am and I don't care a pin what the stupid slut looks like. You know Hyppodamia is a seer, truly Gifted, and she *Saw* that the girl was totally antithetical to the worship of love and beauty."

Eros blinked. "That is strange for a person of great

beauty. Usually all they worship is beauty, often only their own faces—or do you mean she did not wish to be confined in the temple, bereft of her normal due of adulation?"

Aphrodite burst out laughing. "Eros! There is no rule of celibacy in my temple, and a rich gift will readily bring permission to enjoy the company of a chosen priestess. In any case, I doubt Hyppodamia would have held firm against the king's order out of sympathy with a girl's unwillingness. And why should she be unwilling? She might have as many or more admirers and lovers as a temple priestess." Aphrodite frowned. "In fact, the daughter must have been willing. Hyppodamia said the girl was angry and disappointed also, but she could not accept her; she . . . she *hated* me."

"No one can hate you, Aphrodite," Eros soothed. "There are many who curse you for the pain they suffer—when it is not your fault at all—but they do not hate you."

"Perhaps, but that is not the point. If I do not do something about this stupid king Anerios, no one will think me powerful enough to worship. And that will mean no more offerings—no more bushels of grain, no more sweet legs of lamb, no more succulent ox rumps, no more tender doves, no more gold and jewels . . . I must go and punish him."

Eros nodded immediately but said, "I, not you. This Anerios sounds crazy enough to toss a spear at you." He smiled and shook a finger at her. "You remember what happened the last time you confronted someone of that type. You were so shocked that anyone could say no to you that you forgot to activate Hermes's spell and were wounded. If his aim had been better, that oaf could have killed you. And this one sounds another of the same kind. I will go."

Aphrodite sighed with relief. "Oh, thank you, Eros.

I am ashamed to ask you to run my errands all the time, as if you were a servant. You are not a servant. You are my friend." She looked up at him. "I think my only friend."

She put out a hand and Eros took it and kissed it. It was true enough. She was as cursed as he. Every man, and not a few women, who looked at Aphrodite desired her madly, too madly to have the balance necessary for friendship. Not that Aphrodite felt as he did about that. She enjoyed the passionate longing, sometimes satisfying it and sometimes laughing at it. There was a light-hearted, light-minded quality in her that could amount to cruelty—but not to him, never to him.

"You want this Anerios dead? And the girl also?"

"Oh, no!" Aphrodite exclaimed. "He must suffer! He must repent aloud and in public! He must kneel to Hyppodamia and beg her pardon and urge his people to pray and sacrifice to me. And he himself must perform some great and shocking sacrifice."

Eros smiled. Aphrodite might look as if she were barely nubile; her big, blue eyes might seem wide with innocence; her delicate features and body might imply gentleness—but none of this was true. She was as old as any of the other great mages of Olympus, about as innocent as a long-lived harlots' madam, and not at all gentle when she was angered.

"I agree," he said. "How did you wish to bring about this reformation?"

Aphrodite bit her lip gently. "About that I am less certain, but it must be owing to some reversal of love."

"Hatred? You want his people to hate him and deprive him of his kingdom?"

"No . . ." Aphrodite drew out the word. "I want to see him hop every time my priestess says 'toad.' And I want the people of Iolkas to know their king is subservient to the goddess Aphrodite." She dropped her head, looked at Eros under her long lashes, and smiled wickedly. "If he loses his kingdom, I will lose half the fun of his repentance."

Eros did not sigh, but he did feel a prick of envy. Why could he not be more like Aphrodite? She was as isolated as he, but she had no trouble laughing, and the light in her eyes testified to her true enjoyment of life. He could be amused, but the laughter was only in his head; it did not lighten his spirit.

"Love gone wrong, then," he said. "The desire of an unsuitable object, one that will make him ridiculous and disgusting in his own eyes as well as everyone else's."

"Perfect!" Aphrodite clapped her delicate white hands, then put the rose-tipped fingers together and propped her chin while she thought for a moment. "The daughter too," she said. "The most beautiful woman in the world, eh? Let her become enamored of the dog boy or the swineherd. You will have to find someone really repulsive, not someone who can be improved by better clothes and education."

"But how could I know that in one godlike visit? If we were truly gods, Aphrodite, I might be omniscient like the Mother, but I am not. I would have to stay at Anerios's court to discover—"

"Would you mind?" Aphrodite asked. "If you do not wish to be bothered, I can just smite them both with some loathsome disease or the whole kingdom with a plague. Artemis will sell me a spell."

"No. They might not connect that punishment with the crime. All that might happen is they will erect a temple to Apollo or Artemis and neglect yours—and I am not so sure of my ability to best Artemis or Apollo in any conflict, not to mention what would happen to me if Zeus heard I had tried. I do not mind going among the natives. One place is as good as another to me, but I cannot stay at court as Eros and I am afraid to ask any of the mages for a disguise. Any mage trading a spell to me would be in trouble with Zeus."

"Oh, Eros," Aphrodite cried, rising and taking his hand. "I did not know you wished for a disguise. Why did you never speak before?" She laughed aloud and squeezed his fingers. "I will get the illusion from Zeus himself, so he cannot blame anyone else. His illusions are best, too, and I will make sure it is not a one-time spell so you can reinvoke it, like the spell of revulsion, any time you wish."

He looked at her, smiled, thanked her, marveling that she could not understand that he had not the smallest inclination to live a worse lie than he lived now, able to live at all only because he carried a spell that made those who felt desire for him feel loathing instead when he invoked it. What satisfaction could it give him to walk among the native people with a false face? Everything about him was false already, like the lovely phosphorescent sheen that plays over the surface of something long dead and very putrid.

He said nothing, however. From the glint in her eyes, and the way the corners of Aphrodite's mouth had curved upward, he knew she was looking forward to obtaining the spell for him. Partly that was pleasure in giving him something she thought he wanted—poor Aphrodite, she seldom had that pleasure because he could no longer find joy, yet he could please her so easily; she took such delight in a trinket or even flowers. But even more, he knew, she was looking forward to wheedling the spell out of Zeus without telling him for what she wanted it. Zeus would enjoy that, too, so everyone would be happy—except Hera? No, Hera would not care, not about a brief tumble with Aphrodite.

She had already turned toward the house, bright-eyed and smiling with anticipation. He accompanied her through the large reception room that led to the antechamber and the outer portico and then, not knowing why but somehow eased by her lightness of heart, across the outer courtyard to the gate. He went no farther, watching her walk lightly up the path to the wide road paved with smooth slabs of stone fitted together so well that no mud ever seeped up through the cracks to soil a mage's elegant shoes.

Now a border of trees and grass lined the road, broken by small paths like the one where he stood that led to Aphrodite's gate. Eros remembered the road when it had been raw, when Kronos had forced slaves, captured natives and nonhumans, to drag and fit the stones. He shuddered and turned away, not from the memory of the brutalized slaves so much as from his memory of his own past.

Once inside the house, however, he could not remember what he had intended to do when he had left his apartment. After looking about the antechamber, hoping vainly for memory of some purpose, he returned to his bedchamber and lay down on the bed, staring blindly at the exquisitely painted ceiling. Slowly the tightness in his chest eased. He had no idea who had painted the ceilings and walls of Aphrodite's house, but the gay, lightly amorous scenes had not the faintest taint of suffering about them. Eros smiled as his eyes closed. Aphrodite had no doubt paid the painter well, and doubtless every payment had inspired him to greater efforts.

Eros woke from the light doze in which he had been lying to an insistent scratching on his door. "Come," he called, sitting up and gesturing at the wall, where a lamp immediately glowed into life.

One of the young children who served as Aphrodite's pages, a little boy not more than six or seven, hop-skipped in. They were a merry lot, coddled and kissed, with few and light duties. Still, Eros had heard Aphrodite blamed for stealing children or demanding them as sacrifice. Perhaps those who criticized her believed she had their own perverted tastes, but the children came to no harm—they would have better lives as well-trained servants to the mages of Olympus than their parents had had—and to him and Aphrodite they were a dire necessity.

Too young to be affected by either Aphrodite's or his own appearance, the children served as an effective buffer between them and the adult servants who did the real work of the household. The little ones carried ver-bal messages when the orders were simple, message spells when they were more complicated, and stood guard at doors to warn adult servants away from cham-bers occupied by those whose appearance could wring their hearts or drive them to foolish actions. By the age of ten, the children were dismissed from their duties and taught the arts of real service. Then they were placed with a mage Aphrodite trusted and approved, who paid Aphrodite handsomely for such perfect, polished help, and treasured them as they deserved.

"Lady Aphrodite is home," the child piped. "She says for you to come to her—if you wish, of course."

Eros smiled and rose. "Run ahead and tell her I am coming, that I only want to wash the sleep from my face."

In all the years, from the first day she had given him living space in her home, stinking as he did of the revulsion spell, angry and bitter, she had never given an order or made a demand. Everything was "if you wish," and, incredible as it had been to him at first, when he said "no," she had accepted it. Now, of course, he never said "no," even when he knew he should. He did not really mind if the other mages disliked and distrusted him, and even he was brought to laughter at some of their antics when he had hit them with one of her love spells.

Those memories were so amusing that he arrived smiling, and Aphrodite jumped to her feet, crying, "You are pleased! Dear Eros, I have the most complete disguise. It is a man in his mid twenties, black hair, brown eyes, a short beard—oh, how silly I am. Let me give you the spell and you can invoke it and see for yourself."

On the words, she put her hands to her mouth. Between her lips a silvery globe began to form. Fed from some source deeper in her body, the globe brightened and condensed, until a blindingly brilliant ball dropped from her mouth to her hands.

"I see how you received the spell."

Eros chuckled as he held out his hands to take the glowing object. Aphrodite and Zeus must have been playing very naughty games. She did not reply, but her eyes had a slight glaze and her perfect lips were just a trifle rosier, a trifle fuller, than usual. In fact, she had the sated look of a cat that had gorged on sweetened cream and was just ready to curl up and sleep.

"Must I absorb it the same way?" he asked, still smiling.

"No, of course not," Aphrodite replied with a slight frown.

She found any implication of sexuality connected with Eros, even at second hand, somewhat distasteful. An anxious glance convinced her that he had only been teasing, knowing her reaction. She smiled as she watched him close his hands around the ball of light, close them tighter, tighter, until the palms were clasped flat against each other. He rubbed the palms together, once, twice, raised his hands to his eyes to peer into the darkened area between the palms. When he opened his hands, the light was gone.

"To invoke it," Aphrodite said eagerly, "you must choose a name and simply say, *'Epikaloumai* whoever.' Each time you say the name while you are in the disguise, you will reinvoke and reinforce the illusion. However, when you are out of the illusion, you must use *'Epikaloumai'* to reinvoke it."

"Thank you."

Eros tried to put pleasure and gratitude into the words and thought he had succeeded this time because Aphrodite's smile did not dim. He was, in fact, grateful that the spell was so easy to invoke. Some required such elaborate voicings that they were hardly worth the trouble. Some mages, Eros suspected, did it for pure spite; others because the spell was dangerous, and recalling the voicings—because if one didn't get them right the spell was likely to backlash—gave the user time to think. In addition, the idea of doing something, even visiting an unpleasant fate on someone, had its charms, particularly when the someone so eminently deserved that fate.

"I got a translocation spell from Hermes too," Aphrodite added.

"My, you had a busy day," Eros said, grinning.

Aphrodite giggled. "Oh, Hermes is a lovely boy." Then she frowned. "But I'm not sure you'll want to use this one. It takes a lot of power, and it will place you almost a full day's walk from the palace in Iolkas. The only place Hermes knew was the top of Mount Pelion, and you know he cannot cast a spell for a place unless he has seen it himself or can take an image from a scryer. You wouldn't want to appear in the middle of the palace or the town square, which are the only places beside the temple my scryer has seen. But I can take you to the temple with my own spell."

"I have never lacked for power," Eros said slowly.

"But there are the love spells for father and daughter, also," she said, looking doubtful. "Can you manage all?"

"I believe so."

Eros looked away as he spoke, as if he were thinking about Aphrodite's question, but he really only wished to hide the bitterness he felt. He knew he could have been a mage, perhaps even one of the great mages, but no one would ever teach him. He had asked more than once, before Kronos had fallen and he had become a scarcely tolerated resident, not citizen, of Olympus. Even then, however welcome his beauty and his body, he had been driven away as soon as he'd made his request. His beauty was dangerous enough, he had been told; that beauty combined with knowledge would be a major catastrophe poised on a knife-edge.

"In any case," he continued, "I will not need to cast all three spells at one time. I will have several days' rest between arriving on Mount Pelion and deciding how best to punish Anerios and his daughter."

"You prefer to go to Pelion?" Aphrodite asked.

"Oh, yes," Eros assured her. "You know the stir your coming will make at the temple. There would be no way to hide the fact that you had brought me. My presence at the court so soon afterward, even in disguise, might be associated with your arrival—I do not imagine the illusion will change my size; Zeus knows quite well that it would look too strange if, for example, a man the height of a native stooped to pass a doorway. No, it will be better if I walk in from Mount Pelion. Then I will be properly travel-stained and can say I come from . . ."

"Where? And what name will you choose?"

"The name . . . Atomos. The natives will not know that means 'a person' in the old language. And Atomos will come from . . . from far Macedon, from Pella, or, no, from Cellae, I think. King Anerios will not know Cellae, and I can be the king's son."

"But why would a Macedonian travel to Iolkas?"

Eros laughed. "Why, to pay court to the most beautiful woman in the world. Why else?"

CHAPTER 2

CHAPTER 2

Translocation spells, Eros thought, lying back on the dry grass in a hollow not far from the huge, flat-topped boulder the natives used as an altar, really did take a lot of power. He was not dangerously depleted, but the fact that he had noticed the drain was significant. He felt a little, rather pleasantly, tired—physically tired, not the weariness of boredom and emptiness that more and more made him sleep away both days and nights.

The air was different here, much cooler than the sheltered valley of Olympus, and the scents that came to his nostrils were sharper, tinged with resin from the pines, an earthy smell of decaying leaves, and a faint acridity from crushed weeds in the hollow where he lay. Aphrodite's house smelled of flowers, always flowers, even in winter.

Lazily he put out a hand to check that everything had arrived safely with him. His cloak was under his head, the travel pack propping it comfortably pillow-high. His bow and quiver were right under his right hand, where he had released his grip on them when he lay down. His sword was strapped around his waist; he could feel the hilt digging into his ribs because the belt had ridden up when he'd slid into a more comfortable position. The pouch of metal bits—gold, silver, and copper, lay on his abdomen. By his left hand was the small clay pot of ashes which contained several coals.

Eros smiled into the dark. He had remembered to put on old hunting clothes but had packed flint and steel in his pouch before realizing his carelessness, removing them, and preparing the firepot. Anerios might have some firemaking tool, but not steel—that was Hephaestus's art, and Hades's, of course. But somehow one did not think of homely things like a firemaking steel in connection with Hades, only miracles like the full-length mirror he had brought Aphrodite after she had reconciled Demeter to the loss of her daughter.

Actually, it was no longer truly dark as it had been when he arrived. Eros lifted a hand out of the shadow of the altar stone and a heavy ring on his middle finger glinted in the pale silvery light from a bright three-quarter moon that had risen. He dropped the hand listlessly. Aphrodite had objected to his leaving that night, saying anxiously there was no need for him to go in the dark, that he could wait a day or even two. He could not tell her the truth—how eager he was to be away. He could not hurt her by admitting that even her kindness was losing its ability to create a vital spark in him, that their idle talk and confidences, no matter how pleasant, had long been insufficient to engage his mind and spirit. He had pointed out instead that Anerios's punishment should follow his crime swiftly and that the day or two would be better spent deciding what that punishment should be. Aphrodite never seemed to understand that he needed something to do, and in Olympus, even hunting for food was unnecessary.

The thought of food surprised him, but his stomach growled in response and he laughed suddenly. Idiot that he was, he had forgotten that he had slept through dinner—not that he had missed it; he had had no appetite for it then. Now, of course, he was hungry as a newly awakened bear. He cocked his head as the word came to mind. Yes, there was a distant rustling in the brush beyond the clearing, and only a bear—or a man—would make so much noise. Bears were indifferent to noise because they did not hunt and were not instinctively careful of alarming wary prey, and men, most of them, were simply too clumsy to be silent.

Eros rose smoothly to one knee, simultaneously moving closer to the altar stone. As he moved he caught up his bow with his right hand and swung the strap of his quiver over his head with his left so the arrows were in easy reach of his hand near his hip. He knelt quietly in the shadow of the boulder, watching. No man, unless he actually approached the altar, would notice him, and probably a bear would ignore him if he offered no threat. Had he been in Olympus, he would have challenged the beast and slain it. Dangerous animals were not permitted near the valley, although some still roamed the mountainsides around it. But here it would be a waste. His stomach growled softly again, and Eros grinned and admonished it. To kill a whole bear for one steak—

On the thought, the crashing increased and the animal roared. Eros cursed softly. He knew he was downwind, but he had not had time to change his position after he became aware of the creature and in any case, he had not thought it necessary. Ordinarily a bear regarded the scent of a human as something to avoid.

The bear burst into the clearing, surprising Eros by blundering into a tree on its left and twisting to slash at it before it came fully out into the moonlight and reared upright. Eros's eyes widened. It was huge, the largest bear he had ever seen. Then he also saw the gleam of moonlight on the pale fur of the muzzle, on patches and streaks around the creature's head that marked old scars, the ragged ears. It was old. Still Eros did not move. Let it live out its life; there were berries and nuts enough so it would not starve and it would probably die peacefully enough during its winter sleep.

Then it swung its head and Eros rose from his crouch, an arrow already fitted to his bow. The whole side of the head was a pale glistening. Something had torn away skin and eye and the wound was corrupted. Perhaps it was testing the air, but it was blind on the side turned to Eros and he had time to loose his arrow. Just as it struck, the bear roared again, coming down on all fours to charge. Eros knew he had missed any vital spot. A second arrow took it in the throat, and it stumbled but came on, shaking its head in pain or fury. The third arrow tore out the beast's good eye but did not penetrate the head. The bear screamed, drowning out Eros's obscenity as he laid a hand on the altar stone and leapt atop it.

The sound of movement was enough. The beast's head swung. Eros had to decide in that split second whether to loose a fourth arrow or draw his sword. He chose the arrow, letting fly into the mass of corruption where he thought the eye socket might have been. Then, having no choice, he leapt backward off the stone, stumbling and dropping his bow in the effort to find his balance and draw his sword. The bear had plunged straight forward, however, right into the altar stone. Half atop it, it scrabbled weakly toward Eros and then stilled.

Eros stood, breathing hard, heart pounding, sword half bared. Then the bear started to slip off the stone, and Eros slammed his sword back into its scabbard and leapt forward to grasp the beast's forearm. Muscles cracking, he dragged it toward him, fully atop the altar. When he had caught his breath, he looked up, smiling slightly.

"That is a rather unwieldy sacrifice, Mother, and I do

not worship Your aspects that demand blood. Forgive me if I use this place merely as a skinning table."

Having said it, Eros drew his knife, looked at the bear, looked back at the knife, and shook his head. No one man, not even Heracles, was going to skin that bear—at least, not in a few hours. And what would he do with the carcass and the skin when he was done? Skinless, the carcass would attract more flies and carrion eaters than the complete corpse, and that would be a sad waste of meat. He licked his lips, suppressed the thought of a sizzling bear steak, and decided he needed help.

A moment's search uncovered his bow. Another few moments and he had settled his cloak around him, his pack on his back, and his firepot into the heavy leather pouch designed to carry it. A quick circuit of the clearing showed one well-worn track, no doubt used by the people who came here to make sacrifice. Eros frowned. Had not the bear come into the clearing just about in this same spot? If it stayed near a track men used—reasonably often, from the look of it—could the bear, because it was old, have preyed on the men, perhaps frightening them from their supplies so it could eat? If so, killing it might make him welcome to Anerios.

He put the idea in the back of his mind to be drawn forth if needed and looked at the track. Although it was bright enough at the edge of the clearing, the moonlight was blocked by a screen of well-leafed trees and did not penetrate far. Muttering what he thought of himself for forgetting to bring a torch, Eros set about finding a suitable stick of green wood with a thick knobbed end and pine trees with oozing galls from which he could scrape the resin to coat the branch. By the time he was ready to light a small grass fire with a coal from his firepot, the moon had reached its zenith and was starting down.

A moment later the torch was aflame, the little grass fire stamped out, and Eros was on his way. The rough-made torch spat and sputtered, flaring and coming near dying. It was soon apparent, owing to the path twisting and turning to avoid steep slopes and places where parts of the mountain had given way, that it would never last long enough for him to escape the wooded area. He grunted with discontent when he thought of the time it would cost to make another torch or to feel his way down the dangerous track like a blind man. Fortunately, neither was necessary. About halfway down, a tiny valley had been carved by a stream. The moonlight showed a small orchard, some narrow fields, and several houses.

"Epikaloumai Atomos," Eros muttered. He hesitated while a feeling like itching or even a mild pain passed over his skin and then went toward the nearest house to pound on the door.

He was surprised at the size of the building, even more surprised when a voice answered his first knock, crying, "Wait, wait. I am coming."

"You are very late," the voice continued, as the door opened wide, exposing an old man clutching a dim lamp in one hand and holding around him with the other a worn and patched blanket. "Come in, come in," he muttered, not lifting his head to look at Eros. "Your supper will be overdone, but I could do no more than set it by the fire to wait for you."

"I am afraid you have mistaken me for someone else," Eros said. "Not that I would not welcome a cooked supper, no matter how overdone, but you could not have known *I* was coming. I did not know it myself. I was camped by the altar at the top of Pelion and I was attacked by a bear."

The old man had lifted his head as soon as Eros spoke, and he gaped stupidly until he heard the last words. Then he looked nervously toward the road and said, "You escaped him. Thanks be to Hermes the swift. Come in, quickly. You will be safe here. The buildings are too strong even for him, and he has not been back since he clawed Georg to death before we could drive him off. That was more than a week ago."

"He will not follow me," Eros said. "I killed him. I hope he was not sacred, but something, maybe a younger animal, tore the skin from his head and it was rotting."

For a moment the old man gaped again. Then he swallowed. "Sacred? No! A plague, rather. How did you kill him? How? I cannot tell you how many hunting parties have tried."

Eros shrugged. "Perhaps he was sick from the corruption, and I am a strong archer. The body is atop the altar on Pelion. I came for help. It seemed a shame to waste so much meat and the hide also, but I could not carry so much."

"Arktos is dead!" The old man uttered a rusty chuckle. "That is good news. Come in. Eat if you are hungry. I will rouse the men and they will go back with you."

"Thank you."

Eros dropped his torch to the ground and stepped on the head, quenching the sputtering flame. The old man preceded him into the large chamber, leading the way toward the central hearth and stopping to light two more oil lamps hung from tall metal tripods. The light they gave was sufficient for Eros to make out a small loaf of bread sheltered behind two covered pots on the edge of the raised stone hearth around which were several benches. He nodded and the old man turned away and hurried back the way he had come. Eros used the edge of his cloak to lift the pots onto one end of a bench and remove their lids.

Bending over, he sniffed the contents of the nearest pot and sighed. Ah well, one could not expect the excitement of killing bears and the elegance of Aphrodite's cook at the same time. He broke off a piece of bread and dipped it into the pot while he seated himself on the bench. The stew had cooked itself into a kind of gluey paste, but with hunger as a spice it was good. The contents of the other pot, once they had cooled enough for Eros to extract them, were even better. Some kind of baked fish, drier than he preferred, but tasty.

He had finished the fish and much of the stew when half a dozen men entered on the old man's heels. As the door opened, Eros heard the protesting bray of an ass or a mule. He rose, smiling, and shook his head when he was asked politely if he did not wish to finish his meal, saying he had eaten enough. The eagerness the men felt to discover whether he had really killed the animal they feared was apparent when hospitality was skimped. No one urged him to eat more, offering instead a ride in the cart if he were tired. Laughing, Eros refused this treat also; he said, most truthfully, if one excluded the use of the translocation spell, that he had spent a very restful day.

He suspected that the jolting of the cart, which was clearly not floored with the bands of leather that absorbed some of the shocks in a chariot, would be less restful than a second journey, even uphill, on his own feet. However, his main reason was to learn something about Iolkas from the men who accompanied him. To his pleasure, they talked freely, but this puzzled him also because their easy manner did not fit well with being subjects of a cruel and autocratic king.

In fact, he learned no ill of Anerios from them. On the way back up the mountain they told him that the small settlement had been established by King Anerios for the convenience of pilgrims who wished to make sacrifice on the mountain. The large central building was the visitors' lodge, the old man its keeper, and the others had been offered the chance to make the land their own in exchange for providing food for the visitors to the lodge.

It was a fair enough exchange, one said cheerfully. There was game in plenty in the forest, and now that they did not need to fear the bear, hunting would be less dangerous, so meat would not need to come from their small herds. Pilgrims usually came in small groups, and not too frequently. For the large processions that were made at seasonal times of sacrifice, the king usually sent extra supplies.

"He is a pious man, King Anerios?" Eros asked.

"He does his duty in all things," an older man walking just beside Eros answered. "My name is Erasmion. King Anerios is a good king, and with many years left to him, I pray, for we have had peace and plenty in his reign thus far, and will have—unless the suitors mad for Psyche bring war upon us."

"Then the Lady Psyche is not yet bestowed?"

"No," the man beside Eros answered, but there was a kind of constraint in his voice.

"Another one!" someone Eros could not see muttered, his voice redolent with disgust.

"I hardly expected she would still be free," Eros said. "I came to look upon this wonder for tale of the beauty of Lady Psyche has reached even to Cellae in far Macedon."

"Macedon," Erasmion said in a musing tone. "Is Cellae on the coast?"

"No, and I am not fond of ships," Eros stated most untruthfully. "I came down through the mountains to Doliche, thence to Larissa, around the lake to Pherae, from where I set out for Iolkas. I have been traveling since spring."

"That is a long way to look on a woman's face, no matter how beautiful," Erasmion remarked.

"Ah, well," Eros said, smiling, "Cellae is a quiet place and I had a desire to see more of the world. If I could also win a beautiful bride, my journey would have a good purpose."

"Did you sacrifice on Pelion for good fortune?" someone just behind asked with a touch of amusement.

"I should rather go to the temple of Aphrodite for that purpose, should I not?"

There was a brief and, Eros thought, uncomfortable silence, and then Erasmion said, "The altar on Pelion serves all the great ones. You can call on any name there."

"Ah," Eros said innocently, "I did not know that, but I think I will save my sacrifice to the goddess for her own place."

The older man glanced at Eros, but did not reply. He might have been saving his breath for the climb, which was steeper at this point, but Eros did not think so. Nor did Eros think Erasmion was much troubled by the king's sanction against Aphrodite's temple, of which he was certain Erasmion was aware. His teeth set for a moment, but he reined in his anger on Aphrodite's behalf. An older man might not have any reason to call on Aphrodite—she was one to whom mostly the young prayed—so Erasmion might think little of the interdict against her temple. That was Anerios's sin, and Anerios would pay.

Doubtless that would have a chastening effect on all, even those like Erasmion, who did not feel the worship of Aphrodite pertinent to their own lives. That they worship and make sacrifice was not necessary; that they respect and refrain from insult was. When they saw Anerios made ridiculous by love of a repulsive object, the men's general good opinion of the king would drive home the lesson that it was unwise and unsafe to scorn Aphrodite even if she could not throw thunderbolts.

The torchlight paled as a sharp curve in the road showed an area free of trees. Less concentrated on the path itself, Eros now heard the sound of the sea and when they came to the open area, he drew his breath as he looked out and down at the ocean. It was a glistening silver, picking up the light far to the east, too faint yet to show color, where the earliest glimmering of dawn appeared, and decorated closer to the shore with tossing fillets of white.

"Do you have no high lookouts in your mountains," Erasmion asked.

"More than enough," Eros replied, "and less safe than this. But we do not have the sea below, no more than a narrow river walled in by another mountain. Here . . . one can see to forever."

"Unless the fog rolls in," the cheerful voice that had spoken in the beginning said. "Then you can fall off, right into forever."

"I thank the gods there was no fog this night," Eros said. "With what looked like a straight road under my feet, I might have walked right off the mountain. I am accustomed to fog and to mountains, but none of ours have roads. I will be more cautious in the future. I could have sat with the bear until morning, but I did not think I would be in danger coming down, once I saw the road."

They turned away from the edge and began to climb again. The light grew stronger as they walked, and they came at last to the clearing, where, to Eros's relief, the dead bear still lay across the altar stone.

Erasmion was the one to draw breath as they approached the animal. "Having been attacked once by a monster like this, did you not fear to go into the forest?"

Eros shrugged. "I am a good archer and a fair swordsman, and I am used to hunting wild beasts."

The men looked at him. He stood a head taller than the tallest of them and when he threw aside his cloak and pulled off his chiton to save it from being stained with blood and other muck, as the others were doing, they flicked sidelong glances at the smooth muscle that played under his skin. All were shivering as Eros plucked out the three arrows that had lodged in the beast, but once they started skinning, the effort of shifting the heavy body and slicing through the hide, then plying knives to free the hide from the flesh, warmed them well enough. By the time the sun was well up, they were all sweating freely and making frequent trips to the spring that welled out of a rise of rock beyond the altar stone.

When they had the skin free, Eros took it aside and washed it thoroughly, taking particular care to clean away all the corruption from the side of the head. He began to scrape away the tissue on the inner side also, but he had not progressed far before three of the men were finished butchering the body. The other three came back from the woods bearing armloads and cloaks full of fresh leaves. These they layered in the bottom of the cart to keep the butchered meat clean and also used to cover the pieces and the sacks into which they had gathered the offal for the pigs and the dogs. Above that Eros laid the skin, and over all they placed a clean cloth wet with the cold water of the spring.

The mule and cart were then moved into the shade and the men set about cleaning the altar and the area around it. Eros himself washed the stone while several of the men gathered any scraps they had missed. A small fire was then set on the stone, the gatherings drenched in oil and set ablaze. The clean ashes were brushed away, leaving all decent for future sacrifices.

When they were about to go, Erasmion stopped suddenly and asked, "Don't you want to leave a haunch as a thank offering?"

Eros shook his head. The bear was probably too old and tough to please Aphrodite's palate, and in any case, he had no way to let her know he had left it for her. To do that, he would have to go to the temple to tell the priestess to tell the scryer when she felt the "call." A trip to the temple would not endear him to Anerios, and even if he went in secret, by the time Aphrodite learned of its presence and could collect it with a translocation spell, the meat would be rotted and no good to anyone.

"I do not make blood sacrifice," he said. "I left a brace of rabbits and five doves on Aphrodite's altar in Pherae when I was there. I will wait. If I think I have some hope of succeeding with the Lady Psyche, I will make a greater sacrifice—"

"Her temple is not—" one of the men began.

"You are wise," Erasmion interrupted. "The Lady Psyche is hard to please. If you see a chance of success, then will be soon enough to make sacrifice."

Eros thought about that interchange as they started down the mountain. Clearly the interdict of Aphrodite's temple was common knowledge. Equally clearly, it was not only Erasmion who did not consider that sacrilege, although the older and wiser man, while not prepared to oppose the king, would prefer that the news did not spread. Eros had plenty of time to control the anger that rose in him over the contempt shown for his friend because the trip down the mountain was no swifter than the climb up. They could go no faster than the mule, and the laden cart had to be braked all the way to prevent it from rolling into the mule's hindquarters. It was midafternoon when they came back to the little settlement; by then Eros was tired and glad to accept the offer of a second meal and a bed in which to make up for his lost sleep.

He woke much refreshed and pleased to learn that news of his "wondrous feat" had been sent down the mountain to Iolkas, and that King Anerios had sent one of his own sons to extend an invitation to the "mighty hunter" to be his guest and to receive his thanks for ridding the road to the altar on Pelion of a menace. Although Eros said he was ready to start at once, Damianos begged him not to deprive the people of the village of a feast of bear meat which would avenge them in small part for the hurt the animal had done them.

To this Eros agreed, smiling and confessing that he had felt a yen for bear steak ever since he had seen the creature. It was true enough, but it had also occurred to him that arriving in the middle of the night would deprive him of an effective entrance in company with the remains of his kill.

He succeeded rather better in that purpose than he had expected, for the king himself came out onto the porch facing the great court of the palace when they arrived in Iolkas during the afternoon of the following day. Eros paused a step ahead of the cart, which displayed the bearskin spread over the sidewalls, and bowed while young Damianos rushed up the few steps to whisper in his father's ear, imparting, Eros was sure, the false lineage he had devised for himself.

"Lord Atomos," King Anerios said, "we welcome you joyfully, as much in relief at your safe arrival in our palace after so dangerous an adventure as in gratitude for being freed from the depredations of a monster."

"I am glad of your welcome, King Anerios," Eros replied. "But I must admit I did not seek out the beast to kill it. It sought me, and I had little choice."

"Your modesty becomes you," Anerios said, smiling.

"Will you permit my servants to take the cart, prepare the meat, and begin the tanning of the hide?"

"With gratitude," Eros said. "Please use the meat for whatever purpose seems best to you. The hide I would like to present formally."

Anerios smiled and Eros wondered if the king thought he would be the recipient. Eros, of course, intended the bearskin for Aphrodite. It would make a perfect trap when he told Anerios he intended it for a sacrifice to the goddess for help in gaining Psyche's favor. Doubtless Anerios would forbid him to offer sacrifice at the temple; then he could cry aloud of sacrilege. But Damianos had not had time in that brief whisper to tell his father that Atomos was yet another suitor for Psyche's hand.

He focused his attention as the king gestured. Anerios was asking him to come within and be refreshed after his long journey. Eros accepted the invitation, with quite genuine gratitude, too. He was gritty and sticky, and even Damianos's best manners could not keep him from occasionally turning his head away from Eros's aroma.

That need was the first attended to, Damianos himself leading Eros to a colonnaded porch to the right. They turned left through a doorway opposite a stair and then immediately right into a short corridor that led to a cool dressing room with benches around the walls and tall racks holding soft, thick drying cloths. Through an open doorway Eros heard the splashing of water into what he fondly hoped was a tub deep enough to immerse himself.

After Damianos told him he would return when his guest had bathed, Eros lost no time in shedding his pack, belt, and weapons, dropping his soiled clothing to the floor and snatching up one of the cloths. At the doorway of the bathing chamber, he stopped and almost backed up, suppressing a simultaneous impulse to throw the cloth he was carrying over his head. However, no astonished cries of joy and submission came from the three women who were filling the tub when they saw him. The eldest smiled politely enough as she invited him to step into the bath, but her smile was only polite, nothing more. Even the two younger women showed only the faintest flicker of interest—and more curiosity in a stranger than real interest in a man.

Their calm acceptance reminded Eros of his disguise and he came forward with confidence, allowing the women to bathe and anoint him and finding occasion when he thanked them for their service to say the name "Atomos" to reinforce the spell. He felt no change beyond the slightest drain of power and relaxed further. Zeus's illusions were truly the best; apparently he could count on the disguise remaining stable for more than a day without reinforcement.

He found Damianos waiting in the antechamber with a handsome chiton and cloak, which he begged Atomos to accept as a small token of his father's gratitude.

"I thank you as messenger, your father as giver," Eros said, smiling and casting aside the drying cloth. As he drew on the fresh chiton and closed his own belt about it, he went on, "I am especially grateful because I brought no fine garments with me. I do have in my pack a kilt that does not smell of sweat and dead bear. It is the formal dress of my own people, but I do not know whether a kilt is acceptable in Iolkas."

"Were you not offered giftings on your way?" Damianos asked in a rather shocked voice.

"Yes, indeed," Eros replied hastily. He had forgotten the native practice of offering gifts to "noble" guests, and if he had truly come on foot, he would have collected a wagonload of offerings by now. "But if I could do so without offense, I returned them, or offered them at the next place of guesting. On so long a journey, for so uncertain a purpose, it seemed foolish to burden myself with different styles of dress." He patted the pouch that hung from his belt. "I brought the where-withal to buy appropriate clothing, in case your sister was still free and your father should favor me with his approval."

Damianos sighed. "I do not think my father will forbid you to address Psyche. Between us, Atomos, the king would be glad to see her settled."

"Is she such a shrew that he cannot command her to accept the man he thinks most suitable?" Eros asked, half laughing.

"She is not a shrew at all," Damianos said with a wry smile. "She just explains to you how much more trouble would be caused by doing what would make her un-happy—and she's right, too."

"You mean she looks into your eyes and your brains are melted to mush by her beauty?"

"Oh, no." Damianos shook his head vigorously. "I am her brother and I am so accustomed I hardly see her. Anyway she could always get her way and she was not always a beauty. In fact, she was the ugliest little child—"

"Not always a beauty," Eros echoed, blinking.

Damianos shrugged. "Horexea and Enstiktia—those are my elder sisters—were both pretty children. Psyche was the baby, but she was tall and skinny and clumsy and she was no pleasure to look upon. Her eyes were too big, her nose and chin too small—her face was all wrong." He laughed without humor. "I suppose one grew into the habit of not looking closely at Psyche."

"Then how did she become what she is? By sorcery?"

"I am sure not," Damianos replied a trifle stiffly. "We have no great sorcerors in Iolkas, and Psyche did not begin to study sorcery herself until after we realized how beautiful she had grown. No one really noticed her looks until a visitor tried to take her by force. She fought him off and came crying to my father and he *looked* at her—hardly believing that anyone could want her enough . . ." He made a gesture of helplessness. "And he saw what she had become."

"I am growing more and more eager to meet this marvel," Eros said, having barely prevented himself from exclaiming in surprise when Damianos admitted that his sister had *studied* sorcery.

The native people did not usually welcome the Gifted among them. Some drove them out. Some killed them. Some allowed them to practice because of a mixture of fear and desire to use their abilities. Iolkas seemed to be of the last type, but even so, to permit a daughter of the king to study sorcery was unusual. How strongly Gifted was this Psyche? He would know when he met her, Eros thought. Many of the Gifted, he among them, could sense the ability in others and could nearly always sense the use of power. For him a spell always had a visual aspect, so if Psyche were enhancing her appearance, he would "see" it as an aura—but the ability was a sword that cut two ways. Would Psyche "see" or "smell" his disguise?

He worried the point, replying by instinct to Damianos's next few remarks. It had occurred to him that if Psyche had created her own beauty and maintained the illusion day and night for years, she must be very powerful. The drain of being Atomos was slight and he could sustain the illusion for several days, perhaps even for several weeks—but for years? And if Psyche were strong enough to do that, would Aphrodite's spell be strong enough to affect her? The moment of doubt passed as swiftly as it had come, and Eros smiled. He had remembered that Aphrodite's spells were strong enough to make even Zeus act the fool.

Fortunately, the smile was appropriate as Damianos gestured widely to the portico of the great central building of Anerios's palace. Eros said something complimentary about the smooth plastered pillars—those in Olympus were of marble polished until it was as smooth as silk—to go with his smile and Damianos glowed with pleasure. As they passed into the vestibule, Eros saw several beds already standing against the wall, recalled that one of those, or perhaps a new one, would be his, and barely managed to repress a grimace. He was accustomed to his privacy and had forgotten until this moment that guesting with natives offered little of Olympus's graces.

He hoped Damianos had not noticed the faint change in expression and was reassured as they entered the megaron. The light was dimmer, and Damianos was looking eagerly ahead toward the central hearth—Eros stifled a sigh; another discomfort he had forgotten was the meandering smoke that managed to avoid the smokehole in the roof. Damianos had hesitated, his eyes scanning the already well-filled benches. Eros's eyes went beyond to the lesser folk, sitting on their cloaks on the floor, but not so crowded together as to make trouble for the servants, who were setting small polished tables by the benches of the greater folk. And then Damianos led him toward an empty bench, right beside the throne chair of King Anerios.

A swift glance around told Eros that no woman was present. Iolkas might not drive out its Gifted, but adhered to the custom of native folk in not sharing their meals with their women. Eros had another brief struggle with his expression when he thought of the reaction of the female mages of Olympus to such a practice. Even Zeus's lightnings would pale in the blasts that would correct such manners.

Of course, the native people did not know the power

of the Mother and thus gave less honor to women. Eros felt a twinge of guilt as he returned Anerios's greeting and took his seat. The great mages of Olympus had intruded themselves between the common people and the Mother, usurping the worship owed the true Goddess. And he was aiding and abetting that practice by enforcing Aphrodite's will. Not that the Mother cared for worship. She was not so petty and small-minded as a mage. Eros restrained a shudder. She had Her Own set of weights for Her strange scales.

For his purposes, he told himself, the custom was a benefit. He would find it easier to examine one victim at a time. He lifted his cup—a very fine one of silver hammered thin and engraved with an intricate pattern—which a servant had filled, poured a few drops in libation, and proceeded to respond to Anerios's polite questions by describing his "homeland" and his "journey." He had remembered the passion of the native people for hearing of happenings in other courts and cities and had come prepared with tales gleaned from Aphrodite's temples and her gossip with other mages.

Between bits of news from Cellae, Pella, Doliche, and Pherae, they ate. And ate. More accustomed to the small dainty meals with which Aphrodite coaxed his minimal appetite, Eros found himself grateful to be able to cover how much less he ate than the others with talking. When he ran out of news, there was the tale of the killing of the great bear. Eros blushed as he related it to cheers from the listeners, hoping that Atomos's dark skin would conceal his embarrassment. The telling was taking much longer than the event. He would have been hooted out of the hall in Olympus for making so much of what had been a plain necessity, not an act of heroism, but these folk delighted in hyperbole.

Later, after he withdrew from the center of attention, laughingly claiming he had been drained dry and his voice was hoarse, he asked Anerios if he might be deemed worthy to propose himself as suitor for his daughter Psyche. The king nodded. "You are acceptable to me. Whether you will be acceptable to Psyche is much less likely. There are five others here—" Anerios's eyes flicked to that number of young men, all dressed in gorgeous chitons and overrobes, seated well apart from one another "—whom she has refused."

Proud bitch, Eros thought, feeling within himself the small center of angry, pulsing red that was Aphrodite's spell of obsession. That would tame Psyche's pride.

CHAPTER 3

In the women's chambers above the queen's megaron, Psyche listened to her mother without expression.

"He is from Cellae in Macedon," Queen Beryllia said with considerable emphasis. "He said he began his journey here midspring. It is now nearly time for harvest."

"I doubt he was pressing on with any haste," Psyche murmured, her eyes on the hands she had clasped in her lap. "He must have rested as a guest in many places, and for all we know, for considerable time."

"I see you are set against him already because you assume he did not rush to throw himself at your feet without pausing to eat and drink."

"No, mother!" Psyche exclaimed, looking up with shock marking her lovely face. "I was only trying to understand how far Cellae really is from Iolkas. What good would it do for me to accept the man—" her lips twisted as if she had bit into something very bitter "—if Cellae were close enough to cry blood feud and launch an army?"

"Well? What do I tell your father?" Beryllia asked, without making any reply to Psyche's remark. "Do you go down or refuse even to meet the man?"

"The others will make trouble for him," Psyche said.

Beryllia laughed briefly. "I do not think so. He stands a head taller than any of them—and he slew the bear Arktos all alone, without help."

Psyche hastily lowered her eyes to her hands again, afraid the spark of interest she felt would show. He sounded a most worthy man—but not for her, she reminded herself. No man, no matter how worthy, would be suitable for her. Even if his city was too far to launch a war on Iolkas, would he not kill her out of jealousy? Why, oh why, had the priestess refused her a haven at Aphrodite's temple? What if she did hate the goddess of beauty? She had no power to harm Aphrodite.

Something had to be done. Something. Anything. It had not helped to isolate herself in the women's quarters. The suitors still came, still threatened her father if he would not force her to come down, still quarreled among themselves no matter how firmly she refused them. Perhaps the priestess of Aphrodite would change her mind when the lack of sacrifices made life in the temple thin and meager.

Psyche shivered slightly. More likely she would not. Psyche remembered the priestess's blind-looking eyes as they stared into her, seeing under flesh and bone what Psyche hid from everyone else, remembered her fear when Anerios struck her, and remembered that the fear had not bent the woman's will. Would it not be better to accept this man, go with him to his far city, and let him kill her? Psyche shivered again. She did not want to die, but if there were no other way . . .

"Yes, of course I will go down," she said to her mother. "To refuse would only delay the meeting for a day or two. I will dress now and be ready."

The torches in the well-wrought metal stands were alight by the time Beryllia led her youngest daughter and the wives of the other noblemen at court down to join the menfolk. Stools had been set beside and slightly behind each bench, except a low chair near Anerios's throne for the queen. There was a stir among the men as soon as the women approached, three of the five Anerios had indicated were suitors rising to their feet.

"Lord Atomos, this is my daughter Psyche," Anerios said, clearly and loudly.

Eros turned his head from the three who had stepped forward, but paused when they heard Anerios's introduction and began to mutter to each other. He raised his eyes to the woman standing beside the king, drew breath, and slowly got to his feet.

"My," he said with widening eyes. "Oh, my! You are something else again!"

So she was. Eros was intimately familiar with the most exquisite beauty, but what he saw was nothing at all like Aphrodite's scarcely nubile, ethereal face and figure. Psyche was very nearly as tall as he, full breasted and with voluptuous curves that could not be concealed completely by her modest garments. Her large eyes—he could not make out the color in the torchlight—met his squarely. Her skin seemed flawless and very pale; her hair was so black as almost to be an absence of light where it flowed free. The nose was straight and fine but not thin or delicate, the lips—very unlike Aphrodite's rosebud pout—full, the whole mouth generous, except that it was pinched in at the corners as if to give nothing away. In fact, each feature by itself was not so special; put together, even Eros—accustomed as he was to his own perfect face—was almost overcome.

The face, which had presented only a frozen blankness, a perfect carven mask, during her father's introduction, quivered into life in response to his remark, the brows lifting slightly in surprise. "Something else from what?" Psyche asked, taking in the stranger's dark, thick-browed face.

There was, amazingly, none of the dazed adoration

with which she was all too familiar. Admiration she did see, but that was covered as soon as she spoke by an expression of startled caution. That seemed odd, but Psyche was not sure of what she had seen because Lord Atomos swept an arm across his chest and bowed deeply enough to hide his face.

He was smiling when he straightened, and he said, "You must know, Lady Psyche, that you are different from every other woman."

"I know nothing of the sort," she said, her voice gone utterly flat, the warm burr, which had made her surprised question a delight to hear, absent. "I can prove to you in any number of ways that I am exactly like every other woman."

"Psyche!" Anerios muttered.

Her eyes flickered to her father and she caught back what more she had been about to say. Again her mouth felt bitter as gall. All he cared about was that this Atomos lived far enough away so that his people were unlikely to declare war if he should marry her and then go mad with jealousy. He did not care that she would be too far away to be protected by the responsibility of father and brothers to a wedded daughter and sister.

A burst of laughter brought her eyes back to her new suitor. "And so you are!" he exclaimed, with every sign of delight, "But my reasons for saying so may be very different from the proofs you promised me. So, Lady Psyche, will you not please be seated on this stool and explain to me why *you* say you are exactly like every other woman?"

Psyche read amusement and, again, a kind of wariness in him. For the first time in five years, a faint light of hope glimmered through the dead ashes of her dreams. She sat down as he had asked, aware of her father sending the refused suitors back to their seats with questions as to whether they were finished eating

and wished to take their leave. Their protests over Anerios's presenting his daughter to the stranger, rather
than offering her a choice of partners, was drowned out
in a babble of voices from her father's men and their
women, who had heard the same protests a thousand
times over the past few years. Other men stood. The
"slighted" suitors returned to their places. Psyche's
eyes came back to Atomos, who smiled at her.

She looked down at her hands and said, "I must
warn you that many of my proofs and arguments are
philosophical. You will have to take on trust the fact
that my physical parts are exactly like those of any
other woman."

Now, she thought, he would tell her no proof could
make her less than perfect, and thus, by definition,
different from all other women, or he would totally
ignore what she had said and begin to extoll her beauty.
She had not looked up again and thus was totally unprepared for either tone or words.

"Well—" Somehow Psyche heard laughter, although
his voice was grave. "I can see that you have the proper
four limbs, but do you not think I should require more
than philosophical proof that all of you is really you?"

Psyche's astonished gaze leapt to his face to find his
eyes were on her full breast. Her lips parted, but nothing came out, and when he lifted his eyes to her face, she
found herself blinking with shock.

"With a proper female guard, of course," Atomos
went on, and she could hear the quiver in his voice that
marked his effort to retain his sobriety. Again her lips
parted—this time to laugh, although she dared not yet
grasp at the hope his teasing manner aroused, and he
spoke again, this time with a touch of . . . contempt?
. . . saying, "I would not wish to damage a reputation
as flawless as your face."

Psyche swallowed a mingling of indignation and

amusement and opened her eyes wide. "Oh, are you planning to bargain for me by the pound?"

"Holy Mo—Aphrodite, no!" Eros exclaimed. "You would cost a fortune by the pound. Cellae is rich in the red gold sown through the mountains, but there is a limit even to the gold of Cellae. Would you not rather wear it on your neck and arms than have me pay it to your father because you would make two of most other women?"

A kind of cold shiver had passed over Psyche when Atomos swore by Aphrodite, an icy douche to cool the rush of warmth that followed her astonishment at his answer to her first remark. The little frisson of fear evaporated completely by the time he finished, and she laughed aloud.

"Clearly I am too much of a handful for you—"

"Not at all," he interrupted, holding out his hands. "As you can see, I have fine, large hands. They managed a bear the night before last. I imagine they can manage you."

"You plan to shoot me with arrows?"

To Psyche's surprise, Atomos blinked as if she had slapped him. But then he smiled and said, "Only with arrows of love."

The lightness had gone out of his voice, however, and she shook her head and said, "Love is not for the beautiful."

She spoke so bitterly that Eros drew a sharp breath, his heart clenching with sympathy. She understood! And so, was it such an evil in her to hate the goddess of beauty, when beauty had done her so much ill? He remembered the slight flinch when the suitors rose to approach her. Or was he reading into her words what he wished to hear?

"What else is there to kindle love but beauty?" he asked.

"Many things that are a great deal more durable," Psyche snapped, annoyed at having expected more and hearing instead the same trite argument she had been offered more times than she could count, more times, she felt, than there were grains of sand on the shore. "Thank the gods that there are some men with brains left in the world, like the princes of Apheta and Olizon, who saw soon enough that beauty is a shallow thing and courted and married my sisters Enstiktia and Horexea."

"But why take second best, even though I am sure your sisters are lovely women, when they could have had you?" Eros asked.

"They did not take second best," Psyche replied, even more annoyed. Why had she hoped? This one was like all the others. "My sisters are truly beautiful women, not accursed as I am with an unnatural perfection. Also, my sisters will be of value to their households forever. Horexea is a weaver of surpassing skill, and Enstiktia's embroidery almost lives and breathes."

"I am quite sure that you have skills to equal those of your sisters."

She laughed without mirth. "None that a man would think would fit me to be a wife. I have a very ready tongue, but I have found that little valued by men." Her lips twisted. "In fact, it is the one thing that can sometimes clear the glaze from their eyes. I have some learning about the beasts and birds and plants in the wild, but men who prefer to immure a wife inside the house think that unwomanly. And I have a substantial knowledge of spells—" She hesitated, cocked her head, as if waiting for an expression of horror, and when Eros only smiled, went on wryly, "Only the spells are useless because I have not the power to bring them into full potency."

That was true, Eros thought. There was not a flicker

of magic about her. He was rather surprised that her astonishing perfection had not reminded him to "look" and "smell" for sorcery, but she was so different from what he had expected, with her ready sense of humor and her feelings—so like his own—about what she called her unnatural perfection. Then he remembered what Damianos had told him was the reason for her study of sorcery.

"But to me what you offer is very precious," Eros said gently. "There are servants and slaves who can weave and embroider, but the winter nights are very long in Cellae, and a woman with a ready tongue would be a great prize. And in Cellae, we do not confine our women. You would be free to hunt and fish and gather, if you desired, so you would benefit my household much through your knowledge of the plants and animals. I am not certain what use your spells would be if they do not work—perhaps to teach others of greater power?"

Teach me? Eros wondered, realizing that he had barely substituted the name Cellae for Olympus when he said her skills would be precious—realizing, too, that he had been *feeling*, truly feeling, since his first moment of astonishment when he had looked at Psyche and instead of accepting his remark as incense on the altar of her beauty she had almost laughed. He had been speaking more for Eros, a man going wooing, than the minion of Aphrodite seeking for what would most hurt one who had offended her. Mother help me, Eros thought. *I* want her.

Psyche stared at him for a moment as if she did not believe her ears. "Do you mean—" she began, and then laughed. "I dare say you would find my learning less precious if it were stored behind a different face."

Of course he would, for she would not have learned the bitter lesson of the evil inherent in superlative beauty, but he could not tell her that. It would be ridiculous coming from a man with Atomos's face.

"I do not know," Eros replied. "And the point is moot, because if you did not have the face of a goddess, rumor of you would not have flown all the way to Cellae. But I admit I would not have come so far to look at a woman with a ready tongue."

"More the fool you, for learning and a quick wit will last through a whole life, whereas the shape of eyes and mouth will change, hollowing and falling in with the passing years."

"Many years," Eros said, smiling. "By that time a man might have been dead of old age, or illness, or accident. The more fools the princes of Apheta and Olizon who yielded up the golden treasure of your beauty for the silver coin of your sisters' skills."

"A gilded phantasm, oh foolish Atomos, not a golden treasure. How long would a man who lived with me see my face? Have you never had a companion of surpassing ugliness? A friend with a terrible scar? If you loved those men, did you see the scar or the gross features after a few days?"

This time it was Eros's mouth that opened and closed without producing words. It was true! Unless some special reason made him *look* at her, he hardly saw Aphrodite. And she watched his expression, not his features. He shook his head, not in negation but in a kind of wonder at Psyche's keen perception.

She misunderstood the gesture and sighed wearily. "A man can sell weavings and embroideries and still enjoy the warm pleasure of a wife who loves him and who takes joy in creating more weavings and embroideries for his good and the good of his household. Beauty is a cold and sterile thing; it finds no room within itself for the love of others. Any man who took me would have nothing but what he could see, and that would become meaningless in a few days or a few weeks at the most."

Again Eros's gut twisted. Was he so full of his own beauty that he had no love, no warmth to offer? Could it be that those to whom he had responded—some out of pity for their anguish, some out of his own physical need—had felt the lack of love in him and were thus driven to jealousy and to inflicting fury and misery upon him until he abandoned them? But Psyche could not know that, unless his mask was slipping and she had caught a glimpse—

"But I, Atomos, do not believe you are cold and sterile," he said hastily, and knew his disguise was still perfect. There had not been even the faint quiver of draining that he had felt when he had said that name in the bath earlier. So, likely she had spoken in simple pride, knowing herself matchless and unwilling to take less than her equal. "I think the right man could awaken within you a warmth to match your matchless beauty—"

"I hope not!" Psyche said, laughing. "If that warmth was as excessive as my beauty, my lover and I would both go up in flames."

"The flames of love," Eros said, lips twitching, "are rarely fatal. And no matter how painful, that agony is equally joy."

"If you do not mind," Psyche snapped, "I prefer a well-wrapped hot brick in my bed in the winter, not a shovelful of lighted coals."

Eros choked and then roared with laughter. "I too," he gasped, then added plaintively, "but a few coals to light the fire to heat the bricks would not be amiss."

Psyche put out her hand. "Perhaps not—" she began.

There was a cry from the benches to the right. Psyche snatched back her hand, stiffening, and her eyes flashed toward the five suitors. The nearest, who had not joined the general conversation, had leapt to his feet. Now he rushed around the seated folk and came to stand beside her, glaring down at Eros.

"Psyche," he said, "do not listen to this man's blandishments. Cellae is a poor, miserable collection of mud huts, and Macedon is full of nothing but savages who wear animal skins and eat their meat raw. If you go with him, he will harness you to his plow like an ox—"

"A cow," she said. "I know I am a big woman. It is not kind to call me a cow—but an ox is impossible."

The suitor gaped at her. "Psyche!" he exclaimed. "I never had such a thought! I—"

"I do not remember ever seeing a woman harnessed to a plow in Macedon," Eros said, with such specious thoughtfulness that Psyche had to bite her lip. "Following the plow, yes, but—"

"Hush," she hissed at him. "Are you trying to start a brawl?"

"No." His eyes met hers with a purpose they had not held before and he smiled slowly. "But I am beginning to think you would be worth the price even if I did have to pay for you by the pound." He lifted his brows. "After all, you might be able to draw a plow—"

"Monster! Psyche, you cannot consider—"

Her face had been alight with laughter, which added so much to her loveliness that even Eros had found himself a trifle bedazzled. At the interruption, all animation died out. Her face was no more than an exquisite mask when she turned to the suitor, whom she had apparently forgotten.

"Ignatius, it is not your affair what I do or do not consider. I have refused your offer—more than once. Why do you not leave me in peace and go home?"

"Because I must have you for my wife. I must!"

"Even though I am unwilling? That is stupid!"

"But you are so beautiful. I would not speak of harnessing you to a plow. I would never ask you to do anything at all. I would enshrine you in painted rooms, dressed in fine garments and bedecked with costly ornaments like a precious jewel in a perfect setting."

"I do not wish to be enshrined. I am neither a corpse nor a deity. Ignatius, close your eyes and try to *think*. What good would I be to you?"

"I could look at you. No one could desire more."

"You fool! I have told you over and over that when I am no longer an object out of your reach but your own possession, you will no longer see me. *You* will not notice me any longer, but every visitor will, and every visitor will desire me and beg to become my lover. Do you know whether I have the character to resist? If you take me unwilling, will I even try to resist?"

"A good woman does not even think such thoughts!"

"Who told you I was a good woman? Not I!"

A choke of laughter, stifled but unfortunately still audible, wiped out the expression of uncertainty that had flickered across the suitor's face. "You are too beautiful to have an ugly soul," Ignatius cried. "Whatever he offers you, I will offer more."

With a sound remarkably like a beast's snarl, Psyche jumped to her feet. "And you are no better!" she spat at Eros, whirling on her heel and striding from the megaron.

"Psyche!" Anerios exclaimed, but his daughter only tossed her head and continued toward the door that led to the queen's megaron and the stairs to the women's quarters on the second floor. Ignatius followed her, but neither Anerios nor Eros watched. The suitor would stop at the stairway. It was death to invade the women's quarters. One shout from Psyche or even a maidservant would bring all the men of the household to the defense of their womenfolk. As soon as it was clear that Psyche had no intention of attending to him, Anerios had turned to Eros and shrugged. "I am sorry, Lord Atomos, for my daughter's bad temper."

"I do not believe she is bad tempered," Eros replied, still choking a little on suppressed laughter, "merely exasperated. One cannot blame her. She is clever and must be sickened by having her conversation limited to her own face."

Anerios glanced at him, almost hungrily, and then said, "But you were not praising her beauty and boring her to tears. So much the more must I apologize for her. One moment I heard her laughing and the next she was dreadfully rude. What made her so angry?"

Eros grinned. "She had very nearly discouraged Lord Ignatius, which I believe to be a dearly desired purpose, and like a fool, I laughed and spoiled all her careful reasoning." The smile disappeared from his lips and he looked grim as he added, "Jealousy knows no reason."

"This is the sad truth," Anerios said, looking equally grim, "and is the reason why I dared not simply choose a husband for Psyche. Unless he is a monster, a husband has little reason to fear unfaithfulness in an ordinary woman, but Psyche—"

"Would certainly be offered many temptations. Yet I think that where she gave her faith willingly, of her own choice, she could be trusted."

Anerios's lips parted, but he obviously swallowed the words he had been about to say, and with a smile that was patently false, began to extoll Psyche's good sense and modesty. What he said was utter nonsense, self-contradictory—if Psyche were modest, far from being sensible, she would be an idiot—but it was almost certainly what the king believed Eros wished to hear. Yet there was scarcely any need for Anerios to encourage a suitor, particularly one from such a far place, when there were surely enough from close by, persistent despite the firmest discouragement.

Eros had to swallow a laugh, recalling the scene between Psyche and Ignatius, but the impulse dissipated as it occurred to him that the favor Anerios was showing him might be *because* his pretended homeland was far distant. Anerios was well aware that, whether for her fault or not, Psyche's husband might become violently jealous. Was his charm for Anerios that Macedon was too far away to "hear" if Psyche's husband did become insanely jealous and treated her unkindly, or even killed her?

Eros was surprised. Until this moment, Anerios had seemed a thoughtful and honest father, rightfully if regretfully warning the suitors of the dangers of marrying his daughter. He was relieved that Anerios was not quite as good a man as he had first thought. Nonetheless, Eros still felt twinges of regret for the punishment he would have to inflict for Aphrodite's sake upon one who seemed a worthy man. And as for Psyche . . . he would not think about that now.

His friend came first, of course. Aphrodite, understanding the curse of his beauty, had taken him into her home, fed him and clothed him, when every other person in Olympus, mage or common, had turned from him in loathing and horror. Through all the years, she had never failed him. Neither the delightful sensations of life—laughter, sympathy, even desire—that had wakened in him since Psyche had spoken to him, nor the concern he felt for inflicting shame and possibly loss of his kingdom on a man who had made the single mistake of offending one of the "gods" of Olympus, could deflect his purpose.

Little as he liked it, Eros now knew enough to choose the punishment that would inflict the keenest torture on both Anerios and—and Psyche. Unless it was possible that the priestess had exaggerated or initiated the conflict?

"You need not fear I do not appreciate all your daughter's good qualities," Eros said, at the first pause in Anerios's eulogy. "And not because I expect to be enchanted forever by her beauty."

"No, indeed," Anerios said, trying to look as if he believed it. "There is more to Psyche than her face and form. She is very wise."

"I agree. In fact, I think her too wise to be willing to follow me to Macedon, so far from the protection of her father and brothers." He saw the slight change in Anerios's expression that confirmed the suspicion he had had, but it was irrelevant, and he went on as if he had not noticed. "Thus, what I must do is be sure she is touched with the madness of love and will dismiss all doubts because of her desire for me."

"She has already shown you more favor than any other suitor," Anerios said. "I will arrange for you to walk with her in the garden tomorrow. When you are not plagued by her unsuccessful suitors—"

Eros shook his head. He guessed that Anerios's indulgence to his daughter was ended. Psyche would be ordered to profess love for Atomos, perhaps with a taste of the whip to encourage her "sincerity."

"Of myself, it would take me a year to convince her," he said, interrupting Anerios. "But I will take my case to Aphrodite, who is the goddess of my people. I have heard of your famous shrine to Aphrodite—I came as much to see that as to see your beautiful daughter, who I was sure would be wed before I arrived."

"The shrine is closed." Anerios's voice was cold and loud enough so that the conversation of the others stilled. "The priestesses were corrupt and would not accept my commands. There can be only one ruler in the kingdom of Iolkas."

"The goddess is not subject to the commands of mortals," Eros warned, his voice also loud and cold.

"Perhaps the goddess is not," Anerios snapped, his mouth twisting into a sneer, "but the priestesses are mortal, and they are subject to the king."

"I cannot take a wife without Aphrodite's approval." Eros stood.

Anerios stared at him as if he could not believe a man could resist Psyche even for a goddess's favor. "Then you will not wed Psyche," he said.

CHAPTER 4

Eros left the megaron feeling the eyes of everyone on him. He had no doubts about the necessity of Anerios's punishment any longer. Zeus would have blasted the whole palace for such pride. Aphrodite must not be slighted. He was so angry at the sneer with which Anerios had said perhaps the goddess was not subject to his will that he was tempted to invoke his natural form and punish him at once. However, he had not yet chosen the object for Anerios's unnatural passion, and for some reason he did not examine, he did not want the disguise of Atomos too closely associated with Eros.

In the vestibule he looked around uncertainly, until his eyes fell upon a bed on which were piled his cleaned hunting leathers, his pack, and his bow and quiver. It took no more than a few minutes to divest himself of the gift chiton and cloak and pull on his own clothes. Upon the clothing he laid a chunk of silver. To pay for his food and reject the gift of clothing was to reject guest-claim and all association with Anerios and his family.

He had just fastened his pack when Damianos came hurrying out. He looked at the clothing on the bed and the piece of silver. "Surely you are not leaving now," he cried. "Do you not at least wish to speak again to

Psyche before you go? It is nearly dark. It is dangerous to be abroad in the dark."

"Not so dangerous as to be in a household that has scorned Aphrodite," Eros said. "She is the goddess of love, but love can be very cruel—and so can she. Beg your father to make amends to the priestesses and to pray for Aphrodite's pardon. For your own sake, for his, for the sake of the household—Aphrodite has a tender heart, perhaps—"

"I cannot do that," Damianos interrupted stiffly. "He is the king as well as my father. His word is law."

Eros turned away and started out. In the doorway, he looked back at Damianos. "He will not be king for long. Aphrodite will so besmirch him that his people will not tolerate his rule. I have seen it happen before. I do not wish to see it happen again."

He went across the porch, down the steps, and through the courtyard, stretching his legs to his fullest stride. He was not certain that Damianos would tell his father what he had said and that he had rejected guest-obligation, but he wanted to be well away if Damianos did and Anerios decided to take offense and set his men on him. But aside from the guard's curious look at someone leaving the palace so late, no one paid him any attention. That made him angry again. Whether for bravado or real indifference, his warning had been dismissed with contempt.

Eros did not take the direct road to the temple, but he was tense for the first quarter stadium down the road to the town. Until he had passed bowshot range, he was not safe. No arrow or javelin followed him, however, and he slowed his pace, turning aside from the main road that went into the town onto a path that meandered through the small fields and scattered farmsteads that made up the northern outskirts. On a slight elevation to the west was the temple, which he had visited from time to time on errands or to pick up offerings for Aphrodite.

Night had fallen by the time he reached the road that went from the town to the temple, and as he turned into it he saw above him firelight. Since he did not remember the priestesses lighting their doorway—they did not want the temple to be confused with a whorehouse and required those who desired holy congress with a priestess to come during the day and make their offerings to the goddess publicly—he used a hunter's caution in approaching. His care was rewarded by the sight of two guards watching the road.

Eros paused only long enough to whisper, *"Epikaloumai* Eros," and for the crawling sensation that passed over his face and body to abate before he slid farther into the trees that bordered the road. He removed his kilt from his pack, bundled everything but his sword, bow, and quiver into his cloak, and jammed the bundle into a convenient tree crotch, where it was virtually invisible in the dark. Then he made his way past the guards, back onto the road behind them, and pulled vigorously on the rope that set a bell clamoring.

The guards shouted and leapt to their feet, one plunging a torch into the fire and rushing toward Eros only to stop at the sight of a black arrow nocked to his bow.

"It is forbidden to enter the temple," the guard shouted.

"I am Eros. You can forbid me nothing."

"Eros, my ass," the man sneered, "you've paid to get your rod dipped and don't want to lose your—" As he spoke he hefted the torch higher then still higher; when the light caught Eros's face, he stood transfixed, mouth open.

"I have arrows of gold and arrows of lead," Eros said. "The leaden arrow is nocked. Do you wish all men and all women to turn from you retching with revulsion? Go away from this place and tell your king that Eros has come to wreak vengeance for his slight to Aphrodite."

The door in the wall opened behind him and a priestess cried out, her voice shrill with shock, "Divine one! Eros!"

He turned his head and ordered, "Fetch Hyppodamia," and heard running footsteps, then faintly, at a distance, repeated calls of, "The god Eros is come, Lady Hyppodamia."

The guard looked uncertainly from the open door to the black arrow, and again at the unearthly beauty of the face. He became aware that his fellow guard had not come forward to reinforce him and began to back away.

"I do not want to see you or any other of the king's guards blocking the way to the temple in the morning," Eros said, and turned away without waiting for a reply to enter the doorway. He faced outward again, but when he saw the guard retreating toward his fellow, he relaxed his bow, put the arrow back into its quiver, and shut the door behind him.

"What will you do if they do not obey, Divine Eros?" Hyppodamia's voice asked breathlessly from the shadows.

"Do you have a Seeing, priestess?" Eros asked. "Even the gods do not know all the weaving of the Fates."

"Not for this, but I know the king. If you kill the guards, he will use it as an excuse to attack and destroy the temple, not acknowledge a divine act."

"You need not fear I would be so clumsy, priestess. The minds of mortals are not hidden from us, and I knew your refusal to take the Lady Psyche as your replacement was assumed a defiance of his authority by

King Anerios. He said as much to a guest in his house today. What I will do to the guards may cause their deaths, but their punishment will not come from any physical attack by my hand or by that of any person in this temple."

Eros heard a stealthy sound behind him and turned swiftly, sword half drawn, but it was only the younger priestess, who had opened the gate, creeping closer.

"Away!" Hyppodamia ordered sharply. "How often have I told you to keep your eyes on the floor when one of the divine ones honors us with a presence? Do you wish to be consumed by an unslakable thirst? To your chamber. On your way, bid Glaucia come hither to watch by this gate. And do not dare set a foot outside of your cell until I come for you." She waited until lagging footsteps faded along a passage to Eros's right and then, in a murmur Eros could scarcely hear said, "Will it please you to use Aphrodite's apartment, my lord? You will be safe there from intrusion."

"Indeed," Eros said, smiling. "And you will have fewer problems if I am out of sight. But do you come with me, Hyppodamia"—she had better come with him, he thought; he hadn't the faintest idea of how to get to Aphrodite's rooms, since he had never seen this part of the temple before—"as I have some questions."

He then graciously waved for the priestess to precede him and followed her from the short corridor into an antechamber, which they crossed to a doorway in the back of the right-hand wall. That led into a large guest room, with its bath and naked beds. On the back wall was a graceful fresco of a young priestess holding out her hand. Hyppodamia placed her hand on that of the painted priestess, pressed inward and twisted, and the wall pivoted, opening into a chamber furnished with couches and chairs and well lit by lamps burning a sweet oil—one of the rooms Eros knew.

The wall closed behind him and he saw that a similar fresco on this side concealed the pivot release. Beyond to his left was a narrow doorway that led to a bedchamber, the room through which he usually entered. The pivoting wall on that side had a garden scene in which a blue bird played the role of the lady's hand, which was why Eros had not recognized the device. Both rooms opened wide double doors onto a tiny, completely walled-in garden.

Eros smiled very slightly. The bedchamber held a large, low bed that Aphrodite occasionally used to toy with native lovers. Vaguely Eros remembered using it himself, which immediately called to his mind an image of Psyche. Would that be punishment enough? To love her and leave her? An inviting thought, but one Eros put aside. Psyche might be sufficiently punished, but she was too proud, Eros was sure, to speak of her torment. That would not satisfy the need for the whole kingdom to know what happened to those who flouted the "goddess's" will and make them fear her wrath.

A pang of deep regret surprised Eros. It had been so long since he had desired any woman, particularly a mortal woman. He had not used any temple of Aphrodite for such a purpose in . . . he could not even guess at the years, but long before Hyppodamia had become high priestess. His eyes moved to where she stood, head bent, waiting silently on his pleasure and he barely prevented himself from uttering a gasp of surprise. She was old! How many years had it been since he had visited this shrine? Yet he could remember nothing of the intervening time. He might as well have been dead, for all that he recalled of living during those years.

Then he saw the bruises on Hyppodamia's face and arm and he was recalled to his purpose. "If you would like to sit, please do," he said, laying his bow down on a table as he passed behind her to throw open the doors. The scent of sweet oil from the lamps was cloying.

He grinned when he turned back; although she had murmured a thanks and sat down on a stool near the pivoting wall, her eyes were firmly fixed on the toes of her shoes.

"Your will, my lord?" she asked.

"A sow," Eros said, "recently farrowed so her dugs are prominent, large and ugly if possible, but of a docile enough disposition that she would not savage a man who tried to caress her. Do you know of such a beast? When the guards are gone, could you send some servants out to enquire?" He laughed at her expression. "Divinity does not include the knowledge of every pig in the area."

"No, lord, of course not," Hyppodamia concurred doubtfully, "but such a beast would not be very toothsome . . ."

"So I think also, which will make it all the more strange for Anerios to suddenly develop a mad passion for it."

The priestess was so startled that she almost raised her eyes to Eros's face to see whether he was serious. He saved her from any further doubt by adding, "How long do you think he will keep his throne when he pursues such an animal with tender words and kisses, even tries to mount it?"

Hyppodamia shuddered, then sighed, and again bowed her head. "It must be as you command, my lord, and I see that an unnatural love for an utterly loathsome creature is a fitting punishment for scorning my lady's power."

"But you are troubled, Hyppodamia. Speak your trouble aloud, priestess. I will not touch your mind, for you are faithful and honest, and there is no need to violate the privacy of your thoughts."

"Thank you, Lord Eros. I am troubled by the loss of Anerios as king and his sons with him. It is true enough that he is very jealous of his power, but usually that jealousy is controlled by reason, and I honestly believe his purpose is for the better quiet of the state."

"He closed the temple of Aphrodite for the better quiet of the state?"

"In a way, yes. He has become desperate for a solution to the problem of Psyche. He is not such a monster as to slay his own daughter. While she lives, however, his house is infested with suitors who will not leave even after she refuses them, who quarrel among themselves and with any new suitor who comes, causing disruption of his household and a constant threat that one will be maimed or killed to begin a blood feud. He dare not give her to any man who lives close enough to bring an army against Iolkas, for that, he is sure, would be the result of the jealousy soon wakened in any husband by the constant temptations offered to Psyche."

Eros, who had been standing near the doors he had opened, blinked and started toward a large gilded chair set beside a small table. So that had been the charm of Atomos to Anerios, not only the fact that he would not need to hear that Psyche had been hurt or killed, but that the husband would not find it practical to seek satisfaction. Hyppodamia had continued speaking and he forced himself to attend.

"He thought he had found the answer when he brought Psyche here," she was saying. "I wish I could have taken her into the temple, but she was unfit, totally unfit. To have her serve the goddess would have been a defilement in itself. She *hates* beauty and does not believe in love. I had to refuse her, and his rage drove him to desecration and blasphemy. Once he had gone that far he began to think how much more secure he would be if he controlled the temple as well as the throne.

Thus, desperation led to rage and rage to evil thoughts, but usually Anerios does not oppress his people and has been a good king."

"Your bruises, priestess, cast shadows of doubt upon your words. Is there not something else besides your pity for Anerios? Do you fear for the safety of your temple and your underpriestesses if punishment is visited on Anerios?"

She sighed again. "You see deeply, Lord Eros, even when you do not 'look'—and I know you have not because you have spoken of the nearer, most obvious fear. I am not much concerned over revenge. I think so much terror will be aroused by Anerios's fate that the temple will be protected against any attack even by his sons, who would be the first to wish us harm. But I fear there will be war in Iolkas if Anerios and his family are judged accursed and driven out. Because he is so strong a king, there is no preeminent noble who could succeed him peacefully."

"Then we must hope that there are guards on the road and that Anerios takes warning from their fate. If he comes to beg mercy and make restitution to the temple, I myself will tell Aphrodite that you are willing to forgive him and plead with her to be merciful. If he resists, he must go down. Aphrodite prefers love, but she must not be thought of as less than divine for that reason. When the offerings of love are withheld, worship must be extorted by the whip of fear."

"You are merciful, lord." Hyppodamia bowed her head and then asked, "Is there any service you desire of me or my priestesses?"

"Nothing tonight. Breakfast and the hunt for the sow tomorrow."

She rose, bowed again, and withdrew. Eros made a moue of distaste. He always hated the pretense he had to make of godhead when he came among the native peoples in his own form. He thought it wrong, but Zeus and Poseidon had started the practice, hurling thunderbolts and raising terrible storms to coerce worshippers to make generous sacrifices—which increased their wealth and their herds. Athena and Apollo had adopted the notion with deep enthusiasm, and within no long time all the great mages had temples and were enjoying the sacrifices.

Not Hermes, Eros thought suddenly, and began to laugh. Hermes had grown so rich selling translocation spells to the "gods" and "goddesses" so they could appear and disappear that he was totally indifferent to native worshippers. He had some; messengers—and thieves—prayed for his ability to disappear and reappear in some far distant place. Thought of the young, merry-eyed mage, always ready for mischief, made Eros feel light. His perfect brows drew together: to feel light assumes an earlier feeling of heaviness. To feel at all was a pleasant change, but what went so deep that he would be burdened by it without conscious thought?

He followed his thinking back from Hermes to sacrifice to the need for fear to Anerios's punishment—to Psyche. The weight he had cast off when Hermes came into his mind slid back onto his heart. How could he bear to force Psyche into the demented adoration of a halfwit who would even more dementedly adore her, preventing her from the exercise of body and mind in the name of keeping her safe and perfect, and thereby inflicting on her the cruelest suffering through frustration and boredom?

Poor Psyche; she had done nothing wrong. That she had been born beautiful was through no fault of hers. For the sake of her family and her homeland she had agreed to serve a goddess whose attributes she loathed. That was not so heinous a sin. Eros chuckled sadly. If it were, he would be afflicted with all the tortures of

Tartaros, since he hated love and beauty as much or more than Psyche and yet he served Aphrodite and lived with her and loved her. He could not bear the injustice, and yet Psyche had to be punished or Aphrodite's reputation would suffer.

Eros bit a fingernail, thinking that if he pleaded for her, Aphrodite would exempt Psyche from punishment. She would even give Psyche to him. Eros's mind checked on that, aware of the leaping of his heart, thrusting aside the desire with the knowledge that his satisfaction would do harm to his friend, his only friend, who would indeed put aside her own interests to please him, would gladly come and fetch Psyche herself to bring her to him. Whatever he felt, whatever her true guilt or innocence, for Aphrodite's sake, Psyche must be punished, must be given to a monster . . .

Suddenly Eros burst out laughing, having found the perfect solution to his problem in a combination of his desire to spirit Psyche away to save her and the idea of giving her to a monster. That would be Psyche's punishment! For her scorn of Aphrodite, she would be set as a sacrifice on the altar on Mount Pelion, condemned to be a monster's bride.

Eros gnawed his lower lip. But if Anerios took the warning and made contrition . . . Well, Eros thought, that would not matter. Even after begging pardon and promising amendment, Anerios must make a sacrifice in expiation of his rebellion. The expiation would be to sacrifice Psyche. Again Eros began to laugh. Even if Anerios did grieve over the "terrible fate" of his daughter, it would be a sacrifice he would be eager to make.

The solution to his problem left Eros pleasantly relaxed. He blew out the lamps in the room and went into the bedchamber where he opened the doors to the garden. For a time he stood there, enjoying the cool air, thinking of Psyche's quick-witted responses and the faint stirring of interest she had shown in Atomos. And Atomos was thick-browed and heavy-featured. Would she not be even more interested in him when she saw—

"No!"

The fact that the word burst out of his mouth aloud expressed the depth of his rejection of the idea. He had responded to Psyche's interest in Atomos because that interest was in the being of the man, not in the mask that anyone could see.

Eros removed his clothing and went to lie on the bed, contemplating a new problem. He could take Psyche, but once he had her, what would he do with her? If he showed her Eros, she would either reject him or, despite her knowledge of the worthlessness of his beauty, become enamored of it. If she did, she would soon turn jealous, particularly if he took her to Olympus, where all the female mages were beautiful. Nor could he wear the disguise of Atomos. He was strong, but he could not be Atomos day and night without respite for very long—and Aphrodite would not like it. Nor did he want Psyche to love a false image.

He wanted her to love what Eros was under the skin—and he had hopes she could because the thoughts and words to which she had responded were from his own heart and mind. But how could he hide himself and still not show her a face to which the characteristics she had learned to love would become attached? By not showing her any face at all! If she could learn to trust and then to love—what? Not empty air. It was too unsettling never to know from where a voice would come. Constant shock, Eros thought, did not lead to trust and must preclude the growth of love.

He stared out into the darkness, where a breeze had found its way over the wall and was rustling leaves and slowly smiled. A blot of darkness—that would be monstrous enough to fulfill her punishment so that he would not be made a liar. But from that darkness his voice would come, speaking reassurance, and when she gathered courage enough, she would be able to put her hand into that darkness and feel a man.

Then he lost the smile. Not in Aphrodite's house. Aphrodite would like a blot of darkness walking about even less than she would like Atomos, and a spell of darkness would take as much or more power as the disguise of Atomos; he could not wear it constantly for long. But there was no place but Aphrodite's house ... oh, yes there was! The hunting lodge Aphrodite had given him in the mountains above the valley of Olympus. He could be Eros in Aphrodite's house, sleeping away half the day, as he usually did. Only now he would not be trying to escape the weary hours of nothingness but resting to gather power so that at night he could be Psyche's "monster." An enormous relief washed over him and his eyes closed on a delicious sense of anticipation.

He woke early, full of energy, washed, and then pulled the silken rope above the bed, which he knew would bring a priestess. Hyppodamia herself came and he asked for food and whether the guards were still at the gates. The tray and the news that not only were the guards there but the force had been increased came back with her so quickly that Eros knew both had been prepared and waiting. Eros smiled.

"So Anerios sent more men, did he? Ah, well. The more men the merrier the rout will be. Thank you, Hyppodamia." He chuckled at the look on her face. "Trust me. No matter what their orders, when I have done with them, far from attacking the temple, they will not even recall its existence."

"Thank you for your care of us, my lord."

"Aphrodite never fails those who love her faithfully,

and I am Aphrodite's servant and messenger. I will
come when I have eaten."

When she had withdrawn, he sat down at the table
and began to eat and plan his strategy. There were two
gates, the one he had entered last night and another on
the other side of the temple in the wall surrounding the
gardens and orchards of the priestesses. Unfortunately
they were not in sight of each other, but possibly the
shouts of men fighting would be heard. Eros's jaw set.
He could not take that chance. He would have to run
along the wall to the other side. His perfect lips twisted
into an unhappy grimace. That would be most ungodlike. The priestesses would expect him to fly.

Eros closed his eyes and sought within himself. Faint
as a dying breath came a memory of words, *tuphlox tha
ommata,* and moving with that breath, thin and light as
a ball of cobwebs, there was a spell. Aphrodite had
given it to him at some time long ago to hide him while
he cast on the Mage-King Zeus the enchantment that
infatuated him with Europa. Eros frowned momentarily; sometimes Aphrodite's mischief had very unexpected results.

Then his mind came back to the old spell. He had no
idea whether it could still be used and was afraid to
bring forth the fragile thing to examine it. Safer by far
to tell the priestesses to gather in the inner shrine—
where they would hear little and see nothing—to pray
for Aphrodite's help.

Yes, that was right. He could try to infuse the spell
with power and use it at the time he needed it. If it
worked, his movement from one part of the temple wall
to the other would seem like a miracle to any priestess
that peeped or to any soldier not stricken with a spell;
if it disintegrated, he would be no worse off than if he
did not have it at all or had forgotten it—but he never
forgot a spell.

More essential were the spells he must use as weapons. Eros brought his mind and will to bear on what he imagined as a little box just beneath his breastbone. In it lay tiny balls, some warm, bright gold, some a putrid orange-green, and some dead black. At one side were two of an unpleasant pulsing red—one of those was for Anerios. The other had been meant for Psyche, but he would not use it. Another jolt of anticipation made Eros chew faster, laugh aloud in wonder at his eagerness, and finally tell himself that if he did not stick to business, he would never get her.

Hyppodamia said there were ten men at each gate; he would have neither sufficient individual spells nor the time to deliver them in his usual way—which was just as well because full strength the spells would last a year and there was no reason to utterly destroy men who were only obeying orders, even if they should have known better. If the diluted spells lasted a day or two, the lesson would be sufficient. But how to deliver them if he could not use his bow? His mind ranged over the weapons that wounded at a distance and came soon to the sling. He was not so expert with the sling as with the bow, but he was not seeking to hit a single target only to spread a scattering of magic over the whole group.

Taking a last bite of his bread and cheese, which he washed down with warm goat's milk, Eros summoned Hyppodamia again and told her that he was finished with his meal and it was time to begin. For her own safety, she and her acolytes, lesser priestesses, and servants should gather and pray in the inner shrine. He saw her stiffen and the tray, which she had lifted, began to shake in her hands, but she bowed without speaking and slid through the pivot door, which he opened for her.

When she was gone, he returned to the table and spread his hands, staring at the space between them until it was filled with the image of a broad-bellied sling. Then he lifted one hand and cupped it beneath his breastbone. In a moment the vision of a little black ball formed in the palm. Freed from its confinement in his body, the ball expanded. With his mind, Eros plucked it in half, then each half into half, halving the four pieces once more into eight pieces. Rolling those into smaller balls, he willed them to remain separate and watched to be sure they did not join, after which he spilled them into the belly of the sling. Then he repeated the process with a sickly orange-green ball.

He reached for the sling and picked it up as if it were a real thing, hefting it to judge its totally imaginary weight as he opened the pivot door and went out through the empty visitors' chamber and anteroom. Beside the gate through which he had entered was the now empty chamber in which the gatekeeper usually sat. Within it was a ladder that the gatekeeper, or more likely a manservant, could use to climb up on the flat top of the chamber to look over the wall.

Eros set the ladder and climbed up, hoping none of the priestesses was watching and had her faith shaken by seeing one of the gods do something as prosaic as climb a ladder instead of covering the space in a single bound. He did crouch as he climbed so the soldiers would not see his body rising slowly above the edge of the wall and guess at his mundane method of arrival. He wanted to surprise them. The less chance one of them had to throw a spear or shoot an arrow, the greater the chance he could maintain the illusion of godliness.

When he was ready, he popped upright, calling, "Soldiers of Anerios, you were warned!"

A few were sitting and watching the gate already. Others were lounging about, half convinced that the guards who had fled to the palace the previous night babbling of seeing the god Eros had been the victims of a trick of the priestesses or possibly of townsfolk who valued the temple for varying reasons. At the sound of his voice, they all leapt to their feet, looking first at the gate and then upward. Most simply stared open-mouthed. Two had reached for their spears as they jumped up but stood frozen by his appearance, one clutching his weapon, the other with his hand extended toward it.

Eros's voice continued without a hesitation, although he felt rather weak with relief. It would have been shockingly out of character for a god to need to dodge a mortal's weapon. That would have implied too strongly that the "gods" were as vulnerable as men.

"Since you have chosen to obey a mortal master instead of an immortal goddess, you have invited a dreadful fate. Yet such is the mercy of Aphrodite, that those of you who survive a week of living under her curse will be given a second chance to amend your ways and love and worship her. And one of you will be spared to tell your master that worse will befall him if he does not come to humble himself to the goddess and make full reparation for his transgression."

As he spoke Eros raised his hand, whirling the sling, which no one but he could see, around and around. On the last word he released it, spraying outward the dead black balls and those of putrid orange-green.

Instantly one of the soldiers screamed at the man whose shoulder his arm had been embracing before Eros cast his spell, "Monster, evil, disgusting worm!"

Eros could see the black pall of the spell of hatred dropping like a veil of shadow over the man, who drew his sword and would have struck the other man. He, on whom Eros watched the spell of revulsion spread like a green slime of vomit, stood transfixed, crying, "Beloved! What is wrong?"

He would have died in that moment, only such violent revulsion struck the lover who now hated him that he retched and his blow missed. The entire group was now embroiled—two lay dead and three fled away pursued by four others, who struck at each other as often as at those who fled them. One man, who had been nervously watching the gate when Eros first appeared and had thrown himself face down on the ground soon after Eros began to speak, crawled backward, weeping. The spells had flown over him and he was untouched by hatred and revulsion. Nonetheless, because he knew himself to be the messenger appointed, he expected to die by Anerios's hand just as surely as his companions were dying by each other's.

As he watched the chaos of screaming, fighting men blunder off toward the town, Eros fed power to the cobweb that had once bestowed a kind of invisibility. To his surprise, instead of shattering or crumpling into nothing, the fragile threads strengthened until the ball gleamed like silver. That must have been a very powerful spell—well, it would be, since it was intended to deceive Zeus.

There was something about the web . . . Hecate! That was who had cast it. Eros hesitated. Should he use the spell again? Hecate was *very* strange. Even Zeus did not meddle with her, and she was as old as he—or older. What could Aphrodite have given her in exchange for such a spell? Eros rather balked at the notion of Hecate using a spell of love. Hate? Revulsion? Despite her strangeness, he doubted Hecate needed or desired such spells.

With a mental finger Eros plucked at a strand; like a true spiderweb, the threads were very strong, ensuring that the spell was sound. And the color they made in his mind, full-powered now, was wholesome. He disgorged the ball of web into his hand, let it swell, whispered,

"Tuphlox tha ommata," and cast it over himself. He felt it unfold, touching his hair, his cheeks, his bare shoulders gently as a floating spiderweb. The feeling was pleasant, protective—not a sensation he associated with Hecate.

He looked upward and whispered, "Thank you, Mother."

The Goddess, it seemed, was willing to indulge him. Not only had She honored his words to the soldiers by preserving a messenger who could recount his words and their effect but surely, no matter how strong in magic Hecate was, it was She, the Mother, who had kept that old spell viable. It was only a teasing indulgence, possibly to show that She had taken note of and approved his reawakening, because it would not have mattered if all the men had been affected. Possibly they would all kill each other, but even if they did not succeed, Eros was certain none would know who died when and each would believe some other had been spared to be messenger—and had suffered the fate of bringers of ill tidings.

He prepared the second batch of spells as he walked along the wall to the other gate, climbed to the roof of the gatekeeper's chamber, and whispered, *"Heimi oraton,"* while imagining the webbing passing through his skin and reforming into the ball, which shrank to almost nothing as it took its place in the box. When he saw himself, he breathed out softly in relief. Sometimes an old spell malfunctioned by being hard to reverse. And then he thought, Forgive me, Mother, for my doubts . . . I am only human.

His speech and spell-casting against Anerios's men were equally successful this time, except that he spared none. He did feel a little guilty because all the men were kneeling and begging forgiveness for being where they were. However, that they were there, begging pardon or not, instead of running off against Anerios's orders, was an offense—a confession that they still feared the king more than they feared Aphrodite.

He watched them turn on each other, leaving three groaning with wounds, but still trying to kill each other as the other seven ran along the road toward the palace striking and screaming. Eros hoped that some would stay alive long enough to reach Anerios, then he shrugged and came down to put away the ladders, and, eventually, to give the priestesses a thrill by "appearing" on the altar beside Aphrodite's statue.

"They are stricken with hate and loathing," he told the supplicating priestesses, "fitting curses on those who will not accept love and beauty. Let them spread the news of what befalls any who fail to honor Aphrodite as she deserves. If Anerios does not come to confess his transgression and make restitution before dark, I will lay the goddess's curse on him tomorrow."

CHAPTER 5

Eros woke before dawn, full of resentment. He had given warning after warning in the hope that Anerios would yield and bow to the power of the "goddess." Had Anerios done so, he would have found Aphrodite very merciful; the restitution required would have been well within his means, and the problem of his daughter would be solved. The king had remained adamant, however, even sending another force against the temple. Eros had sprayed the front ranks with hate, and those bespelled had turned on their fellow soldiers. The few who continued to try to advance despite the chaos, Eros had made so loathsome that they could not even endure each other.

After that, Hyppodamia's scryer reported, heated conferences had taken place in the palace. The queen, her family, and her youngest son argued strongly for placating Aphrodite, while Anerios blustered and threatened that if Eros showed his face in the palace, he would strike him dead despite his beauty. Aphrodite had once been wounded by a spear, he said, and if Eros was only her servant, he must be more vulnerable. Psyche had taken no part in the discussion, the scryer reported. She remained in her chamber, speaking to no one.

Despite that good news, for if she were consumed by guilt she would be more ready to be "sacrificed" to remove the curse from her family, Eros was furious. Anerios's stubbornness complicated everything. Now he would have to wait until the people killed or drove out their king. If they drove him out instead of killing him, he would have to arrange Anerios's death without open involvement, lest Psyche fall under the taboo against taking as lover the person who killed her father. Atop all that, he would have to have Psyche watched to be sure that she was not harmed as the cause of all the trouble.

As he rose from his bed and dressed in his Olympian kilt, he caressed the ugly pulsing spell of obsession with his inner eye. He was so eager to start the process of Anerios's destruction that he did not call for breakfast. He could eat when he returned to the temple.

In the inner courtyard where the living tributes to Aphrodite were kept until they were translocated stood the ugliest sow Eros had ever seen. Her skin was mottled and she was old and gaunt. She looked up when Eros opened the pen but made no move to rush at him, and when he picked up the pail of slops set ready and called, "Pig, pig," she came toward him with interest, but no great hurry. That reassured but did not surprise Eros, who had given instructions that she be well fed the night before. She followed him out through the gate nearest the direct road to the palace and along the road, showing no impatience to get at what he carried but interested enough in it to keep close—as long as Eros did not hurry.

Since he could not increase the sow's pace, Eros watched the lightening sky with some concern; however, the walls of the palace came in sight before the sun rose. He went off the road then so the gate guard would not see him, and when he and the sow reached the wall, he dumped about half the food in the pail on the ground. The sow moved to the food and began to eat contentedly. Eros smiled at her. Despite her appearance she was a nice old beast. He would do his best to see that her service to Aphrodite was well rewarded.

Eros fed power to his cobweb of invisibility, feeling a greater drain of his strength than he had the first time he renewed the spell. As he cast the net over him, Eros examined the threads. They seemed sound. Well, if they would not cover him again, he would find another way. Slipping his bow over his shoulder, he began to climb. At least, even encumbered by the pail, he had no trouble getting up the rough stones of the cyclopean wall and down the other side. Then he walked to the gate, lifted out the bar under the starting eyes of the guard, and pulled the gate open.

"This house is accursed," he intoned. "No gate can lock out its doom." The guards sank to their knees, sweating with fear. Grinning, Eros set down the pail. "Go!" His voice, coming through his cupped hands, acquired an even odder tone. "Pray at the temple for mercy and you will be saved."

It was fortunate that he was standing to the side or the guards would have run him down in their rush to avoid the fate of the men Anerios had sent to attack the temple the day before. When they were gone, weaponless, running along the road, Eros picked up the pail and went to fetch the sow, who had finished what he'd left her and was wandering along the wall—fortunately, in his direction—snuffling hopefully. She seemed not at all disconcerted by what she must consider a delicious smell emanating from nothing—or perhaps, Eros thought, she was not affected by the spell and could see him. Whatever the reason, she promptly lifted her head and trailed behind him at her own stately pace, not balking at the gate or at the noise and movement coming from the inner courtyard.

Eros was feeling more and more kindly toward the accommodating beast, and he paused under the gate, dropping a handful from the pail to keep the sow busy while he drew from his store of spells a tiny, tiny flicker of golden light which he set upon the sow's brow. She was just as ugly, just as dirty, just as old and gaunt, but he doubted anyone could harm her now. Then a truly nasty smile twisted Eros's mouth as he realized that the liking everyone would feel for the old beast would make more repellent Anerios's unnatural sexual desire for her. Grinning, he walked out of the passage, the sow following quietly.

In the courtyard, servants were going about their morning duties and nervous soldiers were gathered in groups. One by one, as they saw the sow crossing the open space, they stopped, fell silent if they had been talking, and stared. To their eyes, the dirty old animal, coming from what they believed was a locked and guarded entrance, was walking all alone, quite purposefully, head up, not snuffling along the ground, toward the portico that led to the king's quarters.

On the lowest step, Eros dumped the remainder of the food, invisible to him and to everyone else except the sow, who selected something from the mass and began placidly to chew. Everyone watched her with a kind of nervous intensity that wavered between amusement and terror. Meanwhile, Eros ran quickly back across the courtyard to the side porch and up the stair to the right. He passed the first landing, which opened on the corridor of the women's quarters, and climbed a ladder, coming out on a flat roof no doubt used for drying and bleaching clothes and yarn. He drew the ladder up and closed the wooden flap that kept out the rain.

From the place near his heart, he drew out the pulsing red thing, his lips curling away from his teeth at the unclean feel of it. This time the sphere lengthened rather than swelled, conforming to the image held firmly in Eros's mind. Between one breath and the next, a red arrow, throbbing and glittering, at the same time beautiful and repellent, lay in Eros's hand. He went to the far end, took his bow in his hand, and breathed, *"Heimi oraton."*

Visible, he took a deep breath, and called aloud, "Hola, people of Iolkas! I am Eros, servant and messenger of the goddess Aphrodite. Call forth your lord and his daughter to hear the will of the goddess."

There was a frozen, horrified silence. Two menservants and several women collapsed on the ground. Eros blinked. He had done nothing to them. Other women, and a few men, began to scream.

"Anerios has transgressed against the divine Aphrodite." Eros's voice rose, clear and pure, like a fine hunting horn, above the sobs and wails. "So far, cowardlike, he has sent others to suffer the lash of her displeasure. Now it is time for him to face his own doom."

"My brother was sent against the temple, and now he is dead," one soldier called out to the crowd.

"My cousin and I were closer than brothers, and he was turned into something so loathsome that my gorge rises at the thought of him," another echoed.

And half the soldiers in the courtyard set up a shout of "Anerios, come forth and be champion to your cause."

Eros thought he heard footsteps going down the stairs, but his eyes were fixed on the entrance to the vestibule where Anerios would appear. The soldiers shouted again, and Eros began to wonder if his voice would carry over the din, but a silence fell as Anerios appeared at the top of the steps, hair tangled from a restless night, a spear in one hand, the other clutching a himation loosely around him.

Eros set the image of the sow into the head of the red arrow, notched the arrow to his bow, raised it, and fired. As Anerios's eyes lifted, following the gaze of those who still stared at him rather than the king, Eros saw the arrow sink deep. The spear, half raised, fell from Anerios's hand. Although the king could not yet have discovered at what his people were staring and thus from where the threat to him and them came, he lost all interest in everything but the glorious, delicious, ultimately desirable female creature he knew was waiting for him. His eyes sought and found the sow, still rooting around the bottom step of the portico for tidbits only she could see. Anerios uttered a strangled cry, his grip on his himation relaxing so that it slipped to the ground.

Eros's voice rang out into near silence, overriding the gasps of horror at what the falling himation disclosed. "This is the curse of Aphrodite: those who do not honor love will be dishonored by it."

"Father!" Psyche shrieked, bursting from the side porch and running across the courtyard.

She caught up the himation and cast it over her father's shoulder, although it was too late to hide both his violent erection and the object of his lust. He shoved her away but she clung to his arm, mouthing into his ear words that Eros could not hear. However, Eros could see the dulling of the ugly, glittering strings of red that had spread from the arrow over Anerios like a net, and their throbbing slowed. Psyche had countered his spell!

Admiration for her courage and loyalty almost quenched Eros's fury at her interference, but he could not allow Aphrodite's power to be challenged. Psyche must be punished instantly. Eros drew out the second spell of obsession, but as he lengthened it into an arrow, he realized he had no object for Psyche to love. All that was left to him was to inflict on her an undirected, unquenchable lust that would make her couple with anyone, anything, constantly, until exhaustion felled her only to make her rise to renewed lust. Tears rose to Eros's eyes. How could he do that to a woman so clever, so witty, so charming? How could he ignore his debt to Aphrodite for any other woman?

Eros fitted the arrow to his bow and let his eyes find their target. Then he saw Psyche's face. She was white, even her lips, and she trembled, clinging to her father as much for support as to restrain him, her eyes drooping half shut with exhaustion. He remembered now that she had told him her spells did not work because she had so little power. Plainly it had taken all she had within her to subdue the utter madness of Anerios's obsession. The compulsion to love the sow remained. Aphrodite's spell was the stronger, and as Psyche's counterspell faded, Aphrodite's would regain its full power. Eros let the bow point down toward the earth, took the dreadful red pulsing thing back within him, and shut it away among the other spells.

He tore his attention from Psyche and fixed it on the crowd. "Hear me!" Eros bellowed.

Every eye—except Anerios's, which remained fixed on the sow—turned to him. A silence fell so deep that Eros could hear the snuffling of the sow and Anerios's panting breath. He drew himself to his full height, imagined himself even taller, broader, more beautiful. A huge sigh of terror and longing lifted to him from the watchers.

"For his hubris in claiming his power greater than that of divine Aphrodite, Anerios is smitten with a foul perversion of love. Look at your king, panting with lust for a sow! Yet she is the instrument of Aphrodite, and no harm may be done to her."

A moan of terror rose and fell. A curse on Anerios that was not lifted would carry over onto his whole family. That could mean death or slavery for nearly all in his household. The king's three sons, who had come from their quarters with weapons in hand to support their father and had frozen with horror as the scene played out, dropped their weapons and turned to kneel with hands upraised toward Eros.

"Mercy!" they cried, showing him empty palms, and the whole crowd knelt and cried, "Have mercy!"

Eros looked sad—with some difficulty, since the scene was evolving much as he desired. Beside that, he did not know whether anyone could make out his expression.

"Since you cry for mercy," he called, "I am permitted to tell you that the divine Aphrodite is tender of heart. When Anerios bows down to the goddess before all the people and makes sacrifice and restitution, the curse will be lifted. For his violation of her holy person, the restitution will be set and must be made to the priestess Hyppodamia. To Aphrodite, the greater sacrifice: Psyche must be brought to the altar atop Mount Pelion and left there for the goddess to do with as she pleases."

"No!" Damianos cried. "Poor Psyche, she—"

Eros felt like kissing the young man for providing an excuse for a pretense of rage. "Enough!" he roared. "I have not come to chaffer like a merchant. I am Eros, Aphrodite's voice. My part is to convey her commands. Your part is only to obey those commands with tears of contrition and grateful hearts. Remember that the goddess could have bade me destroy you all with hate and loathing. You have one week to bow down to Aphrodite's will. If not, you will learn what befalls a realm whose king desires only to swive a sow."

On the words, Eros again invoked the spell of invisibility, but as the glittering net dropped over him, he had to catch at the balustrade edging the roof. A wave of weakness had almost brought him to his knees. The spell was too thin; invoking it had drained his power to the dregs. He would not be able to invoke it again. He could only cling to the balustrade and thank the Mother because it seemed he would not need to do so. From the courtyard came cries of fear and amazement as he appeared to vanish, and then shouts arose for Anerios to obey Aphrodite's commands.

Relief only made him weaker. Eros slipped down onto his knees. When he tried to stand again and could not, he swallowed hard. A little more draining might have been fatal. He took a deep breath and then another. What he wanted to do was simply lie down until the trembling of weakness left him, but he didn't dare. He had no idea how long the weakened spell would hold. If he reappeared, prostrate as he was . . .

Eros forced himself to crawl on trembling limbs to the rain shield. It took him three tries to lift it and long agonizing minutes to bring the ladder to its lip. A cold sweat burst out on him as he struggled to prevent the ladder from falling with a crash. Summoning his last reserve of energy, he crawled down the rungs and made his way across the courtyard. The sow lifted her head as he passed her, but no one else noticed. They were all still on their knees. Some were staring at the roof where he had stood; others were watching Anerios, who had stopped struggling with Psyche but who could not tear his eyes away from the sow, his face twisted with both horror and longing. Still others had fallen flat and begun to beg Aphrodite to forgive them, promising rich tribute.

Stretching a hand forward to steady himself against a column, Eros was horrified to see that the glittering net, which should have covered him, had gaps and its light had dimmed from sparkling diamond to barely gleaming silver. Terror lends strength. Eros leapt up the remaining stairs of the porch and into the shadows of the vestibule. There he snatched up someone's cloak and drew it around him. Pulling a generous fold of the cloth over his head like a man in mourning, he made his way out the side door into the long corridor that ran between the megaron and the storerooms. At the end of the corridor, he found a door, which, to his relief, led outside.

Had he not been staggering with weakness, it would have been no great feat for him to find his way to the unguarded gate and slip across the road and into the woods. As it was, reeling with exhaustion, he barely made it into the shade of the trees where he was somewhat concealed before he dropped to the ground, sobbing for breath. He was aware of little beyond the aching hollow inside him, much like hunger . . . After a moment Eros turned on his back and laughed softly. Idiot that he was, it was hunger. Now he recalled that in his hurry to finish Aphrodite's business, he had not broken his fast.

When Eros remembered that he would have to make his way to the temple before he could get something to eat, he stopped laughing. But he needed food and he dared not remain so close to Anerios's palace. It was not likely that anyone would think of hunting for him, but it was barely possible. In their desperation, Anerios's sons might take the chance of adding blasphemy to sacrilege by proposing that the avenging servant of Aphrodite was only a mortal who could be caught and forced to remove the curse.

Groaning, Eros levered himself to a sitting position. He had put a hand, which was quite visible now, against a tree to help himself rise to his feet when he realized he had no notion from which direction he had come nor which way he must go to find the temple. He sat still, frightened by this loss of his normally reliable sense of direction, only to find that his head had turned toward what he suddenly knew was a path in the undergrowth. It was barely marked—a broken twig, a few crushed stems among the sparse grass, a little branch bent at an unnatural angle.

He almost turned away, thinking it was a wood-gatherer's track and would lead nowhere, but then he frowned. Surely a wood-gatherer's track would be far better marked. This looked as if care had been taken to leave as little sign as possible of those who passed. And he wanted to walk that path. Slowly, Eros came upright, holding to the nearby tree until he could steady his shaking legs. Then, a trembling step at a time, he followed the faint trail.

Fortunately he did not have to follow very far. Scarcely two stadia from where he had begun he came to a huge olive tree. Beneath it, a tiny spring filled a wooden bowl above which, on a large, flat stone, stood a roughly carved icon. Eros stopped dead, then dropped to his knees.

"Mother," he whispered, "did You call me? Will You chastise me for driving those poor people to worship Aphrodite in your stead?"

He waited, silent and with bowed head, but oddly he felt comforted rather than more frightened, less exhausted . . . welcome. An impulse made him lift his eyes and he saw at the foot of the statue oatcakes piled on fresh leaves. A warm joy filled him; She *had* called him, not to punish, but to sustain. The true Goddess, Eros thought, was not living flesh. She had no need of material offerings and was immune from the petty spite that was proof the great mages of Olympus were *not* gods. With a humbled heart, Eros gave thanks to the Mother, then went and gathered up the oatcakes. Nestled at the foot of the stone on which the image stood, he ate the offerings, drank the clear water, and curled up to sleep.

Anerios and Psyche had not knelt to cry for mercy with the others. Anerios had not made any sense of Eros's words because he was locked in a titanic struggle between the sane knowledge that Psyche's counterspell had given him—that he must turn his back on that sow—and the insane compulsion that drove him forward against his will to caress the beast. Psyche heard but did not care. Since she had no hope of being pardoned, she had nothing for which to pray—and she did not dare let go of her father because she could feel him pull against her weakening hold.

"Help me!" she cried to her brothers. "Help me bring our father within. And pen that beast!"

"No!" Anerios gasped, dragging her forward.

They would both have fallen down the steps had not Damianos caught his father and blocked his path. Gillos rushed forward to help him and Otius grasped the nose of the sow and led her away. The people watched in horror as Anerios fought his sons to follow or bring back the animal, but the two were too strong for him and dragged him back from the porch, through the vestibule, and into his private bedchamber.

Psyche had gone with them, but she stopped outside the room. Her mother had been within it, no doubt, and perhaps other women, but Anerios dealt with his daughters only in the public chambers or in the women's quarters with their mother present. She could hear the struggle and her father's groans as he alternately fought himself and his sons, but she only leaned against the wall and closed her eyes. After a while she slipped down and sat on the floor.

The weakness that afflicted her was not like that after great physical effort. That also caused a trembling of the limbs and a need to sit or lie down, but that weakness was of the outer body. This was far more terrible. There seemed to be a huge hollow void at her core that was sucking at her, drawing strength from her body into itself. Psyche knew that if too much were drawn, she would collapse in on herself and die.

Vaguely she heard Damianos protesting and Gillos's angry reply, which was broken off to shout "Father!" and "Hold him, Damianos."

The sharp command caught her attention and she heard clearly her father's groan followed by several gasps and then his voice, strained, but rational, "I did not even know I had moved. We cannot give her up. She saved me. Until she whispered that spell in my ear, I had no mind. I knew nothing except—" His voice cut off, then continued thin and breathless. "At least she broke the spell a little. I know now what horror I desire." Another silence. More creaks of the bed and thuds. Then Anerios's voice, gasping. "I cannot help myself, but I know. We must find another sacrifice, not Psyche."

"Do not be foolish, father," Gillos said. "Do you still think you can befool the goddess? Eros warned that he would make no bargains. Perhaps Aphrodite is envious of Psyche's beauty and wishes to remove it from the world. Where will you find a face and body to match hers? You will only get us into more trouble if you try to keep her. If you give her up as well as a few oxen and sweet words, you will not need her. The curse will be lifted from us."

"Gillos!" Damianos cried. "She is our sister. Would you see her sacrificed like a lamb or a heifer?"

"I would go myself, if that was what Aphrodite ordered," Gillos snarled. "Do you not understand that this curse has besmirched the whole family? Even if Otius were to take papa's place on the throne, the people would not accept him. You heard them screaming that the goddess must be pacified. Father must humble himself to Hyppodamia and Psyche must be chained to the altar on Mount Pelion or we will all be driven out as scapegoats."

"Not chained!" Damianos exclaimed. "Eros said nothing about chains."

Slow tears trickled down Psyche's cheeks. If Damianos would do no more than protest against her being bound by chains to the altar, certainly no one would try to save her. She and Damianos had been particularly fond of each other in happier days. They liked many of the same things, most particularly to discover how wild creatures lived, and they had often shared ventures. Wearily she wiped the tears away. Gillos was right. What good could any protest do? She knew she had to be the sacrifice, since it was she the goddess demanded. Only it was . . . lonely . . . that no one cared enough to make more than a token protest.

"Psyche! What are you doing here?"

Otius stood looking down at her. But before he could order her away or Psyche could offer an explanation, Anerios howled like a wild animal. "I smell her," he shrieked. "I smell her. Let me go."

Otius leapt into the room to help his brothers control his father. Psyche closed her eyes and prayed for strength, knowing what must be the end of the struggle. She heard Gillos shouting that Otius should go away and wash the scent of the sow off him and Otius yelling back that he had washed, not being a fool. She heard Damianos sobbing and the sound of blows striking flesh and then of cloth tearing and incoherent shrieks of rage. And in the gasping silence that followed the struggle to bind her father, he began to scream like a woman in labor, begging his sons to have mercy and let him go to the sow.

"Can I live like this?" he wailed. "Let me empty myself and I will be better. I must go. I must."

Then came the bellow she had been expecting, "Psyche!"

Otius burst out of the room and pulled her roughly to her feet. "Do something," he snarled. "You quieted him when the spell was first cast. Quiet him again."

"I will try," she whispered, "but I spent my little power on the first counterspell. I do not know whether I have strength enough to cast the spell again."

She could feel the hollow within her. She knew that light and power should fill that well, but it took weeks to renew herself, and even then her well held only a light mist, not the strong glow she had felt in the wise woman with whom she had studied. She wondered, as Otius snapped that she must try and pushed her into her father's bedchamber, whether the casting would kill her. And for one resentful moment she thought it would serve her family right if Aphrodite would not lift the curse because her chosen victim was dead and she had been deprived of the pleasure of torturing her.

Then she saw her father bound, writhing with unsatisfied lust, and she could not bear to see him so bereft of strength and dignity, even humanity. She leaned over him, stroking his face and his body. The words of the counterspell poured out and a soft, blue mist seemed to float gently from her fingers over and then into his body. Her life flowed out with the mist. The room dimmed. For a moment she felt the edge of the bed cutting into her thighs and a painful pressure on her arms, and then . . . nothing.

CHAPTER 6

Psyche felt herself being lifted and a spoon pressed against her lips. She opened her mouth and her eyes at the same time. For a moment, no one realized she had regained consciousness. Enstiktia had her eyes on the broth she was spooning into Psyche's mouth, and Horexea, who was supporting her, was watching the process. Psyche swallowed, which kept her silent, while she wondered whether she was dying.

As the thought came, she knew it was ridiculous. She did not feel ill. Yet tears streaked Enstiktia's face and her eyes were red and tired looking, as if from much weeping. A movement behind Enstiktia caught Psyche's eye. Her mother came into view, and she looked far worse than her sister. Her face was drawn, the cheeks hollow, and the eyes, although dry, ringed with dark marks, like bruises. It was she who uttered a cry of surprise—but clearly not of joy—when she saw that Psyche's eyes were open.

"My poor child," she breathed, leaning down and stroking Psyche's hair.

Psyche blinked. She could not remember when her mother had last called her "poor child." And then memory flooded her. She remembered the hateful, haughty, blinding beauty of Eros, the agony of her poor accursed father, the casting of the counterspell, the pronouncement of her own doom. She had apparently survived the second spell-casting but had lost her senses.

"Papa?" she asked.

Horexea clutched her tighter and began to sob aloud. Enstiktia dropped the spoon into the bowl and hid her face in her hands.

"Your father has been granted some remission. Your brothers carried him to the temple of Aphrodite after you fell, but they had to—" Her mother's mouth and voice began to shake, and she had to pause to steady them. "They had to take the sow with them. He fell into convulsions when they tried to carry him away without her." She swallowed. "Still, when she walked with them, he had sense enough not to scream of his desire. Your spell held well enough to permit him to speak to Hyppodamia and promise restitution."

As she spoke, Beryllia drew a stool to the side of Psyche's couch and Psyche freed herself from her sister's arms and sat up. The queen's mouth trembled again. "Child," she whispered, lowering her eyes to her tightly clasped hands, "we promised everything. Your father offered his whole herds of cattle, to have a golden statue made to honor the goddess, to abdicate, to pass the rule of the kingdom to the priestess, anything . . ."

"Hyppodamia would not listen." Psyche said flatly.

"No, no." Beryllia shook her head and met Psyche's eyes again. "The priestess demanded no revenge for the hurt done herself. She asked only such temple attendance and sacrifice as would reinforce the king's acknowledgment of Aphrodite's power. And she wept for your father and for you. She prayed to Aphrodite to accept some other sacrifice. It was Eros. He came . . ."

"He did lighten the curse on our father so that he can

resist his desire enough not to disgrace himself and us," Horexea said quickly.

Beryllia nodded, but her eyes slid away from Psyche's. "The mercy was only for your father," she said faintly. "Eros forbade the priestess to intercede for you again. You must go . . ." Her voice failed altogether.

Psyche patted her mother's clasped hands. "Perhaps it is for the best," she said, staring into nothing. "What had I to look forward to? No man could see *me* past this face. I believe it is better to die by the goddess's hand and restore peace to papa and to our lands and people than to be married to a man who would torment me bitterly out of jealousy and then, perhaps, destroy my home and my family too."

"It is not fair!" Enstiktia wailed. "No one valued you when you were a little girl because you were unlovely, and now, because you are too lovely, you must suffer a terrible fate."

"That is not certain," Horexea said sharply. "Eros said only that Psyche was to be left at the altar. You know the creatures offered to the goddess are never slain and that she sometimes demands children as sacrifice. A few have even been returned, those who could not be comforted by her kindness. They say the other children are well and happy."

"Yes, of course," Beryllia said, forcing a smile. "Perhaps Aphrodite desires a beautiful handmaid."

A handmaid who hates her? Psyche thought. But she did not speak the thought aloud. She did not think either her mother or Horexea believed the comfort they were offering her, but she was warmed by her mother's and sisters' grief. She felt less cold, less alone, strong enough to do what she must with dignity.

Whether that feeling could have sustained her for long she did not know, but at first her relief that she would not dissolve into incessant weeping or mindless shrieks allowed her to realize that she was starving. She finished the broth Enstiktia had been feeding her and then a lavish meal. Her attention was fixed so firmly on filling her empty stomach that she did not question the succession of elegant courses that were brought up until she was nearly full. While she was toying with a tart/sweet concoction of fruits and nuts, it occurred to her to ask how the cooks could have known she would wake just when she did and be so hungry.

Both her sisters burst into tears and her mother grew so white that Psyche thought she would faint. Then she recalled that the other women had eaten very little and her heart leapt into her throat. A funeral feast! Insane laughter vied with shrieks of terror inside her, but the obstruction in her throat denied any outlet to both. *Her* funeral feast! She had been devouring her own funeral feast!

She swallowed, swallowed again, and finally managed to whisper, "How long have I been senseless?"

"Six days," Beryllia said. "Tomorrow morning we must take you up the mountain." Her voice was still flat, but tears filled her eyes and then spilled over as she added, "I hoped . . . I hoped you would not wake, that you would not need to be afraid—" And then she hid her face and moaned, rocking back and forth. "To lose a child is hard," she sobbed, "but to know that child is afraid and be unable to offer comfort . . . I cannot bear it. I cannot bear it."

Psyche knew what her mother meant. She remembered a little brother's death and how her mother had sat with him while he slipped away, smiling, assuring him that she was there and that there was nothing to fear.

"Well, I am afraid, mother," Psyche said, touching her mother's shoulder. "But remember how frightened

Enstiktia was when she was bearing her son." She pressed her sister's hand, which had been extended toward her. "And she came through that fear into great joy. Who knows? Perhaps what the peasant women whisper to each other is true. Perhaps there will be a kind Mother waiting to welcome me."

It was not much to cling to, a belief that the noble families laughed to scorn. But Psyche remembered that the wise woman who taught her had spoken of the Mother from Whom, she swore, she received the power she used. Psyche had not believed her; and when she tried to tap that source, she could not find it. Now, sick with fear, she reached for any lifeline and found a little thread of hope.

Between that and the fact that she felt ashamed of weeping and wailing for herself, she found the strength to make herself busy. She spent the evening gathering up and apportioning to others her possessions. Usually for the youngest daughter that would be a light task—a few gowns, a few ornaments. But Psyche had been the recipient of lavish gifts from suitors for several years. She had rejected those that she could, but many she had to keep to avoid offense. In addition, during her studies and explorations she had accumulated valuable recipes and a knowledge of herbs that she did not wish to be lost because of her death. Nor did she wish to leave behind her bitterness and envy by giving too much to one or by giving the wrong thing to the wrong person.

The jewels took most of the time. She worried so much about arousing enmity between her sisters or envy in their husbands that she forgot the purpose of dividing her possessions. And she was so weary when at last she felt almost content with her decisions that she was able to sleep until her mother woke her at dawn.

The shock of seeing Beryllia with her hair full of ashes, her face and gown streaked with tears and dirt, froze out fear, froze out all emotion. Like a soulless simulacrum, she explained to her mother how she had apportioned her goods and begged her to give them to the designated persons. Fresh tears washed some of the ash from Beryllia's cheeks, but she thanked Psyche for saving her the pain of deciding whether to keep or distribute her possessions, and she promised the packets would go to those she had named.

Then her sisters, ash- and tear-smeared and with rent garments, entered to help her dress. For a moment, emotion stirred in Psyche as she prepared to resist being dressed as a mourner, but she crushed the faint stirring of resentment, fearing that any feeling, even rage, would unloose the hounds of terror that would tear her apart.

Her distaste for being presented as a penitent was not challenged, however. Enstiktia's and Horexea's hands were clean, and they helped her into the garments she had prepared without protest. She needed neither breast band nor girdle, for her full breasts were also firm with youth and exercise, as were her belly and hips; nonetheless, she donned them to keep her chiton from clinging if her body grew wet with fear. A simple white chiton, embroidered with a single row of leaves in a clear violet, came next, and above it, a violet peplos embroidered in white.

When she had tied her outer girdle, Beryllia said, "There is food—"

Psyche nodded, and Horexea went away and returned with a tray. What was in the dishes, Psyche never knew. None had any taste and all smelled of the ashes that covered her mother and sisters. Nonetheless Psyche ate heartily, wondering as she chewed and swallowed whether that was how the dead perceived food, all dusted with the salt and ashes of grief.

When she was done, she rose and said, "I am ready."

Enstiktia placed a large, thick cloak of soft wool over her shoulders. When her sister's hand brushed Psyche's, she thought that Enstiktia must have a fever, so hot was her skin, and then she realized that Enstiktia was not specially warm: her own hand must be cold as ice. But she did not feel cold. And when she wrapped the cloak around her, several layers of thick wool, she did not feel any warmer. Was it the goddess's mercy that she could not feel, Psyche wondered, and then thought, no, it is the Mother's mercy. Aphrodite may be kind to those who please her, but she is not merciful.

Whoever had given her the gift of unfeeling was merciful enough not to withdraw it. The strongest emotion Psyche felt all that long day was one quiver of surprise at the very beginning of it when her brothers closed around her to lift her into the open litter that would carry her up the mountain. Not that she felt anything about that, not even when Damianos kissed her cheek and wet it with his tears. It was the fact that there were four litters that surprised her.

The open one was hers, so all the people could see that it was she who was brought to Pelion and set upon the altar. One closed one held her father—she could hear his heavy weeping—and the other was for her mother. Her sisters and brothers were walking, her brothers among the bearers who would carry her litter, so who— A low grunt answered her unfinished question. Psyche thought if she could feel anything, surely she would be amused. The sow was in the fourth litter, and her father was probably weeping more because he could not ride with the beast than because he was going to lose his daughter. She suspected that moment could not come soon enough for him, both because it would banish his dreadful compulsion and because her death would solve a great many political problems for him. She said as much to him when he marveled at her courage because she ate a substantial dinner at the little village where Atomos had asked for help in skinning the bear. "No, I do not grieve," she said, curving her lips as if she were smiling. "I am consoled by knowing that giving up my life will make your life and my brothers' so much easier."

Her older brothers did not react, though Damianos's breath caught, but her father had grace enough to lower his eyes and murmur, "I never wished you harm, Psyche."

She thought that was probably true and knew, too, that most of her father's stupid overreaction in the temple had been in a sense her fault. If she had not felt such loathing at the idea of being priestess to a goddess of what she abhorred, she would not have been rejected by Hyppodamia. But she felt no remorse for what she had said, and when they set out again, she actually fell into a doze from sheer lack of interest.

Even arrival at the summit did not break her calm, nor the final farewells, nor the heaping of the altar with comforts for her "journey." Psyche sat, blank of mind, dead of heart, watching with indifference as the sun sank behind the lower mountains to the west and twilight faded into dark.

The first break in her stupor of indifference was caused by a mild sense of surprise when she found she had broken open a jar of olives which had been left as an offering for the dead and was munching on a handful. That reminded her with what appetite she had eaten her own funeral feast, and she burst out laughing.

The sound was shocking in the silence, but not nearly so shocking as the voice that echoed her laughter and then said, "So you hate love and beauty enough to laugh at your fate? Your monster has come to fetch you, Psyche."

She jumped to her feet, whirling to face the faintly

familiar voice, but the brief hope she had felt fled, pursued by terror. She could see nothing except a blacker blackness stirring at the edge of the forest. "Monster?" she repeated faintly.

"Did they not tell you what your punishment for rejecting love and beauty would be?" The familiarity of the voice was lost in mocking laughter. "You are to be the bride of a monster."

Then the blacker blackness detached itself from the edge of the forest and flowed toward her, and all the fear that had been suppressed throughout the long night and the longer day rose up and fell down upon her, crushing her. She was so terrified she could not draw breath to scream, and a blackness within her drowned her senses and flowed outward to meet the shadow that stalked her. She felt herself falling but had not strength enough to put out a hand to save herself, but she never seemed to reach the ground.

When Psyche's eyes opened, she saw stars. Not the kind of stars that might bedazzle her eyes if she had hit her head after falling off the altar on which she had been standing, but the small, distant stars of a night sky. Nor was she surrounded by blackness. She lay, wrapped in her warm cloak, on soft grass in a glade well silvered with the light of an almost full moon. For a moment she wondered whether she had fallen asleep in the woods of Iolkas and all the horrible events had been a dreadful nightmare. Breath catching on hope, Psyche hurriedly untangled one of her arms from her cloak and pushed herself upright so she could look around.

Hope died instantly. Although she was no longer on top of Mount Pelion, she knew her father's obsession and her appointment as a sacrifice had been no nightmare—nor had the blot of blackness that had spoken to her. Somehow, she had been transported from the altar on Mount Pelion to . . . where? One glade in a forest might look much like another, but she was certain she had never seen this place before. This was no forest glade in Iolkas; it was trimmed and pruned, forest tamed into a garden, and—she drew a sharp breath. There was a house just beyond a fountain, whose burble and splashing she had thought must be a stream.

A house. The bride of a monster. Was it waiting in the house? She sat and stared at the place. She could run away. She shuddered. To have that flowing darkness following on her heels would surely be worse than confronting it. And if she ran, would Aphrodite consider that a violation of the terms of lifting the curse from her father? She had expected to die. What could the monster do to her worse than that? But she knew there were worse things than death—slow torture, pain, and humiliation for days, weeks, months, years. Running away would not spare her that. There was only one thing she could do. Psyche bit her lip and got slowly to her feet. She could enrage the beast until it struck out at her and killed her.

It took her a long time to get to the house. She kept stopping and trying to find an alternative to what she was doing, but she knew there was no escape for her. And sometimes her limbs trembled so much she had to stop just to keep from falling. Most horrible of all, the door of the house stood open, creating a warm, inviting, golden pathway of lamplight. In Iolkas, such a pathway promised a safe haven against the terrors of the night. Here . . . Psyche shivered as she stepped into the golden glow, but a kind of hysterical desire to be finished, to be done with waiting, made her hurry. She hesitated only once, when she actually stepped across the threshold, and that was out of astonishment; she had walked into a total anticlimax.

No monster waited for her, no pall of blackness covered any part of the small courtyard, which was paved with a beautiful mosaic and well lit with lanterns hung from polished wooden columns which supported the gallery of the upper story. Four old servants, two men and two women, stood in the courtyard, and apparently they had been waiting for her, because all smiled and bowed respectfully and one woman gestured for Psyche to step into the long vestibule. That, too, was brightly lit, and at the end to the right was the open door of a reception room in which Psyche could see a chair and bowls and towels for washing a traveler's feet.

"Where am I?" she asked, turning back to look at the servants who had followed her in. "Who are you?"

All four pointed to their mouths and shook their heads. Mutes! Servants who could never tell what they had seen. Psyche's heart clenched and she glanced fearfully over her shoulder, but the courtyard was empty, not a shadow anywhere. And the servants did not look frightened or haunted, as those who had seen monstrous cruelty surely must.

"Where is the master of the house?" she asked then. This time the men shrugged. One tried to convey something in signs, but Psyche could make nothing of it. Meanwhile, the other man and one woman went into a doorway a bit to the left of center and the other woman went into the reception room, laying out the towels and beckoning Psyche to come to her and sit in the chair. Almost immediately, the other old woman came in bearing a pot of steaming water and the man followed with a pitcher. The first womanservant poured the water, tested it, and washed Psyche's feet. When they were dry and her cleaned sandals had been replaced, she was led to the andron, which in a private house such as this served the purpose of the megaron. She braced for at last confronting horror when she saw where she was being taken, but the chamber was empty and the servant gestured for *her* to sit or recline. In moments a manservant brought a table to the couch and the first course of an excellent meal arrived. Like an automaton, Psyche began to eat, wondering whether her placement on the central couch in the chamber usually used by the master of the household was supposed to mean that she was the mistress here.

Her mind could not come to grips with the facts; she had endured too much stress and was too exhausted to try to reason out an answer to the question. She found herself nodding over her food and gratefully followed the old woman who came to lead her back out into the courtyard and up the stair to the gallery. Two doors faced the stairhead. The one on the right was opened by the maidservant to show a handsome bedchamber. The other old woman was waiting. Together they removed her clothing and she slipped into the bed and slept.

If she dreamed, she did not remember. Psyche woke pleasantly to sunlight, to the sound of birdsong and the distant tinkling of the fountain, and, when she saw the strange room, to a heart pounding with renewed fear. Only there was nothing to fear. Her heart steadied but did not lift. She felt at the same time foolish and weighted with dread.

There was a bell on a small table beside the bed. One of the old women came in answer to its silvery peal and opened a chest full of handsome garments—all new, all made to the measure of her tall, well-fleshed body. Many garments. Did that mean she would live in this house for many days? Weeks? Months? Years?

She chose the simplest among the rich chitons and peploses and dressed. She went downstairs to find breakfast waiting. She ate. She wandered out into the garden. No one stopped her. No one came after her when she went to where she had awakened and beyond that into the woods. But she knew there was no escape. For one thing, she had no idea where she was. For another, the freedom granted her made her very sure that she could be easily found and brought back.

Shrugging, she returned to the house and began to examine it. When she came across a servant, the woman or man smiled and nodded at her, making her welcome wherever she appeared. It was a lovely house, every room beautifully furnished and decorated, but she could take no pleasure in the tastefulness and convenience. There was nothing to fear, but something constricted her throat and lay so heavily on her breast that she could barely breathe. And then, having been in every room on the ground floor, she climbed the stair, opened the door on the left of the chamber in which she had slept, and stood transfixed.

She had found a long-unfulfilled dream—a real book room. Psyche stood blinking in the doorway, the heaviness in her breast lightening as she took in the deep shelves stocked with scrolls, the racks of wax-filled frames for writing notes or first drafts that needed correction, the wide table on which were supports for three sets of brass rods for holding open the scrolls and a stand for styli. For the first time since reentering the house, she hesitated before crossing a doorsill. This was too good, too much what she desired. Could it be a trap?

But the room was very well lit. There was no shadow, no corner in which a blackness might lurk. Psyche stepped in, walked quickly to the shelves, and pulled a roll from the top. No black shadow appeared, no voice protested. Psyche untied the ribbon and unrolled the top half, expecting to see squiggles she would not recognize. Her heart leapt when she recognized the symbols, then sank when she could not understand the words. She took another scroll from the shelf below, but that, too, was unintelligible. Sighing, she rerolled and retied both scrolls, replaced them, and turned away.

She did not leave the room, however. After a moment of standing irresolute, she shrugged and went back to the scrolls. What else had she to do? It was better to be busy, even only rolling and unrolling scrolls, than to spend the long hours dreading every moment.

By the time she had been through the highest shelf, Psyche had begun to doubt her reasoning. It was just as boring, she thought, to keep looking at gibberish as to do nothing at all. Nonetheless, she did not want to leave the book room. Something about it—perhaps the well-worn chair in which she was sitting; whoever heard of a monster that sat in a chair and read books?—was comforting. She moved another unintelligible scroll from right to left, untied a new one, and gasped with joy. Here at last was something she could read. It was not very interesting, a treatise on beekeeping, which she was certain she had seen or heard before, but it proved there were some works in her own language.

The fourth shelf, the one that could be reached from the chair merely by stretching out a hand, was her reward. Most of the scrolls were in familiar dialects and, the greatest of treasure troves, there was also a listing of equivalent words in several dialects, and in one language totally unfamiliar. Psyche stroked the thick book—four scrolls rolled together—as if it were a living creature she wished to praise and make docile, but she put it aside, eager to see what else she would find.

There were several texts on hunting, a text on philosophy, and one on birds with charming sketches. She was startled when one of the menservants scratched on the door and then entered with a tray of food—bread, a bowl of olives, three different cheeses, a pitcher of

wine, and another of milk, and cups to drink each. He
set the tray down beside her as if it were the most
ordinary thing for him to bring food to the book room.
Psyche almost smiled. Did the monster eat bread and
cheese and olives while it read? But the thought brought
a chill with it, a memory of that black nothingness
flowing toward her, and she reached hastily for another
scroll from the pile.

The title made her freeze for a moment and then
slowly reach for the scroll holders. *The History of the
Olympians,* she read. This *must* be forbidden to her
people, Psyche thought, and was swept again by the
conviction that the book room was a trap. But she was
already caught and already condemned. What worse
could befall her than to be drawn into the blackness and
be lost?

Curiosity was a stronger impulse in her than fear, she
found. Although self-preservation bade her roll up the
scroll and look for something safer, she found herself
reading. The beginning was harmless enough . . . perhaps. It was an explanation that the author felt a translation was necessary because continued and increasing
dealings with the native peoples was making their language more familiar to the Olympians than the old
tongue they had brought with them.

Brought with them? Psyche wondered. Did gods
come from somewhere? She twisted the roller to expose
the next section of text and began to read about
Kronos's quarrel with his father, his attempt to seize
power, and his expulsion from his nation together with
those who had supported him.

It seemed only moments before a sustained ache in
Psyche's neck and shoulders forced her to straighten
her back. Only then did she realize that the light was
failing and she had been hunched forward, leaning
closer and closer to the manuscript in an attempt to see

better. She sighed and rose, shaking out her creased gown while she wondered whether she should restore the scroll to its original place in the hope of concealing what she had been reading. Before she could decide, a glow lit the gallery outside the open door and one of the menservants holding a lamp gestured to her and made a sign of eating.

Psyche decided to leave everything the way it was. Was not her purpose to enrage the monster? In fact, she was tempted to take a scroll down with her, since there was no one to whom she could talk while she ate, but she could think of no way to prop up the manuscript or to protect it from stains. However, with her head full of the descriptions of the homeland and conflicts of the Olympians and the powers wielded by its rulers, she hardly noticed her solitude or the food she consumed. At last, still thinking about whether power alone should define what was a god and wishing she had someone with whom she could discuss the question, Psyche pushed away the cup of wine with which she had been toying and left the table. She would walk in the garden for a while, she thought, and then go to bed.

The vestibule was empty, the door to the courtyard open. Seemingly, this house had nothing to fear from thieves or attack. Psyche looked up as she stepped out, noting the bright stars in the clear sky and the brilliant moon.

"I hope the house is to your taste," a man's voice said.

CHAPTER 7

Golden lamplight and silver moonlight alike were swallowed up into the utter blackness Psyche confronted. Its spreading base seemed to cover half the courtyard and its rounded apex appeared to reach the tops of the trees. Shock, disappointment, and rage followed each other and filled Psyche to the exclusion of fear. She had begun to be happy with the books and her thoughts. It was not fair to have that happiness snatched away before she had really tasted it.

"Begone!" she ordered. "Begone, you foul thing!"

"Why do you call me foul?" The voice was ravishingly beautiful and held no threat. "I have done nothing to merit your insult."

"I agreed to be sacrificed to Aphrodite," Psyche spat. "I never agreed to be a monster's bride. You had your chance to do what you wished with me when I fell senseless. Now I am awake, and I will resist you to the death."

A very human chuckle drifted out of the dark. "But does not the fact that I did you no harm when you were helpless imply that I may be trusted?"

Psyche shuddered and shook her head. Her fear was diminishing, but her revulsion for the blackness that seemed to swallow into nothingness everything it touched was only increased by the lovely voice and the warm laughter.

"Trusted?" she echoed. "No! It tells me of your cruelty. You want me awake and suffering. I will not yield. I did not make this bargain and will not keep it. I will not be befouled by you."

"I can promise that you will not be befouled by me, for I am the cleaner and more honest of us." A cold note, steel-hard, somehow did not lessen the music of the voice. "I do not believe that you would have watched your father futtering a sow—a very nice sow, I admit, but not at all attractive—for the rest of his much shortened life. I do not think that you would have allowed your whole family to be made scapegoats, or seen your sisters and their children driven from their homes as well as your brothers. You know you would have agreed to any terms. You are lying and dishonest, seeking a crack in your promises so you can ooze out of your bargain."

Psyche winced. What the creature said was true, and it hurt. She stared into the blackness as hard as she could, but she could see nothing. The inky shadow did not eddy or swirl. It was as if a piece of the world had been cut away and replaced with pitch. She shuddered again. She had no answer to the monster's accusation, but she could not agree to yield herself. She could not even conceive what torture a mating with such a being would cause or what could be the result of such a mating.

"I will not," she cried. "You are a monster!"

"Who is the monster between us?" the black cloud asked. "Your face and form are beautiful, but your spirit is monstrous—a lying, cheating thing hiding its self-interest in a pretense of noble sacrifice. Is it not monstrous to break your word and your promise to be a sacrifice—no way was specified—to expiate the sin against Aphrodite? Is not the punishment meet and fitting, that she who claims to hate love and beauty be mated to monstrosity without love? Which of us then is more monstrous? I—upon whom it is better not to look, but who has tried in every way, even cloaking my monstrous form in darkness to spare you—I, who will honestly try to fulfill my pledge to be a good husband, or you?"

"Perhaps you are right." Psyche's breath rattled with her trembling. "But it does not matter. I cannot yield myself. I cannot. I am too afraid." She caught her breath on a sob. "I beg you," tears spilled over and more sobs made her words almost unintelligible, "kill me and be done. Do not torture me. Just kill me quickly."

A slight movement in the black pall, a swelling toward her, made Psyche retreat a step in acute terror. She realized as her lips parted to scream and no sound emerged that she had expected more reassurance, more concessions—not death. She had no longer believed the monster was dangerous and was acting a part, lying to it—and herself—hoping to shame it into giving up its claim. The movement ceased. The shroud of darkness stood quiet.

"Psyche, I will not torture you or kill you, even if you refuse me forever. I will do you no harm for any cause. I will live in the hope that you will come truly to understand what you have been known to say, that beauty or ugliness is no mirror for the soul beneath."

The voice, soft now, was pure music. Yet for a moment, Psyche thought there was a kind of familiarity to it. She could not pick out exactly what was familiar, though, and the overlying qualities, the smooth music and rich timbre, were not associated in her mind with anyone. Moreover, having the reassurance she sought, she guessed that the monster had never meant to threaten her, had possibly been reaching toward her to comfort her. On the other hand, it gave no sign at all of giving up its claim to her.

"You say you will not kill me. You imply you will not force me. Then what do you want from me?"

"For the present, your company. For the future, your willing acceptance of the sacrifice you promised."

She wanted to cry, "Never." The thought of willingly offering herself to be swallowed by that black nothing was too horrible, but silence would buy time. As long as the creature kept its word, she could live; and life, as she had learned a moment ago when she thought she was about to die, was sweet. What she did not know was how she would endure being in the presence of the black emptiness day and night. Surely she could bargain for some time alone.

"How much of my company?" she asked cautiously.

A hearty laugh burst from the cloud. "And you call me a monster!" the voice cried between chuckles. "First you plead not to be tortured only to be killed quickly, and when I offer you a fingertip of kind assurance, you bite off my whole arm, demanding guarantees about how your precious time will be spent. Should you not be down on your knees, thanking me for my mercy?"

"Should I?" Psyche asked, shame making her waspish. "You have been lauding your moral superiority to me. Would it not decrease the perfection of your soul's beauty if you enjoyed the groveling of your victims?"

"Ouch! That prick hurt," the cloud said, trying to sound wounded, but clearly amused. "And my feet are starting to hurt too—"

"You have feet?" Psyche asked, glancing down. She could see nothing, but the remark somehow was reassuring.

"Large ones," the monster replied, and Psyche knew it was doing what served it for smiling, "and easily made to ache by the weight they carry. Will you not invite me to sit down?"

The amusement made her more waspish. "I? Invite you? This is your house, is it not? I assume the bride is brought to the bridegroom's house—"

"The house is Aphrodite's. We are both her servants—and, I suppose, have equal rights to her house."

Involuntarily Psyche took a step toward the cloud, asking with sympathy, "Are you too a victim of the goddess of love and beauty?"

"A victim? No. And neither are you, although you have not yet understood Aphrodite's forethought, kindness, and mercy. As for me, when others would have condemned me to death for no reason save my appearance, she saved me, gave me a place to live, looked on me without flinching, and has never failed or faltered in her kindness."

Psyche's lips parted to make a caustic reply, but she thought better of it. There had been no laughter in the voice at all when it spoke of Aphrodite. The creature loved the goddess and might be more enraged by an insult to her than any challenge to itself.

"We see with different eyes and feel with different hearts," she said moderately. "But if the house is as much yours as mine, you must feel free to sit where you like and when you like without needing to wait for my invitation."

"Then let us sit in the garden," the monster said. "If you sit on one end of the bench near the fountain, perhaps you can imagine that you are talking to a suitor sitting in the shadows at the other end."

"Very well," Psyche agreed, but she did not move.

"Go ahead and pass me, Psyche," the cloud urged softly. "You must learn to trust me."

"I am afraid to pass too close." She heard the high tight tone hinting at hysteria, swallowed, and tried to explain. "I cannot bear the thought of being swallowed up into that blackness."

"There is nothing in the cloud that can or would harm you, Psyche. Nor will it swallow you. It only conceals what enters it; it changes nothing. It is a disguise to hide my appearance."

"It is a horrible disguise!" Psyche exclaimed, but she gathered her courage and hurried past the black blot. Her skirt even brushed the darkness, confirming what the creature said, for the cloth disappeared as it entered and emerged unchanged as she pulled it away. "If you are allowed a disguise," she snapped back over her shoulder, "why did you not choose that of an ordinary man?"

She shuddered and faced forward again as the darkness began to move, flowing across the courtyard behind her. She had to grip the bench to keep herself still as that blot of blackness advanced across the moon-silvered grass, but when it shrank down onto the other end of the bench and blended into the shadows, the horror diminished. She had almost forgotten her question and was surprised when the beautiful voice came from the shadow.

"I had most excellent reasons for choosing this disguise. The most important to me is that I did not wish you to form an affection for any face other than my own, which you might well do if I wooed you wearing the disguise of an ordinary man. Another reason, perhaps more important in the abstract, was that to disguise myself as an ordinary man would have violated the terms of your punishment—that you be bride to a monster. I am Aphrodite's servant and I am obliged to fulfill my obligations to her."

"Then why do you simply not force me and be done with your obligation?" Psyche snapped.

"Because I want more from you than to be an unwilling sheath for my shaft. That, I can find anywhere. Like any being, I desire a home, love, children. For me to have that, you must be happy, Psyche. And when you are happy, you will admit that your punishment was just and that Aphrodite is wise and kind and gladly acknowledge her power—so we will all be content."

"If you are going to preach at me all the time we are in each other's company," Psyche said nastily, "I will begin to doubt your promise not to torture me."

"For someone in the last extremity of terror, you have a venomous tongue," the blot snapped back.

"If you are going to pretend to be a suitor, that is what you must expect from me," Psyche retorted. "I was not very welcoming to the richest, noblest, and handsomest of the men who came to court me, so how can you expect to be more gently handled when you tell me you are a servant and so ugly that you must hide your face in a black blot?"

The cloud sniffed with disdain. "Black blot, indeed. I am more awesome than a blot. And the circumstances are different. Those suitors bored you to death, not to mention that they were so jealous they would have made your life miserable and perhaps—"

"If the rich and handsome would be jealous, am I to believe that the poor and ugly will be less so?"

No answer came from the shadow, and Psyche was suddenly remorseful. She had been cruel, and whatever was in that blackness had done its best to be kind and reassuring. Likely the poor creature had no more choice about what it did than she. It had said it was Aphrodite's servant. Servants do not do their own will, but obey.

"Forgive me," she said softly. "I have been so frightened and so despairing that I have lost all sense that others have troubles and sorrows. My tongue is naturally sharp, but I fear it is now spiteful because I am overworn with waiting and expecting a dreadful doom."

"Of course," the darkness said. "I must ask forgiveness too. I meant to give you time to grow accustomed and came in the night so I would blend in a little and you would not be reminded every moment of my strangeness. I did not mean to increase your fear by making you wait for your 'terrible doom.' Even the sweetest lyre is shrill when it is strung too tightly. Go and rest, Psyche, in the knowledge that your doom is nothing worse than to sit, thus, and talk to me."

Psyche jumped up as if she had been released from bonds that fixed her to the bench. "Thank you," she said, and then posessed of a dreadful thought, added, "Where will you go?"

"Not into your house," the monster replied. "I will not come again until tomorrow night. You may meet me here in the garden, or if it rains, let the servants darken the house and I will come within so we can talk in comfort. You need not fear that I will mistake that invitation for another. I will leave you when you wish to be free of me."

Guilt stung Psyche again. "You said Aphrodite allowed you to live in this house. Do you have some other place to go? I—it is not fair that you should be cast out of your home."

"There is one other place where I am welcome. I will not sleep under this roof until you are ready to call this 'our' house and welcome me into your bed."

Psyche paused, the rigidity of her body showing her denial. Then she turned and fled. Eros remained on the bench, wrapped in his cloud of darkness, which was no more than a faint, dull mist to his eyes. Smiling broadly, he watched her cross the courtyard and enter the vestibule. Probably it was now safe to dispense with the cloud, but it was not necessary. He felt no significant drain in power while he wore it. He was not sure whether that was because he was bursting with the Mother's Gift or whether Hecate had woven a specially durable and economical spell.

He had been a little surprised at Hecate's willingness to accommodate him without Aphrodite as an agent, but only a little. He knew that Hecate was unaffected by his beauty and indifferent both to the Olympian prejudice against him and to Zeus's orders—perhaps because she was not an Olympian. She came from someplace in the east, the same area in which that mad boy Dionysus had spent his youth and early manhood—and Dionysus had never avoided him or tried to seduce him either.

Eros shook his head. Come to think of it, compared with Dionysus, Hecate was positively ordinary. But Eros did not think Hecate had accommodated him out of personal peculiarity or indifference to Olympian opinion. Nor had she been much interested in the payment he offered for the spell. She had accepted the jewels he brought, but had put them aside without a glance after touching his hand: she had smiled at him—and Hecate rarely smiled—and called him Mother-blessed.

Eros looked around. When Psyche was ready, he would build a shrine to the Mother here; She might not come to it—but She might. Since he had laid himself down in the woods near the palace to sleep at the Mother's shrine, it was as if he had Her special blessing. During that sleep, his power had not only been restored but doubled, tripled, and from that time, everything had gone right for him. The spell on Anerios continued to work perfectly. And like a private miracle, an impulse had sent him to watch with the scryer just when Hyppodamia had begun to pray for the lifting of the curse.

The scryer knew he had been dealing with the problem in Iolkas, so she was satisfied when he said it was unnecessary to trouble Aphrodite with Hyppodamia's prayers. Thus he was able to translocate to the temple and forbid any more prayers for Psyche's pardon while bribing Anerios with the offer of a week's mitigation of the curse and complete lifting of it if at week's end Psyche were sacrificed.

Eros chuckled softly. It was just as well Aphrodite knew nothing of the "sacrifice" of Psyche. The chances were that Aphrodite would have responded to Hyppodamia's prayers with a pardon for her. Her anger assuaged by Anerios's abject submission, Aphrodite was not the kind to hold a grudge. But her basic indifference, once her power in Iolkas was assured, would have created endless trouble. Psyche had to be removed from Iolkas to ensure the peace and stability that Hyppodamia had convinced him were necessary for the prosperity of Aphrodite's shrine—and for Psyche's own good, too. At his wits' end because of the trouble caused by trying to make her a priestess, Anerios might well have resorted to more drastic methods to be rid permanently of his daughter.

Poor Psyche, he had not wished to make her suffer, but sometimes one had to be cruel to be truly kind. She was the most amazing woman. Eros laughed suddenly, remembering the casual way she had sat on the altar, eating olives. Delight had drawn him out of hiding sooner than he intended. Then he stopped laughing, recalling his disappointment in the way she fainted when he came out of the trees where he had been waiting for the sacrificial procession to arrive.

Of course, the faint made transporting her to the house Aphrodite had built for him in the mountains above Olympus much easier. Violent struggles and intense terror created energies that could disrupt a translocation spell. But at first he had thought her courage might be less than would be necessary for her to grow accustomed and then to love something so dreadful it had to be hidden in a black pall. The round answers and barbed pricks she offered once her initial shock had passed, however, promised well for the future. Still, he must remember she had pretended to be much calmer than she really was when she nibbled olives on the altar. He must be patient.

Eros stretched and yawned, then smiled as he rose and moved off toward the forest that bordered the garden. The thought of needing to muster patience was so strange—and so wonderful. There had been nothing he'd wanted for so many, many years, nothing to be impatient about. Now he could scarcely wait for the next day to dawn because the night when he could begin to woo Psyche would follow it. And for more than a week he had been alive, aware of every hour.

Emotions he thought he had forgotten swept him by turns—eagerness, anguish . . . When Psyche had said that the rich and handsome would be less jealous than the poor and ugly, he had been torn by the desire to reveal himself. But it was not his own jealousy he feared; it was hers. Better to be patient and win her to love the being, whatever it was, whose physical form was hidden from her.

From the dark under the trees, Eros looked back at the house. The door had been closed—Psyche's hint that he should keep his promise and stay out? Irritation pricked him, knitting his brows and thinning his lips, and he began to laugh again over his vehemence. Even the sensations he had not lost completely, like irritation and amusement, were sharper and fresher. He laughed again, recalling how infuriated he had been after he managed to catch Psyche before she fell and hurt herself when he saw that the altar was heaped with grave goods.

It had not been, as he said, consideration for Psyche that had kept him from remaining with her until she woke from her faint and trying to reassure her that she would be safe. He had actually had to go back to the altar on Mount Pelion to remove the jars of food and bolts of cloth, spindles and needles and yarn, and who knew what else, so that anyone returning to the altar would see that Aphrodite had accepted the offerings. In fact, he had had to make three trips to get all the grave goods stored. Even his Mother-enhanced power had been strained by such heavy use of the translocation spell.

Having thought of the offerings left with Psyche, Eros wondered again what her family had been thinking of to virtually cover her with funeral gifts. They knew Aphrodite did not favor blood sacrifice—she liked to get all those white heifers and rabbits and doves alive; they kept better that way. Aphrodite complained that stasis spells left an odd taste in slaughtered sacrifices. Besides, Eros had told Anerios and his sons that Psyche would be a bride, not a corpse.

Ah! Right! He remembered her denial that her menfolk had told her about the "bride of a monster" doom. The grave offerings were to convince her . . . no, not her, she would have accepted whatever fate had been set on her, poor child. Instead, the funeral goods were to convince Anerios's townsfolk and noblemen that Psyche would die. It accounted, too, for the excessive display of grief by her mother and sisters, who, after all, must have found her a source of nothing but envy and trouble for years.

A light came on in the chamber to the right of the midline of the house. She was going to bed. Eros yawned and stretched again. The Mother's gift notwithstanding, he had done more in the last week and a half than in he knew not how many years. Smiling at looking forward to even so common a thing as going to bed, Eros dismissed the cloud with the same words that lifted Hecate's spell of invisibility and invoked the one that would bring him back to Aphrodite's palace in Olympus.

A cherubic child, thumb in mouth, was asleep in the middle of his bed. Eros sighed; apparently he was not going to get to bed, at least right away. But he was too happy, too much aware that his happiness was owing to the task Aphrodite had set him—even if she did not know it—to resent what must be a summons.

He smiled at the little angel, tripped as he walked to the bed to rouse it, and then shook his head when he saw the havoc wrought among his game boards and pieces—not that it mattered; he never cared much for them, except that they had been gifts from Aphrodite intended to help him pass the dull hours. He leaned over and stroked the child's curls.

"Does Lady Aphrodite want me, little one?"

The child yawned and squirmed. "If you are not too weary, the lady said."

"Off to your bed, then. I will tell her you faithfully brought her message."

"Carry me," the child demanded.

Eros laughed and lifted him. "I should spank you. Look at the mess you have made."

The little head nodded trustfully against his shoulder. "You took so long."

Eros frowned over that, wondering if the child had been waiting for him all day? It was odd that Aphrodite had been so persistent. Having handed his burden to the old woman in charge of the little pages, Eros made his way to the front of the house. The reception rooms beyond the courtyard were all dark, however, and Eros crossed to the other wing of the palace. Here the corridor was alight and he could see that the door of the antechamber to Aphrodite's private suite was open. He quickened his pace. A shadow fell across the doorway, and Aphrodite emerged, looking very anxious.

"Eros! Thank the Mother you have come."

He hurried closer, took the hand she held out to him. "Is something wrong, Aphrodite?"

"No, not really, but where have you been? I have been worried about you."

He laughed. "Mostly in Iolkas. Yesterday I was watching to be sure Anerios fulfilled every vow and promise of submission. Today I was cleaning up some spells that lasted longer than I expected. Before that—I really don't remember, exactly, but I've been back here several times. I must have missed your message, if you left one for me. But why were you so worried? I've been gone longer times before."

"Never when you were so sad. The last time I spoke to you, I felt as if you could not wait to close your eyes and turn away from me . . . forever."

"Oh." He smiled, thinking she was more perceptive than he had realized. "No. I have never wanted to turn away from you, Aphrodite. Only from my own life."

"Eros . . ."

He shook his head and his smile broadened into a grin. "But no longer." He went down on one knee and held up his hands as if in worship. "Oh, wise and puissant one. Oh, Aphrodite," he chanted, "you knew the answer."

"Eros!" She drew back a little shocked.

He burst out laughing, jumped to his feet, and hugged her hard. "No, I haven't lost my mind. Once you sent me to Iolkas, I was too busy to be sad. For a while I wondered whether I would have to defend your temple single-handed. When you said you were worried about me, I thought you were afraid I had got hurt bringing Anerios to heel. I am not as likely as you to get spears thrown at me. Still, I must tell you that I was right when I said Anerios was the type to try. Fortunately your spell hit him too fast. He had brought the spear to throw, but he dropped it to admire the sow."

"The sow?"

"The inappropriate object he fell in love with. You remember, don't you, that that was what you agreed would be the best method to tame him? It was indeed. The trouble in Iolkas is settled. Your power is supreme there and will not be questioned again. When your priestesses say 'toad,' Anerios will jump as high as she desires."

"Oh." She uttered a little giggle. "I had forgotten I said that." Then she turned and drew him into the room, gestured for him to sit, and curled herself onto her favorite cushioned long chair. "Tell me."

"I had a bit of luck to begin with. When I arrived on Mount Pelion, I was attacked by a bear."

Since he was clearly unhurt, Aphrodite laughed. "Not everyone counts it lucky to be attacked by a bear."

Eros grinned. "For my purposes it was good luck. For the poor beast too; it had been hurt and was sick and suffering. Anyway, I killed it, and because it seems to have been plaguing the countryside, that brought me a welcome into Anerios's palace and made me worthy of his personal attention. Thus I was able to learn quickly that in all but his pride and his desire to have no one, not even a goddess, set above him in authority, he was a good ruler. Hyppodamia said so too and begged that if it were possible and would not conflict with your best interests, your curse not deprive him of his throne—at least, not in such a way as to put the rulership into contention."

Aphrodite frowned. "That is not Hyppodamia's business. I do not wish my priestesses to meddle with who rules. This time the ruler brought the trouble to my shrine, but if my priestesses favor this man above that, every temple will soon be neck deep in trouble."

"In the past, I would have agreed. And even now, if the quarrel rises from among the people without reference to any temple, neutrality is best. But more and more the great mages are meddling—particularly Zeus, Athena, and Poseidon. If you wish to keep your worshippers faithful, I think you will have to instruct your priestesses to pay attention to the political climate, particularly to those who espouse the worship of other gods."

The frown on Aphrodite's forehead deepened. "Is it worth it?" she asked. "I enjoy the sacrifices, but to me they are not worth contesting with Zeus or any of the others." She smiled sensuously. "I can get what I want in other ways."

"That is most certainly true." Eros chuckled. "And would double your pleasure in the getting. Still, it would not be right to abandon a faithful priestess. And in Iolkas, where the trouble had been created by the king and it was the priestess who suffered, I felt I had to take into consideration what Hyppodamia desired. Fortunately what she desired fell in exactly with what you had ordered."

He went on to explain why civil war was almost certain had Anerios and his family been expelled and pointed out that Hyppodamia feared that in the violence of a war the temple might have been destroyed before Aphrodite could muster protection for it.

Aphrodite watched his face and listened to his voice more than to the sense of what he said. She was glad, of course, that her priestesses would be safe and that more worshippers than ever would bring offerings, but she would have sacrificed that shrine and others, too, to have brought back the lilt in Eros's voice and the light in his eyes. They glittered like emeralds and his whole face was alive as he explained how he had used her spells to rout the attacks by Anerios's men and how that had enhanced her power. He was enjoying the memory of his strength and cleverness, but Aphrodite knew the change in him was owing to more than that. Something had happened in Iolkas that had nothing to do with her shrine or her influence.

Probing delicately, she asked, "Did you enjoy wearing the disguise?"

Eros's long lashes dropped over his eyes. "In a way. I had the pleasure of being bathed by several young ladies of Anerios's household and not one of them made an improper gesture or suggestion." He glanced up, then down, and the corners of his perfect lips curved up. "It is very interesting and enlivening to have a lovely woman look down her nose at you and ask why you deserve her favor. Have you ever thought of going awooing instead of being pursued?"

"No, I fear I am too proud."

Aphrodite's lips, as enchanting as those she was looking at, trembled with fond amusement. So Eros had at long last begun a new love affair. She was glad, but she had no interest in obtaining any more information. Assured that, at least for the immediate present, Eros was happy, Aphrodite cared nothing about the man or woman he found enthralling. Neither was in the habit of confiding the details of love affairs to the other—unless something went painfully wrong and comfort was needed.

The hint that Eros needed to overcome reluctance in a lover before he could value what was usually laid at his feet without his asking was amusing. Aphrodite thought he was quite mad—she enjoyed doing nothing, yet being pursued by a passionate lover. However, it was entirely his affair and she was relieved to return to her own interests with her growing concern for him assuaged.

"But the reason," Aphrodite continued, "aside from wondering why I had not seen you in so long, that I sent the child to wait for you is that I have had an unusual number of callers this past week."

"I am surprised and flattered that you had time to worry about me."

"Well, I was in a fine temper and could have used your good sense. Hephaestus came—"

"Hephaestus put you into a temper?"

Eros was truly surprised. Under pressure from Zeus and Hera, Aphrodite had married their crippled son many years in the past. She had been fond of Hephaestus, but had not understood—despite Eros's warning—that vows of marriage meant a great deal more to Hephaestus than to his father. Her own infidelities, as meaningless to her as a smile cast at a stranger in the street, hurt Hephaestus deeply, and he had revenged himself for her repayment of a debt to Ares by entrapping them together and holding them up to ridicule.

Aphrodite had been thoroughly annoyed—particularly since Hephaestus was not exactly pure himself, although she later acknowledged he had taken no lovers while they lived together. She had dissolved the marriage and had gone back to her own establishment and the comfort that Eros offered, and he had been very careful indeed to refrain from saying, "I told you so." But as time passed, Aphrodite and Hephaestus had become reconciled; they found they could be good friends now that they were not bound in marriage.

"No, not Hephaestus," Aphrodite replied. "Well, not at first. Dionysus was here when Hephaestus arrived, and—"

"Dionysus?" Eros was surprised and a little annoyed. Had Hecate sent Dionysus to warn Aphrodite that he had bought a spell from her? "What in the world did Dionysus want?"

"Who can ever tell what Dionysus wants? Perhaps he wanted—or needed . . ."

"You?" Eros asked, astonished at the relief he felt that he would not need to explain to Aphrodite why he wanted the spell of darkness. Was he trying to hide Psyche from Aphrodite? Why? She had never cared whom he bedded. But loved?

Aphrodite had shuddered delicately at his question. "No. He's as indifferent to me as to any man or woman. I had always accounted him hemaphrodite; he is so beautiful and graceful—feminine, and yet not feminine at all." She looked at Eros, eyes wide. "But there was desire in him this time. Only, I could not read it. I thought maybe you had awakened him?"

"Not I," Eros said. "He was never interested in me, although he was willing enough to be friendly. I like him . . . only . . ."

"Only it *is* uncomfortable to look into his eyes. He is a true seer, you know, but his Gift is so erratic that he cannot control it—or he has never cared to learn how. In any case, it's near useless to him and can drive others mad. But I would guess that he had Seen something. He was only idling until Hephaestus came, and then he wouldn't go when I hinted he should. I sent for you. I thought you would draw him away, but you weren't here."

"He wouldn't go?" Eros repeated. "But that's not like Dionysus at all. Usually he's too quick to think he's not wanted."

"Yes, which is why I felt he had an incomplete See-ing. He knew Hephaestus would come here, and he knew that what Hephaestus would ask was important to him—but he didn't See what it was. So he began to tease Hephaestus—and poor Hephaestus doesn't take well to teasing. I really *needed* you, Eros, and you weren't there."

"I'm sorry, Aphrodite. I didn't know."

The words were the right ones, and he meant them—and yet did not mean them, Aphrodite thought with a sense of shock. He *was* sorry he had not been there when she wanted him, but he did not wish he had been there. Aphrodite realized that the love affair he had started in Iolkas was more important to him than her need. Jealousy pricked her. Eros had had many love affairs since he had come to live with her, but this was the first time he'd put his lover above her.

"And don't care, either?" she snapped.

"Of course I care," Eros said, looking surprised. "But I was doing necessary business for you. I wasn't off amusing myself. I cannot feel guilty for not being in two places at once. My, my,"—his fine brows lifted—"whatever happened *has* put you into a temper."

Perhaps she was misreading him, Aphrodite thought. He had not been "alive" in so long. It was true enough that no matter how great their powers, the mages were not gods and could not be in two places at once. She shrugged.

"Yes, because I am still not certain what to do, and I have *no* idea what Dionysus made of, or will do about, the problem Hephaestus brought to me. It seems that Poseidon answered a prayer from a king called Minos of Crete, who requested that Poseidon send a bull from the sea to confirm him as ruler. Minos's brothers had questioned his right to the throne and he wanted a sign from a divinity. Minos promised to sacrifice that bull to Poseidon—and then reneged on the promise because Poseidon had sent a truly magnificent animal, one of

Apollo's, I think. Apparently Minos intended to breed from the beast and improve his own herds."

Eros shook his head as if to clear it. "Without wishing to offend you, Aphrodite, Poseidon is far more powerful than you and more than strong enough to fight his own battles. Why does he need your help? And how did Hephaestus get involved?"

"Oh, Hephaestus got involved because Tethys begged him to approach me. You know Hephaestus will do anything for Tethys, and I don't blame him for that. Hera can be a cold-hearted bitch, even to her own child, and Tethys mothered him. And Hephaestus knows Poseidon will not come here. Poseidon doesn't trust Zeus—or he's afraid that Zeus will suspect him of trying to foment discontent. What Hephaestus said was that Poseidon doesn't want to punish all of Crete with an earthquake or a tidal wave. As to why Poseidon needs my help—" She smiled sensuously. "He may be able to move mountains and whip up wild storms, but he cannot raise lust. Poseidon wants Minos to suffer and to suffer in a way specifically related to that bull. He wants Minos's wife, Pasiphae, to conceive a passion for the bull and mate with it."

"With a bull?" Eros gasped. "But a bull has no interest in a human woman. And even if you could get that kind of a spell to work on an animal, which I'm not too sure of, the woman would be killed. Don't do it, Aphrodite—and don't ask me to do it! Why should Minos's poor wife die in such a horrible way for her husband's misbehavior?"

Aphrodite hesitated, staring at Eros. She could not remember the last time he had cared enough about anything to remonstrate with her. The man or woman who had caught his eye had worked a miracle. Although she was glad for Eros, she was resentful over the years of effort she had expended. He was *her* friend.

Who but she had any right to bring him to life again? Almost instantly she suppressed the flicker of jealousy. It didn't matter; as in all the other cases, the affair would soon be over.

"No, no," she said, laughing. "It wouldn't be the bull that coupled with her, not really. It would be Poseidon."

"Oh." Eros laughed too. "What a fool I am. I should have understood that without being told. Well, why not do it? Hephaestus seldom asks for anything, and I might need a favor or two from him. Minos will be punished. Pasiphae and Poseidon will probably enjoy themselves—" A huge yawn interrupted him. He rose from his seat, yawning again and shaking his head. "I'm perishing for sleep. Forgive me."

Aphrodite watched him go toward the door in astonishment. Never, not once since she had brought him to her home, had Eros so casually dismissed a problem she felt worth presenting to him. Whatever worried her worried him doubly. Her lips thinned. He had not even realized that she was worried. She didn't like that at all. A love strong enough to draw Eros's attention away from her? No, she didn't like that at all.

Then Eros stopped at the door and turned, frowning. "Be sure to tell Zeus before you actually provide the spells or send me to Crete. He won't object. He has no interest in Crete and he doesn't want to annoy Poseidon if he doesn't have to. But he'll appreciate the fact that you informed him of the contact with his brother."

Aphrodite nodded and smiled, her normal good humor restored. "Goodnight," she said, appeased. He had told her when he came that he was tired, but he had been thinking about what she told him all the time, and his last thought had been for her.

CHAPTER 8

Psyche did not expect to sleep. In fact, she would not have slept for pure spite—so she could tell the monster that even the thought of being in his company was enough to keep her awake all night—but her body played her false. With the real assurance that no more would be expected of her than to talk to him, the tension that she now realized had kept her quivering, even when she thought she was at peace, left her, and she did sleep, quietly and deeply, and without dreaming, so far as she could remember.

Without fear to spice every moment, her morning was very dull. Among the women at home, she had had her duties and they were truly a necessary part of the smooth functioning of her father's household. Here, she was not essential. The household had been established, possibly long established, with no place for her; she was no more than a toy for a monster's amusement. Not that she was denied occupation. When she entered the kitchen after breaking her fast, the old women made way for her. Had she wished to cook, to choose spices, she was certain they would have allowed it, even cooperated, but her interference was totally unnecessary. No guests would come. No one would eat the meal beside herself. Why bother?

An exploration of the chambers on the upper floor she had not examined the previous day because of her fascination with the books in the book room had disclosed a woman's workroom to the right of her bedchamber. A loom stood ready; beside a comfortable chair were two baskets of clean wool with spindles lying atop them; on a table lay folded cloth and beside that, hanks of vibrantly dyed thread and a small polished wooden box, which Psyche knew contained needles and pins. She had no doubt there would be facilities for dyeing cloth or yarn below. She could spin, weave, embroider—but to what purpose? The gown she was wearing and the others she had seen in the chest were finer than any she could make, and it would be years before she would need more clothing.

Passing the book room, which was another kind of frustration because she had no one with whom to discuss what she read, she found a large and luxurious bedchamber at the other end of the upper gallery, clearly a man's room. Weapons hung on the walls, most notably several magnificent bows, and by the wall, below the bows, was a table with feathers for fletching, a glue pot, fine line for binding. Beyond the table, under the window, was a wide bed covered with heaped furs. Psyche backed out before she saw more, knowing whose room it was and feeling a pang of guilt that its occupant should be banished by her unwillingness to have him in the house.

She stood for several long minutes before the door of the book room, but at last she turned away. There was the anodyne for her boredom, but she was reluctant to take the draught. She knew that going back to the book she had been reading, or to any other that would interest her enough to make the hours pass, would only raise a fever of need for someone with whom to talk. And the creature in the cloud had been very conversable. No, she told herself firmly, turning her back on the room. I will go out and walk myself tired.

In the garden, however, her eyes were drawn immediately to the bench where she and the black cloud had talked. Like magnet to lodestone, she was drawn to it. The bench was whole, no part of it had been absorbed into the darkness. Standing there, she remembered what they had said to each other, remembered his sharp rejoinders, how clearly he had seen through her posturing. Seen through her posturing . . . The words repeated in her mind. The monster had not been at all bemused by her beauty. He had called *her* a monster!

Without being aware of it, Psyche turned and plumped down on the bench. Would not one think that something so horribly ugly that it had to hide in a cloud of darkness would be more enchanted by her beauty than a normal man? Well, perhaps not, not if the being was aware that he was not a monster inside. He would know then that the external appearance meant little, that an ugly man could be a good one and a beautiful one evil. He had said that, that he wished to be a good husband to her.

Psyche jumped up and a small sound of revulsion pushed its way up her throat. No! She would not mate with something so horrible that it dared not be seen. What if she got with child? What would that poor child be? Tears came to her eyes. Had the creature been born a monster? What did its mother do, kill herself? Who had raised it? Surely someone had been kind to it, or how could it know enough to be kind to her?

She hurried away from the bench around the back of the house where she had never been so the area could wake no memories. Here she found the true garden, rows of vegetables and beds of herbs, and flowers—a wild profusion of late-summer flowers. At first she smiled, but as she began to wander through the beds, her brows knitted. She had never seen such flowers, such vegetables. The lushness, the richness of every plant was unnatural. Raising her skirt so she would not spoil it, Psyche knelt to examine the earth more closely. It looked ordinary except for being blacker and richer and there was something about it, a smell? No, not exactly a smell, more a feeling of fecundity . . . Yes, but that was not natural either. And then she understood. Some power, some blessing, had been given to this garden, not a spell but an outflowing of fertility.

She rose from her knees at once and brushed the loam from them as if it might contaminate her. As she backed out of the garden, however, she took herself to task. Was she not being as prejudiced a fool as those who held all magic suspect? There was nothing evil in the power that lent richness here. The plants were in no way forced or deformed; they were only larger and denser than those in the garden of Iolkas. And that raised a new question in her mind. Why should the garden of a monster be so blessed?

Then Psyche reminded herself that it was not his garden; it belonged, like the house, to Aphrodite. Instinctively she brushed at her knees again and then laughed nervously. The power that fructified this garden did not come from Aphrodite. Aphrodite was only goddess of beauty and of a barren kind of love. The goddesses who enriched the earth were Demeter and her greater daughter, Persephone. The well within Psyche seemed to ache for a moment like an empty stomach asking to be filled. To have that kind of power? She sighed. It was not a spell; it was a Gift that created that richness, and Psyche knew she had no Gift—except perhaps one for trouble.

Her lips twisted wryly and she turned away from the garden with its seductive aura of power. She had very little. She had been grateful for that. Those with a true

Gift were not tolerated; mostly they were sent to the caves of the Underworld, sacrificed—sometimes to Persephone to ensure the richness of the earth or to Hades when there was plague or some other inexplicable evil abroad in the land. Sometimes a more direct ending took them. The Gifted were greatly hated and feared because a Gift could be used instantly right from the mind of the Gifted one. Such power was too dangerous.

Learned magic was different; spells had to be spoken, gestures made in the presence of those who were to be bespelled. A witch or sorceror could be overpowered or even killed long before a spell was completed and was thus vulnerable to physical attack and punishment. The vulnerability made most workers of magic, even those who were very strong, useful without permitting them to become too powerful.

Psyche found herself wondering again who had blessed the garden to make it so lush. It did not seem reasonable that Demeter or Persephone would need or wish to do Aphrodite a favor. The monster? Could he have done it himself? She tore her eyes away from what she knew as knee-high plants, but which reached her waist here. There was no way she could reason out the truth, so it was silly to tease herself about it. She turned about to return to the house, nearly stamping her feet with ill temper.

Suddenly Psyche stopped and smiled. True, she had no way to reason out the truth, but she could ask the monster directly. Yes, indeed. He had promised not to hurt her no matter what she did. Why then should she not broach even forbidden topics? Possibly she would make him so uncomfortable that he would not want her company.

With that not-so-laudable purpose in mind, Psyche went happily back to the book room. With a leisurely break for a light midday meal, which she occupied with framing questions she sincerely hoped would embarrass the monster, she gorged herself on the most fascinating information from *The History of the Olympians*. They were the most shocking people!

Psyche was not particularly troubled by the fact that when the Olympians had finally crossed the mountain range between their homeland and Hellas—what an epic that was!—they had captured and enslaved some ancestors of her people and those of many other tribes. After all, stronger nations among her people did that all the time to weaker ones. What horrified Psyche was that the Olympians seemed to hold nothing sacred.

She had got up to the part where Kronos, whose Gift was the withdrawal of heat, had tried to freeze his eldest son, Hades, so that he could kill him, when she was interrupted by a servant silently summoning her to dinner. She went down and ate, wondering how all sense of family had been lost to the Olympians. What held them together at all if a father could not count on the support of his sons and daughters, even of his nieces, nephews, and cousins? What woman would dare marry if she did not count on her father and brothers to punish a husband who was unreasonably cruel?

She paused a moment in her chewing, recalling that her own father had not been perfect on that score, but then she resumed eating. Her case was exceptional. Ordinary modest behavior and common sense, even extraordinary precautions, could not ensure that her husband would trust her. But for the Olympians, unnatural attitudes of parents to children—and vice versa—seemed to be the natural order. How dare the monster call her unprincipled in the light of what his people considered ordinary.

By the time Psyche had consumed her sweet, she was as eager to see the black cloud as she had been fearful the preceding day. She almost leapt from her eating couch as soon as she felt it was dark enough and seized a thick, warm himation. She did not want to feel chilled and need to allow the monster to depart until she had got the answers she wanted. Only when she approached the bench and realized that a third of it had disappeared did she hesitate.

"Good evening to you," the beautiful voice called softly. "You are earlier than I expected."

"Well, I have some things I wish to say to you," Psyche responded, her doubts much assuaged by the pleasure she sensed in the creature's voice.

"I hope you have found nothing amiss in the house? The servants have been instructed to bring you anything you desire—"

"No, no." She came forward and sat at the other end of the bench surprised at her lack of reluctance. "I am very comfortable—too comfortable, to tell the truth. I'm bored to death. However, now that you mention the servants, do they have names? Since they are mute and I am not very good at guessing charades, they have no way of telling me."

"Yes, of course they do. The men are Kryos and Titos and the women are Hedy and Melba. I cannot think how to tell you which is which, but if you call a name, that servant will answer."

"I think I might have reasoned that out in time."

A chuckle came out of the cloud. "I am afflicted with ill-tempered and unreasonable females. You snap at me for trying to be helpful and Aphrodite was very put out with me because I could not be in two places at the same time."

"Do you spend much time with Aphrodite?"

"Yes. I told you I was her servant."

"I suppose it is she who gave you your taste for beautiful women."

There was a slight pause. Then the lovely voice said slowly, "I have no particular taste for beautiful women. In fact, I find most of them as dull as ditch water. They are too fond of their own faces and have no interest in any conversation beyond their appearance."

"And Aphrodite?"

"Aphrodite is what she is and has long ago recognized how unimportant and irrelevant is her appearance or that of anyone else. She is a happy person, kind, a little lazy, sometimes mischievous, but indulgent not only to herself but to everyone who does not deliberately offend her."

Again, as at other times, Psyche felt the creature was smiling. Morever, there was such warmth and affection in his voice that she knew she should not press her irritable questioning further. Nonetheless, she could not help asking, "You love her?"

"Very much. I have told you already how good she is to me."

"But not good enough to grant you her favors." The words were out before Psyche thought and she caught her breath as a movement rippled over the blackness at the end of the bench.

"I love Aphrodite as a friend, a comrade, a person who saved my life. I do not desire—have never desired—Aphrodite as a man desires a woman . . . as I desire you."

The voice was calm, no threat in it, and the final phrase was spoken with a kind of husky depth that wakened a response in Psyche. A quick glance at the place where the other end of the bench disappeared into nothing curbed that response, but it occurred to her that a being who lived with Aphrodite and was constantly in her company might be inured to beauty.

"But Aphrodite must be more beautiful than I," she

remarked, and then asked curiously, "Why do you want me?"

"Not for your beauty." The warm chuckle almost drew a smile from Psyche. "I want you because you value your beauty even less than Aphrodite values hers. I want you because you are not crouching in the house, whimpering with fear. I want you because you have the courage to knit your brows at a sorcerous blackness and cross-question it."

The answer was so flattering that Psyche barely choked back a sincere "Thank you." What a clever beast it was to praise her for just those qualities that she herself thought of worth. To defend herself from falling into the trap of friendship the creature was constructing, she said sharply, "If you like questions, I have a great many more, some I fear you will not like."

"Why should I not like your questions? My purpose is to talk to you until your fear of me passes. There is only one question I will not answer if you ask. I will not describe my appearance."

He *was* clever! Admitting his purpose prohibited her from complaining that he was trying to deceive her. She ignored that remark and pretended a shudder. "Ugh! Why should I want to know that you are a slimy blob with tentacles or covered with warts and hair or—"

A burst of hearty laughter interrupted her. "You will never guess what makes me monstrous," he said, still chuckling, "so do not work your fertile imagination overtime."

It suddenly occurred to Psyche that even a monster should not be amused by his deformities. For the first time she felt a flicker of doubt. Was he really so horrible to look upon? Nonsense, she told herself. Why else should anyone hide himself in such a chilling fashion? She shrugged.

"My imagination is not so fertile as the garden of this

house. If you are so willing to answer questions, tell me why your earth grows grape clusters the size of barrows."

"I have no idea," the monster replied—Psyche could hear his grin. "I have nothing to do with the garden. I doubt I have been in it twice in ten years."

"I knew you would say that," Psyche remarked, with a little sneer. "It *is* the easy way out, isn't it? To pretend you are ignorant when you don't wish to betray a secret to a common native—too common to know the truth but not too common to be the whore of a monster."

"That's not fair, Psyche. You were brought here to be my bride, my wife in all honor. I will swear to you that you will be my only woman—I will take no concubine or other—"

"I don't suppose there's a long line of applicants waiting to be concubines to a black cloud hiding a repulsive monster," Psyche interrupted with a derisive snort. "It makes your fidelity a little less valuable as evidence of my worthiness."

"If you are trying to exasperate me, you are wasting your time," the monster remarked, and Psyche could hear him grinning again. "If you really want to know why the garden is particularly fertile, I will promise to find out. If you will accept a guess, I believe Demeter or Persephone gave it more of a nudge than usual."

"Are you implying that Demeter and Persephone need Aphrodite's spells and purchase them in this way?"

Although there was a disbelieving note in Psyche's voice, it did not have the full thrust of cynical contempt she had intended. The monster's first remark had removed half the purpose of her question. Plainly the creature was very good-natured, and it was virtually impossible to annoy it. All she would acheive by asking was having her curiosity satisfied.

"No."

Psyche ground her teeth. Far from making the whatever it was so uncomfortable it would avoid her, she
seemed to be amusing it. That single syllable, slightly
drawn out, was a clear challenge to pursue the subject.
Psyche almost jumped to her feet and stamped away—
but she was too curious.

"Very well," she said with a sniff. "I will ask the
question you so clearly want asked. Why, then, did
Demeter or Persephone expend so much power in your
garden?"

"Now, that I can answer," he said. Ignoring her
comment on his maneuver, he went on to explain
Aphrodite's part in reconciling Demeter to her daughter's marriage to Hades. "Actually, it was probably
Persephone who blessed the garden," he finished. "She
is the more powerful of the two and the more grateful
because she is so very happy with Hades. Demeter still
likes to think of herself as ill used, although she is much
happier too in the worshipful admiration of her native
priestesses at Eleusis than she was with a restless, angry
daughter who wanted to live her own life, so she sometimes shrugs off the help Aphrodite gave her."

Psyche had been enthralled by the monster's tale,
listening in delighted fascination as he described Persephone's courage in enslaving the King of the Dead.
Surely, she thought, black-browed, dour Hades was
more fearsome than a poor, deformed creature who
had shown himself to be both kind and good tempered.
But she could not allow the monster to think she had
not recognized its purpose. It *was* Aphrodite's servant
and apparently was dedicated not only to inducing her
to yield to it but to acknowledge Aphrodite's "goodness."

"I thought we agreed yesterday that you would not

preach at me," Psyche snapped—but only after the monster had finished speaking.

She saw the blackness move higher against the silvered leaves of the shrubs behind the bench, as if it had drawn itself up in indignation. But to her immense surprise she felt no fear, only a slight shock as she realized so much time had passed that the moon had risen. And did she feel, too, a flicker of regret that they must soon part?

"I was not preaching!" the shadow said haughtily. "I was speaking the exact truth about what happened—and, I hope, proving that no secrets are being kept from you because you are a native woman."

"Are they not?" Psyche asked, but less aggressively than with true interest.

"Well, I would not tell you a private secret about Aphrodite or her friends any more than you would tell me a secret private to one of your sisters. What is public knowledge in Olympus, I am perfectly happy for you to know."

"Then we are in Olympus?"

"No. We are north of the city in a hunting lodge on the flanks of the mountains that surround the valley."

"I am not good enough to be in Olympus?"

The monster hesitated, then said softly, "It is nothing to do with you."

Psyche's hand went out in mute apology, but she caught it back before it touched the black nothing. When they sat in the dark like this, it was so easy to forget with what she was talking. She hadn't meant to hurt the creature, hadn't meant to force it to acknowledge that it was not welcome in what seemed to be its home city. She wanted to make it leave her alone . . . didn't she?

"So you do not mind that I know what is public knowledge in Olympus? Even that the gods are not gods at all?" Psyche said hastily, hardly knowing whether she wanted more to divert the monster from his thoughts or herself from her own.

Again she saw the darkness move against the silvered brush and she drew breath and bit the inside of her lip. Had she gone too far?

"Now, how did you deduce that from what we have said to each other?"

Still no anger. A kind of interested and amused admiration in the musical voice—and an implicit acknowledgment that what she had said was true. Psyche let her breath trickle out slowly, not wanting the creature to know that she had been alarmed and regretting her daring. He wanted her because of her courage, didn't he?

"I am not as clever as that," she admitted. "I have been reading a book called *The History of the Olympians.*"

"Reading?"

"Is that supposed to be forbidden to the common natives?"

"I don't know and I don't care. I was only surprised that you had learned to read because your people keep their women in subjection."

That remark stung, the more because the creature seemed simply to be stating a fact without any intention to offend. "And Olympian women are free?" she snapped back.

"Ah . . . yes." A chuckle. "Not out of the generosity of the men, but because I don't think any of them has yet thought of a way to control an Olympian woman. I hope I am not a coward, but I freely admit I quail at the thought of making any challenge to Athena or Artemis. The one tends to cast Gift-aimed spears when crossed, the other is at least as expert as I with a bow. When Zeus made the mistake of offending Demeter, all

Olympus nearly starved. And mage-king though he is, Zeus has been known to back off from an open confrontation with Hera. She cannot blight the crops and is less likely to skewer you with a spear or use you for a target, but Hera has her ways of making her displeasure known."

"And so do native women," Psyche said, "though their ways are also more subtle than spears or arrows."

"Is that so?" There was real interest in the question. "I meant no shame, only that men are stronger than women and have the use of weapons, which seem to be withheld from native females."

"Among us there are laws and customs for the protection of the weak that cannot be violated without calling down the opprobrium of the whole community. But mostly it is sufficient for a woman to refuse to join her husband after dinner or to sit sullen and silent to show she has been injured. If stronger measures are needed or she wishes to keep the quarrel private, she can refuse to come to her husband's bed, and meals can be cold, ill prepared, and ill served—or not served at all."

The monster laughed softly. "But none of those could explain why you were permitted to learn to read. I hope you will tell me what subtlety you used?"

The creature's warm laughter tempted Psyche to laugh also, but the truth was that when she had learned it had taken no subtlety. No one had cared what she did, the ugly youngest daughter of three, unlikely to be of much value for a political marriage when she had two handsome and talented older sisters.

Reminded of a long misery that had altered with her appearance only for the worse, Psyche turned her face away and did not answer, only saying bitterly, "But I am not an Olympian woman and have no subtleties to use against you. I suppose if you had known I could read, you would have removed Aphrodite's books."

"The books are mine." The voice was gentler, almost as if the monster understood that the anger in her had nothing to do with Aphrodite. "No, perhaps they are Aphrodite's, since she obtained them for me, but Aphrodite has little interest in books. And, no, I would not have removed them. I'm glad you can read."

"Even though I have discovered the most discreditable things about the 'gods,' who are no gods?"

"So, we have come around to your original point. But Psyche, how do you know that the Olympians are not gods?"

"Because the book I read describes the homeland of the Olympians and their struggles across the mountains."

"Indeed, I remember."

"You remember?" Psyche gasped, temporarily diverted. "But that was centuries ago."

"Yes." There was a long silence, Psyche turned her head again to stare into the blackness. Then the creature said, "I am very old, Psyche, and in all my life I have known little happiness because of how I looked. Kronos—you read of him?" She nodded and the voice went on softly, "Kronos used me. I was young. I did not understand—or, perhaps, care—what I was doing. Many suffered because of my carelessness and indifference—that was monstrous. Later, I tried to resist, but it was too late. When Zeus overthrew Kronos, I was accounted as an enemy by all and I was punished. Only Aphrodite understood and . . . spoke for me."

The darkness surged upward so suddenly that Psyche flinched, but it swept by her blotting out all light for a moment. Then it was gone, gliding across the grass toward the deepest shadow under the trees. For a moment Psyche simply stared after it, then, as horrified understanding came to her, as she realized that he had not been born deformed but had been changed as a punishment, she jumped up and cried, "Wait," but the black cloud was gone.

CHAPTER 9

The lamps flared alight when Eros appeared in his bedchamber, but no little messenger waited for him, and when he crossed the courtyard to Aphrodite's suite of rooms, he found them dark and empty. He returned to his own chamber, shivering slightly with an inner cold he had not felt for many years. In speaking with Psyche he had recalled, as if it were happening anew, the horror of those first years of Zeus's rule.

He had needed to see Aphrodite to assure himself she did not again need to clench her teeth and swallow and swallow to control the hatred and revulsion his presence woke in everyone. She who had cast the spell had been least affected, but even she could not long endure him. That was when she had had the hunting lodge built for him so he could hide himself.

In those years, before he learned to control the spell that Aphrodite had been forced to lay on him, he had been utterly outcast, completely apart, cut off from other living beings both physically and mentally. Even those who pitied him because they knew he had not been Kronos's tool at the end, that he would gladly have welcomed a cleaner ruler, could not bear his presence. He stood shaking, reliving his rage at what had befallen him and his later horror when he came truly to understand what he had done. His heart pounded with the violent emotions, only beginning to slow when he recalled how he had found peace by embracing his pain, enduring life only because he felt he deserved his suffering.

"Have I not suffered enough?" he whispered. "Mother, You gave to me so richly when I slept at Your shrine. And You gave me Psyche! I thought it was a sign that I was forgiven—"

The whisper cut off abruptly on an indrawn breath, which whooshed out a heartbeat later in an embarrassed chuckle. What a self-pitying fool I am, Eros thought, crossing the room to sit on the bed and pull off a shoe. I should have been more careful about what I asked for. I forgot I might actually get it. I thought I wanted to live again—and I *am* living again. Now I remember. Life hurts!

The clear statement of the fact in his mind made him laugh aloud. Barefooted, he stood again, unclasped his belt, drew off his tunic, and threw it in the direction of a chair. A slithering sound hinted that it had fallen to the floor, but Eros did not move to pick it up as he would have done only two weeks before when all he had left to cling to was the perfect order of his life. The precise placement of every object, like the exact response of smile or frown, so he could retrieve the article or the pretense of emotion and appear alive, was no longer necessary. Uplifted by joy, tormented by rage, and wrung out with despair, Eros no longer felt any need to "appear alive."

In fact, what the slithering sound of his tunic falling had brought to the forefront of his mind was not a need for order but his nakedness. And the nakedness brought into sharp focus the need to get Psyche into his bed—quickly. He had almost forgotten himself and drawn her into his arms when she asked him if she were not good enough for Olympus. There was not one of them, no, not even Aphrodite, beautiful and good as she was, who came near Psyche. If Psyche was not so good, not so generous, as Aphrodite, she had what Aphrodite did not—a conscience and a measure of judgment in which self was recognized but did not outweigh everything else.

To Eros, that was irresistible. He had nearly died twice from the lack of that balance—once physically, and again out of pure indifference. Such a wave of desire had passed over him in response to her question that his self-control had nearly drowned in it. He had almost forgotten that he had said he would not force her and that she would have all the time she needed to come to him willingly.

Her own gesture, the snatching back of her hand, away from the well of blackness that he appeared to be, had reminded him. He intended to keep those promises—Eros dropped back onto the bed and drew the covers over him—but that did not preclude the use of "accidents" and "temptations" to hurry along that willingness.

What sort of temptation can a blot of blackness offer? Eros chuckled aloud, recalling the cynical lift of Psyche's brows as she remarked that long lines did not form for a chance to be a black cloud's concubine. The memory only renewed and reinforced the urgency of his desire. However, it was clear that temptations were out of the question. Accident, then.

What sort of accident? She had to touch him, to learn that there was a real being, not a devouring emptiness, inside the dark. Touch him—he thought again of her hand reaching toward him. If their hands met . . . Warmth pulsed in his loins at the thought of even so innocent a touch. He lay luxuriating in the sensation, thinking that he had never touched her, except for carrying her from the altar to his house, and she had been unconscious then. A limp, unresponding body held no lure for him.

Eros sighed and turned to his side. It might take weeks for her to find the confidence to reach out to him. His eyes, moving idly over the familiar room, fell on the pile of game boards and pieces that the servants had picked up from the floor and laid on a table. For a moment he stared unseeingly at the jumbled toys, mildly irritated by the disorder because it had broken his train of thought. Why had the stupid servants not put them away? But the question hardly rose before the answer came; they did not know what belonged where. He had his own particular place for everything.

He began to speak the words that would quench the lights and hide the mess he did not wish either to clear away or see but stopped abruptly, lifting himself on his elbow so he would have a better view of the beautiful boards inlaid with colored, scented wood and the exquisite pieces carved of gold and silver and ivory and semiprecious stone. His lips curved upward.

Had not Psyche said she was bored? What more suitable gift to while away dull hours than games? And what easier path was there to an accidental touching of the hands than the movement of pieces on a board? Eros hopped out of bed to examine what he had and to choose those games in which such a collision was most likely to occur.

Actually, Eros could have fallen asleep without making any plans to win Psyche. Psyche's conscience was presenting better arguments for accepting him than either temptation or accident could. Her first reaction to the monster's swift departure had been to call him back and comfort him. Having been deprived of the ability to make restitution either because he was already gone or pretended not to hear her, she had sunk back onto the bench, biting her lips to keep back tears of remorse. The monster was not at fault for her family's early indifference and later resentment toward her. She had no right to claw at him because she was angry. How could she have been so cruel as to remind him of so dreadful a punishment?

Then she shook her head, thinking back on what she had said. She had made a sharp remark about his depriving her of the books, but he had not minded that. He had seemed to understand that her waspishness was not really directed at him. And she hadn't meant to be cruel when she spoke of the Olympian trek from their homeland. How could she have known he could have been any way involved with the exile of Kronos? Well, that was one topic she would avoid in the future.

The thought reminded her that she had set out to make him so uncomfortable that he would leave her alone. She pulled the thick himation closer, aware of a chill. But the air was not cold and she knew what had chilled her was the prospect of being alone with nothing to do and no one to talk to . . . forever. Surely that punishment was too severe for a cruelty she had not intended.

She rose slowly and went back to the house. At the door she hesitated, tempted to leave it open so that if he returned he might see it as a symbol that he was welcome. Then she remembered he had said he would not enter the house until she invited him to share her bed. No. Not that. She was not ready for that. How could she lie with some terrible creature that might not even be human in form? She turned to look out at the bench, but no shadow had swallowed any part of it and she shut the door, took the candle left ready for her, and went up the stairs.

She used the candle to light the lamps in her room but shivered when she looked at the bed. Then she picked up the candle again, frowning slightly, and went to the last room on the left. Holding the lamp high, she examined the bedchamber of the monster.

The bed was narrower than her own; he was certainly not monstrous in size, although the dark shroud that surrounded him could have hidden a giant. The bows hanging on the wall were longer than those her brothers used, so he was taller, but nothing about them bespoke any deformity. The grip was surely shaped for a human hand. Hesitantly she approached a clothes chest, set the lamp on a table nearby, and knelt before it.

This was surely forbidden; Psyche bit her lip, remembering that the monster had said he would not answer any questions about his appearance. But he had not forbidden her to try to find out in other ways. Psyche stared at the lid of the chest. It was *very* bad manners to open another person's chest; it was an invasion of privacy. She uttered a soft bark of laughter. Thinking of manners and ordinary conventions in her situation was ridiculous.

With a quick intake of breath Psyche flung open the chest and drew out one heavy cloak, another, and then, at last, a well-worn tunic. She held it up, turned it front and back. It was a perfectly ordinary tunic, large, but with no extra cloth, no worn patches, that could betray a deformed body.

Sitting back on her heels, Psyche contemplated the tunic, the weapons on the wall, the bed. Slowly she folded and replaced the clothing in the chest, then rose and left the room. In her own bedchamber, she sat down on a chair and stared out the window. The bench, still silvered by moonlight, was empty.

An ordinary man, she thought, does not hide himself in a black cloud. Then it occurred to her that her doom was to marry a monster. Her heartbeat quickened. Was it possible that the being in the cloud was an ordinary man and the cloud itself was designed to make him appear monstrous to fulfill that doom? She drew a long breath, almost released a sigh of relief, and then remembered that he had spoken of punishment, a punishment so terrible that even now, centuries later, he had physically fled the memory.

Psyche bowed her head. She was afraid to contemplate a form so terrible . . . Her head lifted again and a frown creased her perfect brow. But he joked about it. Well, perhaps not joked, but spoke very lightheartedly about being a monster. How did that fit with a pain so sharp he had fled to conceal it? Because it was not pain? Could it be rage, recalled when he remembered those who had inflicted the monstrous form on him as she still felt rage over her family's treatment? Could he have feared inflicting that rage on her—as she had done to him in spiteful words only a moment earlier—and thus taken himself to where he could not hurt her? A very kind and noble monster.

She knew that already. Psyche sighed. She was, as he had said, the more monstrous of the two. She was selfish, concerned only with her own hurts and feelings. How could she still be angry with her mother and sisters when she had seen their grief for her? Grief? Guilt, perhaps, because they were relieved to be rid of her. As the thought came to her mind, Psyche flushed with shame. The black cloud was right, she *was* a monster.

Thought of the monster overrode her guilty shame. Surely he had been hurt more deeply than she, and whatever his crimes, even if they were worse than his admitted carelessness and indifference that had caused others much suffering, he could not have deserved centuries of pain. Why had he not been forgiven and released? Her lips curled contemptuously. Because the gods who were no gods were creatures as petty as humans—cruel, vindictive, and indifferent to his suffering.

A new idea burst into Psyche's mind like a flash of light so that she blinked. Could giving her to the monster have been not only a punishment for her but a deliberate attempt to renew *his* agony? Clearly from the almost amused way he spoke of his monstrosity, he had grown accustomed to it. Was it known that he desired love, a home, children? Was it assumed from her rejection of the worship of Aphrodite that nothing would make her accept the monster? Would that not tear him apart, to be with her whenever he wished and yet be deprived of what he so desperately needed?

It would serve them all right if she accepted him! Psyche almost rose from her chair to impart her resolve to him, and then first chuckled at her impetuosity and finally shuddered at the ultimate in cutting off one's nose to spite one's face. Perhaps she could learn to love the monster and welcome him into "their" home, but children? Poor, deformed creatures who could never have any happiness? Tears formed in her eyes and ran unheeded down her cheeks. Could she inflict that on herself, on the children, on the monster, who . . .

Oh, what a fool she was! She wiped the tears from her cheeks and shook her head, half smiling. She did not doubt the monster was good and kind and that he knew the effect of his appearance on others. Could such a being desire to have children *unless he knew they would not be deformed?* Doubly a fool. She should have realized that as soon as she understood the monster had not been born a monster. Unless the spells that deformed him were designed to afflict all his progeny? No, surely he would have discovered that. He, above all, would not want a child if he knew it would have a life of misery, ashamed to show its face, shunned by the whole world.

So she could no longer use the excuse that to mate with the creature would produce monstrous children. Nor could she believe it would damage her physically to couple with him—the furnishings in his chamber and the clothing in the chest all gave evidence of a large, but not abnormally large, man. Suddenly Psyche shuddered. Only it might not be a man. It might be the same size and have hands and yet be some kind of slimy horror, or be covered with ulcerated sores dripping pus, or . . .

She thrust away the nauseating horrors that had filled her mind. There was no need to commit herself irrevocably and immediately to the ultimate act. Even if she could not see into the black cloud, the monster had assured her he was there, a real . . . whatever . . . within it. She could discover a great deal about him by touch, and she need do nothing until she was quite sure that his deformity was something she could endure, like a single eye in the middle of his face or a humped back or an extra pair of arms. That was a soothing thought. Psyche uttered a long sigh, stood up, and began to remove her clothes. Having made her decision, she felt relaxed and drifted off to sleep almost happy.

Morning brought no change in her determination. In fact, she hurried through her breakfast, eager to get to the book room and find some unexceptional subjects that could be discussed safely and might lead to a touch. There were lots of scrolls concerning hunting; Psyche sighed. That would be safe enough, but no better than the talk in her father's house. She could listen, but aside from a few questions her monster would surely guess were only an excuse to make conversation, what could she say? He was too clever, she thought, to enjoy the pretense.

Patience was rewarded eventually. She found a treatise on plants, sensibly divided into sections on food, healing, and magic, in which she was truly interested. She spent most of the morning reading it, smiling in recognition of some uses, surprised and doubtful about others, and eager to discover specimens that were entirely new to her. A summons to lunch caught her just as she had started on the section about magic.

As she ate, she wondered whether her monster practiced magic. The thought brought a brief sense of the nearly empty well within her, but she diverted herself by pondering whether any of the plants with healing or magical properties were likely to grow nearby. That was a question she could ask her monster—her mind checked, backed up: *her* monster? When had he become *her* monster? Psyche thought about it and could not remember specifically when she had changed her mode of thinking, but the term was certainly not new to her. She had used those words before.

Well, so he was her monster; he had been inflicted on her, and whatever he looked like, he was a gentle soul. All the more reason to be certain her questions would not hurt him. But she was sure he would like to have his advice asked about the plants and also whether it would be safe for her to wander alone in the woods beyond the garden. Psyche's hand paused with a bite of food halfway to her mouth. If the woods were not safe, did she wish to ask the monster to accompany her? Would she be comfortable with that looming blackness so visible in the light of day?

She had found no answer to that question by the time she returned to the book room. Leave it, she thought. He had said she could invite him inside in case of bad weather and he would not assume too much. Then it would be safe to invite him to come to the book room to look at one of the scrolls. One had to have light to see a book, and she would be able to determine how she felt about having the darkness looming over her shoulder or beside her while he read. And if he put out his hand to hold the scroll, she would see the darkness bulge and she might touch him—by accident.

A little thrill went through her, but before Psyche could decide whether it was a thrill of fear or of excitement, she was shocked by an entirely different thought. How could she be so sure her monster would return? He had not said he would. He had not waited to hear her call to him—or if he had heard, he had not responded. Doubtless he had run to his precious Aphrodite for comfort.

Psyche set her teeth. Precious little comfort he would get from Aphrodite. She had "spoken" for him, had she? Poor fool, he called himself Aphrodite's servant, but he didn't seem to realize that she had been using him all these years. Then Psyche sighed, her ill temper diminishing. Aphrodite's selfishness assured her that her monster would return. He had told her more than once that his mating with her was her punishment, a duty set on him by Aphrodite.

No matter what misery that duty caused . . . Psyche hesitated, sought for a name, and was shocked anew at her own unkindness. She had never asked her monster's name. Well, she would! When she invited him in, she would apologize and she would call him by name, not "Creature" or "Monster."

Reminded of her purpose, Psyche hurriedly put the treatise about plants aside and began to search for one that presented a problem she could reasonably ask him to examine. Like a good omen, when she reached into the shelf below, the first scroll she drew forth provided a subject. The unknown squiggles were the first marks to catch her eye. She was about to return the book to the shelf when the new position revealed another row of symbols, and these she recognized. She looked at the positions of the two lines, feeling a stirring of excitement. There was no way to be sure, but she believed the second line was a translation of the first. Now all she needed was to be certain the subject would not cause her poor monster pain. The title didn't tell her much: *Whispers in the Breeze.*

Perusal of the scroll showed that, provided it was a translation, she held a book of poetry. Why bother translating poetry? If you could read it in the original, it was far better to do so. Did that mean her monster could not read the original language? No, that was ridiculous. He had said Aphrodite had obtained the scrolls for him. Would she get him books he could not read? Psyche looked with a sudden greater interest at the scroll. Had the monster done the translation? For Aphrodite? For someone else? The monster had indicated clearly that he had no other friends.

In a fine temper, Psyche rerolled and tied the book of poetry. It would serve her purpose well enough, but she did not need to read a lot of silly love poetry, which was all Aphrodite would care about. To soothe herself, she unrolled the history. She could not discuss it with . . . she sighed. She did need a name for him. However, there was no reason why she shouldn't learn what she could. Perhaps his fate was mentioned and she could discover what he had been and what he had become.

That was so intriguing an idea that Psyche began reading at once, but she soon forgot the monster and her original purpose. She found the information in *The History of the Olympians* fascinating, even though some of it was also horrifying. The way Kronos had used the slaves his tribe had captured—her people and others among the coastland natives—had been brutal beyond necessity. But the result . . . She cocked her head and twisted the scroll holders to return to the description of the plan for Olympus. If it had been fulfilled, it would be a city fit for gods.

The slaves had done much, but as much or more had been accomplished by the use of the Gifts. Gifts from whom? The Mother? Had that been the true worship? Had the Olympians interposed themselves between the people and the Mother? Psyche was sure that the Olympians were not gods, most of them not even godlike. They were only Gifted, she thought, staring past the open scroll. In fact, the gods were more strongly Gifted than anyone she could even imagine.

How was it that those who were not Gifted or less Gifted were not so afraid that they destroyed them—as her people had done and still did with their own Gifted. Certainly the Olympian Gifted were dangerous, which was how so many of her people could be taken prisoner and carried away. Kronos had been responsible for the capture of thousands. Yet despite his strong Gift, Kronos had been overpowered.

At that moment the manservant, whom she had discovered was Titos, scratched and opened the door. Psyche sighed and allowed the scroll to close. Too bad she could not ask the monster how the Gifted could be controlled. That would be a truly useful piece of knowledge for the people of Iolkas to have—but she was not likely ever to be free to bring it to them. She shrugged and followed Titos down the stairs; in any case, she did not intend to mention that scroll and take the chance of hurting her monster again.

She ate quickly, bored with her own company. She had reason to regret her haste to be finished as soon as the meal was over. Now she had nothing at all to do, not even picking over sweets and savories she did not want. The sun had barely set and the sky was full of light. It was much too soon for her monster to come . . . if he were coming. She bit her lip. Doubtless Aphrodite would drive him back to her in the end, but it might not be today or even tomorrow.

Pride forbade her to go to the bench and wait. And all her preparation in the book room might have been in vain, so she had no desire to go there. Desperation drove her to the workroom, and she lit the lamps because though it was still light out, inside the room it was rather dim. She began listlessly to turn over the pile of cloth until it occurred to her that although her chest was full of the finest clothing, all new, the tunic she had seen in . . . she must learn his name . . . his chest had been worn. She could make him a new tunic. She looked at the cloth again with far greater interest and began to open the folded pieces to see if any were large enough.

When she next looked up, Psyche realized it was very dark outside. With a gasp, she ran out and down the steps. As she hurried toward the bench, the dark cloud surged to its full height, spilling out of itself a cascade of objects that glittered faintly and clattered as they fell. Psyche jerked to a stop, horrified at what seemed like parts of a metal simulacrum falling out of the creature.

"I thought you weren't coming," the monster's beautiful voice said, a touch reproachfully.

"I am sorry to be late," she replied automatically, still trying to absorb that cascade of metal objects. "I was looking at the cloth and—" Now she did not know whether that tunic had belonged to what was in the cloud or not, and even if it did, she could not admit that she had been so ill mannered as to look in his chest and notice his tunic was worn. "The fabric is very fine," she continued, her voice trembling just a trifle, "and—I am afraid women are easily distracted by the prospect of elegant garments, even when they have been gifted with a whole chest full of beautiful new clothes. I forgot that time was passing."

He laughed. "And there I was last night, tossing and turning with worry because you had said you were bored."

"I said I was bored?" Psyche repeated. "When?"

"When I asked if the house was satisfactory. You said you were too comfortable, that you hadn't enough to do. So I brought some games. Oh, blast! I forgot them when I saw you running. They're all over the ground."

"Games!" Psyche exclaimed, and burst out laughing.

The shadow had shrunk down. Psyche guessed he had bent or knelt and then had the distinct feeling that he had paused to look at her when she laughed. A moment later, her eyes now having adjusted to the dark, she saw a board appear on the bench, then another, then several smaller, shiny bits—pieces. Then, thinking about how the objects had spilled out of the shadow, she realized they had been carried within it, fallen out, been reabsorbed, and come out again. She sighed softly with relief. Her head had always known her monster told the truth about the shadow hiding but not swallowing what was within it, but her heart welcomed the evidence.

"I'll help you," she said, coming closer and kneeling down.

The pieces that had not fallen into the grass were easy to find. They shone faintly and she gathered them up and reached forward to set them on the bench. As she did so, her hand and part of her arm disappeared. Before she could withdraw or even gasp, her hand collided with another, warm and solid.

"I am so sorry," the beautiful voice said softly, as the shadow withdrew and her hand and arm reappeared. "I was not looking and you moved so quickly—"

Psyche licked her lips. "No need to beg pardon," she got out. "When two people"—her voice shook a little, but she steadied it and went on—"are scrabbling around in the dark, touching is a likely accident."

"I am a person," he said calmly, having picked up what she feared. "It is not good to look upon me, but I am a man like any other."

What touched her had felt like a man's hand. She could still feel a knuckle and the division between two fingers. Psyche almost asked him to let her touch him and be sure he was a person, but she was still too shocked by the disappearance and reappearance of her arm. It was all very well to "know" that would happen, to have seen it happen to pieces for a gaming board, but to have it happen to her, to see her own arm disappear and reappear, was different.

"Of course you are," she said, gathering her scattered wits. And then, recalling her determination to stop calling him creature or monster, she said, "People have names, but you have never told me yours. I am ashamed not to have asked sooner."

"My name?" He hesitated, and then said slowly, as if he were trying to remember, "Teras. You are kind. But why not call me 'monster'? I will answer to it."

Was that what his kind and generous Aphrodite called him? Psyche was appalled and said sharply, "Perhaps I do not wish to call you 'monster' because I do not wish to think of you as a monster any longer. You have been much kinder to me than I to you. I am beginning to think you were quite correct when you called *me* a monster. In the past few days, I have had more time than usual to think, and I have discovered some very unpleasant things about myself."

"No! You must not spend your time tearing your heart to shreds. There is nothing unpleasant about you."

The voice was high and thin with pain and anxiety, the voice of a man who had torn his own heart to shreds and wished to spare anyone else that agony. Psyche did not even realize she had stretched out her hand. She had closed her eyes for a moment, as one does to shut out the sight of a face ravaged by pain. She felt her hand taken in a firm, warm grip. Her eyes shot open to see her body end at her shoulder. She must have gasped, because the hand let go and the dark shrank back, but what remained with her was the feeling. She had not lost sensation, even where Teras had not touched her. She had felt her arm extended, the brush of her sleeve against her flesh as she moved. The darkness around Teras did not swallow her up any more than did the night.

Slowly Psyche put her hand out again. "May I touch your face?" she whispered.

CHAPTER 10

"Close your eyes," Teras said, and when Psyche shook her head in denial, he first laughed and then sighed in exasperation. "Silly girl, did you think I was going to stick out my hand and somehow bring a normal man for you to feel? Keep your eyes open if you wish, then. I only suggested that you close them to save you the sight of your hand disappearing, which seems to bother you. But you are free to touch my face or any other part of me to your heart's content."

Afraid her courage would fail, Psyche thrust her hand into the blackness at the level of her own head.

"Hai!" Teras cried, "Gently. You almost put out my eye."

It was horrible to see her arm disappear, but Psyche had felt the glancing blow and now a face was pushed against her reaching hand. She felt the cheek, slid her fingers down along it to a chin, raised them to pass along lips, which moved against their tips, pursing in a kiss.

"Stop that," Psyche said crossly, and closed her eyes.

Teras laughed. A hand seized her other hand and drew it toward the face, urging her without words to examine fully. The flesh was warm and dry, without unnatural knobs or ridges or any sign of an open sore, the cheeks, chin, and lips clean-shaven but with the faintest bristling that showed a beard could grow. She felt a nose, two eyes, a broad forehead above which was hair covering a rounded skull. Sliding down again her hands encountered two ears, a strong neck, broad shoulders. Psyche withdrew her hands and opened her eyes.

"You are not a monster," she said, her voice accusatory. "You have been frightening me for amusement."

"No." The blackness bulged forward; her thigh and hip disappeared as her hand was seized. "I said it was not good to look upon me. That is the truth."

"You mean an illusion of monstrosity is upon you?"

There was a brief hesitation. Then he said, "I will not answer that question. I told you I would not answer questions about my appearance. You will find nothing to disgust or frighten you when you touch me. That is all I will say."

"If you had children, what would they look like?"

He did not answer and Psyche gripped his hand, which she thought was about to withdraw. "I am sorry if I hurt you," she cried. "But I must know whether the punishment set on you will descend to your children."

"It was not that you hurt me. I thought you were asking the same question in a different way."

"No. What I meant was . . . I could not bear it if my child looked so horrible that it did not dare face the world."

"Your child!" It was a joyous exclamation. "Then you will marry me, Psyche?"

He would not answer! He would not admit to her that a mating with him might produce a monster. All he wanted was to satisfy his lust. She pulled her hand away.

"Marry!" she spat. "What sort of husband is so eager to mate that he will not warn the woman he calls wife that his children would appear deformed? What sort of handfasting can there be when you and I are alone, without witness? Not even the servants could swear to your promises. Are they not mute? When I bear you something so loathsome that it needs to go veiled in blackness, what claim could I make on you, whom I have never seen? Will you not drop me back on the altar, like refused offal—"

Her hand was seized again, held hard against her struggle to free it.

"Psyche, my love"—the voice was throaty music—"I am sorry my joy at the hope of your willingness to marry me overcame my sense. I did not mean to refuse to answer you. Beloved, I swear there is no reason in my past ill-doing or in my punishment for our child to be marred in any way. The spell set on me will not befoul my descendants. And witness or no witness, I will be faithful to you, will protect you and succor you until the day I die. There is my blood in your hand to warrant my swearing."

She felt something hot and wet on her hand and cried out in disgust. Then the grip on her was released, and when she jerked her hand back she saw a wet stain in the palm, black in the pale light of the new-risen moon. She stared at it, shuddering in revulsion, so filled with horror that at first she could not move to rid herself of it.

"Wipe it carefully and save the cloth." Teras's voice sounded as if it came through lips tightened against pain. "With my blood, freely given, you can work any magic you desire upon me. If I fail you, you can kill me, or draw me back to you to serve as your slave."

"No!" Psyche cried, staring down at the little puddle in her palm.

She had already realized that she could not simply wipe the blood onto the earth. If something evil smelled it and collected the grass and dirt, great harm could come to poor Teras. Carefully she blotted up the blood on the corner of her himation, rolling the smeared cloth inward so that no smallest fleck would touch another surface. The blackness bulged and a knife was lying on Psyche's knees when it withdrew. She cut the edge off the himation, folded it still smaller, and tucked it into the bodice of her gown between the upper and lower girdles so that it could not be lost. Then she stood up.

"I will go in and burn it now," she said. "No person should be so enslaved."

The blackness had swelled upward when she rose. Now it moved to block her path. "Psyche . . ." The beautiful voice was very gentle. "That you have said those words is reason enough why I desire a life-bond with you. Do not burn my keepsake—at least, not yet. Hold it as a surety of my goodwill. You can burn it any time"—there was a soft chuckle—"but I do not wish to stick my knife into my hand again the next time you express a doubt of me."

"I did not ask for any surety."

"No, but what you said was all true, and it will be easier for you to believe my promises if you have so strong a token of my good faith. You do not know me well. I understand. It *is* hard to know one whose face you cannot see, whose expression is a mystery to you. I am satisfied that you should hold my life in your hand because I know, though you do not, that what you fear will never happen. In any case, my life matters little, Psyche, because you already hold my soul. You are the vital spark that has relit my inner fire. I do not believe I can live without you any longer—"

Psyche had been standing quite still, looking a little to the side of the shadow that could not be pierced, almost hypnotized by the beauty of Teras's voice and the beauty of the sentiments he expressed. And not once had he mentioned her appearance. She was just beginning to wonder whether he might be blind and perceive what was happening around him by other senses when the last sentence jerked her to alertness. If she listened in silence much longer, he could claim she had agreed to far more than she was ready to yield.

"All I did was ask to touch your face," she snapped. "That was no invitation to you to touch me or—"

"I did not mean it that way. I meant that I need to be with you, to speak to you." A brief pause; when he spoke again, it was plain that Teras was smiling. "Alas, I will survive without coupling if you deny me, although—" a heavy sigh "—not with much comfort." A plaintive note changed the normal music of his voice. "It is very—ah—irritating to be always ready."

The tiny giggle that forced its way past her lips surprised Psyche and rather diminished the force of what she intended to be a repressive remark: "No man can be ready all the time."

"No?" Now the laughter was open. "Would you like to test me?"

Psyche knew she should say coldly, "Not at all. Do not be so vulgar." What she did say was, "It would serve you right if I said yes, first claiming that I was only investigating the truth and not offering any invitation to a similar investigation of my person."

"If you investigated long enough, you might reduce my state of readiness—for a while," Teras rejoined in a rather choked voice. "In that case, I fear you would suffer more from the prohibition than I."

"Hmmph!"

It was all Psyche could manage because she knew if she opened her mouth to speak she would bray like an ass with laughter instead. Talking to Teras was an utter delight. He was the only match she had found since her own wits—and beauty—had matured. The thought woke a feeling that that was not entirely true. Someone else had not been struck dumb by her face, but at the moment she could not recall who, and it was not wise to let her mind wander while she was conversing with Teras. One careless word had proved that already.

"If I promise not to take advantage," his voice was now blatantly wheedling, "will you not 'investigate' just a little?"

"Stop that!" Psyche ordered. "You promised not to importune me."

"I never did! Never! Do you think me mad? I must do something if I wish to ease this state of readiness. I promised not to force you, but I fully intend to importune you as often and as persuasively as I can."

"You are infuriating!" Psyche exclaimed, stamping her foot. "Your mind runs on a single narrow trail without branches or turnings."

"It did not before." He sighed gustily. "It was your suggestion that you would—"

"If you say 'investigate' again, I will do something quite dreadful," Psyche said.

"What?" Teras asked with bright interest.

She gave up and laughed aloud. "Throw myself on the ground and drum with my heels! There. You expected something quite different, I suppose, but I refuse to give you any further chance to importune me." She hesitated, and then said softly, "I am not ready, Teras. Not so much because I doubt you, or even fear you, but—but—"

"Must I go, then?"

"No, don't go. Come into the house. I have been reading and have come across several things I wished to ask you about." The darkness moved aside, and Psyche, thinking he was retreating, added hastily, "Not any question that will hurt you or remind you of the past—"

"I will not run away again," he said. "Sometimes an old wound needs to be probed to make it clean."

"Not by one who is so ignorant that the cautery goes too deep. But this book is harmless—a treatise on plants—"

"Plants! Oh, I forgot your question about the garden. I'm sorry. I will have an answer for you tomorrow."

"No, no, these are wild plants. I want to know which grow nearby, if any do, and if it would be safe for me to gather them. Come inside and look at the book."

"Will you grow uneasy with me again when my . . . black shroud is so apparent?"

Psyche turned her head to look directly at the place seemingly cut out of the world. "That is part of what I must learn, is it not? It is growing colder. Soon we will not be able to spend much time here. If we are to be able to sit and talk so that I can come to know you it must be in a sheltered place."

"You are right." He chuckled. "And coupling out in the countryside, although it is lauded in poetry, is much less pleasant in reality than in verse."

Psyche drew in her breath, but before she could speak, he continued. "But let us not jump into the deepest part of the ocean from a ship to discover whether we can swim. Let us wade out slowly and avoid the danger of drowning. Go tell the servants to darken the house, except for a lamp for yourself."

"Very well," Psyche agreed.

Turning to go, she trod on something hard and sharp, cried out, and stumbled. Instantly, she was blinded by utter blackness, clutching wildly at support, caught in a firm embrace, steadied, and put out into the silvery light of the moon a moment later. Despite the brevity of the experience, she had a strong impression of a big, straight body without deformity and the feeling that she might have clung a little longer regardless of the absolute blackness.

"What did I step on?" she gasped, unwilling to think about the experience.

"One of the game pieces I dropped. See, there it is. I forgot them."

"I did too," she said. "Shall we try to pick them up?"

"It would take all night. Tell the servants to do it in the morning, when there is light. Come, I'll walk with you a little way to be sure you don't trip again."

To her relief, Psyche found that she felt no renewal of horror when Teras entered the house. In fact, the light from the lamp she carried, being centered around her, showed less of the blotting out of reality than the moonlight, and when a side-glance showed the disappearance of a chair or the stair rail as Teras passed, she did not find it as chilling. She realized she was growing accustomed.

In the book room she set the lamp on the table, untied and unrolled the scroll, and held it flat, turning her head into the dark behind her. "You see," she began, and then stopped as she saw the blackness retreat. "Whatever is the matter?" she asked, turning back to look at the scroll.

It was the book of poetry she had unrolled, not the work on plants. She had forgotten that she had left that one out, planning to ask him to point out which words in the translation matched those with which she was familiar and so manage to touch his hand "by accident." She heard a ragged sigh.

"I am so sorry," she cried, springing up and letting the scroll reroll itself. Tears started to her eyes. "Teras, I swear I unrolled the wrong book. I had no idea—"

"You couldn't know this had any more meaning to me than any other, of course." His voice was flat. "No, don't cry, Psyche. It's all right."

"I never meant to hurt you," she sobbed, closing her eyes and running into the dark, clutching him to keep him from fleeing, murmuring she knew not what to soothe away the pain.

She could not know how successful her maneuver was. The unfaltering grip, the hand that drew down Eros's head to kiss his face, the soothing murmurs would not have been possible at the time he had translated those poems. Her nearness assured him as nothing else could do that he was no longer so obscenely loathsome, so revolting, that he had to leave the house before the servants could cook or clean. They had used to fall to the floor, writhing and vomiting, barely able to crawl outside if they accidentally entered when he was there, even when he was upstairs and they below. That was over, ended. The wound was clean and could heal.

As joy wiped out remembered misery, Eros began to return Psyche's caresses. He moved his head just a little so that her lips met his instead of falling on his cheek. He felt her tense and whispered, "Please," against her lips—and she did not withdraw. Then he put his arms around her, first barely embracing her so she could pull free, and when she did not, he used one arm to press her against him. The other hand he raised to run gently over her ear, down her jaw, along her throat, and up around her ear again. She shivered a little.

He lifted his lips from hers just enough to form the words, "Can you bear to be this close to me?" and she pressed closer to reassure him in defiance of her fears and doubts, as he knew she would. He kissed her again, moving his mouth from hers to her throat, her ear, and back to her lips, which were fuller than when they first met his.

Perhaps it was unfair to use her guilt, especially when she had done no wrong, to make her willing to yield to him, but the sooner they were together, the sooner her doubts and fears would be at rest. Eros slid the hand he was holding her with down her back, stroking, then cupping her buttocks and holding her tight to him so she could not mistake the urgency of his need. He brought his hand up again, stretched the fingers until they touched her breast. She made a little sound. Eros twisted his body and stretched farther until his longest finger just slid against her nipple, which was so hard and erect he could feel it through the cloth of her tunic and peplos. Her arms tightened around him and dropped to pull his hips closer.

"Psyche," he murmured, his lips moving against hers, "if you still feel you cannot let me love you, send me away now. I may not be able to stop later. But please . . . I need you so much."

Now or later, Psyche thought muzzily, what did it matter? In the end she would yield to him, and he was warm, and straight, and strong under her seeking hands. So let it be now. Her lips throbbed softly and she stretched her neck to press them against him—it did not matter where. His hand stroked her and she shivered again as a finger rubbed her nipple. It tickled and did not tickle; she wanted to wrench away and she wanted to push her breast hard against the teasing hand. And her nether mouth felt moist and swollen and at the same time gapingly empty.

The hand that had been playing with her ear ran down her neck to her shoulder and began to push down the loose neck of her gown. The mouth followed the hand, kissing down her throat, down her chest, down her breast, and seized the nipple. Psyche's knees loosened, but her monster was ready. The arm that had bared her breast was behind her shoulders, the other behind her thighs. She was lifted and carried. Dimly an alarm bell rang inside her, but she could not listen. Her gasps and sighs drowned it out.

When she was laid down on a bed, she knew why the alarm had rung, but it was too late—and she did not care. A hand had slipped under her skirt and was gently caressing those swollen lower lips. She cried out, clutching tighter to her the head that sucked her breast, lifted her hips to drive the fingers in, in to fill the void. They moved, but only to touch and touch and make her more frantic until she let go of her lover's head and tried to seize his hands. She found instead his naked hips and then one hand, which guided hers to the blind, seeking shaft.

Psyche had never known a man, but she knew what she held and she knew where it belonged. A moment later the sword was poised above the sheath, but it did not plunge in and pierce her. It went a little way, filling the lips but leaving the throat empty, and then withdrew. Psyche heaved upward in pursuit, only partly aware that a hand had returned to her breast, rubbing and squeezing gently at the engorged nipples. She was, however, violently aware of the sensations produced, that tickling that was not a tickling coursing down her body and intensifying the need to be filled.

He had come in again, farther but not far enough, and then withdrawn almost completely. Having heard more than once of inconsiderate husbands who satisfied themselves and left their poor wives still craving, Psyche locked her legs around her lover's hips and drove him down just as he himself thrust downward with what he hoped was enough force to tear her maidenhead but hurt her as little as possible. The combined power was more than either had reckoned on. Both shrieked with pain and stopped moving, but Eros was well lodged.

Psyche felt the ultimate fool. With the return of the ability to reason, she realized first that Teras could not possibly have satisfied himself yet, and second that his slow invasion had been meant either to ease the pain of the loss of her maidenhead or to excite her so much she would not notice. She was about to explain that her mind had flowed away into the sensations of her body when Teras's lips came down to barely touch hers.

"The pain is over, love. Now is all joy," he murmured.

Nor did he fail in his promise, largely because the shock he had experienced had reduced his engorgement. For a few strokes at least, his thinned shaft passed easily. And for those few strokes he had been busy with lips and tongue and fingers, putting her back into the trance of sensation in which there could be no fear. That cause for tightened muscles missing, her own blood and moisture eased the pain of stretching into one more sharp peak of pleasure, which built and built until it exploded into an agony of joy that made her cry aloud and tighten her grip on her lover until he gasped for air.

That grip and the convulsions of her body ignited his so that only moments after she had subsided into limp satisfaction, his climax came. Fortunately, she had been very limp, far too exhausted to raise an arm to push him away, not because she was sated and selfishly did not care about him, but because her mind was too blank to understand why he was still moving. By the time the tempo of his thrusting had quickened frantically and he had stiffened, uttering choked cries, thrust once, twice more, groaned, and collapsed, Psyche was alert enough to enjoy his climax almost as much as she enjoyed her own. Both lay quiet, still entwined, too tired and content to consider greater comfort.

After a time, Teras breathed, "Am I crushing you?"

"You are no lightweight, but I am strong," Psyche replied, smiling.

Teras chuckled and rolled off her but lay close, still

touching. From the utter blackness around Psyche when she allowed her eyes to open for a moment, she knew she was still within the black cloud. Although she no longer felt the horror of being engulfed that had filled her earlier, she closed her eyes again.

"You certainly are strong," Teras said, his voice reproachful. "I think I may be permanently bent from that push you gave me."

Psyche forgot the blackness surrounding her and burst out laughing. "Don't be so silly. I may be innocent, but I'm not so innocent as that. It can't be bent like a piece of metal."

"Is that so?" Her hand was seized and laid on his rod, which was now limp and a little curved as it lay against his thigh. "See, it is bent."

"I am blind within your blackness, but what I feel is that if I keep my hand where it is, your 'bent member' will straighten out at once."

"You flatter me. I am not so strong as that." But even as he spoke he could feel himself swelling and he laughed. "Perhaps I was wrong. Apparently you are a greater inspiration to me than any other woman."

Psyche removed her hand. "I am not sure I wish to be one among many."

"You are not, Psyche, nor will ever be." The beautiful voice had become strained and harsh. "I was dying—not my body, but inside myself. You saved me—not by your beauty, but by your disdain of it, by your willingness to laugh, by your honesty and your courage. There will be no other woman, ever."

"That is a strong avowal," she said softly.

She had meant to mock, having heard from other women that every man promised faithfulness as instinctively as a dog barks at a stranger. But there was in the voice and in the slight tension of the body resting against hers an intensity that she could not mock. It occurred to her suddenly that she was ten times a fool. All that talk of women . . . poor monster, how many women could he have known? She felt the shoulder beside her shrug.

"It is true." The voice was light with laughter again. "But if you are going to be jealous of a monster, you are quite mad."

He had just stated her own thought aloud; nonetheless, she was speaking the truth when she said, "I cannot think of you as a monster when you are so perfect to my hands." Then she added, "But jealousy is stupid anyway. Even if you were as beautiful as Eros, it can only bring grief, often unmerited—as I know too well. No, Teras. I will not seek causes to accuse you of betraying me with other women."

"Would you care?" He turned toward her and drew her to him so that their bodies were pressed together.

Psyche thought for a long moment. "Yes and no," she responded at last. "I suppose pride forces me to want to be first." She smiled. "If I knew you had another lover . . . I might resent it, but I think you would have to fling the fact in my face. It was the way you said 'any other woman' as if I were one in a long string stretching far into the past and far into the future . . ." Her voice faded, and then she said, "But if you have already lived so long, Teras, there will be a future for you far beyond mine. You will watch me grow old and die . . ."

"I will not live long beyond you, my Psyche," he whispered against her lips. "As for growing old—I did not choose you for your outer beauty, although it caught my eye, but for that inner being which can only grow stronger and more perfect with age. And as for dying—remember, I am already very old. All that there can be in life I have already experienced—except love. You have brought to me the last, the best, that life can offer. Without you, for me, there can be no life. I will not mind dying."

Only words, Psyche told herself, but she clutched him closer, somehow convinced by the casual, almost smiling, tone of voice of her inestimable value to him, not for an accident of birth, which another accident like breaking her nose could wipe away, but for what she had built for herself. The arms that welcomed her in a comforting hug now loosened enough for the hands to begin to wander over her. Psyche sighed.

"Are you too sore, beloved?" he murmured a little while later, lifting his lips from hers. "You do give an old, old monster surprising strength, but I can wait if you need to rest."

Psyche chuckled breathlessly. "I notice you did not ask sooner, you monster. Now, sore or not, I am too eager to deny you."

"Perfect," he sighed, arching his body so he could kiss her breast. "Eager, yes, but not ready. You can still talk sense."

With that he brought his mouth down and soon, as evidenced by her incoherent cries, she was ready as well as eager.

CHAPTER 11

The following morning, Psyche half awoke, stretched her hand to touch her lover, and came fully alert with the shock of realizing he was not there. For a moment she was furious, feeling that Teras had used her and left her. In the next moment she recalled what she would have seen—half the bed, half her body swallowed into a black nothing. Involuntarily she shuddered. Teras knew how she felt about the blackness; he had left her to spare her.

Nonetheless, while Psyche summoned the servants, bathed, dressed, and breakfasted, she worried at the subject. She knew she was being deprived of one strong link between a mating pair—the early-morning pillow talk, the planning together of the work of the day. The question was, could she bear to hold such talk with "nothing," or worse, a blackness that was a negation of everything?

In the dark, it did not matter much if her eyes happened to be open when part of her was outside of his aura. Mostly she kept her eyes shut and thus was unaware of anything except the feel of his warm, strong, straight body. But in the daylight, keeping her eyes closed would not help. One sees light through shut eyelids when there is light to see. To be constantly reminded of the black cloud by alternating dark and light beyond her closed eyes would make coherent thought impossible.

She would prefer a tusked, horned, gray-skinned horror, she thought. Her mind stopped on the exasperated phrase, and she examined the idea. Would she really prefer to see Teras in his monstrous form? Could she separate what her eyes beheld from what her hands felt—or would she feel the disfigurements because she could see them? And there were far worse forms, far more disgusting deformities, than what she had been envisioning. Better leave well enough alone, she decided.

Naturally, she could not. Even when she found on the table beside her bed the carefully wrapped piece of himation stained with Teras's blood, she could not focus her mind on it enough to decide what to do. Fearful that any method of destroying the "keepsake" might harm her poor monster, she found a small box into which to place it and buried it at the very bottom of her clothes chest.

It was a long day. Whatever she began, she soon found her mind drifting to the surprising delight the monster—no, Teras—had wakened in her body, which only brought her again to the question of whether she could accept him better as a creature frightening to the eyes or something that froze the soul from not being there at all. Again she ate too fast at dinnertime and found herself with nothing to do when the meal was over. This time, however, she did not need to pretend to herself that she was not eager for his company. She went out at once and sat down on the bench to wait.

Psyche had hoped the sight of her would bring Teras sooner, but to her chagrin it was quite dark before she noticed the blotting out of a portion of the lawn that flowed toward her.

"You are late," she said, standing up and holding out her hands.

They were seized, drawn into the cloud, kissed. Psyche thought the breathing she felt was quicker and harder than usual. Did that mean he had been hurrying? From where?

"Teras," she said, looking into the dark about where his head should be so she would not see her arms, faintly pale in the starlight, disappear completely at the elbow. "Oh, Teras, is your monster form so very horrible? Do you think I might become accustomed to it so you could be with me during the day as well as at night? It is really very dreadful to see parts of my body disappear, even though I know they will reappear unharmed. I am not sure I could bear that in the full light of day, but I was sorry to wake and find you gone."

She was enveloped, kissed soundly, and then held more gently as Teras murmured, "Thank you. I am well assured that I did not hurt you or frighten you, that I did pleasure you. I wish I could have stayed with you, but—" he sighed. "I see what I did was wise. If you think my monster form preferable to this darkness, I did well to go. But Psyche, my love, I could not spend much more time with you right now in any case."

"You are so busy?" Psyche asked in amazement. Aside from her own desire for company, she had been envisioning poor Teras crouched in some secret place, waiting miserably for darkness to fall. "What do you do all day? Do you make 'monster' appearances or something?"

He laughed ringingly. "You mean to frighten naughty children into good behavior? No, I do not 'appear' in monster form like an actor strutting a stage. I've told you more than once that I am Aphrodite's servant. Sometimes there is little for me to do, but right now I am arranging a most tangled business for her."

"Yes, you have told me, but I cannot imagine Aphrodite using a monster or a black nothingness to deliver her orders. Eros was very beautiful—at least, his face and body were beautiful, but his heart was colder than death."

"Colder than death . . ." Teras sighed. "Yes, it was, but do not blame poor Eros. He is as old as I, and as you should know, beauty can be a heavy burden to bear for a long, long time."

"You have borne worse, and your heart is not dead."

He had relaxed his grip on her while they spoke; now he pulled her tight against him again and kissed her lips, her cheeks, and then her lips again.

"My heart was dead as his until I found you, Psyche. Your vital spark has lit again the fires that were quenched within me. But Aphrodite does, indeed, need my services. She is small and frail, not at all fit to defend herself if that should become necessary, and—" he chuckled "—I fear she is most easily distracted. In a complicated matter like this, it is best if I manage the affair."

"What affair? Oh, I had better not ask that, since it is Aphrodite's business."

Psyche heard the sharpness in her voice and was rather ashamed, but Teras either did not notice or did not care. He laughed aloud.

"Actually, it is not Aphrodite's business at all," he said. "She is doing a favor for Hephaestus, who is doing a favor for Tethys, who is doing a favor for Poseidon. It is very amusing—except that Dionysus is involved and he has Seen something that he does not understand and that troubles him—and *that* troubles me."

For a moment Psyche was numb with awe. God-names one after another tumbling from Teras's mouth in a way that bespoke long personal knowledge. Then she reminded herself that they were not gods, only

Gifted beings from a land over the mountains. And she remembered, although it seemed like years ago, that she had said so much to Teras and he had not been angry. Nor had he confirmed or denied her deduction. This seemed like a good time to press for that answer.

"But I thought that Poseidon was supposed to be a god. Why does he need Aphrodite's help? Moreover why does he take so circuitous a route to it? Why not ask her himself?"

"Ah," he said, "I see you have not got much further in *The History of the Olympians,* or you would have discovered that Poseidon does not come to Olympus."

As he spoke, he turned her so that she faced forward keeping one arm firmly around her waist and drawing her arm around him. When he began to walk, she knew they were going toward the house, although she was totally blind. She was surprised by not being the least afraid; in fact, she was distracted from fear by how much her sense of touch was heightened. The play of his muscles as he moved was strongly apparent to her, and she matched her stride to his, stepping forward confidently. He kissed her temple.

"No," she said, "I haven't read any more because that kind of book needs to be discussed with someone and I dare not ask you the thousand questions that come to my mind."

"Why not?"

He sounded honestly puzzled and realizing that she could not spend the rest of her life walking on eggshells she said, "I do not wish to ask questions that will hurt you. I would be glad to know more, but the history of your people is no life or death matter to me. To cause you pain merely to satisfy my curiosity is unfair."

"You are as caring of heart as you are beautiful Psyche. But you need not fear to ask questions. I think you have healed me."

Healing of a hurt so deep it drove poor Teras into instinctive flight one time and into mute endurance another did not come that quickly or easily, Psyche thought. But if he felt enough ease to urge her to ask questions, she could pursue her point, at least concerning those he had mentioned without stress. "Well, then, perhaps you will give me a straight answer. Is Poseidon a god? Is Aphrodite a goddess? And Zeus?"

"In one sense, no," he said. "We are certainly not all knowing nor all powerful. But in another sense, compared to your folk, who fear and destroy your Gifted, the more powerful among us are like gods." He stopped and pushed her gently forward. "We are at the door, love. Go in and take your lamp."

When she emerged from the utter blackness of Teras's embrace, Psyche blinked in the golden glow for a moment, hesitating between going to the andron or to the book room. A moment later, she had lifted the lamp and turned toward the stairs. She was halfway up before she realized that the vague notion of showing Teras the book was ridiculous. She knew Teras was familiar with the work and was unlikely to demand to see her source. Color rose in her face, but she went on without faltering, smiling a little despite her blush. Her real reason for choosing the book room had nothing to do with books at all. It was the proximity of the bedchamber, not of the scrolls of text, that made that room so inviting.

She smiled again when she passed her bedchamber door, but she did not hesitate. A brief memory of the pleasure to be found there stirred in her body and she let it come and enjoyed it without even a glance at the door. That was for later, the sweet crown of her few hours of companionship. If Teras could not come to her in daylight or would not because his undisguised form was so dreadful he did not believe she could bear

it even now when she knew it was just a seeming, then
it behooved her to turn night into day. She would enjoy
talk and his company first, then they could go to bed.
If she slept late in the morning, so much the better; it
would make the following day shorter.

She had not responded to what he had said while
they moved within the house. It was too awkward to
talk to someone who kept to the shadows behind her,
but she had not forgotten her purpose of clarifying
just what was worshipped above the altars of Hellas.
In the book room, she went and sat down at one end of
the table, setting the lamp beside her. A chair from the
other side of the room, barely visible outside of the
glow of her lamp, disappeared completely. A moment
later she heard the scritch of its feet as someone heavy
sat down and slid it forward.

"Like gods, you say, but that brings me back to what
I asked you first. Why does Poseidon need a favor from
Aphrodite? Can he not accomplish his purpose without
her help?"

"As I said before, yes and no." The monster's warm
chuckle and the tone, which implied a fuller explanation would follow, soothed away her irritation before
she was fully aware of it. "What I mean is that Poseidon
has enormous power. He can whip the sea into mountains that will cover the land and move the waters so
that the land above them shifts and rises and falls. The
trouble with using that power to punish those who
disobey him is that he might well wipe out the whole
population around the guilty. That would not be hu-
mane—" The chuckle sounded again. "I am not sure
that would much trouble Poseidon, but wiping out the
population would also result in a great diminishing of
worshippers, which would not be to Poseidon's benefit."

With wide eyes, Psyche said, "Is there no way for him to use his power more moderately?"

"Perhaps, but how could Minos know that a mild storm or a little trembling of the earth was a sign of Poseidon's displeasure? Look, let me tell you the whole tale and you will see why Poseidon has chosen the punishment he has—I must admit, I think it appropriate—and why Aphrodite was involved."

She listened with great interest, agreeing that Minos had no right to break his word just to enrich himself with Poseidon's bull's get, arguing about whether Minos's wife should be involved in her husband's punishment, but in the end, coming back to her original question.

"I still do not see why, if Poseidon can shake the earth, he cannot beguile Pasiphae as well as Aphrodite."

There was a momentary silence, and then, in a mildly puzzled voice, the monster said, "It is not his Gift." Then he added thoughtfully, as if it were the first time he had thought about it, "Power over water is his Gift. I do not know whether he ever learned any magic or whether the power that maintains his Gift can be used to evoke spells. That is why I said we are not gods. As far as I know, no matter how powerful each is, there is a sharp limit to our use—"

"We? Our?" Psyche interrupted. "You count yourself among them?"

"I was born an Olympian. I have my power too. I did wrong and was punished. But I still say we and us, yes."

"Forgive me," Psyche said. "No matter how far from the subject I begin, I always seem to end reminding you of your misfortunes."

"No," he said, a kind of surprised wonder in his voice. "Far from it. I have just come to understand that to be punished is not to be cast out. I am beginning to wonder now how much of my grief I made for myself."

She put out her hand and the darkness bulged out and covered it. His grasp was warm and strong, but Psyche turned her eyes away from her truncated arm despite the comforting pressure of his fingers. Less and less did she believe that Teras had committed any crime worthy of the agony inflicted on him. His sweetness of disposition, his willingness to take all the blame on himself, made her wish to lash out at those who had hurt him, pointing out their cruelty and unworthiness for making him still wear the horrible seeming cast on him. She wished to snarl that it was time that he be freed—but that would only hurt him more. Besides, Psyche knew that much of her fury against those who had deformed him was pure selfishness. She wanted to see him as he must have been, tall and strong, clean-limbed, with a proudly held head. With closed eyes and the image strong in her mind, she rose, pulling on his hand so that she could walk into the black cloud.

"I am not hurt, beloved," he whispered into her hair, "but I will not refuse the comfort you offer me."

Later, she thought that the utter blackness that enveloped her was not all bad. As she had noticed earlier, the total inability to see heightened her other senses. It seemed that every change in Teras's breathing sang a clear message of rising passion, and her skin could feel the warmth of his fingers before they touched her. She was eager, then ready, then fulfilled, but as they lay murmuring light-hearted nonsense before they slept, she remembered how shocked she had been on waking alone in the bed.

"Teras," she murmured. "Wake me before you leave, and say goodbye."

"Why should I break your sleep, love?"

"Because morning is the time for starting the new day, the time when a husband says: I will order the ploughing of the west field today, or a wife says: My women will finish bleaching the linen today, so if you go into the town, bring me some crimson dye. We cannot have the morning, but I need that feeling, the sense that life will go on, that you and I are merely parted to do our separate duties and will come together at our day's end."

"Those are very sweet words, Psyche, and very wise ones. When I left you yesterday, I felt sad, as if I had left something unfinished. Now I know what it was. I will not fail to wake you."

He did not, and to her intense pleasure she saw gray streaks around the shutters that betrayed the coming of dawn. He had lain with her all night. And he had not waked her only to say that he was leaving. He talked of what he would do on the coming day, saying he would be off to Aegina to talk to Poseidon. Psyche warned him to be careful as to how he introduced the idea of Pasiphae and the bull, lest the message that Aphrodite received had become garbled in its long path to her. After a moment's startled silence, he thanked her most heartily, admitting that there was a chance of deliberate mischief in involving Aphrodite.

While they talked, Psyche could hear him moving around in the bedchamber, pulling on his clothes, washing—no doubt in water he had wakened the servants to bring while she still slept—cursing once when he bumped into a chest. It was all so much as she imagined a husband might speak and act when making ready for an early hunt that when he left she sank back to sleep with a strong sense of satisfaction.

She woke to the same feeling of comfort and a need to be busy. With a clear mind and a newly sharpened housewife's eye—the glaze of doubt and fear having been removed—she found that all was not as perfect as it first had seemed. She was happily employed in household tasks that day. The servants neither helped nor hindered her; when she asked for supplies or told them to do something specific, like move the furniture—which she now realized had not been touched for years—they obeyed, but with worried looks, as if they were not sure obedience to her orders was permitted.

That diminished her satisfaction a little, but she soon realized that Teras could not tell them they must obey her lest she order them to help her escape. She thought briefly of pointing out to him that she had nowhere to go but a moment later dismissed the idea. She did not want to know it if he still did not trust her; nor did she want to hear that the servants were Aphrodite's and would not obey him either. The notion might have rankled, except that night her thoughts were given a new direction.

Teras came early, calling to her from the edge of the forest as soon as she arrived at the bench. It was barely dusk, so she went in under the trees where the darker splotches cast by trunks and branches broke up and disguised the deeper blackness Teras cast. They strolled about while he told her of his day's accomplishments and she, suddenly reminded by the tale of his "leaping" to Aegina and then to Crete that her monster was not only a victim but a creature of great power, woke to another reason the servants might have been uneasy. If Teras had arranged the house, they might fear to alter anything; thus she confessed that she had ordered the rearrangement of the andron and her workroom and said she hoped he did not mind.

The blackness stopped, half hidden by a tree trunk. Psyche could sense that Teras was staring at her. "No one had touched it for years," she said defensively. "It was dirty, and—"

Then he laughed and said he would not mind if she hung all the furniture from the roof—except the bed, of course—but that he thought it a sad waste of her time. Whereupon she pointed out, with perhaps a touch of bitterness, that time was one commodity of which she had a superfluity.

"But did you not tell me that you wished to gather and try out the plants described in that scroll on magical and medicinal herbs?" he asked.

"Magical and medicinal herbs?" Psyche repeated, totally at a loss, and then remembered that she had used that scroll as an excuse to invite him to come into the house.

"You asked me if it would be safe for you to gather them, and—oh, I never answered you."

"That was my fault," Psyche said, adding hastily so he would not think too long on the poetry that had distressed him so deeply, "but what in the world reminded you of the herbs?"

"I went to Hermes's house to get the translocation spells, and Hera's maid was there complaining bitterly to one of Hermes's servants about needing to be transported to Hera's shrine to obtain some poultice or other. It came to my mind like a revelation that there is no source of simples in Olympus, and that you and I have no source of metal and barter goods."

"You wish me to gather the herbs and prepare the medicines or magical mixtures for you to sell in Olympus? But Teras, will this be permitted? Would it even be possible?"

"Why not?"

She could not ask whether a being under sentence for evildoing would be allowed to establish a business or whether it would be conducive to trade to have a monster serving at the stall. She asked, "Is it not necessary to get permission to begin a business? And who will serve the clients?"

"I cannot see why permission would be needed, and

there are plenty of old servants who would enjoy attending to a shop. Come, let us go look at that scroll and see if I can remember anything about it. You know, until now, all my wants have been provided by Aphrodite, but I do not think it fair, now I have a wife, that she should pay for all."

Any other objections Psyche might have had were silenced. She knew that his services deserved fair compensation, but for herself . . . She shuddered with disgust at the notion of being permanently dependent on Aphrodite's "kindness and generosity." Simultaneously she realized that having his own source of income might free Teras from his enslavement to the goddess. Perhaps he might not yet realize that he wished to be free, but the less he needed Aphrodite's "kindness," the greater the possibility, Psyche felt, that she could wean him from his dependence.

That night they studied the scroll with care and Teras explained where it would be safe for her to go. In the dawn when he woke her, he told her he had ordered the menservants to accompany her and that as soon as he had finished the arrangements for Poseidon's revenge on Minos, he would go with her himself for those plants that were best collected at night or before the sun rose.

Over the weeks that followed, he did more. Even though he was nearly certain the places she could reach in a day's exploring were free of dangerous beasts—and he came to comb the forest himself on many a day to kill or drive away any threat from an even broader area—he wished to be more sure that no harm could possibly come to her. So he taught her, himself standing in the shadow at the edge of the forest, to use a hunting spear and cast a javelin and even to shoot a small, light bow. She took such delight in her lessons that he continued them, although as the autumn deepened into true winter, there was little to gather and little purpose to going into the forest.

Psyche missed her wandering a little; she was less aware of being cut off from everyone except Teras when she was in the woods. It was a familiar activity from her life at home, and if she did not consciously think she would return to her family, nor suffer any shock when she did arrive at Teras's house, the gathering trips touched some comfort buried deep inside her.

Still, she was busy enough practicing her skills with weapons when the days were crisp and bright, working with the herbs when the wind howled and the snow fell. Winter brought a ready market for syrups to soothe coughs and sore throat, pungent aromatics to clear a stuffed head, and creams and lotions to comfort chaps and chilblains. The great mages might still use magic to cure minor ills, but everyone else found Psyche's draughts and drenches and creams and lotions less expensive and easier to obtain than spells. The shop began to prosper.

And every evening Teras was with her and they talked of the people and doings of Olympus, the errands on which Aphrodite sent him, their own plans for the future, and their dreams. They played games with the exquisite pieces on the gorgeous boards, and they made love. They made love with their eyes amid jests and laughter, they made love with words without ever touching, and they made love abed with their bodies, every inch of their bodies.

Little by little as the months passed and Teras's passion seemed to grow rather than diminish, Psyche came to believe that his need for her was not based on her appearance. He had told her that, of course, but she had needed proof, and had it. She knew her beauty must now be dulled by possession and familiarity, and it was always words, a teasing remark or an ethical argument, that set the black cloud to swelling in her direction with warm, seeking lips and hands that played her like a harp.

Equally important, the more she knew Teras, the better she liked him. In some ways he was truly a monster, not seeming to know good from evil—except as it struck him at the moment; if a thing amused or interested him, it was good, and if it bored or annoyed him, it was evil. This, she discovered, as long winter evenings passed in talk and as she spent daylight hours reading *The History of the Olympians,* was no special fault in Teras but was common to the Gifted among his people. But he responded swiftly to reason and seemed to enjoy learning the code of values that governed her actions.

The pity for him and recognition that she could not change her fate, which had led her to accept the monster, became flavored with respect and admiration. Boiled together by the heat of their coupling, those tepid emotions—like a mixture of innocent herbs that could be seethed into a powerful potion—transmuted into love. Week by week Psyche's happiness and security washed out the stains of resentment and bitterness that had sullied her. She was not aware of that. What she did feel was an occasional pang of guilt for being so deliciously happy when her parents and siblings probably mourned her as dead—or worse.

With the arrival of spring, the pangs of guilt became somewhat more frequent, especially as the days lengthened and her time with Teras grew shorter. Aphrodite's need for him also seemed greater in the spring; he even missed coming for a night now and again, and there never seemed to be enough time to say what needed to be said, let alone make idle conversation.

The long, lanquid days of summer only made matters worse. The plants in the forest were mostly dry and sapless and not worth seeking, the heat was too great to make any exercise out of doors pleasant, and Psyche had little to do but comb the book room for material that would hold her interest—and nothing did. She began to feel cut off from life, bitterly lonely for some other voice than Teras's, much as she loved that voice. She found herself longing to tell her sisters about Teras, to praise her man to them as they had praised their men to her, to discuss with her mother whether she dared dismiss the spell she had invoked to keep her barren. She desired Teras's child but feared that he did not fully understand the nature of the curse on him, or, desiring her greatly, had not told her the truth to make her more willing to lie with him.

Psyche knew there was no remedy for her discontent and that it would be useless and unkind to confess her loneliness to Teras. It was Aphrodite, not Teras, who had condemned her to live in this house cut off from all humankind except the "monster" and the mute servants. Thus it would be cruel to bewail her fate to Teras, who had already done everything he could to make her "punishment" a joy.

Despite her growing desire to have more human contact, a more normal life, Psyche found to her surprise that she felt little personal bitterness toward Aphrodite. How could she be bitter to the one who had given her her monster? She did resent the goddess's skillful manipulation of Teras and remained determined to free him, but now that she understood how Olympians lived, she could no longer blame Aphrodite for punishing those who flouted her authority. Nor could she still hate and reject the "goddess of love and beauty." Love she had found *was* worth praying for, and beauty was coupled to love, the beloved always beautiful in the eye of the lover. She knew that was true! Was not a black cloud of nothingness beautiful to her because she loved the being inside it?

Because she loved Teras, Psyche did her best to hide her growing sadness. And because he loved her, she could not be successful. First he increased his attentions to her, bringing her jewels that took away her breath, ever finer clothing, and delicacies from the far corners of the earth and the vast depths of the sea. Later, when he saw that she brightened more for a loving word than for any gift, he asked her again and again how he had failed her, what he could do to bring back her joy, and she tried to laugh and insisted that she was happy or kissed him fondly and assured him that if she was not full of joy, it was no fault of his.

Matters came to a head as summer drifted into autumn. Psyche was turning out the clothes chests, putting the lightest silks and thinnest linens in the bottom of the chests and taking out the middleweight woolen and heavy linen tunics and himations to be aired. She felt more cheerful than usual at her task, looking forward to the lengthening periods of darkness when Teras would be with her more. She was thinking fondly of the long, cozy evenings in Teras's arms when they had time to talk of anything and everything and to the busy days in her workshop, when she came across the gown she had worn on the day she had been sacrificed.

She sat staring, turning the gown over and over in her hands, the memory of her mother's and sisters' terror and grief tearing at her peace. She remembered: it was this time of year, this very month, when they had left her on the altar. With a shock, she realized that it was almost the same phase of the moon; in fact, the very next week would bring her family to Mount Pelion—since she had no grave or place in the family mortuary—for the formal "release of her spirit."

Psyche burst into tears, all her own joy ashes in her mouth, at the memory of the ashes in their hair, the rent garments and scratched breasts. She knew their grief must be excoriated because they did not know what had become of her, and further embittered by remembrance of slights and unkindnesses that could never be amended. Once she had started to weep, the well of her loneliness opened and she could not stop crying. Eros found her with her face swollen, her breath still catching with sobs.

"Beloved, beloved, what is wrong?" he cried, catching her into his arms, half afraid that she would shriek as the darkness swallowed her or push him away.

Instead, she clung to him confidingly, resting her head on his shoulder. "I am sorry you found me this way," she sighed. "I tried and tried to stop, but—oh, Teras, did you realize that it is nearly a year since I was left at the altar on Mount Pelion? Next week my family will make the prayers for setting my spirit free . . ."

"But my dearling, that cannot hurt you. The Mother will not draw your soul to Her just because your family is not aware that you are safe and sound."

She began to sob again. "That is what I cannot bear. If they thought me dead, I would miss them, but I would not feel my heart wrung. Teras, all my joy is embittered by the knowledge that my family may think of me, not dead and at peace, but screaming and writhing in an eternity of pain and horror. My punishment was to be married to a monster. How could they know that my monster is a better and kinder man than any I have ever known?"

He kissed her forehead and then her lips. "I never thought! That is a more severe punishment than was intended. You will think me cruel, but I am afraid I had forgotten all about your family."

"It is not your fault," Psyche said, holding him tight.

"But it is," he said softly. "I have known that you were sad for so long, and I never guessed at this reason. Do you miss them so much? Have I done you such an ill, Psyche? I could think of no other way to protect you. The insult to Aphrodite had to be punished, and even if she had pardoned your part, which she would have been willing to do if I asked, I assure you, I could see only a tragic end to your situation. You were too much a focus of trouble in Iolkas."

"You!" She pushed away from him, not with a jerk of anger, but as one held in a close embrace moves back to see a too-near face. Before she completed the movement she checked it and rested her head on his shoulder again, knowing she would see no more outside his darkness than within it. "What had you to do with my fate? I thought you were as much Eros's victim as I."

She felt his breath draw in sharply, but after a moment he said, "No. Eros and I are equal partners in your fate. I planned it; he accomplished it."

"But Aphrodite ordered it." Psyche uttered a sobbing sigh and then tried to smile. She had never been able to understand whether or not Teras could see inside the blackness, but she knew that he could sense her expressions and gestures and would know she was smiling. "There, I am better now. I know there is nothing you can do. I will try—" Her voice shook and she drew another trembling breath to try to steady it. "I will try not to think about it anymore."

"That is ridiculous," Teras said. "Trying not to think of something only brings it more often and more sharply to mind. My indifference to all except you, my love, is at fault. A year of doubt and fear for your family is enough. I will have to think of a way to let them know that you are safe and happy."

"Aphrodite will not permit it," Psyche said, clutching him tighter. "She will punish you. No. I could not bear that. I swear I will not cry anymore or worry about my family ever again."

He burst out laughing and kissed her. "You do not

listen to a word I say about poor Aphrodite. She will not punish me because she will not *care.* She is not in the least vengeful once she is satisfied, and she has most likely forgotten all about you and your father or she would have bade me return you.''

"Return me?" Psyche barely got the words out. Horror had all but suspended her breath. It had never before occurred to her that Teras's love for her would give Aphrodite a deadly weapon to use against him.

"Well, she returns children who are unhappy in her service. If she knew you were grieving for your family and they for you, she would send you back to them.'' Teras stopped abruptly, as if he had just understood his own words, but then he went on. "I have told you over and over that she is the kindest of women.''

"Teras, do not tell her that I am unhappy. Do not mention me at all, I beg you. I do not wish to leave you. I do not wish to live with my family." Her voice faltered as her empty days, bereft of companionship, rose to mind, but then she thought of her nights and she went on more strongly and surely, "I only want them to know I am not suffering.''

He did not reply at once, and Psyche pressed herself closer against him, fearing her broken voice had conveyed the dissatisfaction she knew he could not cure. He was so good to her. Fervently she repeated that she wished only to remain with him.

"I am glad of that, beloved," he said softly. "Because I do not think I can live without you. Do not fret about your family. I promise I will find a way to prove you are well and happy and even to carry you a message from them.''

CHAPTER 12

The next morning, Eros carried in Aphrodite's breakfast tray. Her eyes opened slightly wider in surprise as she lifted herself to a more upright position and tucked pillows behind her.

"I cannot remember the last time you brought me my breakfast," she said.

"That is because you cannot remember the last time I had a problem," he replied, laughing as he set the tray in front of her.

"My dear Eros, I can remember easily enough when your life consisted wholly of only one problem—whether it was worth the effort to go on breathing. But that question has not troubled you for a year, not since you found this new lover . . . Ah, is the beast unfaithful? To you?"

He laughed again. "No, not that. She has been attacked by pangs of conscience. Because she is happy, she feels guilty because her parents and siblings do not know what has become of her and might be grieving."

"Oh, you naughty boy! Do you mean you did not woo her and make arrangements with her parents to carry her off? You will ruin my reputation if you demand grown women as sacrifices in my name."

"Nothing of the sort!" Eros exclaimed indignantly.

"You know I would never use your worship in such a fashion. Of course, Psyche *was* 'sacrificed,' but that was her punishment for rejecting you and part of the reparation her father made for striking your priestess and forbidding worshippers access to your temple in Iolkas."

For a moment Aphrodite looked perfectly blank as she nibbled at the food on her tray. Then she nodded. "Oh, yes, I remember." And then she began to laugh and her eyebrows rose as high as they would go. "Was that not the girl who was said to be so beautiful that she thought herself superior to me? Oh, Eros! I never thought I would see the day when *you* would fall victim to a pretty face. And for a whole year!"

"Psyche is more than a pretty face," he said, feeling uneasy as he spoke.

There was an odd bitterness under Aphrodite's laughing words, and he recalled how Psyche had begged him not to mention her to Aphrodite. But that was nonsense. Doubtless Psyche feared Aphrodite would be jealous, but Aphrodite never cared whom he took for a lover—so long as he did not evince any desire for her. And then he felt relieved. Aphrodite, like any of the great mages, resented any challenge to her power. Indeed, that was what had got Psyche into trouble in the first place. He came and knelt beside the bed.

"Psyche never thought herself superior to you, Aphrodite. She just felt that beauty had brought her nothing but grief, and she could not bring herself to worship the goddess of that attribute."

"Beauty brought her you. Are you nothing but grief?" Aphrodite asked sharply.

Eros sighed. "She does not know me as Eros. The punishment you named for her was that she love a monster. I . . . You remember I went to Anerios's palace to discover what would most quickly bring him and his 'haughty' daughter to heel. I found Psyche far from haughty. She felt about her beauty much as I feel about mine. I could not punish her for that—and I could not remit her punishment lest the lesson of the evil consequences of defying your power be weakened—so I ordered that she be brought to the altar on Mount Pelion to be the bride of a monster. I bought a spell of darkness from Hecate and carried her off to the lodge. That darkness is all she has ever seen."

"So she is not jealous and does not plague you. I see." She smiled at him and beckoned him to sit on the bed, holding the tray with one hand so he should not tip it. When he was settled, she poppped a small tidbit of spiced cheese into his mouth and shook her head at him. "Eros, I know you think you have been very clever, and in a way you have, but how long can this last? No woman can resist a mystery forever. Has she not asked you to show her your true form?"

"Yes," he admitted, grinning. "And I have been clever about that too. All I said, most mournfully—and truthfully, as well—was that looking at a black cloud was far better than looking upon me. I have no doubt that her imagination has conjured up horrors I could never have devised."

"But that must fail as soon as she touches you."

Then he laughed aloud. "Aha, I have been even cleverer than you thought. I told all the truth. I said a spell had been cast upon me that made me repulsive, but that inside the darkness she could feel what I truly was. She pitied me, of course, which softened her heart toward the poor, suffering monster, and being a most courageous girl, she soon entered the black cloud that surrounds me. Naturally her hands found only the features of a normal man."

He had been speaking merrily, but then he grew serious, frowning a little. It was plain to Aphrodite he had not said all he wished to say. She continued to eat and sip her warm wine and watch his face; suddenly she called herself a fool. Because he had been sleeping very late in the morning but was alert and responsive when she had a task for him, she had assumed he had returned to "normal." For more years than she cared to remember, Eros had been sleeping away his empty days when no external impetus propelled him into action. During most of that time, he had come alert when called upon, ready to be interested and amused by any task she had found for him.

Little by little that interest had died, until Eros seemed like an animated corpse. She had assumed his new lover had wakened him from that state and been half annoyed and half grateful—but she had been deceiving herself. The Eros frowning into space as he sought words to describe something of great importance to *him* was not the Eros she had known since Zeus had deposed Kronos. There had never been anything important to Eros himself in all those years. This Eros was not only alive but *caring*. His expression had a kind of softness, and there was a new thoughtfulness and depth in his eyes when they lifted to meet hers.

"You know I have lain with many women," he said at last. "And with men and nymphs and dryads too. Never in my life have I had from any the pleasure Psyche gives me—and not because her body is different or because she knows any devices to heighten passion. She knows only what I taught her, and what her own clever mind can devise based on those lessons." He sighed with a kind of exasperation. "I cannot explain. All I can say is that—that there is *more* to our lovemaking than the pleasure of the body."

Aphrodite swirled the dregs in her cup and gazed down into the moving liquid as she said, "It is no business of mine, but you must know I think you are a fool and treading dangerous waters. Love should lie down with laughter, and rise up with joy to seek a new partner. It is obsession that binds two together so close that they can take no pleasure in others."

"You do not think what Hades and Persephone have is good? They are one flesh, one blood, one bone."

She shuddered. "It is not worth the agony they can inflict upon each other—not even by intention, but by accident, and worse, by mistaken goodwill."

Eros shook his head. "Perhaps you are right," he said, "but I cannot believe it." He took her hand caressingly. "You will not abandon me just because I am happy?"

"It is you who have abandoned me," she said, but her voice was light and she smiled.

"Indeed I have not," Eros protested. "Have I not come running to you with my first problem?"

Aphrodite laughed. "So you have. I had forgotten you carried in my breakfast tray in payment for a favor."

"Not in payment," Eros said, smiling. "I could not pay you for the favors you have done me if I could give you all the precious stones and precious metal that Hades could command. Bringing in your tray had a double purpose—to cozen you into wanting to help me . . . and to warn you I was going to disturb you with my troubles."

"You are trying to cozen me now so just tell me this trouble. You may have told me already, but I was not attending."

"I am troubled because Psyche is unhappy. She imagines her parents and siblings miserable because they fear she is tormented by a cruel monster. To speak the truth, I am certain they were all glad to be rid of her and probably have not given her fate any thought at all, but to tell her that would hurt her—and she probably would not believe me because *she,* sweet, loyal, and just soul that she is, is suffering from imagining them suffering."

"You are an *idiot* to get involved with natives," Aphrodite exclaimed, laughing heartily. "They create mountains of tragedy over pebbles of woe. What can it matter if Psyche did suffer her whole life? That is so short, it is like you stubbing your toe."

A sharp pang of fear made Eros catch his breath. The past year, full of interest and joy, had indeed flown by, seeming shorter than many single days before Psyche had come into his life. He suppressed the fear. However short, each day had been full of excitement and pleasure. He would not look ahead, but enjoy what he had to the fullest. Taking Aphrodite's hand, he laughed.

"But I do not like to stub my toes," he said plaintively. "Even if the pang is brief, I do not wish to endure it. And I do not wish that Psyche be sad because her sadness spoils my pleasure."

"Ah, your pleasure. Well, that is a good reason to make her happy." She shrugged. "Send her home—"

"No!" Eros cried, jumping to his feet, nearly overturning the tray. "Do not bid me return her as you return an unwanted child. I cannot! I *need* her. I—I do not believe I can go on living without her."

Aphrodite had snatched at the tray to prevent the dregs of her wine and the remains of a sweet curd in a bowl from spilling over the bed. She felt like saying: Oh, do not be ridiculous; you sound like the silly clunches you shoot full of arrows of love. But the panic in his voice recalled to her the change in his expression; she knew what bound him was deeper than a spell. It was something that made her very uncomfortable the few times she had sensed it, as she had in Persephone and Hades, because it was beyond her control. Opposition, she knew, could have no effect but to heighten that bonding; it could be undone only by those who had made the bond. By the time she put the tray aside and looked up, her expression was bland and she laughed lightly and shook her finger at him.

"Do let me finish what I was about to say. Have you not just told me you want her to be free of imagining her family is in torment? They will never believe you if you simply tell them, and she will never believe that they are at peace unless she sees it with her own eyes. Even if you bring her a message, she will fear that you forced it from them. The best solution to that problem is to get a spell from Hermes to take her to Pelion and to return her to the lodge. Let her go and tell her people that she is content. If she cares for you as you do for her, she will return."

Eros seemed completely unaware of the warning in that last sentence. His face cleared and he leaned forward to hug Aphrodite hard. "You are always my best and wisest mentor. Of course, that is best."

Aphrodite smiled at him. She was almost certain that the girl would not return. What girl who had been the object of such adulation as Psyche had would give that up to live all alone with only a lover she believed was a dreadful monster hidden in a black cloud? And when she did not return, Eros would see that she was mean-spirited and deceitful, not worthy of the love he had given her, and would be cured.

Aphrodite would have been well content had she been present at the scene between Eros and Psyche when he told her she might go home. Instead of seeming doubtful or refusing outright to go so that he would have to convince her of the wisdom of Aphrodite's suggestion, joy lit Psyche's face.

"I cannot believe it!" she cried. "Oh, Teras, is it true? Will Aphrodite permit you to send me home?"

"I told you she was very kind," he said, staring at her radiant face with a sinking heart. Until he saw how her joy illuminated her beauty, it had not occurred to him that her happiness in his company might have been simulated. "How long will you wish to remain in Iolkas?" he asked.

"A few days should be enough," she said. "I hope you will not want me to come back immediately after I arrive and prove I am alive and well."

"I want you not to go at all," he said sadly. "I am missing you already."

She ran into the cloud and hugged him. "I will miss you too, love, and I would ask you to come with me, but I am afraid my family would not be made very happy at seeing me disappear into a black cloud." She smiled, knowing he would sense it. "Once I have convinced them that I am happy, I need not think of them anymore."

"Will you need several days to convince them?"

She buried her face in his breast. "Oh, Teras, I fear there is a sad lack of generosity of spirit in me. I know my sisters probably made much of their joys in marriage mostly because they were envious of me. But *I* was horribly envious of them. I want time to tell everyone what a wonderful husband I have and time to wear some of my jewels and beautiful gowns. I want to tell my mother and father and brothers about our fine shop—even though I have never seen it—and about the fine profit it makes—"

"Very well." He could not help laughing. Her eager recounting of her satisfaction, particularly that in the shop which could not continue to make a profit without her, lightened his spirit. "I can see that it will not be possible to accomplish all that boasting in a few hours.

But—" he tightened his grip on her "—do not forget that while you are enjoying yourself, I will be sitting alone in the dark and sleeping alone in a cold and empty bed."

"Must you be alone, Teras?"

"If you mean does my punishment condemn me not to seek out others, no, but memories are long among Olympians, and few desire my company."

"But you are changed!"

He did not like her insistence that he could find other company. "Am I? Perhaps. But you have spoiled me, Psyche. Now I do not want their company. They are shallow and greedy. I can no longer live without you, beloved. I would rather be alone."

"I almost wish I did not have to go," she said slowly, "but I must. I really must. Perhaps I will not stay only to boast of my happiness, but I must be sure they will no longer grieve for me."

"I think that is true," he agreed, feeling more cheerful. And, although he was not easy about her answer, fearing it would raise new doubts in him, he asked, "When do you wish to leave? I have the translocation spell and can give it to you any time."

"Can you discover when my family will go up the mountain? I would wish to be there when they arrive."

"You do not wish to flee me at once?"

"I do not wish to flee you at all!" she exclaimed. "I sometimes wish . . . No, Aphrodite has been generous enough. I will ask for no more."

Eros was delighted with that response. He had no idea what favor she might desire from Aphrodite, but did not ask. He was certain he could obtain whatever she wanted, and he intended that she should have it after she returned, to wash away whatever sadness she felt at parting from her family. He hugged her tightly and then pushed her out of the cloud.

"You will want to begin your packing."

"No, I will not," she said laughing. "I can do that during the day, when you are not with me. I want my revenge for that game of tables in which you beat me so soundly. I think you cheated!"

He had not cheated. He had not needed to give more than half his mind to any game they had played for months because she had suggested the games only to avoid conversation. She was so clever. Was she now suggesting a game so he would not see how happy she was to leave him?

"No," he said. "I want to see what you will take."

"You want to bite on a sore tooth, you mean," she protested, laughing and slipping back into the cloud and into his arms. "And you will no doubt sigh lugubriously every five minutes so that I will have a guilty conscience. Well, I will not play that game." She reached up blindly, found his head, and drew his face down to hers. "But I will play another and prove to you how very much I like being with you."

She proved, at least, that she had learned the lessons he had taught her very well, teasing him into such high excitement that he very nearly lost control and outstripped her. Not that it would have mattered, because he had barely caught his breath before she was at him again, and that time, drained as he was, he was able to bring her to sighing and singing a full three times.

They slept awhile after that, but when they woke, Psyche dragged him to her workroom and went over the list of sales from the shop, planning what she would need to prepare before she left and what supplies he must collect while she was gone so that she could make new stock as soon as she returned. She lured him back to bed when the plans were set and seemed content to lie quietly in his arms. Toward dawn, however, she woke with a start and clutched him and whispered, "Love me. Love me."

Eros was so tired when he left at dawn that he went to Aphrodite's house to sleep before he translocated to the temple at Iolkas to ask Hyppodamia to discover for him when Psyche's family intended to "release her soul" and whether they did, indeed, plan to have the ceremony on Mount Pelion. It took some time for the priestess's messenger to go and return—although Hyppodamia's messengers were treated with profound respect and he was not kept waiting at the palace—so Eros was very late in arriving at the lodge.

Psyche greeted him with near frantic relief, as if she thought some ill had befallen him—or was it because she had not taken the translocation spell when he offered it and she feared she had lost her opportunity to escape? She did not make him any happier by refusing to answer when he asked her why she was upset, only clinging to him and hiding her face. Then she said she had seen a shadow slinking past a thicket in the woods somewhat farther south than she usually went. The beast, if it was a beast, had not attacked her, she admitted, but it had frightened her from going farther, to a meadow rich with asphodel beyond. Would he please hunt it or drive it away—or make sure that it was not a beast she had seen?

Eros assured her the forest would be cleared of any danger when she returned, but he did not think the shadow in the thicket—if there had been a shadow—was what was troubling her. Nonetheless, she did not ask for the spell. Better yet, she shuddered and clung to him even more tightly when he explained why he was late and told her that they had been out in their calculations and that the ceremony on Mount Pelion would be the very next day.

Then he said, "No beast frightened you, my love. What do you fear?"

"I do not know," she whispered. "I do not know. I do not want to leave you, Teras. And yet I must. I must see them. I must. The image of their grief instills bitterness into every sweetness you have brought into my life. Soon I will hate that sweetness and myself. I must go."

"But Psyche, it does not sound as if you feel they were so kind to you, so loving, that you should be certain their grief will be deep and wounding."

"Oh, no, they were neither kind nor very loving, except Damianos, and even he agreed to sacrifice me. But that is why! Do you not understand, Teras? It is because they know as well as I that they were unjust to me, blaming me for what I could not help. That is what will gnaw at them, and I cannot bear it. I cannot bear to be so very happy while guilt is a canker in them and perhaps will make them truly evil when they were only selfish and thoughtless before."

Psyche left at dawn the next morning, Eros looming black behind her as she fetched what she would take. He had said he would carry it down to the garden for her, half expecting to see a chest packed with all her clothing and jewels. His suspicions had been again aroused by the passion and inventiveness with which she had made love. Why should she feed on him so, he wondered, when she expected to be gone only a few days? He had a speech all prepared, explaining that it took more power to move inanimate things like garments and that she might not have enough, but he never made it. Laughing, she handed into the cloud a small packet, which surely could not contain more than two gowns and a few necklaces, bracelets, and earrings.

Still, the way she held to him when he said he would

give her the spell made him uneasy. Why should she cling? Why should she tell him again and again that she would come back as soon as she could?

"When I have given you the spell," he said, "you must invoke it by saying, *Dei me exelthein Oros Pelioze.* And when you want to return, *Dei me exelthein xenodocheionse.* Say the words over a few times. You must not forget them, and you must pronounce them correctly."

She practiced dutifully. Her ear was good and in a few tries she had accent and emphasis correct. He handed her her packet and called up the spell, seeing it rise into his palm as a loose ball of sparkling silver. When it was complete, he touched the ball to the top of her head and saw a mist of silver motes fall over and cling to her body. He put her out of the cloud and said, his voice harsh with anxiety, "Go. Go now! No, do not speak to me again. Go!"

"Teras—" Psyche breathed, but the black void was retreating, going back to the house, and she did not call aloud.

She understood that he had turned his back because he could not bear to see her disappear. Tears rose to her eyes. There was no one as wonderful as Teras. Though he knew himself ugly and frightening, he had played her no jealous scenes, had uttered neither threats nor pleas. For a few moments longer, until the blackness was hidden by the closing of the door, she stood looking after him.

She hoped her qualms had not communicated themselves to him. After the first flood of joy when Teras told her Aphrodite had given permission for her to visit her home, a dreadful sense of foreboding had taken hold of her. She had tried again and again to cast it off, but she could not rid herself of the fear that Aphrodite's permission had an evil purpose. Had the goddess sensed that Teras was no longer so dependent on her, that he might break free of her hold on him? Had Aphrodite bade her priestess to have Psyche held—or even killed—to be rid of the person who loved Teras and was loved by him, the person who had provided him with a way to make a livelihood without serving her?

Psyche drew a deep, trembling breath. She had not dared mention her fears to Teras; whether or not he believed her, to hint to him that Aphrodite wished to separate them would be a disaster. If he had not believed her, he might have thought she was making an excuse in advance for not returning and forbidden her to go. But as much as she believed ill would come of this visit, equally she knew that if she did not purge herself of her responsibility to her family, worse evil would befall. And worse still would befall if Teras believed Aphrodite had deliberately allowed her to go in order to part them. He would have flown into a rage, perhaps even challenged the goddess. Heaven alone knew what punishment would have been visited on him, and Teras had suffered enough.

Psyche sighed again. She had done everything she knew to convince him she would come back, except say it over and over in words, until she felt him drawing himself out of her arms. And of course, that had made everything worse. Now he probably suspected she would not—Psyche deliberately cut off the thought. She was coming around to the beginning. She must either go now, or return to the house and tell Teras she would not go at all and live with the nightmare of the corroding souls of those who had thrust her into damnation to save themselves.

"Dei me exelthein Oros Pelioze," she said clearly.

The little mist in the well inside her congealed. More power flowed in from her muscles, from her organs, from her very skin so that she grew cold, and colder.

Her vision began to dim, the garden wavering around her. And she was falling, falling as she had fallen in her father's chamber when Otius had forced her to use the counterspell again. She cried out in despair, thinking she had tried to invoke the spell and failed, but then she heard shrieks and shouts, many men and women, and felt lumps and sharp edges bruising her all over.

She was barely strong enough to raise herself on an elbow and cry out, "Do not fear. I am Psyche, not a spirit or a demon."

There was a dead silence and then Beryllia came forward slowly whispering, "Psyche? Are you not torn to pieces, my poor child?"

"Oh mother," Psyche said, levering herself upright. "I feared that was what you would believe and that you would make yourself miserable. That was why I begged to come home for a little while—and merciful Aphrodite granted my prayer."

She almost choked over those words, but she would not give Aphrodite—if she was scrying what was taking place—any chance to tell Teras that she was ungrateful.

"How can we tell you are really Psyche and not some simulacrum sent to fool us into leaving the rites incomplete so that Psyche's unquiet spirit may torment us further?" Otius snarled.

"For one thing," Psyche snapped back, sliding to the edge of the altar so that she could get her feet on the ground, stand up, and rub the sore spots where she had come into painful contact with bowls of grain and small jars of oil, "you can look at the bruises I got landing on your offerings. I never heard of a simulacrum that could get black and blue."

"That's our Psyche," Damianos whooped, pushing past his older brother to take her in his arms and hug her tight. "Oh, sister, I am so glad to see you! I cannot tell you how glad." He clutched her tighter and burst into tears. "I could not sleep for hearing you scream and scream."

"Psyche!" Her father's voice had a softness she had never heard before. "Are you truly whole and unchanged?"

"I am not unchanged, father. I have changed in many ways, but I am your daughter, Psyche, and my spirit is still in my body. There is no need for rites to release it from your house or from this altar."

"That is what I expected you, whatever you are, to say," Otius remarked with a sneer.

Psyche laughed. "Then finish the rites, by all means. They can do me no good and no harm, but I have not come to haunt you, only to relieve your minds of any fear for me. I am happy. I desire that you also be happy. That is all."

"But you are so pale," Enstiktia said, coming closer. "And I see you are trembling."

"You are cold as ice," Horexea cried, having reached for Psyche's hand and then shrunk away.

It must be true, Psyche thought. She had barely enough strength to stand and felt as if she were a brittle frozen shell around an aching hollow, all her substance drawn out of her. In fact, she would have slipped to the ground if Damianos's arm had not supported her.

"Pale and cold as a ghost," Otius said.

"But she is real!" Damianos cried. "She is solid and breathing. I can feel it."

Otius seized her arm and pulled her away from Damianos. "Get back on the altar," he said, and lifted her to the center of the rock slab. "Let us see whether or not the rites to release the spirit will not banish you."

CHAPTER 13

Psyche had made no protest. She had been glad enough for a reason to sit down, even on the altar, for her head was swimming and she feared she would faint. Perhaps she did sink into a kind of unconsciousness, for she was hardly aware of the chanting, the burning of some offerings, the pouring out of others, the anointing of her cheeks, forehead, and breast with unguents. She remembered saying, as she was helped down from the altar, that her weakness was owing to having come so far in so strange a way. That was the last thing she remembered until she opened her eyes and saw her mother sitting beside her bed.

"Teras," she cried, pushing herself up, terrified for a moment that she had created her life with him in a beautiful dream to ease her fear and that she had wakened from that dream into the time before her sacrifice.

"Who is Teras?" Beryllia asked.

"My monster," Psyche replied, anxiously examining her mother's face. "The monster I was to marry and did marry."

"You call for him?"

Psyche breathed a sigh of relief. Beryllia's frightened question assured her that her mother had gone with her to Mount Pelion and left her there. She had not dreamed it. She had been sacrificed—and had returned.

"He is the dearest monster in the world," she said, smiling. "The gentlest and cleverest being I have ever met, so good to me, so kind. My life would be a perfect dream if only—"

"Is he very horrible to look upon?" Beryllia's voice trembled.

"I have no idea," Psyche replied, still smiling. "I have never seen him. To spare me he wears a cloud of darkness. But his looks, whatever they are, are only a seeming. When I touch him, I feel an ordinary man, tall and strong. He—"

She stopped. She did not wish to tell her mother that Teras had not been born deformed but had committed some unnamed crime for which he had been punished by an illusion of horrible malformation. Psyche no longer believed her wonderful Teras had done evil, even though he assured her he had and that his punishment had been just. Nor did she wish to admit that Teras's illusion of deformity had been cast on him owing to some offense taken by the selfish, greedy beings that dwelt in Olympus. However mean and petty and ungodlike, the Olympians were very powerful mages. To think of them as she now did would be very dangerous for her people, who might be led to scant their sacrifices or speak or act in other ways that would bring down Olympian wrath.

"You were forced?" Beryllia sobbed, shuddering.

"I was not forced, mother. After I came to know him, I went willingly to him." She had been speaking seriously, but suddenly her eyes danced. "And it was the best thing I ever did. He has taught me to make love in the most delightful ways. Mother—"

Beryllia's breath drew in sharply. "You are ensorcelled, Psyche. Do you not remember your father's passion for that sow?"

For one moment, Psyche stared at her mother, transfixed with horror. Then she drew a breath and laughed. "No, no I am not. For a moment I was afraid, but I do not wish constantly to couple with Teras. We do so many other things, read together and talk—and quarrel about his—" she cleared her throat; she had almost said "his disgusting people" and continued hastily "—history. Mostly we talk about history and the shop we own together. One does not quarrel about the management of a shop with the object of an obsession."

Beryllia shook her head and sighed deeply. "Well, it does not matter. Aphrodite has released you. You are home now and free of him."

Psyche felt a slight chill at her mother's mention of Aphrodite. It might well be that Aphrodite's intention was to "release" her, as she was known to release some of the sacrificial children. "Free of Teras?" she said. "No, indeed I am not. I do not wish to be free of Teras. I love him dearly."

"Love? A monster? A creature so ugly that he must hide in darkness?"

"Mother, my appearance is more monstrous than his," Psyche cried. "Poor Teras only frightens or disgusts those who see him. I incite men to lust, to jealousy, perhaps even to war, and women to envy and hate. Which of us is the more monstrous?"

Beryllia gaped for a moment, then got her mouth under control enough to say, faintly, "That is nonsense. You are beautiful."

The truth of Psyche's words, however, were forced on her mother and on her sisters, who at first also pleaded with her to regard the permission she had received to come home as a pardon from her punishment. Horexea and Enstiktia were sincere enough. Both had suffered nightmares and moments of misery that spoiled their own contentment over the past year. And doubtless the sight of the exquisite jewels, the web-fine chitons and incredibly smooth peploses, the delicacy and fantasy of the real gold thread embroidery on the robes, and Psyche's descriptions of her house and servants might have lent an extra intensity to their assurances that their sister would be happier if she remained a recluse in her father's house than returned to be the toy of a monster.

Under no circumstances would she consent to the life of a recluse, Psyche told them, with such heat and force that the sisters recoiled. The one, single part of her life with her monster that was not perfect, she explained, seeing that she had frightened them, was that although not confined in any way, she was utterly isolated except for Teras.

Psyche's father and brothers also urged her to stay. Damianos gave no reason and from his anxious looks he might have spoken out because of concern for her. Her father, Otius, and Gillos did not even trouble to disguise the fact that their only interest in Psyche was to avoid further offense to Aphrodite. The goddess had sent her away and might not want her back. It had not been Aphrodite's purpose, Otius pointed out, to make Psyche happy, but to punish her; and the feelings of the goddess's monstrous servant, since he was her servant, were of no account.

By the second day, Psyche was more than ready to go home to Teras, knowing she would never call Iolkas home again. Here, with a house full of people to talk to, she was lonelier than among her mute servants with the knowledge that Teras was coming. Only she *could* not go home. There was nothing inside her except a great, empty void. She had not realized when she invoked the spell that she would have to supply the power to make it work, nor how much power it would take. Teras had not mentioned it; perhaps he did not know. Now her

little reservoir of power was completely empty, and so
much strength had been drained from her that for days
she walked very slowly and had to cling to the walls
when she went down a flight of stairs. As for going up,
she could barely climb at all, except with rests every few
steps.

Had Aphrodite obtained the spell to go and return
for Teras and concealed from him how much power the
invoker would need? Was that Aphrodite's subtle way
of making Teras believe that his Psyche did not love
him and had lied about wishing to come back to him?
Well, she would get back, Psyche swore to herself, no
matter how long it took to restore her power. She
would go back to her teacher of sorcery or seek another
who could tell her a way to draw power from elsewhere,
even from others.

In the past Psyche had always feared to try to increase her power lest she be thought dangerous and left
in the caves of the Dead as a sacrifice to Hades and
Persephone. That was the common fate of the Gifted.
What had she to fear now? Psyche thought bitterly. She
had already been sacrificed to Aphrodite and no one
would dare take her from one god to give to another.
But even though she believed herself grimly determined
to reclaim enough power to invoke the translocation
spell, something inside her closed tighter at the thought,
intensifying the ache that called for the warming mist to
comfort it.

As if her family's suggestions had convinced her to
stay, Psyche stopped insisting that she would return to
Teras immediately, but it was not long before everyone
else had also changed the tunes they had been singing.
Events all too soon demonstrated that far more immediate harm would come from keeping Psyche in Iolkas
than from sending her back to the goddess.

Once she discovered mere numbers of people could

not provide companionship, Psyche kept to the women's quarters as much as possible. It was, however, too late to immure herself. The first evidence that matters had got out of hand appeared as soon as Psyche was strong enough and went to seek the witch she knew and to ask directions to others. Although she went heavily veiled, rumor went before her. Townsfolk rushed into the street as soon as she appeared, calling her name, calling her by Aphrodite's name—as if she were an avatar of the goddess. Psyche was frightened to death and uttered frantic denials that were not heeded. Her only comfort was that Aphrodite was *not* a god and therefore not omniscient, and that she would be most unlikely to waste her scryer's time watching townsfolk.

Unfortunately it was not only the townsfolk who had an exaggerated idea of her importance to Aphrodite. Anerios had grasped at Psyche's return to prove he was completely pardoned by the goddess, that he had even become a favorite with her. He sent word to all his nobles and to the neighboring kings hinting that Psyche had been specially blessed. Naturally, most of those he had informed—and not a few to whom they had passed the word—rushed to Anerios's court to see this marvel.

It was impossible for Anerios to refuse to show Psyche to them; the last thing he wanted was to seem to hide her, for a rumor to grow that she had not been blessed but had been lessened or even mutilated and then rejected to express Aphrodite's displeasure.

Psyche was not pleased and refused at first to be exhibited like a prize heifer; however, when she understood what her father feared would be said if she remained hidden, she agreed to come down to the hall each night until all accepted that she was perfect. What was more, she spoke praises of the kindness and generosity of the goddess Aphrodite and made the point that she was only on a visit to her parents. She would soon return, she insisted, to the kind and indulgent husband to whom she had been married by the goddess's order. No one doubted her husband's kindness and indulgence when they saw the richness of her dress and ornaments.

In her innocence, Psyche had told the tale of her marriage, expecting it would protect her from the men who were already licking their lips as they examined her. To her horror, the knowledge that she was no longer a virgin seemed to stimulate lust even in those who had done their best to ignore her in the past. One night a man lay in wait beside the stairs to the women's quarters and tried to drag her outside. Having regained her physical strength and learned how to strike in her weapons practice, Psyche knocked him endwise. Another tried to seize her just outside the latrine. At least he furnished Psyche with some amusement; she invited him inside most dulcetly, and when he would have embraced her, tipped him into the filth. Even the princes of Apheta and Olizon, her sisters' husbands, found opportunities—the one to take her hand and try to pull her close, the other to whisper a lewd invitation—to importune her.

The next day Horexea said, "I wonder, sister, if the monster is really a monster at all. Did you never think, after you found he was a perfect man to the touch of your hands, that the goddess might have bidden him wear the disguise of darkness so that you would *think* you were married to a monster? It seems so strange to me that Aphrodite, who is goddess of beauty, should have a hideous monster as her servant."

Amused by her sister's sudden conviction that Teras was not monstrous—which, compared to the lecherous prince of Olizon, perhaps he was not—Psyche said blandly that Teras had told her that Aphrodite used him as a servant out of kindness, to protect him. Horexea laughed and shook her head and said she thought Psyche too believing. If she went back, she could dispel the darkness by magic. Doubtless she would discover it was with one of Aphrodite's beautiful boys that she was lying abed.

Later in the day it was Enstiktia who idly wondered that Psyche, professing so much love for her Teras, now seemed in no hurry to be restored to the joys she had left. Perhaps it was because no matter what she claimed, Psyche imagined greater horrors than really existed. Rather than abandon so much wealth and luxury, Psyche should try to discover if the monster was truly dreadful. If she found him too repellent, why then, kind Aphrodite had let her come once; surely the goddess would let her come again.

Two days after that her father told her that one of the neighboring kings had wished to set up a statue to *her* in Aphrodite's temple. Hyppodamia had sent a messenger with an angry complaint. "Why did Aphrodite send you here?" her father asked. "Is this some testing of my obedience? Are you opening a way to a greater punishment to us all?"

With some difficulty Psyche prevented herself from laughing in his face. She strongly suspected that Anerios himself might have hinted his daughter—perfect in her beauty as she was—was an avatar of the goddess. He had hoped for silent awe and an increase in his influence owing to his connection with Psyche. Now he had been trapped in the muck he himself had spread, so he blamed her for his greed and ambition.

Psyche knew him already and suffered no disillusionment. Since she did not expect to see him ever again, she wanted to know he was at peace, at least with regard to her, so that she would have no further responsibility to him. Therefore, she assured him most truthfully that she fully intended to return to Teras and also assured him, somewhat less truthfully, that the goddess expected her to return and probably would not permit her to visit Iolkas again.

"Then when will you go?" Anerios asked. "I do not mean to drive you out, but doubtless it would be best if you went back to your monster as soon as possible. You would not wish him to grow impatient, and you did say you wished to be with him."

With all impulse to laugh gone, Psyche blinked back tears of fear and frustration and said that she could return only at the time set by the goddess, that she must wait for a sign. She shivered inside with fear when she said the words. She had already been in Iolkas a week longer than she had told Teras she would stay, and she was terrified about his reaction. She could not decide whether she hoped he was too angry at her to grieve or whether she wanted him to miss her grievously and be so glad to have her back that he would not be angry.

Her eagerness to return made no difference, however; the sign she was waiting for was the strength to invoke the spell. At the moment, she was helpless. Her old teacher could not (or would not) explain how to draw power from the world around her and claimed she had no answer to the inquiries she had sent out to other sorcerers.

Several times Psyche had thought about going to Aphrodite's temple to beg the priestess to send word to Aphrodite, and through her to Teras, that she was too weak to invoke the translocation spell. She did not actually go for several reasons. One was that she recalled too vividly Hyppodamia's horror of her rejection of the goddess. Psyche suspected that her current feeling about Aphrodite, far more personal than her past general resentment and made up of equal portions of distrust and dislike, would be even more offensive to the priestess. Atop that stupid king's notion that she was a fit subject for worship, the result would more than likely be for Hyppodamia to curse her and cast her out rather than listen to her.

Even more discouraging was her growing certainty that trapping her in Iolkas had been Aphrodite's intention and that she would get no help from her. Worst of all, Psyche feared that the message that came to Teras might not be the message she had sent. Maybe, Psyche thought, staring with longing at Mount Pelion in the distance, it would not be so very long before her power was restored. There was still no mist in her well, but the echoing hollowness, the cold brittleness, the feeling she was about to collapse in on herself were all gone. Only the constant small ache that seemed to draw in a mote of mist at a time reminded Psyche of her emptiness.

Eros spent the first two days of Psyche's absence fulfilling his promise to scour the forest for leagues around the lodge to drive out any animal likely to be dangerous. It was a good time of year to rid the area of bear, which might frighten Psyche or even attack her out of irritability because they were seeking dens, and he could set traps in any likely places that would drive them out. Wolves would not trouble a person until deep snow and starvation drove them to desperation; at this time of year game was too plentiful for that. The only danger might be mountain cat. They came and went as they wished and he could do little about them, but again, there was game in plenty. Usually the great cats clung to the higher crags to prey on the mountain goat and would not come downslope as far as the lodge.

The third day he kept busy collecting the supplies Psyche had told him she would need to make her creams and syrups for the shop. That night he did not sleep at all, moving restlessly from room to room, expecting her to appear at any moment. On and off he called himself a fool, knowing she would not come at night. She would be afraid to go the the altar on Mount Pelion at night. But he could not sleep.

He waited at the lodge all the fourth day, telling himself from hour to hour that it took time to get up the mountain and that it was too soon to expect her. When night fell he comforted himself with the notion that she must be enjoying her family's discomfiture and not realize how much time was passing. He lay down in Psyche's bed that night. He had hoped the feeling of her nearness would comfort him, but what repeated over and over in his mind was how her caresses had seemed insatiable, as if she were trying to wear him out. But surely that was so he would not desire any woman in the immediate future. That had to mean she knew it would be longer than she would admit before she returned—but that she would return, surely she would return.

He lived through the fifth and sixth days with diminishing hope, sipping at the bitter draught of rejection, learning anew that old as he was, he was not yet wise. He had taken a woman by force and she had defended herself as women had from time immemorial, by submission and deceit. By the dark of the moon he had stopped reminding himself that Psyche had not been the least submissive, the pain of renewed hope that memories of her brought to him was too acute. It was better to slip back into the little death in which he had lived so long.

He could not find oblivion in the lodge, however. Every room held memories of Psyche and signs that she had left to assure him she would return—deceit, all deceit. He went back to Aphrodite's house to lie in his bed and stare sightlessly at the painted walls. On the evening of the fifteenth day—he still counted the days;

he could not help that—Aphrodite came and laughed at him, saying she had told him not to meddle with the light-minded natives and that a real man would not yield to obsession but cast off an unworthy feeling attached to an unworthy person.

"Forget her," she said, gesturing for the lamps to light, "there are a thousand as beautiful, and if you would only smile at them, you could have them all."

She was half smiling, brows raised in challenge, when she turned from the lamps to cast a sly look at him under her lashes. She was ready to offer comfort or to tease him into laughter, but the smile froze on her lips. She had been a little disappointed not to recieve a furious answer or a spate of complaints. When he had not spoken, she expected to find him flopped over, facing away from her in silent rejection. What she saw was the face of a madman or an idiot with no sign at all in it that he had heard her. His eyes were blind and his cheeks sunken under a week's growth of beard.

"Eros," she said gently, seating herself on the bed and taking his hand in hers. She shuddered and began to sob. The hand was utterly lifeless, as limp as a dead bird; had it not been warm, she would have thought him a corpse. "Eros," she cried, turning his face toward her with her other hand.

Below the half-closed lids a glittering line of tears appeared, but he did not respond to her plea.

The sobs stopped abruptly. "You are ten times a fool," she said sharply, although she could have sung with relief at the sight of those tears. "Once a fool for allowing yourself to be bound to this woman, and nine times a fool for giving her up so easily if she is so important to you. You are forever telling me we are not really gods, but you expect a poor native woman, short as is her life and experience, to behave like a god."

Eros blinked. "But she said she would return in a few

days. If she does not choose to stay with me . . ." His voice sounded rusty and his lips were so dry that one cracked as he spoke and showed a bead of blood at the split.

Aphrodite swallowed as the wave of his longing hit her. "She does intend to return, you utter idiot," she snapped at him. "I have had my scryer look in on Anerios's palace now and again and—"

"She intends to return?"

Eros pushed himself upright and reached for the flask of watered wine set beside the bed. His hand trembled so violently that Aphrodite took it from him and held it to his mouth. He drank long, but then caught at her wrist.

"If you have told me this to bring me back, you have done the first cruel thing that you have ever done to me—and so cruel that all the good you have done before is as nothing. I will never forgive you, and your trick is useless. I am already dead without her and will take a shorter path to find some peace—"

"Oh, la, la, la! Play me no more heroics. I cannot read your Psyche's mind. If she is lying to her family, it is no fault of mine, but she has said over and over that she wishes to return to her 'Teras'—and what in the world made you choose to call yourself 'monster' in the old language?"

"She asked me for my name." Eros smiled, wincing as he spread the cracked lip, but the smile remained. "She said she did not wish to think of me as a monster and that people had names. I could not think of any name on the spur of the moment, and one does not usually need to *think* about one's own name, so I gave her the word 'teras.'" Then the smile faded and he looked anxiously at Aphrodite. "But if she said she wished to come back to me, why did she not do so?"

"That my scryer has not heard, if a reason was ever

given. I would say it is merely carelessness. Her sisters envy her bitterly, and she is the focus of much attention. A neighboring king tried to set up her statue as an avatar in my temple. She must be enjoying her notoriety and the days are simply slipping by."

Eros had taken back the flask and emptied it. His tongue flicked across his lips, trying to soften the dried skin, but the frown he wore had nothing to do with his physical discomfort. In the past Psyche had not enjoyed the attention she received, but perhaps now that she was free of the fear of a disastrous marriage, she might feel differently.

"She said she would like to stay a few days to show off her dress and jewels," he said doubtfully, "but—"

He was about to say that she had taken very little with her when Aphrodite cut him off.

"Not to rub salt into an open cut, Eros, but it would be better if you acted your age instead of creating a goddess to worship like a green boy in the throes of his first love. Do try to bring yourself to realize that Psyche is an ordinary native girl with a too-pretty face. I doubt you are as important to her as she is to you, which is why she does not realize you might be suffering in her absence."

"That may be true, indeed, Aphrodite," Eros replied with a sad half-smile, "but you do not understand that in my feeling for Psyche I am no more than a green boy. Old as I am, I am new to love. You are my friend, and dear to me as the breath in my body. But Psyche is the only person I have ever loved in my whole life. She *is* the breath in my body. Without her I cannot live."

Aphrodite shrugged. She did not really think, now that she had snatched him back from the edge of dissolution, that he would let himself slip back. She remembered towing him out of the slough of despond more than once, and most often he had been reasonably cheerful for a time. In fact, he looked brighter now than he usually did when he came up after wallowing in despair. Too bright? Aphrodite wondered uneasily and decided not to make any caustic comments about bathos. He was very old; she did not wish to drive him into proving he was truly in love with some desperate action.

"Oh, well," she said, "you know Psyche is weak about her family, and my scryer tells me they have been urging her to stay. Her sisters seem to be jealous of your indulgence and the wealth you lavish on her, and her stupid father thinks he can set her up as a substitute goddess. But it will be easy enough to silence them. I will send a reminder through Hyppodamia that it is time for her to return to you."

It would be better to share him with that stupid slut for a time, Aphrodite thought, than to take the chance of losing him altogether. It was impossible for her to conceive of caring for another person so deeply that she would end her life rather than live on alone, but it was also true that the old dote, rather than loving like the young. If Eros was speaking the truth—and certainly she could not remember him ever claiming before this to care deeply for anyone beside herself—then he was beyond a single sharp lesson to make him reject Psyche. She would have to wait until Psyche's crudity and simplicity began to bore him. And, of course, help his disgust of the stupid girl along any way she could. Forced separation, however, did not seem the way.

Eros felt no more need to wonder why Aphrodite had bidden her scryer watch Anerios's palace than he needed to wonder why he had not asked the scryer for news of Psyche. His refusal to ask was for fear of obtaining proof he did not want, and he assumed Aphrodite had told her scryer to watch for his sake, as she had done so much for him for so long. He did have a brief

flash of doubt about why Aphrodite had taken so long
to tell him Psyche intended to return, but that question
was overwhelmed by the far more painful one of
whether he should agree to Aphrodite's suggestion.

He knew quite well that he should refuse. He knew
that if Psyche only came back because her fearful family would no longer keep her, he could never trust her
as he had in the past. But he wanted her, he *needed* her
so much. The pain that wrenched him was so constant
and so terrible. And why should he not trust her? he
asked himself defiantly. If she were thrust out a second
time by her family, would she not cling more tightly to
him because she had nowhere else to go? Is that what
you want? a little voice deep, deep inside asked sadly,
but he pretended not to hear.

The answer he gave was not to that inner doubt but
to Aphrodite. "Yes," he said. "Send for her. I need
her."

CHAPTER 14

The messenger from Hyppodamia carrying Aphrodite's order that Psyche return to her monster arrived at first light. Anerios came to the women's apartments himself to wake Psyche and pass along the message. She flushed with joy and relief, believing that Teras had asked Aphrodite to bring her home and that out of fondness for him, and perhaps unwillingness to show herself in a bad light, Aphrodite had given him permission to fetch her as he had when she was "sacrificed."

Psyche refused Anerios's suggestion that a new procession be organized. She knew from the speculative gleam in his eyes that he was already planning a ceremony that would imply she was the mortal form of a goddess returning to her immortal dwelling.

"You know I am not being sacrificed," she said sharply. "I am only returning to my home and my husband, and I intend to go today, so there will be no time for any show. There is no need for grave offerings or any more ceremony than you make over my sisters when they return to their own homes from a visit here. I would appreciate an escort to the altar on Mount Pelion, since it is a long way to go alone. Damianos can come with me, but once I am safe there, no one need stay. In fact, it would be better if I were alone when Teras comes."

That remark and the faint frown that accompanied it brought a look of concern to her mother's face, but it soon disappeared. No one could misunderstand the speed and eagerness with which Psyche made ready. Her eyes were bright and her smiles unshadowed as she gave as parting gifts to each of her sisters a gown that sister had admired and to her mother a lovely necklet of pearls set in a lacy froth of gold. She ate with appetite although she hurried the meal along, and she set out with Damianos and two guardsmen with light steps, so swiftly, in fact, that she outdistanced them on the way to the gate and had to wait.

Psyche made sure that Damianos's concience was clear by the late afternoon, when they came to the altar. She wished to leave no grief or doubt behind her, and she showed her eagerness to go in every way she could. In fact, it was no pretense. She had barely been willing to stop at the little village to eat and rest, and when Damianos offered to remain with her at the altar, she kissed him fondly and laughed.

"Teras will not let anything hurt me," she said, hurrying uphill, although she was already breathing hard with the exertion. "Likely he will be watching from the shadows, but he might not come out if you were there. He is shy of showing himself because he is very gentle and does not like to frighten anyone."

She glowed with joy when she thought of the safe haven of Teras's arms, the smiling approval of her servants, the sunlit meadows and shadowed forests that were all her own, where no one lay in wait to seize her and no eyes, filled with lust or envy, followed her. That joy only intensified when they reached the peak of the mountain. Convinced that this was what she wanted, Damianos gave Psyche a final hug and lifted her to the

altar, turning only once at the edge of the road to wave
a final farewell which she returned with a cheerful smile
and a wave of her own.

Psyche had barely prevented herself from making
shooing motions instead of waving, and she had to bite
her lips to keep herself from calling Teras as soon as her
brother's back disappeared at the first curve of the
road. She busied herself by looking around at the trees
that edged the clearing, straining to see a blacker blot
within the shadows. Nothing that might be Teras appeared, however, and when she was sure Damianos and
the men could not hear her, she called softly, "Teras.
Come out now and take me home."

No answer came. Psyche shivered a little. The sun
had not yet set, but the autumn air was now sharp
despite the mildness of the day—or maybe it had not
been so mild just that she had been warm with exercise.

"Teras!" she called more sharply. "Do not tease me.
Come and take me home. It will soon be dark, and I am
getting cold."

Nothing stirred in the woods. No shadow flickered
behind the boles of the trees to hint where her husband
might be waiting for her.

"Do not be so silly," she cried. "I do not care if I see
you all black in the light. I am not afraid of you. Your
darkness is a light in my heart. Come to me."

And when no shadow glided out of the trees, she
sobbed, "At least call to me, Teras. I cannot tell where
you are to come to you."

But Psyche did not really expect to hear the beautiful,
beloved voice. She was sure now that Teras, not knowing that she could not invoke the travel spell, had complained of her long absence to Aphrodite. Surely that
spiteful, evil bitch had told him she would send a message ordering the ungrateful and disobedient Psyche to

return to him—and Aphrodite had sent the message.
But Psyche was certain Aphrodite knew she had not the
strength to obey. Of course, Aphrodite would not have
told Teras that. He will believe I do not wish to return
to him, Psyche sobbed; he will believe I do not wish to
return, that I would rather defy Aphrodite than continue to live with him.

Fury briefly overcame despair and Psyche begged
desperately for strength. Immediately, a gentle warmth
surrounded her. She cupped her hands and a faint glow
seemed to fill them. She watched it, eyes so wide the
whites showed all around, breath panting through her
open mouth. She struggled to give thanks, struggled to
drink in the offered strength. Instead she was caught up
in a whirlwind of cold terror and inside her the mouth
of the well was sealed tight with an ugly cap of ancient
fear.

It did not matter that *The History of the Olympians*
had stated that Olympians were human and mortal,
that she knew many Olympian mages could call power
to them, that their long lives, their high status, their
wealth and power, were owing to their Gifts. A terror
ingrained from birth told her she was not an Olympian;
she was only a common native girl, and natives who
were Gifted and could draw power died.

Psyche saw the little glow begin to fade. Torn between terror and necessity, she cried, *"Dei me exelthein xenodocheionse,"* to invoke the translocation
spell. The light in her hands disappeared, the slight
warmth that had softened the walls of her inner well
disappeared, heat was sucked out of her muscles, out
of her veins and heart, and sucked and sucked until
she fell forward onto the altar, as stiff and cold as the
granite slab would be on a midwinter night. It grew
dark and darker, as dark as when she was within

Teras's blackness, but that was all warmth and love and this was cold and death.

Because he was too eager, Eros missed the proof that would have reassured him and made nothing of the ambiguous words with which Aphrodite woke him. She was leaning over his bed, laughing, and when he opened his eyes, she told him that Psyche was on her way to Mount Olympus.

"You certainly put the fear of me into Anerios," she said, giggling. "He ran all naked to pull Psyche out of bed and send her on her way as soon as Hyppodamia's messenger arrived."

Eros leapt out of bed all naked himself. "She is on her way already? I must go to the lodge to be there when she comes."

"What now?" Aphrodite laughed again. "But it will take all day for her to climb the mountain. Eat. Rest. You are far too thin. Do you not wish to be beautiful for the beautiful Psyche?"

"She will not see me," Eros said, and disappeared.

Aphrodite staggered in the backwash of air that rushed to fill the space Eros had occupied when he translocated to the lodge, but she smiled. It was just as well he had not stayed to question the scryer about Psyche's reaction to the message or to ask her to show him Psyche's progress. The girl's delight and eagerness had somewhat shaken Aphrodite's fixed conviction that Eros would be better off without her. Aphrodite bit her lip gently. She had herself watched in the scryer's bowl as Psyche left her father's palace, and the nearly dancing footsteps, the aura of joy about the girl, had lightened her own heart for a moment.

Then she had reminded herself that Psyche was like a butterfly, alive for one brief summer of joy, then gone.

Eros must be free of his desire for her before her short life ended or he would follow her into nonbeing. Aphrodite sighed softly over his pain, but she did not regret what she had said. Sooner or later he would think of her words and their implication that Anerios had forced his daughter to go would add to the distrust Psyche's lingering in Iolkas had generated in him. Suddenly Aphrodite frowned. Why *had* the girl lingered when she had virtually lit up with joy at being ordered to return to Eros? Then she shrugged. They were very light-minded, the natives. Doubtless Psyche had forgotten all about Eros until she had been reminded.

Having arrived in the garden, Eros gasped with the shock of the cold morning air on his naked body. Then he laughed. He had been in such a hurry that he had not even snatched up a himation to cover himself. Still laughing, he ran into the house and up to his chamber to find suitable clothing. Then he had to go down into the kitchen to dress because it was the only warm room in the house. The servants, of course, had not been told to light braziers to warm the upper rooms.

Grinning like a fool, he told them Psyche would soon be home and to make all ready for her and to prepare a specially delectable evening meal. He was surprised at the smiles that greeted his words. He would have thought the servants would be resigned or need to conceal irritation, since having Psyche living in the house must make more work for them, but apparently they were delighted to know she was coming back. It was another mote of joy to add to his nearly full cup. His appetite was another. It had been half a moon since his food had tasted of anything but ashes; now a simple breakfast was pure ambrosia—not that he actually cared for the sickly sweet stuff, but it was said to be the food of the gods—and he wolfed down bread and cheese and hot wine and boiled eggs and broiled ham.

He ate until he was finally full, then went up for his bow. He had scoured the woods clean, but that had been soon after Psyche left. Now he wished to make sure no beast had come back to alarm her. He wanted to be certain nothing at all would make her sorry, even for the briefest instant, that she had returned to the lodge.

Tracking through the woods in widening spirals that would cover anyplace Psyche was likely to visit took most of the day. Eros found nothing, no spoor, no fumets, except of deer and other harmless creatures. He was about to go home, believing the area free of any danger, when a stirring beyond a thin thicket caught his eye—just such a flicker of movement as Psyche had mentioned. Eros froze, made sure of the wind, and stealthily drew close enough to see.

To his surprise, he found a young boar. More than a day's walk south of the broad hollow on the slope of the mountain in which lay the lodge, the garden, and the woods surrounding it was a precipitous drop into a ravine cut by a small river. Beyond the equally steep rise on the other side was a much more gradual slope, densely forested, that led into the valley of Olympus. Although pigs were common in the forest above Olympus, the ravine, which extended for leagues to the east and the west, kept them out of the area around the lodge.

Eros hesitated, wondering how the animal had found its way into these woods, and then put the puzzle aside while he worked his way, keeping upwind, to where he could get a clear shot. Boars were dangerous, more so than bear, which would avoid humans unless particularly irritated or protecting cubs. They were hard to kill too, being thick skinned, thick boned, and very hardy.

Eros preferred to have companions when he went hunting boar, but this one must be killed at once. It might have been the creature Psyche had seen, and if so, it had already wandered relatively close to the lodge and might hurt Psyche if she came upon it unexpectedly.

Stepping carefully to avoid the crackling of fallen twigs and dry leaves and trying to keep the boar in sight—no easy task, because its coarse gray-brown fur blended so well with the litter on the forest floor—Eros at last found a tree thick enough to shield behind with a space beneath clear enough for him to draw his bow. He came around to where he could see the boar and cursed softly. It was a bad shot; the animal was half under some brush as it rooted in the earth, exposing nothing but its hindquarters. Nocking an arrow, Eros stamped a foot and squealed softly.

With an angry snort, the boar backed out from under the brush and faced around, ears and tail erect, momentarily still as it looked for its challenger. Eros loosed the arrow and saw it plunge into the neck below the jaw, but no blood burst from nose or mouth and he knew he had missed the big veins in the throat. With a bellow of rage the beast spun around toward the pain. Hoping it was distracted, Eros drew another arrow from his quiver and nocked that as the animal came around full circle. He loosed, aiming for the shoulder, behind which lay the heart, but his movements had attracted the boar's attention and it charged toward him. Muttering curses over his miss, Eros slipped behind the tree.

The thud of the boar falling brought him out, but the continual squeals of rage and pain told him that the creature was alive before he saw it. He dropped his bow and drew his knife as he moved, realizing that his second arrow had caught the boar in the hip as it charged at him. Eros ran out, but the beast was already up on three legs and lunged at him, its open mouth showing long, sharp tusks. He leapt right over it, and it tried to whirl around to follow but fell again, giving Eros the opportunity leap astride rather than over, seize the boar's snout, and cut its throat.

For a moment, Eros simply sat on the boar's back, catching his breath and thanking the Mother that the creature had not been full grown. He might not have come so easily out of the contest between them had the boar reached its full size and weight. Then he smiled. There were other reasons to be thankful also. An old boar was tough to chew as well as tough to kill; this one would make better eating.

That thought got him to his feet and made him glance anxiously at the sun. Psyche would reach the altar soon and then would take only a moment to translocate to the garden. If he could carry the animal back . . . Eros stooped and heaved. The boar moved but did not rise. Carrying it was out of the question. He had no rope with which to make a harness to drag the beast, and no way to explain to the menservants where to find it. At that, Eros laughed. Poor old men, the two of them could not manage such a load. His only choices were to butcher the animal or leave it to the scavengers.

Eros glanced at the sun again and shook his head. He was being a too-eager fool once more and making grief for himself. Unless she ran all the way up the mountain and did not stop to eat or rest, Psyche could not arrive before sunset. A needle of doubt pricked him; Eros knew he would have done just that—run all the way. But he did not follow the thought to its uncomfortable conclusion. He turned his attention to the boar, telling himself that he had more than enough time to butcher it, which would serve the double purpose of keeping him busy.

With that in mind, he made a good job of it, skinning the animal first and selecting the most succulent portions to carry back. The remainder he wrapped in the skin and lodged in the crotch of a convenient tree. Perhaps he would bring Psyche to collect it and show her how her dinner had been won. Having allowed the thought of her into his mind, he jumped up, aware of the long shadows. It would be dusk before he was back at the lodge. She would be angry if he were not there waiting. Unbidden there was inside him a faint echo of the words, only a little changed—perhaps she would not be angry.

Eros bundled the chosen portions of the boar into his cloak and set off, restraining himself from running. He was so intent on finding an irritated Psyche waiting that he almost forgot to invoke the spell of darkness. He was reminded by seeing the bench where they met in fine weather . . . empty. A chill of disappointment made him hesitate. He would have waited at the bench. Nonsense, he told himself. Poor Psyche must be exhausted from climbing the mountain; she would want to wash and put on fresh clothes. He ran across the garden, telling himself she would be starving; Psyche had an excellent appetite and would be very cross having to wait to eat.

He bounded up the steps into her bedchamber, holding his hunting trophy out. The chamber was polished to perfection . . . and it was empty. Refusing to believe, he rushed into his own chamber, into the book room. Worse had befallen him than a tongue-lashing. She had not come.

Had the servants been able to see Eros's face, they would have fled the house. As it was they cowered back against the walls when he roared, "Where is she?" at them. No gesture was made to any room he had not searched, but he had known before he asked. He flung his bloodstained cloak and its contents onto the floor and fled the house before he killed them all—and then he remembered what Aphrodite had said: that Anerios had run all naked to pull Psyche out of bed and send her on her way . . .

So she had not been willing to come back; her father had to force her. Then it was not surprising that she was late. Dragging steps took longer to climb a mountain, and no doubt she had stopped again and again to rest, perhaps to plead with Anerios not to force her. Oh, she would come. Anerios feared Aphrodite too much to yield to Psyche's pleas. She would come and kiss him and love him and laugh—like any captive slave who pleases a master because she has no other way to live.

Eros went into the garden and sat on the bench to wait. Dusk deepened into full dark. He knew he should go back to Aphrodite's house and let Psyche arrive in an empty lodge, arrive to a cold welcome of absence and frightened servants so she would understand that her master was angry. He could ask Aphrodite's scryer to show him what Psyche was doing and berate her for deliberate delay. But he did not move, only sat, waiting while rage and despair battled for supremacy.

He was stiff and cold, his mind blank with exhaustion, when he rose at last, intending to seek his bedchamber in Aphrodite's house. Into the emptiness of heart and mind came a thin mental wailing; something tugged at him, something wanted Teras. Teras? Then it occurred to him that Anerios was far too frightened of Aphrodite to allow Psyche to delay this long. Aphrodite had told him that Psyche was already on her way when she woke him. Lagging footsteps and demands for rest would be tolerated only for a limited time. Could some accident have occurred?

On the thought, Eros arrived beside the altar on Mount Pelion to be assaulted by a wild mental anguish, a sense of abandonment so violent that he staggered back, gasping with shock. It was another moment before his physical ears made out a hoarse sobbing and his eyes found the crumpled figure lying on the stone.

"Psyche!" he exclaimed.

The huddle stirred, struggled to rise, fell back, gasping, "Teras?"

He felt the wash of relief and ran to gather her up in his arms. She clung to him with a momentary frantic strength before she went limp and her touch was gone from his mind.

"Psyche," he cried. "What happened?"

She did not reply, and she was cold, so cold that the chill struck through her clothes and his, and for one horrified moment he thought her dead. Then she stirred, one hand feebly seeking to touch him. He caught the hand in his; it was clammy and freezing. He had no cloak to warm her and tried to curve his body around hers to provide some heat.

"I thought you would never come," she whispered. "I called you and called you."

"You fool! You had a spell to bring you back to the lodge. I was waiting there for you. Did you forget it?"

"I tried." Her voice was only a thread of sound. "I had not the strength to invoke it."

"But you had strength to go from the lodge to Iolkas," he reminded her resentfully.

Her head moved slightly, as if she intended to lift it and either could not or thought better of it. "I did not know that going would take so much from me. Why did you not warn me?"

"You know spells take power. You countered my spell on your father."

"That, too, took all I had."

He remembered then that what she said was true. He had known after she blocked the compulsion to desire the sow he had set on Anerios that she was nearly empty. That was why she was so cold! He clutched her chilled, limp body closer and bent his head to kiss her hair.

"I am so sorry, beloved," he said. "I never thought. Give the spell to me and I will invoke it."

"Give it to you?" Surprise gave a little more strength to her voice. "How?"

Did she wish to retain the travel spell so she could use it again? "Just as I gave it to you," he snapped.

"But how? Teras, I was inside the cloud when you gave me the spell. I saw nothing. All I felt was that you touched my head and a faint tingling passed from that place over my body."

Her voice had grown fainter and fainter until he could hardly hear it. And she felt colder to him. Fool that he was to sit here in the cold arguing with her!

Eros leaped back to the garden of the lodge, carried Psyche within. As soon as he saw her face in the light, he bellowed for the women servants to heat stones to warm her bed and soup and wine to warm her stomach. He took her to his own room while they scurried to obey and wrapped her in the furs from his bed. She lay flaccid in his arms, her head lolling when he did not support it. That might be a pretense, but not the pinched face, devoid of all color, or the clammy cold. Psyche was either in an extremity of terror or too drained from spell-casting.

Since he knew that Psyche had not fallen into such a state even when she had first confronted what she believed was a monster who would kill her, Eros seized gladly on the latter reason for her state. He cast all doubt away and devoted himself to warming her and feeding her, and he was so happy when she begged him to come into the bed and warm her with his body rather than using hot stones or sand that he thought the pain he had suffered nothing in comparison with his present joy.

He left Psyche sleeping to explain to Aphrodite why she had not returned, and Aphrodite shook her head sadly and said, "That may indeed be true, but what a stupid girl! If she knew she had not enough strength, why did she not go to the temple and send a message to you?"

To that Eros had no answer, although he said to Aphrodite that Psyche probably had never thought of it. Aphrodite agreed, laughing, that Psyche probably was stupid enough to overlook the obvious. Oddly, Eros felt no inclination to leap to his lover's defense. He knew she was not stupid; her mind was keen and often made sense of what his did not. If she had not gone to the temple, it was not for lack of remembering or understanding.

He stayed no longer, telling Aphrodite that Psyche was still very weak and he wanted to watch by her. And Aphrodite laughed again and waved him off, kissing her hand to him as she murmured that Psyche no doubt needed watching.

Eros winced internally because he had taken the words in their negative sense, which a moment later he was sure Aphrodite did not intend. But Psyche's greeting soothed the prick of the thorn of suspicion. She had wakened during his absence and was weeping softly, but her whole face lit when the black cloud that surrounded him filled the doorway. And when he asked why she wept, she laughed and said it was because she thought he would not return until night—and she reached eagerly into the darkness, no longer looking away or shuddering when parts of her body were swallowed up. Even the sharp contrast between his blackness and the sunlit room seemed to cause her no fear or doubt. She clung to him, half in and half out of the cloud, until she fell asleep again.

Joy returned, warming the few remaining weeks of

autumn and the long, dark nights of winter—but not such a clean, sparkling joy as had filled Eros's days and nights before Psyche had gone home. Here and there, like in the lamplit chambers of winter, lay shadows.

The first of those shadows had been cast by the fact that Psyche did not recover normally from the draining of her power. For days she claimed to be too weak to get out of bed, and Eros could not understand it. He had been drained himself from time to time—in Iolkas when he forced the use of a too-thinned spell he had almost fallen from weakness—but that had lasted only a few minutes. Soon he had found the strength to walk, and before the next morning, the Mother had restored him.

He could not help suspecting that Psyche wished to keep the translocation spell and was claiming weakness so he would not press her to do anything magical. And his suspicions were increased by the difficulty she claimed to have in learning how to find the spell, separate it from any others within her, bring it to some outer part of her body, and touch it to the person or place to which she wished to transfer it. Psyche learned everything quickly. However, the delight with which she did transfer that spell, and then two or three others, and then still more as she grew stronger and was able to cast them, made those suspicions seem foolish, and yet she was so clever . . .

Alternating with his fear that she wished to hold a spell that would permit her to flee him was an even sillier doubt. Because he was afraid to trust her now-open avowals of affection, he leapt to the conclusion that Psyche was claiming weakness to avoid his love-making. That had seemed to be false, too, for she insisted on his joining her in bed rather than resting alone that very first night. And once in the bed, he was kissed and caressed most warmly . . . most intimately . . .

although the hands that touched him were ice cold and trembling. Coupling left her prostrate and weeping— she said for joy. Eros believed her . . . he wanted to believe her.

The light of his joy was also blemished by the fact that Psyche was not eager to talk about her visit. When questioned, she laughed and said it was partly because she had not found it pleasant—she detailed for him her sisters' envy, which she claimed she had not enjoyed as she expected; the hungry eyes and wet lips, the lewd touches and suggestions, the even more direct approaches of the men, like the one she had knocked down by the stair to the women's quarters and the other she had tipped into the latrine—and partly, she added lightly, because her family and Iolkas were no longer important to her. She had removed any guilt they might have about her, and she no longer felt any obligation toward them.

Perversely, the darkest and most ominous shadows arose from what should have assured Eros of Psyche's pleasure in being "home." She called the lodge that for the first time, and when she was strong enough she threw herself with great passion into gathering herbs before the first freeze, examining clothing and supplies, giving him lists of items to buy and bring to her to be sure they were well stocked for winter, and attending to every and any household task with what seemed an almost demented devotion. She laughed and kissed him for no reason and seemed to spend any odd moment in her days thinking of astonishing (and sometimes near impossible) ways to make love at night.

Eros turned his back on the shadows so he could not see them, but from time to time some change in the position of his mind brought them leaping out, stretching ahead of him toward some well of sorrow. And even when they were not starkly apparent, they darkened his mind and spirit. Worst of all was the way a splinter of doubt, illuminated by the light of love and laughter, could be exaggerated into a pillar of guilt.

For a very long time Psyche noticed nothing of her lover's uneasiness. Not only her bodily strength but some quality of soul seemed to have been leached away by the backlash of the failed spell. For days after her return she desired nothing but to cling to Teras, to draw within her the warmth of his body and his love. She cared nothing for the blackness that surrounded him and pleaded with him to stay with her through the day as well as through the night. Then, when he agreed, she grew afraid that his absence would offend Aphrodite, and she sent him back to serve his "goddess." She had got back to her Teras despite all Aphrodite could do, she told herself, but Aphrodite was probably thoroughly annoyed; she had better walk very softly for a time.

Oddly, the real beginning of her healing was when Teras demanded back the translocation spell. Psyche had not the faintest idea how to return it, which she wished most earnestly to do; she had nightmares about invoking the spell by accident and dying of the draining or being permanently lost in a terrible wild country into which Teras was forbidden to come. But no matter what Teras said, she could not conceive of how a set of words, often chanted over a smoke of special herbs, could be gathered together and given to someone who did not know either the words or the herbs to use.

After trying for days to explain, Teras had asked her how she knew she had not enough power to invoke the travel spell. When she told him about her well and the mist within it and he countered with a description of his little box holding tiny balls of silver, Psyche at last understood.

She had always known the glowing mist within her

was her power. Now, examining that with her mind's eyes, she saw that there were shining droplets clinging to the sides of her empty well. Those gave her no strength; indeed, the walls of the well were stiffer and colder where they touched it so they must be spells drawing power to maintain themselves. Having recognized them, she soon found she could make them move. Then she had to gather the courage to pry the cap off the well so she could fish the spells out. That was a struggle, but once the well was open, she discovered that removing something from it did not awake in her the fear that drawing in power engendered.

Soon the cap of fear did not leap back to seal the well the moment she relaxed her will. The well was always open, and she could reach in and bring out a spell anytime and as quickly as she wanted. It oozed into the fingers she touched to her breast and formed into a flattened globe that shimmered with changing colors like the surface of water touched with oil, but it never burst or ran out over her hand. The spell lay in her palm, coruscating with ripples of light, unless she deliberately spilled it into Teras's hand. She could not see what happened as it poured away, but Teras told her that he had received it and taken it in.

Psyche's attention was so fixed on this new skill, which seemed to delight Teras, she hardly noticed that in the absence of the cap, her well had filled with a thicker mist, glowing more brightly than ever before. All she was aware of was that her strength and wellbeing returned, and that day by day she was filled with a bubbling joy and a great need for an outlet for her overflowing energy. She ranged far into the woods, often with Teras, who had told her about the boar and seemed most willing to use that as an excuse to accompany her. When he was away, she steeped and ground and compounded until the shelves of the shop and in her own workroom were filled to capacity. Then she ordered a thorough cleaning of the house, taking on herself the tasks that were too heavy for the two old women, cleaned and repaired the winter clothes, experimented with new recipes for both food and unguents.

Psyche was busy every minute, never tired, hardly able to wait until the light failed and she could get abed with Teras for further experiments even more delightful than those that created good food and scented lotions. Somewhere she had read that the paths of sexual pleasure were infinite, and it seemed a worthy and amusing purpose to try to discover whether the dictum was true. Delightedly, each night she set out to find a new way to tease her and her lover into convulsions of passion.

Sometimes Psyche noticed that Teras was more silent than usual and carelessly assumed it was because she was talking too much or had caused him to assume a position he found ugly or awkward. Psyche herself thought it comical when they became so entangled that lust was extinguished rather than excited and they had to begin again. But perhaps Teras, who often seemed to forget that she could not see him, feared awkwardness would intensify his ugliness.

It was not until the winter solstice had passed and the days were growing longer again that Psyche recovered from the euphoria that had held her and established a more normal emotional balance. She did not think much about what she now realized had been abnormally high spirits, assuming that they were owing to being safe in her own home with the person she loved and having once and for all cast off the burdens of mingled affection and resentment that her family had laid upon her. However, as her emotions steadied, she became more aware of what Teras said, of his hesitations and nuances of tone. It began to dawn upon her that Teras was not as happy as she.

Her first reaction was to wonder whether he was tiring of her, and she listened to him more intently, found excuses to keep her hands on him so she could feel the tensions and relaxations in his body. She began to regret that she could not see his face because it was much harder to discover what a person felt when you could not read his expression. And then she wondered whether his face looked so monstrous that no expression could be read on it. Unfortunately that made her aware, which she had not been in a long time, of the cloud of darkness she could not pierce and gave her a reluctance to have it envelop her.

Her slight withdrawal sparked so quick and vehement a response in Teras that Psyche's question was answered. He was not tiring of her; no man who was growing indifferent would have sensed the little discomfort she felt. And the questions he asked, the accusations he made, clarified the problem. She now realized that the fragile belief he had cherished that she truly loved him, truly wanted to live with him for the rest of her life, had been severely damaged by her eager acceptance of a chance to visit Iolkas and the long delay in her return.

That Teras *knew* she had needed to free herself from the guilt she felt about her family, that he *knew* she did not have enough power to invoke the translocation spell, was irrelevant. Knowledge in the head was no poultice for a wounded heart. She learned from a bitter explosion in reply to her anxious questions, that what haunted Teras was that she had been willing to leave him at all and that she had not returned on her own but had delayed until an order from Aphrodite had made her family unwilling to harbor her longer. There was nothing rational in his accusations; she knew it and he knew it too, because he gathered her into his arms and apologized as soon as the words were out, but irrational as it was, the hurt remained.

Looking back over the months, Psyche realized she had hurt him again and again. What had been an innocent truth to her was a painful reproach to him: when he asked whether she were still lonely, for example, she had readily admitted she was. She was sure she had also told him that her sojourn in Iolkas had taught her that the mere presence of others could not provide companionship. Possibly she had also told him that she was happier in the lodge with him than she could be anywhere else with anyone else . . . and said lightly, as she had said everything during that euphoria, the words would only have confirmed the doubts eating away at Teras's belief that she loved him for what he was, just as he was.

As the sun moved toward the spring equinox, Psyche tried to soothe his hurt, to bolster his shaken belief that he was worthy of love, no matter his appearance. The only result was a series of bitter quarrels in which Teras alternately blamed her for waking him from a peaceful kind of death-in-life to endless suffering and cursed himself for being unable to cast off the idea that because she was a captive she painted a false picture of pleasure over her loathing.

Had Psyche not been by then as emotionally distraught as her lover, she would have had sense enough to box his ears and point out with asperity that sniveling captives did not argue, screaming at the top of their lungs, with the masters they feared. Instead, aloud she begged Teras to tell her how to prove she loved him and did not fear him, and in silence she cursed every day, every hour, she had spent in Iolkas, cursed herself fruitlessly for not listening to her sisters when they urged her to return to her monster at once. The fools had thought she lingered because she found Teras horrible and they told her to dispel the darkness and . . . Dispel the darkness and look upon him as he truly was! *And still take him in her arms and into her bed.* Surely that would convince Teras that she loved him. Surely it would . . . if she could do it.

CHAPTER 15

The bitter question of whether she had been lying to herself for most of her life and truly believed that outer beauty was worthless compared to the inner being made Psyche more miserable. She saw that Teras felt her doubts and fears but this time she dared not explain what was troubling her. Then she began to wonder whether Teras had lied to her about only having the appearance of a monster. Was he truly a monster? Did the spell of darkness only conceal him, or did it also made her feel a normal man when what she touched was far fouler than any natural beast?

Once that horrible thought came into her mind, Psyche knew she could not live with it. She must know the truth, for good or ill. She prayed she would be strong enough to embrace whatever Teras was, knowing as she did his essential goodness and kindness. She promised herself that the sweetness they had shared in the joining of their bodies, the laughter, the work, the talk, would cover with beauty whatever dreadful form he bore.

With her new knowledge of the mental image of spells, she began to seek out the magic that caused the cloud of darkness. It was not long before she sensed a kind of delicate shimmer—that oil-on-water play of shifting color—that overlaid the features, body, and limbs, even each individual hair her fingers knew so well. The fact that what she felt beneath the shimmer was her dear, familiar Teras, gave her confidence. He had told the truth: whatever horror she saw with her eyes would only be a seeming. When she closed her eyes after she banished the cloud of blackness, surely, surely what she would touch would be Teras, and if that were so, she could—she *would*—love him.

During the lengthening days when she was alone, she reviewed all the spells she knew and combed the book room for books on magic where she found other spells. Unfortunately, none would serve her purpose. She found spells of invisibility, spells for casting a glamor of beauty and for a glamor of ugliness, but no spell for darkness nor any counterspell that would banish darkness. When she reached the end of the book room's resources, she could think of nowhere else to look. Besides, there really was no time to look further; Teras was growing increasingly unhappy and suspicious. She must either tell him what she had intended to do and abandon the idea, or she must cast a counterspell.

To cast a counterspell, you must have one. Still undecided about what she would do, Psyche began with the counterspell for invisibility she had found in the book room and added a phrase from a simple household spell she knew that banished dirt. She wove the two together and one day, after another senseless quarrel had sent Teras flying from her bed long before morning, cast the spell. She half expected that it would fall apart and lash her with prickles of undirected energy—an experience with which she had become very familiar from her early studies of magic.

To her surprise, that did not happen: the spell formed just as it should and settled quietly against the wall of her well, quite near the mouth. The droplet that contained it seemed a little larger and brighter than spells she had cast in Iolkas or even those she had cast just for the purpose of transferring them to Teras, but Psyche assumed it was because the major part of the spell, devised by an Olympian mage, was better than the ones her native teacher knew.

That minor puzzle disappeared from her awareness when Teras returned very early, very apologetic for his senseless fury. In fact for nearly a week Teras seemed so much happier that Psyche put the whole dangerous subject of removing the spell of darkness out of her mind. She was also aware that if it did not work, the backlash would hurt her; she had had unpleasant experiences with failed spells when she had been a novice and had mispronounced a word or made the wrong gesture. This time, she had used a simple phrase, but if the spell was not appropriate to its purpose, it would fail and she would suffer.

The spring equinox came. Psyche was not particularly aware of the day, but Teras mentioned it, warning Psyche not to be surprised if Demeter and her daughter Persephone came themselves to bless the garden. And then, idly, he told her the tale of the abduction of Kore, who was now Persephone. Psyche listened, smiling, for there was a kind of parallel between her experience and Persephone's, until Teras's voice suddenly changed.

"She fought to come back to Hades," he said coldly. "She drugged her mother and half killed Poseidon to escape their keeping and return to her husband. Later she would have killed Poseidon for endangering Hades if Hades had not stopped her. She has given up Olympus, the light of the sun, and every joy of the upper world, except for a few weeks in the spring, to live in the dark of Plutos—because she loves Hades."

"And I love you!" Psyche cried. "Tell me what you desire that I give up to prove I love you. Tell me!"

But he did not tell her. He simply stood up and went away and never came to her bed at all that night.

More than a week passed, and Psyche was near despair; he had never before stayed away from her for more than a night. Most of the time she was stupid with misery, dull from lying awake all night praying to hear his step on the stair. She often slept very late, having lost any purpose for her daylight hours, which she endured like a tortured beast, unthinking, almost uncomprehending, huddled in on herself. However, one morning, very early, she was wakened by a slamming door, a shutter crashing wide. She ran to the window, breathless with hope that Teras had come at last, only to bite her lips over the sight of two women in the garden.

Both were very lovely. Half asleep still and aware only of her bitter disappointment, Psyche was sure for a moment that they had come to take her place as Teras's lovers. Before real thought could replace fearful instinct, Psyche looked deep to see what had won Teras's favor. Inside one was a well of gentle green; inside the other— Terrified, Psyche drew back so the wall of her chamber would conceal her. Inside the taller and more beautiful woman was a volcano of power, red and deep brown and every shade of blood and the earth, roiling and bubbling, rich with the smell of fecundity.

Psyche drew a deep breath. Here were no rivals but Demeter and Persephone, who had come, as Teras had warned her, to bless the garden. Gathering her sleep-dazed wits, Psyche wondered why they should bother with a little plot mostly used to feed Aphrodite's servants, and she peered out cautiously to see what they were doing. She took courage when she saw how gently, lovingly, Persephone smiled at Demeter. Teras had not got far enough in the story to tell her whether mother and daughter were reconciled. And then, with her mind's eye, Psyche saw that a trickle of power, just a gentle streamlet of richness and warmth, flowed out of the volcano to feed the soft, green magic.

Transfixed with wonder, Psyche leaned out the window and heard Persephone speak in a pleasant, musical voice. "For the goodness she has brought between us, mother," Persephone said, giving Demeter a kiss, "do not forget to double the blessing on Aphrodite's field."

"I will never forget that," Demeter answered, and not only cast her blessing, but walked the field from border to border to spread her magic more deeply into the earth.

It was the last thing Psyche wished to hear. She drew back, convinced that Teras's agony was all her fault. If she did not so senselessly hate Aphrodite, she could have gone to her temple and begged the priestess for help. Clearly not only Teras loved Aphrodite. She had told herself that it was because Teras was a man that he was blind to Aphrodite's faults. But here were women, and women of power, who also cared for Aphrodite and spoke of her goodness. Psyche's conviction that Aphrodite's beauty covered only meanness and evil was shaken, but her injustice to Teras's friend could not hold her thoughts for long.

The distraction of Persephone's and Demeter's presence and the shock of perceiving Persephone's power had prodded Psyche out of her dull quiescence. Her thoughts reverted to Teras, but now they were truly thoughts rather than a numb despair. She clung to the knowledge that he cared for her, that his absence was out of a fear that she did not return that caring. She almost slipped into the slough of despond again when she considered how impossible it was to prove that she did care, but a sudden spurt of fury over her helplessness saved her. She *would* prove it, even if she had to split Teras's thick skull to pour in the idea.

Tears stung her eyes. She had to be able to reach Teras if she wanted to prove anything to him. If she wanted to see someone in Iolkas she could send a message, but here . . . And then her eyes widened in revelation and she laughed aloud. Why not send a message? If she sent Teras a message begging him to come, he *must* believe she wanted him. She ran down to the storeroom where the old menservants were readying the tools for planting now that the field had been blessed.

"I must send a message to Teras," she said. "One of you must take it to Olympus, to . . ."

Her voice faded as she saw the expressions of horror, the violent head shaking, that rejected her demand. One of the men made frantic signs at her, pointing to himself and then to the floor. And then he pointed south, in the direction of Olympus, and shook his head again, even more violently. She could guess easily what that meant: the servants were not allowed to leave, and even more specially were forbidden to go to Olympus. She turned away before they could sign that she, too, must stay at the lodge. She suspected it was so, but she did not wish to see the signs.

As she climbed the stairs, the idea that had leapt into her mind and made her turn her back so as not to *know* what she intended to do was forbidden took firmer hold. If Teras did not come to her, she would go to him. The trouble was that she had no idea how far Olympus was, and this was a bad time of year to travel through the wild. She could carry food enough for a few days, but after that she would need to live off the land and so early in the spring there would be little to find.

Still, she could not resist setting out her weapons, the bow, the arrows, the light javelin, the long knife and short sword. She got her pack, the one she carried when she planned to be in the forest for a full day. It was a good size to make room for the plants she gathered, some of which should not be crushed. There would be room for food, for a change of dress and an extra pair of shoes, in case she should get wet, and she would need a blanket. The pack would be heavy at first, but it would lighten as she ate her supplies.

Psyche smiled, feeling at peace for the first time in moons. She had discovered a way to prove her love. Teras feared that she pretended passion because she was a helpless slave, that she stayed with him because she had nowhere else to go. But if she left the lodge and went to Olympus, would that not prove that she was *not* helpless and *could* go anywhere she wished, but chose to come to him?

That thought cheered her so much that she turned out her clothes chest, seeking an extra set of coarse, warm garments to pack. At the very bottom was a small box; opened, it showed a packet of carefully folded silk. Puzzled, she drew it out and unfolded the cloth, and then stared dumbstruck at the stained piece of cloth within. Teras's blood! She remembered now that night so long ago when he had given her the token that could enforce her will upon him.

What was she to do with it? She dared not destroy it because she was not sure whether that would hurt him. She was afraid to leave it behind, lest someone find it and somehow sense it was his. And then she realized it might be a lifeline for her. If she should become hopelessly lost or trapped, surely she could cast a simple calling spell, and holding that token, draw Teras to her. That could not hurt him. She refolded the token in its covering and placed it in the pack.

Feeling even more cheerful, now that she had an assurance that she could summon Teras to get her out of trouble, she made a list of what she would need—

things she might forget because she did not take them for a day in the forest, like a comb and the powder she used to clean her teeth—and she propped the list against the pack beside the quiver of arrows. She could add to it as thoughts came to her.

It was dark by the time she finished and the little quiver of hope that began every evening when the light failed had died. The aching longing that made each heartbeat slow and heavy, the pain in her throat that made it hard to swallow, fixed more firmly in her mind her intention of doing something, anything, rather than wait forever in misery.

Thus, Psyche made a very good evening meal. She would need her strength and might not dare to fill her stomach again for many days. She even took a plate full of small cakes up to her room, thinking that she might eat them if she woke in the night. She had lost weight, for despair had dulled her appetite. Now every ounce of fat she could restore would help her on her way. Her eyes flicked over the pack and weapons; her lips thinned and her jaw thrust forward. She would not wait, weeping, for Teras tonight. She would go to bed and sleep. And tomorrow she would leave.

So, of course, Teras came. And Psyche was asleep. She had been afraid that to say she would sleep and to do so would be far different things; however, although her mind seemed busy, planning what she would do if the servants objected to the large amount of food she wished to pack and then laying out the course she would take, it was really at peace. The uneasy hoping against hope that had kept her awake for many nights was over, and the combination of fatigue and the relief decision brings sent her deeply asleep.

To Eros, who had finally decided that absenting himself longer from what he desired more than breathing was accomplishing nothing—neither curing his desire for Psyche nor presenting to him any idea that would cure his doubts of her—the clear signs that she intended to leave the lodge were like a contemptuous slap in the face. He might have assumed she merely intended to go gathering, although it was very early in the spring for that, had it not been for the note so prominently displayed.

Even before he realized she intended to leave, he had received a shock. The early bed hour, the sound sleep, the little dish of cakes by the bed, all bespoke a kind of cozy comfort. It seemed to him that his long absence had assured her he would not come back, at least for some time, and she was more comfortable and at ease alone than she had ever been in his presence. *Lying, treacherous bitch!* He had almost believed she had loved the beast in the black cloud for the person that was Eros inside it.

He turned quickly to rush away from the ugly revelation and saw the weapons and pack laid out and then the note. Bitterness could not really kill hope. He seized the note, hoping it was an explanation addressed to him, but all he found was a list of items that proved she planned a long journey.

The stroke that killed hope bred violence. He whirled back to the bed, seized her, and shook her brutally. "Where did you plan to escape to, you lying whore?" he bellowed.

"Teras!" she shrieked; her eyes had shot open when he seized her, but they were still glazed with sleep. "Teras, help me!"

"Teras will kill you, if you do not tell the truth for once. Where were you going?"

She had begun to struggle when she screamed for help, but when he spoke again she blinked and lay quiet. "To you, you idiot!" she said. "To Olympus, to find you."

"I do not believe you," he snarled.

She burst into tears. "I know, and you have reft from me my chance to prove my words. Why could you not stay away another few days?" she asked bitterly. "If I had come to you in Olympus, you would have known it was you I wanted to be with always. To come so far would have proved that I could go anywhere, that I do not live here and pretend love because I have nowhere else to go."

Eros sat heavily down on the side of the bed. "I do not know what is wrong with me, Psyche. Why am I torturing us both?"

"It is partly my fault," she said, sighing. "I made a mistake. Not in wishing to go back to Iolkas; that was necessary because the old strings around my heart had to be cut. The mistake was in clinging to my hatred of Aphrodite so that I could not go to the temple and ask for help in coming home. If I had come, as I intended, on the second day . . . but I did not, and you were hurt beyond bearing." She hesitated, shrugged. "And partly the fault is yours, because you cannot believe what you know, that the outer appearance is nothing."

He guessed that her next words would be an appeal to show himself in his true form, and he bent and kissed her. Had he only been a monster, he could have solved all his doubts that way. As it was, what would be proved by exposing his physical perfection to her? Oh yes, she would fling herself gladly into his arms and swear she had always loved his inner self, but he would not believe it.

She tried for a moment to push him away and break the kiss, but then she lay still. Nor did she try again to speak when he released her lips. She let him undress himself and opened her arms to him in silence, but when he kissed her again, he tasted the salt of tears. He almost pulled free, almost said angrily that he did not need to take a woman who was so unwilling that she wept, but one hand was stroking his hair with infinite tenderness while the other stroked his shaft with great skill. That was all. She tried no crazy tricks, no lewd contortions, but when he touched her, she was moist and ready and he could feel her quick, eager breathing.

Still when he came into her, legs and hands restrained his plunging. And when he drew slowly and then pressed in equally slowly, she took his face in her hands and kissed it, his brow, his cheeks, his mouth and chin, slowly, tenderly. She stroked his body, embraced it, stroked it again as if she wanted to learn every bulge and hollow, every smoothness and crevice, every hair. And all the while she moved with him, ever so slowly speeding the rhythm until at last she gripped him fast and ground herself against him, wailing aloud in an ecstasy that too clearly was half pain.

Hearing her, Eros wept himself, but he was also inflamed by the peculiar eroticism of mingled grief and passion. He drove himself faster and harder, feeling Psyche sobbing beneath him, but there was no refusal in that weeping. Her hands now stroked his inner thighs and his knotted scrotum and she plunged with him, adding her movement to his own to bring on his climax. His seed poured out in torrents, pulsing and pulsing until he felt as if his vitals would be torn loose and flow out with it, and he cried out in a kind of agony. Yet he could not stop, and he continued thrusting until he fell half-fainting into Psyche's arms.

Half-conscious though he was, Eros did not want those arms to hold him. He rolled off her, limp as a bludgeoned ox, and with nothing to say. In the past he had always kissed her, teased her a little, made clear how much joy she had given him. What she had given him this night, he was sure, had brought joy to neither. There had been something wrong, not false—he could not say false—just wrong, something that made him uneasy about her lovemaking.

That made worse what had passed between them earlier. Although every word she said seemed true, inside him was an urgent hissing: *treacherous, lying bitch.* It was better to pretend he had fallen instantly asleep than to try to find words that would not disclose how much his suspicions had been increased by her peculiar behavior. And it was not long before he did sleep; sleep was an accustomed escape for him. Still, that escape had always been from boredom and nonfeeling rather than misery, so this sleep was not the same and was not deep or easy.

Once he felt a dreadful sense of loss, dreaming that Psyche was leaving, creeping from the bed to run away. He cried out, or dreamt he cried out, and then felt as if hands were passing over his body. That comforted him, and he lay still, lulled, just on the edge of sliding away into the depths of slumber when a glittering mist spun into the cloud of darkness, spread over him, and attached itself mote by mote along the fine black network of Hecate's spell.

So stunned was Eros at the image his Gift sensed that he hardly felt the pain when the counterspell spread over him. He made no effort to protect himself for just a heartbeat—and then it was too late. The glittering motes burst into flame, searing the dark net. Eros screamed, and screamed again as the burning motes sank into him, piercing and tearing his skin, burning deeper and deeper as they sought the root of the spell of darkness. And then the slight misting that marked what was utter blackness to unspelled eyes was gone and he lay naked, panting with agony, under Psyche's startled gaze.

"Mother have mercy," she shrieked, backing away. "What have I done? Tell me you are not truly Eros!"

The words pierced his agony. Had she known he was Eros, she would not have worked the spell! She thought she was attacking a monster. He saw a stained piece of cloth fall from her hand and he knew it was his blood token, that Psyche, frustrated in her plan to escape the monster, had gone one step farther and tried to kill him.

Between his agony of mind and his agony of body, thought was impossible. Instinct cast the travel spell that would carry him to kindness, to safety, to where he would find comfort. But the use of power while spell and counterspell were already burning each other away only added to the conflagration, and Eros was far beyond screaming when his body collapsed bonelessly on the floor of his chamber in Aphrodite's house.

Ordinarily Aphrodite did not trouble herself with Eros's comings and goings. The faint trembling in the air that she recognized as the sign of a translocation spell would not normally impinge on her awareness. Fortunately, that night she was both awake and aware when Eros arrived because she had been too troubled to go to sleep.

For the seven past days, Eros had been what she remembered only from years past in a halcyon period between his gaining control of the spell of revulsion and the onset of remorse—and boredom. He had been alive, awake, interested in everything, eager to accompany her or to make innocent mischief for her. She knew he was not whole; she could sense the bond to Psyche remained, but he seemed to be stretching the tether longer and longer each day. Aphrodite had felt she had reason to hope it would soon hardly hold him. Then, in the middle of an idle game, he had jumped up, shaking his head angrily.

"I am eating my heart out," he said. "Why should I

sit here and suffer because I am away from her? Why should I deny myself the pleasure she gives only because I also suffer when I am with her? If I have the pain in any case, I might as well have the pleasure too."

The suddenness of Eros's action had startled Aphrodite so that she did no more than raise her brows. In any case he left so quickly she would not have had time to argue, but she sat staring at his empty chair and an overturned piece on the playing board just in front of the chair and began to wonder for the first time whether the accursed Psyche had some sorcerous hold on him. And then she realized she knew virtually nothing about the girl. Hyppodamia had said Psyche hated her and was exceptionally beautiful; Eros had spoken mostly of Psyche's cleverness, but he did not speak of her often. Frowning with annoyance, Aphrodite found a warm wrap and translocated to the temple in Iolkas.

She was even more annoyed when she returned, having apparently wasted the energy expended on the translocation spell as well as her time. Hyppodamia could tell her no more than gossip: it was known that Psyche had studied with the local witch. Brought to the temple and questioned, this woman said that Psyche was quick and clever about learning spells and casting them, but that she had so little power that the spells were usually without effect. She admitted a few envious women said that Psyche's beauty was owing to a spell but she knew it was not true; Psyche, she said with mild contempt, could not cast a spell that would remain active. A spell cast by Psyche might bring a flash of beauty, but it would be gone almost immediately. It was no spell that made Psyche breathtakingly lovely.

Hyppodamia herself had sensed no power in the girl at all, but she admitted that she had been so overwhelmed by the fierce flood of resentment and rejection that poured out of Psyche, even while she agreed and then begged to be taken into the temple, that her senses could have been blinded to a small, weak Gift. However, she felt certain that she would have been aware of the kind of power that could force a god like Eros to obey Psyche.

The trouble with that assessment was that Aphrodite knew Eros was not a god and that he was particularly vulnerable and attuned to Psyche because of his emotional attachment to her. Still, it did not seem possible that Psyche could control Eros against his will unless she had far more power than either the witch of Iolkas or Hyppodamia suspected. There was no sense in asking Eros; since he was already bound to her, he would never acknowledge that she was summoning him and he could not resist. Aphrodite bit her lip. If she wanted an answer, she would have to have it from Psyche herself, and she had a feeling Eros would not like that.

Just as she was considering ways in which to intimidate Psyche, she became aware of a kind of shuddering in the direction of Eros's apartment. She uttered a low-voiced obscenity and started to leave the central chamber where they had been playing and to which she had thoughtlessly returned. At this time of night, or morning, really, she should be either with some lover or fast asleep in her own bed. If Eros found her here, seemingly waiting for him, it was too likely he would feel she was trying to manipulate him. But as she stepped out into the corridor to return to her own quarters, she heard a child crying and the sound of running feet, and she turned just in time to receive into her arms one of the little boys who slept on a pallet in Eros's chamber unless he was told not to wait.

"He is dead!" the child sobbed. "He fell on the floor and will not speak or open his eyes. He is cold and wet."

Struck mute by the terror that she would be alone, without a friend, forever, Aphrodite shook the child furiously before she found her voice. "He is not dead," she shrieked when she could speak. "Stop your weeping at once." Then she swallowed hard and spoke in a softer voice. "I will go to Eros now. You run to the menservants. Send two to Eros's chamber to help me get him to bed and a third to bring Asclepius the physician here."

CHAPTER 16

When Eros disappeared, Psyche was furious. Rage alone gave her the strength to stand after the draining of casting her spell. She wanted nothing so much as to tear out those great, luminous eyes that had glared at her when she exposed his deceit. But he was gone! The coward! Unwilling to face her. How could he face her? What explanation could there be for saying he was a monster and blanketing himself in darkness?

Panting and sobbing, Psyche cursed the empty bed, raised her head, and howled curses at the air. She knew now that she had been the victim of a cruel joke. How he must have laughed at her, she thought, all the while she struggled to conquer her fears and be kind to the "monster." It was just the sort of joke that cruel, arrogant pseudo-god would enjoy. And she had loved him!

Psyche bent and scooped up the bloodstained cloth she had dropped when she saw Eros's face. She would tear it, burn it, and hope that that self-satisfied snake would be rent and burnt with it. But she only cradled the cloth against her breast and then burst into tears of rage and pain and shame. She *still* loved him! Trembling with weakness and weeping bitterly, she staggered to the bed and fell into it. She did not weep for long.

The tears added to the draining of spell-casting atop an emotionally exhausting day soon sent her fast asleep.

When Psyche woke, the blinding rage was gone. Only shame and sadness remained, and she lay abed, fingering her blood token, and wondering why Teras—no, Eros—had continued the jest so long. It had been many, many months since she had given a single thought to the "monster's" appearance or had been afraid to enter the black cloud. What pleasure could he have found, then, in fooling her?

The word "pleasure" brought back a flood of memories, of all the time they had spent together talking and working and making love. No, he had not been laughing at her, not for a long time, anyway. Then why keep up the pretense of being a monster? She would have loved him just as much . . . The thought trickled into emptiness, then looped around and repeated: would she have loved him just as much if she had seen him as beautiful?

In fact, Psyche realized at once that she would have resented Eros bitterly had he presented himself to her and said she had been given to him by Aphrodite. It would have taken him months, not days, to convince her to become his lover. Or, if she had yielded to him because of his beauty, she would have been angry and ashamed, which would have lain at the heart of her relationship with him always. For the monster, once her worst fears had been allayed, she had felt only pity and sympathy. Teras had been easy to love; she had assumed he was as much a victim as she, and yielding to him made her feel generous and noble and strong.

Psyche uttered a soft laugh, but then she bit her lip. If that had been Eros's reason, he was devilishly clever and knew far too much about women. Then she burst into loud, ringing laughter. How ridiculous! Of course he knew a great deal about women. With a face like that and Mother alone knew how old, how could he *not* know too much about women? They must leap out on him in the public street—

The grin she had been wearing froze on Psyche's face and changed to a grimace as her lips turned down. It was not funny. She remembered the man who had seized her in the woods when she had just grown into her beauty and the hot eyes, the swollen mouths that hung half open as if they waited to eat her, the hands that reached to stroke her intimately as soon as any man caught her alone. And not one had known her, not one had cared what Psyche truly was. She caught her breath on a sob and shuddered. But was it the same for a man?

A slight frown wrinkled her forehead. Actually, she thought, it must be worse for a man. They were accustomed to choosing their prey and pursuing it. They might not care much what the prey thought or felt, but they wished to conquer, to be master by strength or skill. If, because of an accident of birth, the prey leaped out of the bushes and impaled itself willingly on the hunter's weapon, a man who was not an utter fool would soon feel diminished—as she had felt diminished for being desired only for her face, but even more so.

Women were accustomed, trained, to account physical beauty a thing of great value, so most of them were satisfied to be admired for their outer shell although even those often sought praise for other things also. On the other hand, most men would not be at all pleased to be valued first by their appearance. Men were vain too, of course, but their training put many things before a handsome face: courage, skill in the use of weapons, cleverness, loyalty—

That word sent Psyche's thoughts off on a tangent. Men did not account loyalty to a woman of any value. How many women had leapt on Eros when he shed his disguise during the day in Olympus? She waited for the stabbing and burning of jealousy, but all she felt was an impulse to laugh, for the vision she had was of Eros, hair and garments streaming behind him, fleeing as fast as he could run. Then she shivered. No, it was Teras who would have fled, even if his face was beautiful; it was Teras she knew, not Eros.

Psyche thought for a few minutes about whether Teras and Eros really were the same being, even if they inhabited the same body, then sighed and shook her head. It did not matter; she felt not a stir of jealousy over either one. Teras she knew and loved, and Teras with a beautiful face would have been disgusted by women who seized on him for his appearance. He would, indeed, have run away as fast as he could, and if something, say pity, had constrained him to accept the advances, he would have been ashamed. The simple joy of coupling he could have with her at any time, and a woman who loved only his face had nothing more to offer. Eros . . . she did not know Eros, did not love Eros, and did not care if he coupled in the open street with ten at a time.

Teras was going to be very annoyed with her for exposing him, Psyche thought, as she sat up and got out of bed. She remembered now the shouts of rage he had uttered when he felt the counterspell take hold. She would have to convince him that she was indifferent to his appearance.

"Ekkrino!" she exclaimed, utterly exasperated, and then she laughed aloud, realizing that she had been reading so much in the old language as she learned spells that she had said "shit" in that tongue instead of in her own.

The old language! Teras meant "monster" in the old language. That devil Eros! Her exasperation returned in full measure, but it was not over how slyly he had avoided telling her a lie. She had just realized that she had turned a difficult task into one that was nigh impossible. When she'd cast the spell, she had been trying to convince Teras she would love him no matter how horrible he looked. She might have accomplished that if he had been a monster and she had been able to kiss him and fondle him and couple with him. Could she prove to Eros that she loved only the inner man, that part of him that was Teras?

Psyche shivered a little as she belted her robe and tucked Teras's blood token, which she had been holding all the time she dressed, between her breasts. She drew on a warm shawl then and went down to break her fast. She did not want to prove anything to Eros. She did not want to see Eros. She wanted Teras, her own dear monster swathed in darkness.

The servants were very nervous. Kryos nearly dropped the tray he was setting on the table when she looked at him, and Hedy's hand shook so much when she poured the wine that half of it splashed onto the floor. Psyche could only assume they had heard Eros yelling and perhaps had felt the magic. She had no idea what to say to them to calm them and so she ate quickly, wanting to get away from their anxiety, which had awakened her own. She could explain what she had done, but what if Teras, or Eros, did not come?

Rising, she found she did not want to go either to her workroom or the book room. She was certain that any work she tried to do would turn into a disaster and no book could hold her attention. Fortunately the sun was shining, and though it was chilly, it was not too cold to walk in the garden. Psyche headed by instinct for the bench near the fountain. As she drew near it, she remembered the kindness, patience, and good humor with which Teras had wooed her, and she grew calmer. He might be angry, but he would not deny her a chance to explain herself. She approached the bench and stood smiling down at it.

"You evil devil!"

Psyche whirled about, her eyes and mouth round with shock. Despite the fury of the words, the voice was sweet and pure and the woman—no, girl—who confronted her was so lovely, so innocent looking, that the rage which twisted her mouth and made her eyes burn looked like an ugly scrawl added over a beautiful image. Her face was familiar, too, but Psyche knew she had never met this ethereal creature.

"Ungrateful, treacherous bitch!"

"No," Psyche gasped, recovering a little from her shock and growing angry in turn. "Why should you say such a thing to me? I have never done you harm. I do not even know who you are."

But she did! Even as she spoke the words, she remembered where she had seen those features. The face was that of the statue of Aphrodite in the temple, except that the cold stone could express only a small portion of the beauty of the animated being, even now when the living features were all twisted with rage.

"Murderess!" Aphrodite hissed.

"Whom have I killed?" Psyche asked indignantly, drawing herself up, surprised to find that she was taller than the goddess and not at all overawed.

"You tried to kill Eros, you devil. That you failed, that the only words he said were to plead for you, are why I have not struck you down."

"Tried to kill Eros?" Psyche echoed stupidly. "I tried to counter his spell against my father, but—"

"Last night!" Aphrodite shrieked. "You decided to free yourself from what you thought was a monster by murder, by using a token he had given you in love."

"No!" Psyche cried. "No! I only used a counterspell to break the spell of darkness. I did him no harm. I love my monster. I would not hurt Teras for all the world."

"Liar! He lies in my house near death now. Only Asclepius's skill has kept breath in his body."

Psyche was trembling now, head bent, hands prayerfully clasped. "Lady," she said faintly, "say you do not mean it. Say that you are only trying to punish me for rejecting you. It was only a counterspell to the darkness. I swear. I will show you the spell. I have so little power. I could not have done him harm. If the spell failed, it would only have lashed *me* with loose power."

"But you used his blood token to enforce it, and it burned into his vitals—" Aphrodite's voice was also trembling, and tears misted her clear eyes.

Psyche's head came up, staring eyes round with horror, unheeded tears streaming down her cheeks. "The token," she whispered. "It drove the spell too deep." She clutched her hands at her breast. "I meant no harm. I only wanted to prove that I loved him, that I cared nothing for his monstrous form and would love him even after I saw him. Mother, help him. Help him. I meant no harm."

"You had *better* pray for his well doing, for if he dies, I will tear you in pieces. All the years I have struggled to keep him alive, and you—"

Aphrodite's voice broke and she raised her hand as if to strike Psyche. Psyche's eyes flicked up to the raised hand, but she did not flinch.

"I meant no harm," she said, more steadily now. "You *know* I meant him no harm. Lady Aphrodite, you love him too. Take me to him. Let me nurse him. I am a good physician. Perhaps because it was my spell, I can be of some help. I will do anything. Let me prove my love."

Aphrodite made a low, contemptuous sound and turned away.

"Wait," Psyche called. "I still have his blood token. Please take it back to him."

Shocked at having forgotten something so important, and torn between rage and an uncomfortable knowledge of the true devotion that made Psyche remember, Aphrodite turned. Psyche held out the blood-stained cloth. Aphrodite stepped forward and snatched it from her fingers, her eyes instinctively glancing at the girl's face to measure her reaction. What she saw there made her hesitate. More than weak devotion lit the perfection of feature that was Psyche's face. There was intelligence in the broad brow, courage in the violet eyes, tear-drenched but meeting hers firmly, and great determination in the firm chin and set lips.

"Is that supposed to prove your love?" Aphrodite snapped. She turned and began to walk away. Then, just before she invoked the translocation spell, she looked back over her shoulder and added grudgingly, "Well, you did offer before I wrested it from you, though I am sure you knew I could take it whenever I wished. Still . . . Perhaps I will let you try to prove the love you avow. And if you prove it, perhaps I will let you come to serve poor Eros . . . perhaps."

The words held out hope because Aphrodite had realized as she looked into Psyche's face that if she did not give the girl hope, desperation would drive her to some irremediable act. If she should kill herself . . . Internally Aphrodite flinched. It would not matter to her if Psyche died, but to Eros? She was not sure. It was true that when Asclepius had revived him before sending him off into a deep, drugged sleep, all Eros had whispered was, "Do not harm Psyche. Do not." But there was still a chance that when his wits were restored and he thought about what Psyche had done, he would be sickened and his love would end.

Unfortunately, Eros was not a fool and he knew a

great deal about spells. When his wits were restored, he might just as well recognize that only an uncontrolled and overpowerful counterspell had been used. If so, he might easily work out the same reason for using a counterspell that Psyche had already given. Whether the reason was genuine or not was irrelevant. Once Eros seized on it, he would be only too glad to believe Psyche had not tried to kill the monster. Then, if he learned she was dead, he would follow her into the grave as soon as he could.

As soon as she arrived in her house, Aphrodite went in to look at Eros. A young boy, not one of the little cherubs but a child approaching puberty and the time of leaving her household, sat by the bed, attentively watching Eros's face. It was marked by pain and by two deep grooves between the brows, as if trouble haunted his sleep, but the ghastly pallor and the sheen of cold sweat were gone.

"How is he?" she murmured.

The child started but smiled and bowed from his seat as he turned toward her, replying in a low voice, "Lord Eros ate a bowl of broth, but he was mostly asleep even while he ate, and Master Asclepius gave him more of the sleeping potion." Then the child looked anxious and added, "He asked for you. I told him, as you bade me, that you would soon come, but he was troubled and fought the drug. Master Asclepius was angry. He said he would return in the afternoon, that the drug would hold until then, but Lord Eros is not easy."

Aphrodite bit her lip, then slid between the boy and the bed. She knelt down and stroked Eros's hair and, very gently, the grooves on his forehead. "She is safe, love," she murmured in his ear. "I swear to you, she is safe at the lodge. Rest, love. When you are better, you will think what to do."

He turned his head restlessly, his lips moving. Aphrodite was certain that what he thought he was doing was calling for Psyche. She assured him again and then again that Psyche was safe and well. Finally some sense of what she said seemed to penetrate his drugged mind, for he grew quieter and his frown lessened. Aphrodite rose and went back to her own apartment.

She had been so enraged by needing to offer assurances she did not wish to give that she began to wonder, as she knelt beside Eros, whether she could have the girl killed and leave evidence in the lodge that Psyche had fled. By the time she reached her chamber, she had dismissed the idea. Aside from the difficulty of finding someone who would do the deed and then keep silent, the notion was useless. Eros was far more likely to recover from his love if he thought Psyche was safe and comfortable at the lodge and indifferent to his suffering. If he thought she was miserable or in danger, he would only begin to search for her, and he would continue to search until he was sure she was dead, and then the besotted idiot would kill himself.

The clear progression in her thoughts—Aphrodite was not much given to thinking things out—made her so furious that she upended a small table bearing a collection of priceless crystal ornaments, some of which burst with satisfying crashes when they hit the floor. Idiot! Idiot! One would think a being as old as Eros would have learned to avoid the more violent bonds of affection.

The noise brought her little girls, and she sent them away to get one of the older womenservants to clear up the mess. There was no sense in adding wailing children and bloodstains to her irritation. As she stood, staring at the sparkling fragments, some tiny as grains of sand, her anger at Eros's stubbornness brought to mind the look of grim determination on Psyche's face. The woman was an idiot too! Who knew how long the vague hope she had offered would keep Psyche from some new stupid action to "prove her love"? She would have to set Psyche a task, an impossible task, but one that might seem possible.

The womanservant came and began to pick up the larger fragments, laying them for some reason known only to herself in ordered piles. Aphrodite sighed as the servant set aside a many-faceted globe, unbroken except for a chip that spoiled one edge. Persephone had given her that. Persephone, who loved Hades as madly as Eros loved Psyche . . . Aphrodite sighed again, recalling how desperately—and unsuccessfully—Demeter had struggled to break that bonding. But Persephone had been sure of Hades's love. She had known of his desperate need for her from when he had first snatched her into the underworld. Eros already had doubts. If she could build those doubts gently into disgust, he might not seek oblivion as an answer to pain and disappointment.

Aphrodite's eyes still rested on the maid, piling bits of crystal in heaps. Her surface thoughts were of Eros, but on a deeper level she was still thinking of Demeter, who had accepted her conclusion that the bond was unbreakable and now seemed content to have Persephone with her only when they blessed the fields and the seed. Aphrodite's mind clung to the word "seed," because she did not want her deeper thoughts to come to the surface, and then made a crazy connection among what might make Psyche seem indifferent, the piles the maid was making, and seed—many different kinds of seed, some as small as the tiny, sparkling shards on the floor. Aphrodite drew herself up and smiled a little. She had an answer to the task she could set Psyche—a perfectly safe, incredibly boring task that would not seem impossible but actually was.

While Psyche worked at the task, she would remain

at the lodge. Aphrodite could assure Eros she was safe and busy and *content*. To tell him Psyche was content would make her fondness seem tepid and might cool Eros's fervor. Aphrodite's perfect teeth set hard. Why could the stupid girl not *be* stupid? All the others had cured Eros by their own silliness or ill temper or jealousy.

Aphrodite hesitated, then walked slowly to the central chamber and lay down on her couch to think carefully. Did she really need to do anything, which Eros might learn about and resent? In the past Psyche had thought her lover to be ugly. Perhaps now that she knew her lover was Eros she would be like the rest and make his life so miserable that he would cast her off in despair. But Psyche herself was so beautiful that she might be sure of her hold on him and not be jealous. And she had already held him for almost two years, held him against his own fears and doubts.

In the end, Aphrodite knew, she might be as unsuccessful as Demeter, but she *had* to try to break Eros's fixation. Psyche was a native with little power. She would soon start to grow old. The decay of her beauty might wear away Eros's love, but Aphrodite could not take the chance, because if it did not, Eros would die, one way or another, when Psyche died. If not for that, Aphrodite told herself, she would have accepted the half-loaf or quarter-loaf of affection and attention Eros could spare her while Psyche lived.

Feeling pleased with herself, and rather righteous, Aphrodite sent a little messenger to the temple of the Corn Goddess, requesting a word with Demeter as soon as it was convenient for her. She did not expect any reply until dark because Demeter and Persephone were out blessing the fields all day, and, tired from her wakeful night and the emotional upheavals she had suffered, she slipped asleep on the couch.

She was wakened late in the afternoon by the boy who had watched beside Eros. Before she could feel any alarm, he said that Asclepius had come, but that Eros would not take the medicine he offered until he had spoken with her. Aphrodite hurried to Eros's chamber, where she saw with relief that although Eros's mouth was tight with pain, Asclepius looked merely irritated, not worried.

"Psyche?" Eros said. "You did not harm her!"

"No, of course not, you silly man," Aphrodite said, sitting down on the stool where the boy had kept watch and taking Eros's hand. "I do not say I would not have eaten her alive if I had gone when you first arrived here, but I was too busy getting you to bed and helping Asclepius. After he said you would likely recover, I only went to ask why she wished to kill a being who had been so kind to her." Then her eyes and mouth grew hard in a way that was more horrible because of the look of innocence of the features. "But," she added, "if you die, I *will* have her torn apart—"

"Aphrodite!" Asclepius interrupted. "It will do my patient no good to be terrified. His spirit needs peace and a time to recover. I only agreed to your speaking with him for a few moments to relieve his worries and make him calmer."

Aphrodite smiled sweetly. "But there is nothing in what I said to worry him. All Eros has to do is resolve to live and obey your instructions and his precious Psyche will be safe."

"I am not trying to die," Eros said, smiling faintly. "I want to get better. I must know why—"

"She told me it was a mistake—" Aphrodite lifted a brow "—that she was only trying to break the darkness spell to . . . ah . . . prove she would love you no matter how ugly you were."

It was the truth, Aphrodite thought, and for the moment, because Eros was too tired and in too much pain to worry about the small, suggestive expressions, what she said would soothe him, which was necessary. Later he would remember the lift of her brow and the hesitation and wonder what she had *really* thought.

"Thank you," he breathed, "you are always my friend."

Aphrodite was rewarded by the easing of tension in him. His mouth was still drawn tight with pain, and he twitched from time to time as a mote of counterspell burned itself out, but his hands, which had been knotted together, fell open and one reached feebly for her. Aphrodite took it.

"Yes, I am always your friend because you are always mine. We have each other, no matter what. That was why I took your blood token from Psyche when she offered it. She is so very ignorant about magic. Mother alone knows what more damage she might do you, wishing only to help . . . now that she has seen Eros." She drew the cloth from between her breasts and put it into the hand she was holding.

"But if she needs me . . ." he whispered.

"If you will tell me what good you would be to her in the state she has reduced you to, I will bring it back to her and urge her to invoke it." Aphrodite laughed, bent down, and kissed his brow. "Go to sleep and have only sweet dreams, my love. I will make sure Psyche stays safe at the lodge where she will be quite content to wait for you."

"That is enough," Asclepius said. "You must sleep now, Eros, and go on sleeping until the aftereffects of that spell are gone, or you will twitch forever."

Psyche spent the day in an agony of indecision. One moment she was ready to plunge a knife into her own

heart, sure that her love was dead. The next, she knew
he was alive because she was certain Aphrodite would
not deny herself the pleasure of telling her he was dead
and exacting some terrible punishment. That thought
was soothing. Psyche would welcome any punishment;
no matter how dreadful, it would be less than the agony
she suffered now at having hurt Teras, and to be punished might make that agony easier to bear. Yet her
heart beat fast and thick at the thought of a long,
painful dying, and she shivered with fear. Watering her
terror with her tears made a small hope poke through
the black earth of her despair: perhaps Eros was not
near death, as Aphrodite said; if he were only sick,
Aphrodite would not come.

When the hope came to her, Psyche rose and went to
look over her travel gear, which she had never put
away, wondering whether she should set out for Olympus. If she presented herself at Aphrodite's house,
surely Aphrodite would allow her to tend Eros—unless
he was so angry he never wanted to see her again. No,
Teras would not be so unjust and so unreasonable.
Teras would at least listen to what she had to say.
Surely the return of the blood token would show she
had meant no harm. But Aphrodite was angry at the
damage she had done and perhaps would not tell Eros
about the blood token.

Memory of the rage and of the broken voice in which
Aphrodite spoke of the blood token causing the spell to
burn down to Eros's vitals crushed the tiny seedling of
hope. Psyche ran from the pack and weapons without
touching them. She knew Aphrodite's fear and anger
were neither a lie nor a pretense, nor was the cry about
how she had struggled for years to keep Eros alive and
Psyche had almost destroyed him. Then Eros . . . Teras
. . . was dying. Hopeless tears racked Psyche again and
her body stiffened with tension as she waited for

Aphrodite to come and say he was dead and tear her into pieces. She waited and waited, listening for the condemning step, shaking with grief and fear—but Aphrodite did not come. And when the tears were wept dry, the little hope that had been crushed was well watered and again lifted a slender, bright thread above the dark morass.

Young and strong as Psyche was, there came a limit to her endurance of being racked between hope and despair. In the very depths, while she felt that death was too good for her and any torture Aphrodite inflicted would be less than she deserved, she fell on her bed and sank swiftly through the black hole of total despond into the soft darkness of sleep. Exhaustion sank her deep; horror's hook in her soul pulled her often toward the surface. Thus the soft sound of hurried footsteps jerked her awake and she sprang from her bed still half asleep, feeling her heart pounding in her throat, and not knowing why.

The broad smile on Melba's face as she rushed in to gesture Psyche to come with her made Psyche's heart pound even harder, but with an entirely different beat. The old woman's eyes were bright and such a look of pleasure lit her face that Psyche rushed past her, down the stairs, and out into the courtyard, certain Eros himself had returned. She did not wonder why he had not come to her room himself; at first Teras had never entered the house without her invitation and her heart told her that if Teras and Eros were really the same person, Eros would extend that courtesy again until he was assured she would accept him.

The terrible shock she received when she saw Aphrodite in the courtyard numbed her so that for the moment she felt little. And in the next moment she had taken in Aphrodite's expression, and pain and fear fled and the seedling of hope sent down strong roots. There was severity in the exquisite face and anger—but no pain! No matter what Aphrodite told her, Psyche knew that Eros was not dead and not in danger of dying. The joy made her courteous.

"Lady," Psyche said, curtsying. "I thank you for your kindness. I thank you!"

"You have little cause to do so," Aphrodite said.

"But I do!" Psyche smiled brilliantly. "I know from your face that my Teras is alive and no longer in danger. No matter what else you say, or even if you punish me for the mistake that caused him so much pain, I still thank you."

"He is alive and in no danger of dying," Aphrodite snapped, "but far from recovered from what you did to him. He is very ill and it will be long before he is strong enough to leave his bed."

"I am so sorry, so sorry for his pain." Psyche's eyes filled with tears and she clasped her hands prayerfully. "You must know how much I grieve for my foolishness. Please let me come to serve him. I will do anything, anything at all. I will clean the chamberpot, scrub the floor, wash the linens—anything. I know he is angry. Let me be there—"

"You arrogant fool! You think a few words of grief and sorrow can wipe out the harm you did? Do you think that if Eros sees you doing a slave's work he will instantly forgive you and take you to his bosom again? It will be a long time indeed before you come next or nigh Eros. You will have to prove *to me* that you are worthy to serve as his slave."

Sudden rage sent flags of red to Psyche's cheeks. "How?" she shrieked, meeting Aphrodite eye to eye, her fury such that the goddess blinked. "I have been trying for half a year to think of a way to prove my love. Tell me how to prove love and I will do it."

Aphrodite laughed. "With patience. That is how love

is proved. That is the only tool you have not tried, because you are a greedy, snatching, common slut. I will teach you patience."

She raised her hands, bringing to Psyche's attention a large bag she had been holding. Suddenly she upended the bag and shook it wildly while swinging it from side to side, sending the contents showering out of its mouth over the smooth stones of the courtyard.

"There was, weighed on the finest scale in the temple of the Corn Goddess, exactly one-half stone of mixed seed. Pick them up and place them separately, each seed with its own kind." She laughed again, not kindly. "Eros will sleep for many days recovering from the injury you inflicted on him. If you can separate and gather the seeds before they sprout, he should be awake. I will come from time to time to see how you progress. When you have completed your task, I will tell him of your obedience, and I will ask him if he will deign to use you as a slave."

Psyche was so astonished that she simply stood with her mouth open, rocking a little in the rough movement of air as Aphrodite disappeared. Then she looked down at her feet, watching the seeds disperse even more widely as they were blown by the wind of Aphrodite's passage. She had expected to be ordered to perform some dangerous feat, possibly one that would likely prove fatal or end in maiming or destruction of her beauty. But this was simply useless and silly.

Insane. Aphrodite must be insane. What kind of proof of love could picking up a number beyond imagining of seeds be? Without truly thinking of what she was doing, Psyche squatted down and picked up five long seeds of wheat. As she stared at them, she saw attached to her finger a tiny rape seed. Tiny, tiny and black, almost indistinguishable from a fleck of dirt that also clung to her finger.

Her knees began to ache, but she dared not sit down because seeds would be pressed into the woolen cloth of her dress. Still not really thinking, acting by instinct, Psyche began to brush the seeds together into a heap to clear a space so she could at least sit or kneel. Sitting beside the heap, she began to pick up seeds and put them into separate piles. When she judged a candle-mark had passed, she looked at what she had done and began softly to weep.

The task was impossible. Even if she ordered the four old servants to help—and that, she was sure, would be a violation of Aphrodite's intention—there was no way half a stone of seed could be gathered and separated in a reasonable time. And likely the servants would not help, any more than they would carry a message for her.

Yet if she did not try, Aphrodite would tell Eros . . . Teras . . . that she did not care enough for him to do a task that was not dangerous but was simply dull and distasteful. Psyche's tears flowed more freely. Teras might believe that. He was already unsure that she cared for him. Aphrodite had believed she had tried to kill him to be free of him. Did he also believe it?

Psyche closed her eyes against the stabbing pain of doubt and fear. If Teras believed that, she had lost him forever and she would either be returned to her father—in which case between fear and hatred she would not long survive—or she would be abandoned here, to live alone forever. She shuddered and opened her eyes. Better to stare at the impossible task than to envision that future.

As she looked, a seed in the pile moved. The motion had no meaning for her at first; she assumed it was slipping from an insecure position. But then it slid away from the base of the pile and she saw it was being carried by an ant. Her finger went out to crush the thief before it stole the seed and made her impossible task more impossible, and then her breath sucked in.

Ants were myriad. Within her was a spell for drawing like to like. With no more clear thought, Psyche gently picked up the tiny creature and closed him in one hand. Then she used her arm to sweep the seeds away from a narrow path so she could leave the courtyard without crushing them. In the house, she gathered as many empty vessels as she could carry. Returning to the courtyard, she set one jar on its side and imaged an ant hole with its faint, odd smell, the tunnel into the earth, the many chambers within—magically a nest perfect for every ant. Then, she found the spell in her well that created likeness, and touched the jar.

She felt a slight chill as power flowed from her to the jar, but was too enthralled by seeing an impossible hole in the stone courtyard where the jar had been to consider how much she had been drained. Psyche gently placed the ant in front of it, holding her breath until she saw the ant climb into the "hole," and a little later, emerge without the seed. Hastily she took another seed of the same type and laid it in the ant's path. The creature found it, seized it, and turned toward the hole from which it had come. Psyche began to cry.

"I promise you," she whispered as the tiny creature disappeared down the hole again, "your labor will be repaid. As much as you carry today and more will be laid out for you and your kin."

By the time the ant came out of the jar the second time, Psyche had two more spells ready. One enhanced the sending of messages. Psyche hoped it would also enhance whatever one ant did to bring her fellows to the source of food she had found. The second spell was a spell of binding, which made a particular thing infinitely more desirable than any other, combined with a phrase that extended the spell to all things of the same kind. She recaptured the ant and picked up a third seed. When the ant had taken the seed, she cast the spells and found she had sagged to her knees, fortunately in the cleared path she had made. Gritting her teeth against a wave of nausea engendered by a wash of weakness, she gently set the ant down beside the "nest."

After that she felt so dizzy that her head fell forward on her chest, and for a little while she dared not lift it or open her eyes lest the vertigo sweep her into unconsciousness. Her growing anxiety overcame that fear and she opened her eyes before she was completely recovered. When she did, she almost cried out with revulsion. The courtyard was alive with moving black specks, thousands on thousands swarming everywhere, even over the hand she had placed on the ground to support herself, and the small pile of seeds she had made was heaving and squirming.

Revulsion was replaced by a hope that lifted her head and parted her lips. Out of the pile of seeds and from all over the courtyard, a thread of ants and moving seeds was stretching toward the "nest." Psyche watched the pile with a new anxiety. However, it soon lay still, cleared of the only type of seed the ants were at present willing to regard as desirable. They spread more widely over the courtyard, sometimes running over her, but not distracted by her odor or that of her clothing because they sought only one thing. And even though they traveled farther, more came so that the thin line that went down into the "hole" with seeds and returned without thickened into a cord.

Psyche spared a few moments to go within and tell the servants that they must on no account come out into the courtyard and to find more empty vessels. She returned breathing hard, as if she had run a great distance, but she was able to rest after that, sitting by the "hole" and murmuring little prayers of thanks to the

Mother—the only god she could pray to because she knew the Olympians were not divine. She was alert enough to be troubled somewhat later when she saw many ants running about aimlessly while the rope of them that carried seeds got thinner and thinner as fewer returned to the "nest." Then she realized, with a heart that began to leap between joy and anxiety, that they had collected all the seeds of the first type. Not daring to allow herself to think or doubt, she reached out for the next seed she saw and captured one of the ants on her foot. She recast the spell of binding and placed the ant and the seed she carried some distance from the "nest."

Suddenly the pile of seeds was moving again. Psyche gasped and placed her hand over the original "hole." If the ants brought back the second kind of seed, the two would be mixed and all her effort for nothing. Biting her lips, she counterspelled the "hole" to be again a jar. With the spell still rising in her, she was racked by a pang of grief for the last time she had used a counterspell. A lick of fire seemed to run through her veins as her concentration wavered, but she put aside grief, ignored both pain and weakness, and "saw" a jar, not a hole, a jar—and it was there.

She was shivering with cold, bent over the jar, which she clutched to her bosom, but she was not as dizzy and nauseated as she had been after the first spell-casting. Quickly she laid a second jar where the first had been, imaged a perfect ant nest again, and cast the spell on a second jar. A wave of weakness that covered her in a clammy sweat followed, and her head sank onto her breast, but she forced her eyes up and around and saw her little helpers busily trundling seeds into the new "nest." Triumph sang in her. Psyche lifted her head, straightened her body, and breathed deep. She had found a way to accomplish the impossible.

The triumph bore her up each time she cast her spells anew. She *would* not feel hunger and thirst because she dared not take time to eat and drink lest her helpers escape from her control. She *would* not "look" to see how dry of power was her well. Somewhere she found strength to ignore the pangs of hunger, and bit her tongue and cheeks to bring to her mouth the moisture she needed to whisper the spells. Somewhere, each time, she found the power to feed into the words. And the ants ran to and fro, and the jars filled.

Before night fell, the task was done. Until the last ant emerged from the last "nest" and none returned, hunting restlessly for the last seed, which had already been gathered, Psyche remained upright. Then she drew once more on the aching hollowness within, feeling as if the blood of her body was draining into her empty well. With that last strength she negated the spells she had been using. She watched with dimming eyes as the number of ants diminished; she watched until she saw that the black specks remaining were not moving at all. Tears gathered in her eyes for them—poor, innocent creatures driven until they died for no purpose of theirs. And weeping, she slid away into darkness, and lay in the courtyard almost as empty of life as the little husks.

CHAPTER 17

Psyche woke in her bed, first puzzled by her terrible weakness and then rigid with terror—until she saw on the chest several rows of jars. Melba, who was sitting on a stool, reached out and patted her hand, and Psyche whispered first a hoarse thanks and then a request for water. Having drunk, she repeated her thanks with fervor.

She had never dreamt the old servants would have enough initiative to ignore her command not to come into the courtyard and to gather up the jars as well as bring her in and put her to bed. Never before had they stepped outside their normal round of duties. Later, she realized that they must have been watching—and felt the magic, too—and reasoned out what she had done. Much later she discovered they were truly fond of her. At the moment, however, she was only grateful without wondering why or how. What she wanted was food, and drink, and then more food. She was at first too weak to lift herself or feed herself, but the old women, helping each other, attended to her.

When she had eaten until she could not swallow another bite, Psyche slept. When she woke, she was strong enough to sit up and, with a servant's help, empty her bladder and bowels. Relieved of those pressures, she was ravenous again, and when she had eaten, sleepy.

Psyche was not quite certain how often she repeated the pattern, although she was aware that she was stronger each time she woke. The last time her eyes opened, it seemed to be early morning and she felt no more than her usual appetite. Nor did she feel any need for a steadying arm when she swung her legs out of the bed, so she smiled and shook her head at Melba, who was again watching her.

"Thank you, but I do not need help anymore. I am well now. I cannot say how grateful I am to you and to Hedy and Titos and Kryos for your kindness and care of me. I wish I knew what you desired so I could ask Teras—"

She stopped and bit her lip. Who knew if she would ever see Teras again, or if she did, whether he would wish to reward or punish the servants for helping her. But although Melba shook her head, she smiled. Apparently the servants did not fear that any request to Teras on their behalf would bring trouble upon them. The old woman also made some gestures that Psyche thought must mean she and the other servants were happy and needed nothing.

Perhaps it was true. Certainly the servants were not overworked, although they had enough to do to keep them busy. They were well housed, well fed, well clothed, and probably too old to desire excitement for its own sake. Psyche had no idea what had caused their muteness, but she knew they communicated freely enough with each other. Thus they had companionship.

The word brought her thoughts sharply back to Teras. She looked anxiously at the jars on the chest, but they were all safe and each was covered with a piece of waxed cloth. That made Psyche frown. It indicated that she had been recovering long enough to make protection of the contents of the jars necessary.

"How long has it been since you brought me in from the garden?" she asked.

Melba held up a hand with the thumb curled under.

"Four days?" Psyche guessed.

The old woman nodded, and Psyche thanked her again and went to relieve her bladder. Then she washed and dressed and combed her hair and went down to eat in abstracted silence. She was certain Aphrodite had said she would return every few days to see how she was progressing. She put down the piece of bread she had smeared with fragrant cheese. Titos was bringing in a platter of thin-sliced cold meat.

"Has Lady Aphrodite been here?" she asked.

Titos looked puzzled, then pointed to the courtyard, to Psyche, to his eyes, to Psyche again. She understood and nodded.

"Yes, I saw her four, no, five days ago, when she came. I meant, has she come since then, during the time I was ill?"

The old man shook his head, but not with a nervous jerk or so quickly as to hint he had been ordered to deny something, nor did his hand shake as he laid down the platter. Psyche laid a slice of meat over the bread and cheese and bit into them with satisfaction. Aphrodite had not come. Her chewing paused. Did that mean that Eros was worse? She began to chew again and swallowed with an effort, then laid down the bread, her appetite diminished.

No, she would not believe that. Aphrodite had not fixed a day and would doubtless imagine her picking up one seed at a time, at which rate it would take her forever to separate the seeds. She lifted the bread to her mouth and began to eat again, less because her appetite had returned than because she knew she needed the food. She tried to bring back her joy in her accomplishment, smiling and chewing with more energy when she thought of the happy accident that had made her notice the first little thief. And then she remembered her promise: as much as this, and more. Psyche got up from the table at once and went to the kitchen.

There she explained that she needed dry bread, dry meat, and dry cheese coarsely ground. Altogether she would need more than a half stone of the mixture, but not all that day. "It is for the ants," she said, knowing the servants must have seen them swarming over the courtyard. "They fetched and carried, and not one seed did they keep, poor little creatures. Even a slave is fed for its labor. They must be paid. I will spread their ration today, and each day until they have had what I promised."

She was almost happy as she sprinkled what the servants had prepared around the perimeter of the courtyard so the ants would not need to come out into the open and risk being trod on. Then, sweeping away the dead husks and thinking of how hard the little things had worked, a new hope lifted her spirits. Had her notice of that first ant been an accident? Could a kind Mother have directed her attention? Surely it must have been the Mother who granted her strength to cast so many spells and to make them strong enough to last.

Oh, if only it were true; if only the Mother were guiding her . . . She surely needed a help and a guide. Her lips had formed into a prayer when suddenly it occurred to her that Aphrodite might come at any time, even today. Psyche gasped. "Oh, thank you, Mother," she whispered. "Indeed this is no time to waste praying. If Lady Aphrodite does come, the seeds must be gathered and weighed, ready for her."

In her workroom, Psyche had delicate scales and squares of thin silk in which she ordinarily packed dried leaves and flowers to be laid among the clothing in a chest to keep the cloth smelling sweet. Each square of silk disturbed the balance of her scale, and she placed a small metal weight in the other pan and noted the amount. Then she fetched a jar, carefully poured the seeds onto the silk, and weighed them. She noted that weight, too, then brought the corners of the silk square together and tied it firmly into a pouch.

Fourteen times she repeated the process, trying not to think of the total until she was finished. Then, breathing a prayer to the Mother, she added the amounts, subtracted the weight of the silk, and cried out in triumph. Two grains over half a stone! Her scale must be a trifle more delicate than that in the temple of the Corn Goddess—no surprise, since the latter was doubtless used to weigh larger amounts than hers—but she could not be blamed for that.

Making sure that each pouch was truly tied tight, she set each carefully into a leather bag and tied that tight over the mass so the individual pouches could not shift or rub one another loose. Now, she thought, she had nothing to do but wait for Aphrodite. Full of her triumph and the certitude of the Mother's guidance, she expected Aphrodite to appear immediately. She took her bag down to the megaron and sat with it on her lap for more than a candlemark before she began to laugh at herself.

Seemingly Lady Aphrodite was right about her lack of patience. Guidance, even favor, did not imply instant gratification. Likely Aphrodite would not come until tomorrow or even for a day or two longer. There was no sense in sitting and waiting, growing more and more anxious with each minute until she was sure to say something offensive out of pure nervousness.

The trouble was that Psyche really could think of nothing else to do, until it occurred to her that she must make ready some garments and other necessities if she were to stay in Olympus. She could not take much. Aphrodite would not expend the power to shift a chest of clothes and ornaments. Psyche went to her bedchamber, carrying her bag of seeds with her, and laid out two sets of her most delicate undergarments and two outer gowns that Teras favored. With those, she placed her comb and brush, the fine stone she used to file her nails, and the powder for her teeth. She folded all together and lifted it. She thought it light, but she decided which gown she would wear and which she would leave behind if Aphrodite did not wish to carry so much.

The morning passed. Psyche forced herself to eat, her joy in her accomplishment fading with the day. Aphrodite had been so angry. She had not promised she would take Psyche to Eros if she completed the task. And Eros must be terribly angry too. Aphrodite had said he *might* deign to use her as a slave. Slowly she went above and looked at the gowns she had chosen. Neither would be suitable for hard work. Either would soon become draggled and dirty. She would wear the garb in which she had gone gathering with Eros. It did not enhance her beauty, but Eros . . . Teras . . . cared nothing for beauty, and that dress would remind him of the laughter and labor they had shared.

Night came, and morning, and afternoon, and evening, and night again—and Aphrodite did not come. Psyche carried her bag of seeds wherever she went and tried to keep from her mind the dreadful possibility that Eros . . . Teras . . . was worse. What sparked those fears was that Teras would know how grief-stricken she was over the harm she had done him. If he knew, he would forgive her and want to comfort her. Could he have been foolish enough to try to come to her? Could he have made himself worse? He had grieved so much when he thought she did not wish to return to him.

Could he be grieving again because Aphrodite had not told him she had begged to come to nurse him, to serve him in any way?

Another day passed, and another. Each day, Psyche reviewed every word she and Aphrodite had exchanged. On the morning of the twelfth day, she opened tearstained eyes to a chamber barely gray with predawn light, struggling to free herself from a strange dream in which she ran through a forest searching frantically for Teras and knowing that if she did not soon find him she would lose him forever. She did not feel that the dream meant Teras was in danger. It was she who was in danger of losing his love. But why should she be running through the woods to find him?

She reached automatically for the bag of seeds set carefully beside her bed and wondered for perhaps the hundredth, perhaps the thousandth time, what Aphrodite meant when she said it would take Eros long and long to recover. Weeks? Possibly months. What would Teras think, fearful as he already was that she did not love him, and that perhaps she had even tried to kill him, if she did not come to him for months? He would think she did not care. Before the seeds sprout, Aphrodite had said. But in the courtyard, not buried in the earth, they would never sprout.

When that notion had first come to her, Psyche thought Aphrodite had been implying that she would have enough time to pick up and separate the seeds. She still believed her original notion was correct, but since Aphrodite had not come to check up on her industry and progress, the "comforting words" took on a sinister meaning. Aphrodite did not wish to encourage her to finish her task; she would be perfectly content to have Psyche give up in disgust.

Why? Psyche asked herself. *Why set a silly lengthy task and say she would return to see if I were obedient?*

With the dream of struggling through the forest still in her mind, the answer to that was easy: *Because it was important for me to stay at the lodge so Aphrodite, who truly loves Eros and would do nothing to harm him, could soothe him by saying truthfully that I was safe and busy. Would Aphrodite go so far as to tell Eros that she had reassured me that he would recover and that I was happy and not worried about him?*

Psyche's lips folded tightly. It would not literally be a lie. She *was* happy that Eros would recover, and she was not worried about the care he would receive. She knew that he would be seen at any moment by the best physician who had ever lived, a demigod among physicians, and that if necessary, Aphrodite would nurse him with her own hands. Psyche uttered a frightened sob. But that was not enough. Teras needed a reason to wish to recover quickly, needed to know *she* cared for him. New tears spilled down the tracks of the old. If she had been able to think of a way to prove she cared, she would never have needed to try that accursed counter-spell.

Even if Aphrodite came and accepted the separated seeds and took her to Eros, which she had not promised to do and had not even sounded willing to do, what would that prove to Teras? Might he not think that she came *because* Aphrodite brought her, as he half believed she had returned only because Aphrodite ordered her to return?

Rage dried Psyche's tears and she gnawed her lips with frustration. There was nothing she could do! Nothing! . . . Oh, yes there was. She clutched the bag of seeds to her breast, her eyes wide with joy and revelation. The chance to prove herself, which had been snatched from her when Teras had returned after his week's absence, had been offered to her again.

"Mother," she breathed, leaping out of bed, "Mother, thank you."

That was why she had been running through the woods in her dream, why she felt if she did not quickly find Teras she would lose him. Perhaps Aphrodite had no sinister intention. Perhaps she did intend to take Psyche to Eros, but that would be the wrong thing, entirely wrong.

With trembling haste she dressed in her gathering clothes. The undergarments and a single dress she wrapped firmly around the bag of seeds and thrust into the bottom of her pack. She combed her hair, dropped the comb into the pack, made braids, wound them around her head, and covered them with a woolen cap that came down over her ears. Then she belted on the long, strong knife and the pouch of useful oddments she carried when gathering, and snatched up bow, quiver, and the two light spears Teras had made for her. She started for the stairs, then bit her lip and turned instead to the book room, where she scribed on a wax tablet that, having completed her task and feeling too worried about Eros to remain idly in the lodge, she had set out for Olympus.

First she laid the tablet on the table where the servants would be sure to see it. Then she stole softly into the kitchen and filled her pack with cheese, dried meat, some bread, and a bag of flour from which she could, she hoped, make some kind of flat cake she could eat. She took, also, a fire starter and some tinder in a separate little bag and last a small, flat pan, which she laid on the top of her pack before she tied it shut.

Taking up the bow, quiver, and spears, which she had laid down, she clutched the untidy mess in her arms and went softly out of the house, through the garden, and into the woods, where she set down her awkward burden. With a deep sigh of relief, she went back to the house. Even if the servants should now be awake, she could get away without arousing any doubts in their minds. They would not be surprised by her going out of the house warmly dressed.

Returning to the kitchen, Psyche began to eat—a bowl full of wheat porridge that was always prepared at night and left to swell and stew in a covered crock on the stove, which she flavored liberally with honey, slices of cured ham on bread, washed down with a cup of wine. She realized as she was eating that she had wakened even earlier than she first thought and hurried less, eating until she was stuffed and could eat no more. Even then the sun was barely tingeing the sky with pink, and when she went upstairs for the last time, she heard movement in the womenservants' chamber. Still she was able to put on the furred cloak Teras had given her and take a warm blanket from his chamber, so that hers would be on her bed when one of the women came to make it, and get out of the house again without being seen.

Safe in the woods, she set about arranging the considerable load. When she thought all was secure, she made a wide detour around the grounds of the lodge, set her left shoulder to the brightest light, and began to walk south. Teras had told her that Olympus was south and west, set in a cultivated valley between ranges of high mountains. The lodge, she knew, was on the lower slopes of the northern chain of mountains. She would walk south until the land leveled and then turn west.

Psyche did not discount the difficulty of what she was doing, nor was she fool enough to think finding Olympus would be easy. She had heard tales of men who sought to speak to the gods and tried to find the valley. None had ever done so; those who returned said the mountains were unscalable and that there could be no valley, that the home of the gods was hidden from weak mortals. Many had never returned. Whether they died on the way, were killed when they arrived, or had been allowed to remain, Psyche did not know. However, she had several advantages: First, she knew the city was real and that "gods" were as mortal as she, although longer-lived. Second, if she met anyone from Olympus, she could say that she had been set a task by Aphrodite and was bringing the finished product. Most important of all, she was coming from Aphrodite's villa in the hills and was actually in the the valley of Olympus already. Thus, if it was spells that deceived searchers, those should not affect her, and if there were guards to kill or imprison common folk who came upon Olympus, she could demand that Eros be told of her arrival.

She set forward hopefully but did not travel very far that first day. Unaccustomed to carrying so heavy a load, she had to stop frequently to rebalance her pack, trying different positions for the blanket, the quiver of arrows, and the bow and spears until she found a solution that was both comfortable and allowed her to reach her weapons quickly. She stopped to gather, too, winter cress by a small stream she passed near noon and some very young leaves of krambe. She chewed the winter cress with a little of the bread for a meal soon after she gathered it. The krambe she folded into a damp scrap of leather from her pouch. The leaves would add flavor and bulk to the dried meat and cheese when she ate again after she made camp near evening.

The forest was very quiet and Psyche felt quite at ease in it. Teras had cleared all the dangerous wild beasts from this area, she was sure. Once in a while she heard a rustling and skittering in a patch of brush, but she knew it was only a hare or some other harmless denizen of the woods. Actually her mind was more on keeping her southerly route as the sun changed position by checking the growth of moss on the trees and exposed rocks.

When she was certain of her path, it was offense rather than defense Psyche was considering. She was trying to decide whether she should attempt to hunt, if she came to an open area where she could lie hidden, or whether she should use most of the supplies first. The safe path was to save the supplies and hunt, although fresh meat would add to her load, but lightening her pack by eating her supplies would permit her to travel faster and she might reach Olympus before the supplies were finished.

By afternoon she had decided to lighten her load before she hunted. Her shoulders were sore from the rubbing of the straps of her pack, all the muscles of her back were one painful ache, and her arms and legs felt like boiled straw. Nonetheless she went on putting one foot before the other, her right shoulder now to the greatest light, until she found she was having difficulty judging where the lightest area was and realized that the sun, if not set, was down behind the southern range of mountains. It was time to make camp.

She remembered with a warm rush of love and confidence all the things Teras had told her when they were in the woods together. She knew exactly for what to look and even how to find it and how long to spend looking before she selected a less perfect site. A lighter area above a patch of brush caught her eye and she made her way toward it to find what she sought, a small stream edged with bushes and here and there a larger tree. A little way downstream she found the perfect campsite, a huge tree against which she could set her back, whose lowest branches she could reach and use as a refuge, and whose dense foliage made a shadow that created a clear area around it.

With a sigh of relief, Psyche shrugged out of her pack

and hung it from a low branch. She allowed herself a few minutes to stretch and twist but dared not sit down lest she be unwilling to stand up again before night fell. First down to the stream to carry up enough rocks for a hearth, then to the edges of the brush to cut the driest tops of the grass and scrape dead leaves together to be crumbled with thin twigs, and finally away from the stream into the woods to find windfall, dry branches that would burn. Psyche's first twinge of dissatisfaction came while gathering firewood. She had done it many times when she and Teras gathered together, but Teras had always been there to take the largest burden and to break the sticks for her. She bit her lip. She had forgotten to take Teras's ax.

Dusk was so far advanced when she got back to her camp from the third wood gathering that she simply dropped the branches, put her tinder on a flat, dry stone near the dead leaves and twigs, and began to strike the flint against the starter stone. The shower of sparks was bright in the gathering dark, and only a few strikes brought a thread of smoke. Psyche blew very gently and a small core of red formed in the tinder. With great care she tore the unlit tinder away from the burning patch and dropped that into the nest of dead leaves and grass and broken twigs. Another session of careful breaths and a flicker of flame peeped out of the nest. Psyche added thin, dry twigs. The ungrateful flame quickly devoured the nest that had welcomed it and began on the twigs. Now that the flame was well caught, Psyche gathered up the unused tinder and put it away, added larger sticks, and finally, from several directions, thick branches, which she would push forward into the flame as the burning ends were consumed.

By the time the larger branches were aflame, Psyche was almost too tired to eat, but she got the food from her pack, folded the blanket into a cushion, and unwrapped the krambe leaves. The fresh taste revived her a little, enough to give her an interest in drawing out a stick of dried meat and cutting a chunk of cheese before she returned the food to the hanging pack. She did think of boiling the meat with a little of the flour, but that would mean fetching water from the stream and cutting up the meat, which was just too much trouble. She ate the cheese and sat gnawing on the stick of meat, leaning back on the tree.

Something shrieked in the dark, and Psyche bolted upright, her heart pounding. Nothing, she told herself. It was nothing dangerous to her, only some small creature taken by an owl or a fox, but she pushed the branches farther into the flames so that they would leap higher, and it was a long time before her breathing steadied and she leaned back against the tree again. Tears gathered in her eyes; she had enjoyed the nights she had spent in the woods with Teras. Then the dark beyond what little light the fire gave had been comforting, almost an extension of the dark in which Teras wrapped her with his warm embrace. She pulled her cloak more tightly around her. She had been warm enough while she walked and worked, buoyed up by the thought that she was getting closer to Teras, but now she was cold . . . and lonely.

Later, a moaning that moved around her brought her scrambling to her knees to throw more wood on the fire again, although she knew it had to be an owl disturbed by her presence. Still she shuddered and wept a little, wishing she had brought her book of spells and some magical herbs so she could cast a warding around her camp. Then she shivered again. She had recovered from using her magic to gather and separate the seeds, but she doubted she was strong enough to cast any spell that would last the night. It was better to be fearful and alert than to believe she was protected and fall victim to some unexpected danger. Again she leaned back against the tree.

Once more she was brought upright, but this time by a sense of falling as she slipped sideways. Despite her fear, she had fallen asleep. The fact that nothing had harmed her even though the fire was no more than embers gave her the confidence, once she had renewed the cheerful flames, to spread her blanket and lie down. She thought the feeling of helplessness brought on by being prone, intensified by the ache of longing for the times when she lay safe and warm in Teras's arms, would keep her awake, but it did not take long for the tension to drain from her tired body and for her eyes to close.

A hysterical screeching brought her abruptly awake and in another moment made her laugh. It was morning—a bright, sunny morning. Several birds now perched in the branches of the tree had taken strong exception to the swaying of the food bag below them. She did not laugh for long, however. Her first movement brought a groan. She was so stiff and sore that she would not have moved again had not an urgent need to relieve herself forced her upright.

"Damn you, Teras," she muttered through set teeth, "I'll take this out of your hide for being such an idiot."

Her fury at the suffering she was enduring just because the man would not believe she loved him lent her strength to stagger down to the stream. Once there, she washed her hands and face, wincing and shivering with cold. The icy water brought her wide awake and the activity warmed her muscles, reducing her pain just enough to allow her to become aware of violent pangs of hunger, which drove her to climb up the bank—cursing Teras's idiocy with every step—and peer into the ashes of her fire. Her muttering ceased when she discovered a few live coals and the addition of some hastily gathered dry leaves and twigs brought the fire to life again. Fortunately, there was wood enough to build it up and to cook together in the little pan a handful of flour and chopped up dried meat.

Her execrations of Teras were renewed when, her breakfast eaten, she rolled up her blanket and tried to pull on her pack. The pressure of the straps on the bruises they had made the day before was excruciating. Biting her lips in pain, Psyche unrolled the blanket and folded it so she could lay it across her shoulders as a pad. After she had loosened the straps to fit over the blanket, she was able to bear the pack.

Because she was so late starting, Psyche did not stop to eat her noon meal, although she did dig up some lily bulbs which she peeled and ate while she walked. As her discomfort diminished with the warmth of exercise, she grew more cheerful and stepped out more strongly. She was reasonably sure she had actually traveled at least as far as she had come the previous day and was looking forward to accomplishing an equal distance before having to stop when the increasing brightness of the forest ahead of her made her proceed with caution. Thus, she was in no danger when she came to the edge of the great ravine that broke the side of the mountain.

Across the huge rift, Psyche could see that the forested land sloped downward. The valley beyond was hidden, but she knew that if she followed that valley west she would find Olympus. Only there was no way across the ravine.

Psyche lay down on her belly and inched her way forward until she could look down. The face of the rock was broken here and there, small trees clung to cracks, and bushes had rooted in smaller clefts, but Psyche knew she could not climb down. Worse, the last bit that bordered the river was sheer rock, worn smooth by the rushing water. The other side was no better. It was impossible. Even if she succeeded in getting down without falling, she would have to cross the strong current and somehow find handholds and footholds in the sheer rock of the other side. Slowly Psyche sat up and closed her eyes.

Was it possible that she had been wrong to hope, that there was no way to reach Olympus? Tears of weariness and hopelessness oozed under her lids and down her cheeks. She slipped her pack from her sore shoulders and just sat, her mind essentially empty. Then she leaned over, resting on the pack, whispering, "I tried, Teras, I . . ."

His name coupled with the idea of reaching him brought back a memory of the first time she had planned to leave the lodge to get to Olympus on her own. That time Teras had returned before she could make the effort and he had been furious, thinking she was trying to escape him. Psyche opened her eyes and sat up. He had not sneered and said she could not escape; he had asked to where she intended to go! And when she had told him she had intended to go to Olympus, he had not said it was impossible.

Psyche looked left, then left. To the left, eventually, she would reach the sea and one way or another find a way to cross to the southern headland, but she had no idea how far inland she was, and Olympus should be even more inland. She crept forward again to look down at the rushing water and saw that right was upriver. Usually, the closer to its source, the smaller a river became—usually, except that she had no idea how far away the source was and it might be so far that the river increased in size before it began to decrease. Still, between one uncertainty and another, it seemed reasonable to Psyche to go west, toward Olympus rather than away from it, while seeking a place to cross.

The shock of thinking her effort all in vain, although

it had not lasted long, had tired her more than all the walking she had done. Psyche simply could not bear to lift the pack to her back again. Nonetheless, it would be stupid to stop where she was, without water or a decent sized tree, so she got to her feet and plodded westward, sometimes lifting the pack and clutching it in her arms and sometimes dragging it behind her. Both methods of bringing it along were so awkward that she had stopped to replace it on her back when she heard a sharper tinkling above the faint, dull, rushing sound of the water below. Careful listening brought her to the very edge of the ravine where, not a foot below, a spring burst out of the rock and made a bright, slender waterfall.

Leaving her pack to mark the place, she went back from cliff edge seeking a suitable tree. In this she was unsuccessful, but she soon laughed at herself. She did not need a thick trunk to guard her back. Nothing could come at her up the ravine without making so much noise that she would wake. She began to gather supplies for her fire, including three sturdy branches that she could tie together into a tripod from which to hang her pack.

The advantage to camping with no more than a couple of slender saplings between her and the edge, Psyche thought, as she lay wrapped in cloak and blanket watching the fire with heavy eyes, was that it was quieter. The ravine was too narrow, probably, for birds of prey to hunt with comfort, and no fox would be foolish enough to attempt the climb. Something about the thought seemed significant in a pleasant way, but Psyche slipped into sleep before she was able to come to grips with the idea.

She woke, the explanation clear in her mind, smiling with relief. She was certain the split in the mountain had not been too narrow for a bird of prey to dive into where she had first come upon it. Lifting her head with caution, for she remembered how sore she had been the previous morning, she looked across. It was narrower. Psyche smiled more broadly. She had been more cautious about moving, but with less reason; her muscles ached and the bruises on her shoulders hurt, but both less than they had the day before.

Partly because she found movement easier, partly because she was so eager to discover whether the ravine had been cut by the river, which went all the way back to the northern range of mountains, or was merely a split in the mountain that had filled with water from many springs like the one springing from the rock below her, Psyche was out of camp very early. She walked strongly, trying not to look over at the other side of the ravine, because she knew if she did she would be constantly elated and depressed by accidental widenings and narrowings.

By noon she was starving, and she sat down to eat the last of her bread, which was rather stale, and some gleanings of bulbs and tiny, still curled grape leaves. By evening she was glancing constantly across the divide, wondering whether if it widened again, she could come back to this place and try to jump across. She dared not try in the deceptive half light, but she could not bear to stop and camp, even though she was so tired that her knees shook, because the roar of the river below was louder and angrier. The sound made her hope there was an even narrower place ahead, and she wanted to be there to cross when she was freshest and strongest.

She struggled on and on, after a while needing to pretend it was not too dark to see, until even her fatigue could not disguise the fact that the roar of the water was fading. Then she stopped, knowing her hope had not been fulfilled. The river must be quiet, she thought dully, because the gap had broadened enough to allow it to flow silently. She was bewildered with exhaustion, wondering why she had pushed herself so hard. She must find a place to camp, she told herself, wanting only to sink down and weep. Setting her jaw, she took one more uncertain step—and found no footing.

Off balance, pressed forward by the weight of the pack on her back, and with muscles too fatigued to respond quickly, Psyche uttered a shriek of terror and fell. Her hands clutched wildly and found only grass, which tore free. She shrieked again but realized even as she cried out that she was not dropping into the depths of the ravine. She rolled only until the heavy pack braced her, and she lay, trembling and sobbing, clutching at some tough tussocks of grass until she could find the strength and courage to feel about her, first with her feet and then with her hands. Nowhere did the solid earth drop away to nothing.

When the shock of terror passed, she realized she had only tripped into a hollow in the ground and that she was safe where she was. Faint with relief, she managed to slide the pack straps off her shoulders and pull the blanket around her. Fleetingly, she was aware of hunger and thirst. She thought of a fire, but with a hazy indifference. She had no interest in trying to struggle to her feet and find firewood in the dark. Nothing was more important than rest. Psyche's eyes closed.

Thirst and the warmth and brightness of the sun on her face woke Psyche in the morning. She looked up, not into a canopy of branches and newly budded leaves, but into a clear, bright sky. Turning her head from side to side brought little change in view. She sat up to look around more carefully. Clearly she was in an alpine meadow, which extended some distance back the way she had come, from the east. Slowly Psyche shook her head at the memory of her foolishness. It was only because she had come out of the woods that she had not walked head on into a tree—or into the ravine.

She frowned as the word came to mind and got to her feet to see better. To the south the meadow sloped downward and ended in a border of trees, but she could see no ravine. And the roar of the water was diminished to a faint muttering. She must have wandered far from the edge, she thought, and then shook her head again. How could that be possible? She had been almost blind, going forward only because she was following the sound of the river.

Psyche turned around slowly, listening carefully, and then turned again. She was sure the noise of rushing water still came from the east. She might have been so dulled with fatigue that she had not noticed the sound slowly diminishing, but the last time she remembered hearing it, the roaring was so loud it had nearly deafened her.

She put the puzzle away while she relieved herself and ate some cheese, but her mouth was so dry that she could not completely satisfy her hunger. The puzzle of the sound of the river was more compelling than hunger, partly because the sound meant water and she was desperately thirsty. Bundling everything except the pot she would need for water into her pack, she set out to retrace her steps to the place of the loudest roaring in the hopes that would also be the narrowest passage across.

Close to the edge of the meadow, she found what she sought, and she was so astonished that she forgot everything else. Beyond a rise of ground, which apparently had blocked the bellowing of the struggling water, she found both ravine and river. Both began together where a torrent leapt through a huge hole in the wall of rock that ended the ravine and rushed away down the track it had carved for itself. Beyond the source, the land was whole. She now had no need to cross the ravine.

Had she wandered too close and fallen . . . Psyche first shuddered with fear and then smiled. Surely the Mother was caring for her, guiding her; surely She wanted her to find Olympus. Psyche glanced at the furious fall of water and shrugged. She was not going to attempt to dip a potful out of *that* cataract; she would find a spring or a stream elsewhere.

CHAPTER 18

Four days later Psyche looked out from a patch of woods across tilled fields, already carpeted with sturdy shoots of grain, stretching in every direction. Beyond the fields was a road, and in the far distance she was sure she could see a thread of smoke rising into the sky. She had been aware for the past two days that she was approaching inhabited land. The meadows she passed had shown clear signs that they had been grazed over in the past. That was an advantage; at this season they were alive with young hares and she had eaten well.

A second advantage had been to give her time to think about what she should do when she met someone. Her first instinct had been to ask for directions to the city, but then she realized that would be a terrible error. If she met a stupid peasant who knew only that strangers were to be killed at once, she might never get to say she was coming at Aphrodite's order. It would be best, she decided, to be as near the gates as possible and walk right in as if she knew where she were going. Once inside the city, she could ask directions to Aphrodite's house, saying she was a servant of . . . of Athena—no, that would not do, Athena would not be likely to send messages to Aphrodite. One of the male Olympians.

It was fortunate she had made the decision, for in the

afternoon of the previous day she had had to make an instant choice of being discovered or taking to a tree to avoid notice by a swineherd and his charges. Psyche had approached each meadow cautiously, fearful of shepherd or kineherd and the herd dogs, but she had not expected swine in the woods at this season. She had barely escaped and did so only because though swine were fierce and dangerous, they were not hunters. They would not cluster around the base of the tree yelping and looking up, as shepherd dogs would. Since they did not consider her a danger, they had passed, indifferent, and had not called the swineherd's attention to her.

The encounter had provided another advantage. The swine had left tracks and rooted up places, and since they were going in what she believed was the right direction, they provided a better guide than judging by the sun and other signs. And they had proven a reliable guide, Psyche thought, watching the fields and the road. Olympus must be ahead, along that road. The question now was, how far ahead? Certainly it was not in sight, and if she were caught wandering in the fields or on the road far from the city, the excuse she had planned to give might not be accepted.

She would have to travel at night until she saw the walls, Psyche decided. Then she would have to find a place to hide for the rest of the night so that she could approach and possibly enter the gate with the farmers and tradesmen who arrived every morning. She slipped off her pack, which was much lighter now, and took out some strips of hare, killed in the morning and roasted the night before after she was certain the swineherd was far beyond the light of her fire and the smell of her cooking.

Naturally, there had been nothing to glean after the passage of the swine. She chewed the meat slowly, and took out and then stored away again the last of her cheese. Although birds and hares might be plentiful in the fields, she dared not hunt them in daylight and doubted her ability after dark. Perhaps there would be lily bulbs by the side of the road; they grew there in Iolkas, so perhaps they would in Olympus. If not, she would have to go hungry. It would do her no harm to fast for a day. Water? Her eyes lifted to the thread of smoke in the distance. Where there was a house there would be a stream or a well. She would not go thirsty. And she might reach Olympus this very night.

Psyche not only reached Olympus but walked right into the heart of the city without realizing it. Having managed to sleep a few hours in the afternoon, despite her rising excitement and fear that Aphrodite would turn her away, she set out at dusk. There were no people in the fields or on the road, and she needed some light to pick her way through the growing crop so as not to leave a clear trail of crushed plants.

There had still been a glimmer of light when she reached the road, and she hesitated, fearful of being seen. After a moment she decided to walk on, thinking it would be more dangerous to appear furtive by trying to hide. However, she met no one and continued more boldly as night deepened. The moon rose in time for her to notice a small, placid pool not far from the road. There she stopped to rest and drink her fill. She had been trembling with nervousness before she reached that place, but found herself calmed by the aura of peace. As her stomach stopped fluttering, Psyche realized she was hungry, and she took out and ate her last piece of cheese. She was certain now there was no need to hoard food. The place was not wild, but a carefully tended shrine.

When she stepped out onto the road again, she found it was smoother, the ruts filled. The city must be near, she thought. Confirmation of that thought came in what Psyche judged was less than a candlemark when she came in sight of a walled enclosure. She stopped abruptly, holding her breath with fear that a challenge would come from a watcher on the wall. But no one called out, and she could see no sign of guards. Cautiously she drew closer. The absence of guards was odd, but from the curve of the wall she could see, and from which she could estimate the amount of ground the walls must enclose, Psyche judged that they surrounded a great manor house.

Eventually a closed gate broke the wall. Psyche again held her breath, expecting a challenge, and then, when none came, she darted past the gate to the other side of the road. There, in the shadow of a large tree, she stopped. Beyond the gate, the road changed from smooth earth to slabs of stone. At first she had almost believed it to be a solid stone causeway, then she saw the regular cracks. When she started forward she realized the slabs were so well fitted that she could not detect the joinings with her feet.

She walked slowly at first, peering anxiously ahead, certain that she would see the walls of the city in the moonlight, but there was only the road, curving gently and bordered by tall shadows that must be trees. After a while she walked more quickly, not noticing in the dark the narrow pathways between the regularly spaced trees that led back to hidden manors. She was looking for walls. No city she knew lacked walls. Sometimes a town near a king's walled palace did not bother with defensive enclosure; there the inhabitants expected to be sheltered in the palace in return for fighting to protect it.

Suddenly the road opened out into a wide rectangle. To the right and the left, branches led away from the main trunk, but Psyche barely noticed them. She was looking down the broad vista to its far end where a palace, gleaming white in the moonlight, faced her across the open space. No walls. Olympus had no walls! Psyche shivered. Such arrogance. And then she shivered again. Olympus had no walls because the Olympians had no fear of being attacked. She remembered now that Teras had never mentioned gates or walls when he spoke of the city.

Psyche stared, enraptured by the beauty and chilled by her knowledge of the horrors that had wrought that palace. Zeus's palace—Kronos's really. Teras had told her of the driven slaves who had built and polished that palace when he was trying to explain why the punishment for serving a master like Kronos had been just. Of course, it had not been the plight of the slaves that distressed Teras but how he had been used to apply similar enslavement to his own people.

A rise of resentment banished the awe engendered by the magnificent building. Slaves, nothings, that was all the native people were to the Olympians. She remembered her first conclusion when she learned that Eros and Teras were the same, that Eros had been playing a cruel joke on her, but before she could throw her pack on the ground and walk out of the city again, she also remembered Aphrodite's anguish and that she had said she would not strike Psyche dead only because Eros, desperately ill as he was, had pleaded for her. He did love her, native though she was, and she would teach him, through that love, that people were people, native and Olympian alike.

While she struggled with her memories, Psyche's eyes had dropped from the great palace. Now she looked from side to side, deliberately avoiding that cruel magnificence. She realized that the open space before her was the agora, the open market free to all, and to either side were the long buildings with their covered porticoes that housed the permanent shops. A flicker of warmth surged up in Psyche as she remembered that her own shop would be in one of those buildings. And thought of the shop, which sold lotions and dyes and unguents to make the beautiful more beautiful, reminded her of her tangled hair and odorous clothes.

Panic surged up. She would be seen as an intruder as soon as the sun rose. No Olympian would have a servant who was so dirty. She swallowed. Where there was an agora there was a well. She did not need to be dirty. She could wash, yes, and comb her hair and wear the gown she had carried. Psyche drew a deep breath. She would look no different than any other woman on the street if she packed away her dirty clothes in her pack and wrapped the pack in her blanket as if she were carrying laundry. Perhaps her gown was too fine for a servant . . . but perhaps it was not. Who knew how an Olympian would dress a favorite servant.

The well . . . Psyche looked out over the empty agora, but she could see no sign of a well head. It might be anywhere, she thought, shrinking internally from the idea of searching for it, the one moving figure in that whole empty space. And then she remembered the pool and the peace that surrounded it. If there were no walls, there would be no gate to pass, no guards' questions to answer. She could walk into the city at any time; if she appeared neat and well dressed, no one would question her. And she could ask directions to Aphrodite's house from anyone in the agora. She smiled as she turned and started back toward the pool far more briskly than she had come away from it. When she was in the agora tomorrow, she thought, striding along, she would just take a peek at her shop.

It was a beautiful shop, quite beautiful, with the pots of unguent arranged most elegantly on well-wrought shelves, the packets of herbs for healing potions displayed at the foot of clever drawings that showed a disordered and a cured person, and in small bins the parchment rolls with recipes for possets and poultices. The only thing she did not like were the symbols painted on the doorjamb which said "By permission of the Lady Aphrodite." It reminded her too vividly of how dependent upon Aphrodite Teras really was.

It was not fair, Psyche thought, as she stood at the opening of the lane that led to Aphrodite's house, to which the shop attendant had directed her without the smallest hesitation. She had built the business in that shop with her own hands and wits—and Teras's help. They could live, and live well, without Aphrodite. Perhaps they could not afford so grand a house as the lodge or four servants, but to be free of obligation would be well worth a simpler style of life. If she could convince Teras . . . Her heart sank. Not Teras, Eros. And she did not know Eros at all.

Why was she doing this? Psyche wondered. She did not love Eros. She did not even *like* Eros. In fact, what she had seen of him in her father's palace had given her a strong distaste for Eros. She almost turned away; however, her sturdy common sense pointed out that without Eros she could not have Teras and that she was dwelling on these foolish ideas anyway only because she was afraid to enter and confront Aphrodite.

Shame and a prickle of rage drove her forward along the path to a gate in a wall. Psyche looked at the wall, which plainly was for privacy, not for defense, feeling almost offended. Then she shrugged. What was the use of a defensible wall when a great mage could fly over it or blast it to bits? While the idea had flitted through her mind, she was looking for a bellpull or a gong to strike, but she found none. Exasperated, she put her hand on the gate to rattle it and found it was not fastened shut.

Beyond was a large courtyard, empty and silent. Psyche stopped and looked about nervously. It was wrong. At this time in the morning, servants should still be busy in the coutryard. Nonetheless, she saw all was in order, the stone flags swept clean, the dew dried from the benches. Psyche drew a deep breath and started forward again. Perhaps Aphrodite had her cleaning done by magic. From what Teras had said, Aphrodite had a unique way of purchasing spells—at worst for little cost and at best with a profit of pleasure for herself.

She pushed the disrespectful thought out of her mind and stepped onto the portico with a strange feeling of unreality. The door did have a bellpull and Psyche tugged at it, relieved to hear chimes that sounded faintly on the other side of the door. In only a few moments, the door opened and Psyche stared with widening eyes at an empty corridor.

"Yes, lady?"

The shrill little voice made Psyche gasp and look down to where the sound came from. A cherub smiled brightly up at her, a dear little girl about five years old, with round, rosy cheeks and silk flowers in her dark, curly hair. She was clothed in a dainty tunic.

"Is that for Lady Aphrodite?" the little girl asked, reaching for the bundle Psyche carried.

"It is too heavy for you, child, and I must give it to Lady Aphrodite myself," Psyche said, shaking off her surprise and recalling that Teras had told her that Aphrodite was served by the children "sacrificed" to her and that the mites were well cared for and happy. "Will you tell Lady Aphrodite that Lady Psyche has completed the task set her and has brought the seeds she desired?"

"I will see if she is awake," the child said. "You can wait in the reception chamber."

She stood aside for Psyche to enter, then closed the door, waving toward an arch that opened into a large chamber furnished with groups of chairs and couches. Before Psyche could move or speak again, the little one had skipped along the corridor and disappeared through another opening. Psyche stood biting her lip, furious with herself for not asking about Teras—no, Eros. The child would not know the name Teras. Well, it was too late for that, and Eros might still be too angry to see her. Nor, on second thought, did she think it would be wise to try to circumvent Aphrodite's commands—more than she had already done by coming to Olympus instead of waiting at the lodge.

"Who are you?" another childish voice asked, this one less shrill.

Psyche started and looked down again. It was a boy child this time, older, perhaps seven, also dark-haired and dark-eyed. The question was curious, not insolent, and unafraid.

"I am the Lady Psyche," she said, smiling despite her growing fear that Aphrodite would send her away and never tell Eros she had come, but she still dared not ask for Eros. "I have come to see the Lady Aphrodite."

"Did that silly Chloe forget to tell you to sit down?" the boy asked, frowning. "She is only little and does not know all the proper ways. Where did she go?"

But before Psyche could answer, Chloe popped out into the corridor again and seeing the boy with Psyche said crossly, "It is my turn to answer the door, Daphnis. Lady Psyche is my charge. Go away."

"But you left her standing in the hallway, and—"

"I did not! I told her to go into the reception room. It is your fault she is standing here because you stopped her and were talking to her."

"Children," Psyche said softly, "do not quarrel. You

have both done very well. Am I to go in to Lady Aphrodite now, Chloe?"

"Not yet," Chloe replied. "Lysis said she was awake, but not yet ready to receive a guest. She will come for you when the lady is ready. And I am to fetch cakes and wine."

"I will fetch the cakes and wine," Daphnis said. "You will spill everything."

"No, I will not," Chloe cried, indignantly, turning away and starting down the corridor. "Lysis said I should."

"Lysis is as silly as you are," Daphnis riposted, hurrying away after the girl child. "She should know you are still too young to be serving. You are only starting to open the door."

Psyche, her heart lightening, watched them turn a corner and disappear down what must be a central corridor, then entered the reception room. They were adorable, so eager to perform their tasks, so happy about their duties, and without the smallest anxiety; they must be instructed with love. She was growing more hopeful that she would not be turned away without even seeing Aphrodite. No one who was so kind to children could be entirely heartless.

Aphrodite loved children and was not heartless, but it was neither kindness nor sympathy that prevented her from having Psyche immediately transported back to the lodge. First astonishment and then fury had swept through Aphrodite when Lysis reported that a Lady Psyche was waiting to give her a package. Her next impulse had been to be rid of Psyche as quickly as possible; however, she had realized at once that sending her back to the lodge could serve no purpose and having her killed would be a disaster. She could not hide the fact that Psyche had come. By now probably all the children knew and most of them were too young to keep secrets. Sooner or later Eros would learn, and actually he had foreseen this. Aphrodite bit her lip, recalling the conversation they had had only a week past, when he had said he could bear the separation from Psyche no longer and must go to her.

"Do not be so silly," she remembered saying. "You know it will do you much harm to invoke a travel spell. Asclepius will feed you poison if you undo all the good he has done you and make him start all over again."

"Yes, but you do not know Psyche," Eros had said, frowning but with a hint of pride. "If she grows impatient, she is likely to do something dangerous."

Aphrodite had tried to look puzzled. "Well, she did seem worried about you and asked to come to care for you, but she settled down eagerly to her task. I am sure—"

"Why do you not bring her?" he had interrupted eagerly. "If she is here, I will not be so restless—"

"Eros!" Aphrodite remembered how exasperated she had felt because she believed he was creating the woman he desired instead of seeing what Psyche really was—but she did not say that. She knew that the more she criticized Psyche, the more virtues Eros would see in her. Instead she had said, "If Psyche were here, you know you would not be willing to sleep away three-quarters of every day. You would want to talk to her, play games with her—and that will be fine when you are no longer in pain. Worse yet, I cannot imagine you sleeping quietly at night, when you are aware of her. Behave yourself. You are acting like a two-year-old child."

Eros sighed. "Will you go to her and tell her I will come when I can?"

"There is no need." Aphrodite remembered the irritated patience she had felt. "I have told you before that I set her a silly, harmless task which can be completed only in the lodge itself and promised when it was done that I would bring her to you if you were still ill. She was quite happily employed with it and will stay that way until you are well. Now, drink this and go to sleep again so that you can sooner be with your Psyche."

And last night Eros had been after her again to assure Psyche she was forgiven and that he would come to her, and she had soothed him by promising she would—but it was already too late. It seemed there *was* more to Psyche than a simple native beauty. Aphrodite remembered that notion had crossed her mind before and she had dismissed the idea. She would not do that again; however, she had better tell Eros at once that Psyche had come.

She dressed, drew a cloak over her head, and passed quietly through the inner courtyard to Eros's wing of the house. She found him in his bedchamber, dressed in the tunic he had worn the previous evening and staring out a window, but clearly not seeing anything, because he started when she spoke his name.

"Did you go to bed at all?" she added sharply.

"No," he replied, turning toward her but not looking up. "It is useless. I spent all night thinking over what you said. If I cannot use a translocation spell, I will walk back. She—she does not trust you, I fear, and a makework task will not hold her long. I am physically well now, and the better I am physically, the worse I feel in my heart. I cannot bear being parted from her."

"Are you going back as Teras or Eros?" Aphrodite asked.

The beautiful green eyes met hers and she sighed at the pain in them. "I cannot go as Teras," he said. "And if I go as Eros—"

"Well, you can save yourself the trouble of worrying about it," she snapped. "You were quite right. Psyche did not wait. She is here."

"Here?" He jumped to his feet.

Aphrodite caught at his arm. "Wait and think!"

"But if she is here—" His voice checked and the joy in his face was overcast with trouble. "But how did she come? How *could* she come?"

"You see? Already you are bitten by doubt. You will be eaten alive by it if you do not find some way to content yourself. Listen to me: no person, even if she got the servants to help her, could have completed the task I set her in less than several moons. If she has completed it, it was by magic."

"She is so clever," Eros said, smiling—in Aphrodite's opinion, fatuously. "I cannot imagine how she did it."

"Neither can I, but that is scarcely the point. If she has power, why did she lie to you?"

"I do not know, but she was truly drained near to death when I brought her back from Iolkas. Only . . . only I do not know for what purpose her power was drained. And—and that was no mean spell she used to break Hecate's magic. I do not know." He drew a deep breath. "But it does not matter, my dear friend. She has destroyed me already. If she wishes to kill Teras, I will die gladly. If she wishes to torment Eros, I must endure. I *want* her. I *need* her." He laughed, suddenly, though his eyes were full of tears. "In her presence, even my doubts are half joy, whereas when we are apart, there is nothing but black misery laced with red pain."

For a moment Aphrodite said nothing as she fought to swallow her rage. Before she could speak, Eros laughed again more naturally.

"I remember before I went to Iolkas the first time, that I felt as if I were being slowly encased in ice. I was numb and nothing could touch me except sometimes a little warmth from your kindness, and I was very, very tired. I asked the Mother why I should walk and talk among the living when I was dead already and wished that I were either dead or alive. I was sure, because I had lived so long, that She would bless me with death, but She has a very strange sense of humor."

"Idiot!" Aphrodite said, laughing. "Everyone knows to be careful about asking gifts of the Mother. You are too likely to get *exactly* what you asked for, which was not what you meant at all. But I think She must love you almost as much as I do because She has blessed me with knowledge of a way to assuage those doubts of yours."

"Can you?" He jumped up, seized her, and kissed her. "You are never tired of helping me, and you should be. By now, I should think you would be glad to be rid of me."

"No, love," Aphrodite said, returning his embrace. "I will never be rid of you. You are a part of me."

Eros tilted up Aphrodite's chin so he could look into her eyes. "If you can do this, if Psyche is what I believe she is, you will be repaid manyfold because you will have two friends, two to laugh with." Eros's eyes gleamed with hope and enthusiasm.

Aphrodite heard the words but shut her mind against the incredibly appealing notion of a woman friend, a woman who would not envy and resent her. Ridiculous. Psyche had hated her even before she had needed to try to protect Eros. One last throw of the bones, Aphrodite thought. Either this ploy would assure Eros of the girl's devotion and bring him peace—until he realized Psyche was aging and dying—or he would learn she was a light-minded whore and grow indifferent enough to put her aside . . . or die of his grief.

Unable to resist Eros's eager hope, Aphrodite had smiled back at him despite her dark thoughts. If only

Psyche were not a short-lived native. If only the girl's life could be extended . . . Aphrodite's lip caught between her teeth as what she was about to say made a new connection in her mind. Psyche *had* used power to separate the seeds. If she had power, she might live longer . . . Eros had cocked his head at her extended silence and she pushed the little hope/fear away. It did not matter now. The immediate problem was Eros's uneasy mind. Aphrodite knew her plan must be tried.

"Since Psyche must have used magic to complete the task I set her," Aphrodite said, "I can claim she did not fulfill the bargain and set her another task. I will bid her fetch me wool from the fleece of the burning sheep—"

"No!" Eros exclaimed, stepping back as if Aphrodite had become loathsome. "That is too dangerous." His eyes grew hard and his lips thinned. "Are you jealous, Aphrodite? Are you trying to kill my love?"

"Do not be such a fool!" Aphrodite spat back, both hurt and guilty. "What good would that do me? If she died trying to prove her love of you, would you not hasten to follow her? Would I not lose you entirely? And when have I ever been jealous of any person you took to your bed?" She shuddered delicately. "That is not what I want of you, and you know it."

"Then why so dangerous a task?" Eros asked, frowning. "I would not blame her if she refused to go."

"Blame her? No," Aphrodite said thoughtfully. "If she did refuse, of course, you will know the limit of her love—although that does not mean she does not care for you, only that she does not care enough to risk her life. But I do not think she will refuse. As you say, she is very clever. She found a way to separate those seeds and she found a way to get here. I think she will agree."

"Clever is as clever does," Eros said. "But those 'sheep' would think nothing of savaging a lion, and the way to their 'pastures' is not safe. No, I am not sure I could snatch wool from one of those sheep. I cannot agree that Psyche should try so dangerous a feat alone."

Aphrodite uttered a huge, ostentatious sigh. "I hope Psyche *is* as clever as she seems, because you certainly have lost any fleck of good sense you once had in that beautiful head of yours. I do not intend her to go alone—although it would be better if she thought she was alone. Naturally, you will follow her. You will then be able not only to protect her but to judge how much power she has, how she obtains it, how she uses it, and possibly even why she has kept it secret from you."

Eros stood still, biting his lip, and shaking his head in a worried way. "It would still be too dangerous," he muttered. "If I follow close, she will know I am there, and if I keep my distance, she could be hurt, even killed, before I could reach her."

Aphrodite shrugged. "But if you do not go with her, you will learn nothing."

For another moment Eros stayed silent, biting his lip. Then his face was lit by a beatific smile. "Oh yes, I will," he crowed. "Atomos, the suitor who left Psyche rather than cross Aphrodite's will, will meet her 'by accident' by the river, which she must follow to come to where the burning sheep live. So I can protect her, and Atomos can tempt her to abandon Eros—" His voice shook and he stopped speaking abruptly and swallowed.

"It is a good plan, better than mine," Aphrodite said sharply. "You will know one way or another what she is. If she will take another man while she believes you are still lying ill from a spell she cast, she is not worthy of your pain." He stepped back, shaking his head, and she reached out and grasped his arm so hard her fingers grew white and his flesh ridged up between them. *"You must know."*

He stared defiantly, looked away and dropped his head, then raised it. "She will be true," he said.

CHAPTER 19

In the grip of rising hope, Psyche had eaten the excellent cakes and drunk the wine the children brought. Their compromise had amused her: Chloe carried the silver plate with the cakes, which provided little chance for accident, and Daphnis bore the tray with the beautiful flagon of wine and delicate—but breakable—cup for drinking. She was a little surprised when Daphnis settled onto a comfortable cushion near the door, but only for a moment. Clearly he was there both to provide service and to make sure she was not free to wander about without someone's knowledge.

Again the temptation rose to ask about Eros, to ask to be taken to him, and again she subdued it. To occupy her mind, she asked instead, "Have you served Lady Aphrodite long?"

"Oh, yes," Daphnis responded. "A long time. I was littler than Chloe when I came."

"And did you not miss your mama and papa, because you were so little?"

The child looked puzzled. "I do not remember." Then he laughed. "I cried because I was afraid. All the little ones cry, but nurse gave me food and it was warm here."

The poorest of the poor, Psyche thought. Of course

they are happy—warm and fed and dressed in what they could not dream of—no, they were too young when "sacrificed" to think of clothes. But why so young?

"And do you do all the work of the house?" It seemed impossible to Psyche that these children could move furniture or cook, yet she had seen no one but the two children. "That seems hard to me."

Daphnis laughed. "No, the servants do that. We only open the door and run messages and carry refreshment and suchlike. The servants do not come out of their quarters when Lady Aphrodite and Lord Eros are awake and about."

Psyche's breath caught. "Lord Eros is about?" she asked quickly.

"I have not seen him," Daphnis said. "Did you know he was very sick? A bad lady hurt him." His eyes grew large and round. "He was almost dead—all white and wet and cold, Niki said. Niki was frightened. He cried, and he is too old for crying." The child shivered. "Bad! It was bad to hurt Lord Eros."

Psyche was stricken mute. She could only stare at the child with eyes almost as large as his own. Daphnis nodded. "Bad. If we are bad we are sent away and never come back. We—"

"You are all great chatterboxes."

Although the voice was kind, both Daphnis and Psyche jumped to their feet. Daphnis laughed, seized Aphrodite's hand, and kissed it, and Psyche sank into a curtsy. Aphrodite bent and kissed the little boy's head, then freed her hand and patted him firmly on the buttocks.

"Run away now, love," she said, "and see that we are not disturbed." She watched him go, then turned to Psyche, who had come erect.

"I have completed my task, Lady Aphrodite," Psyche said very stiffly. "Since I knew you would not expect me to finish so soon, I thought I had better bring the fruits of my labor to you here in Olympus rather than wait at the lodge, perhaps for weeks or months. I was eager, also," her voice quivered, and she stopped, bit her lip, and then went on, "to hear how Teras was progressing."

"You are very sly and very bold," Aphrodite said. "What magic did you use to get here?"

"Magic? None. I came afoot—"

"In that dress, with your hair so carefully done?"

"Not in this dress, of course. I carried it, hoping—"

"Put aside your hopes for now," Aphrodite interrupted sharply. "Eros is still abed, and I will not allow you to spoil his recovery by causing him any excitement. You little fool! Did you not guess that was one reason why I set you such a task, to keep you from coming here and disturbing him? It is not possible for you to have completed the task by yourself or even with help. You cheated! You used magic."

"You did not forbid me to use magic, madam," Psyche replied. "So I did not cheat. I will not ask to see Teras if that would do him harm, but I think I deserve to know that you will tell him that I have come."

She had not really expected that her original request to see Teras would be granted and her disappointment over Aphrodite's refusal was not very great. In fact, she was surprised and pleased that Aphrodite had said she must put aside her hopes to see Teras "for now"— particularly after Daphnis had innocently confirmed Aphrodite's accusation that she had injured Teras badly. She hated to admit it, but she felt more relief than pain over escaping the need to face a furious . . . Eros. All Psyche wanted now was to be sure Teras would be told that she had come. Once he knew that,

she did not doubt he would quickly forgive her and
return to her.

"I did not know you had any magic to use," Aphrodite said indignantly. "And stop using that stupid
name! His name is Eros. When you went to Iolkas, you
told Eros you could not return to him because you
could not power the translocation spell. But you can
use magic, so you lied about that—"

"I did not!" Psyche exclaimed. "I did not have
enough power for so great a spell. I drained myself until
I fell unconscious. I never lied to Teras, never." Furious, because she knew what this new accusation meant,
she cried out, "I do not know Eros. I do not want to
know him. I want my Teras, my monster, not your
accursed Eros."

"They are the same, you stupid slut," Aphrodite
snapped. "Give me the seed."

Psyche had to bite back an even more furious retort,
and her teeth ground together as she lifted her bundle
to the table and untied the thongs that held the blanket
around it. Unaware of the open amazement that flashed
over Aphrodite's face, she laid aside her bow and quiver
and the belt that held pouch and knife and opened the
pack. She drew out first her soiled traveling garb, then
the remaining leather-wrapped strips of broiled rabbit,
and finally the leather sack. Having restored the clothing and food to the pack and folded the blanket over
her weapons, she opened the sack and laid out the
fourteen small bags of grain.

Before Psyche had finished setting the little cloth
bags in a row, Aphrodite had untied the mouths of two
of them. The Olympian stared for a moment at the two
piles of seed: One was of tiny, black specks in which any
other seed would show up like a torch on a dark night.
The other was small, round, shiny husked seeds that

would also readily expose contamination with another variety.

"How?" Aphrodite asked. "I will not believe you gathered these up and sorted them in a week's time. You say you did not use magic—"

"I said nothing of the sort," Psyche retorted, expecting this was some new trap. Aphrodite had said she would not allow Psyche to see Eros—for now. That implied she would be allowed to see him sometime . . . provided Aphrodite could find no new excuse to prohibit her visit. "I said I had not enough power for a translocation spell, but apparently I do have enough for small illusions and other small spells. I saw an ant taking a seed—"

"An ant?" Aphrodite repeated, completely at a loss.

"The seeds were myriad, but ants, too, are myriad," Psyche said, and told how she had beguiled the ants into doing the work and how she had repaid them.

There was a silence. Aphrodite's lovely eyes were fixed firmly on the floor and her lips pursed hard. Despite the effort, at last she laughed. Then she shook her head.

"You are very clever; however, the task I set you was not a test of cleverness but of patience. So you completed the task, but all to no purpose, because you failed the test. Eros is not yet ready to judge you, but I will have to tell him, when he is ready, what you have done."

Psyche shrugged. "That will scarcely shock him. Teras . . . Eros knows that patience is not my greatest virtue."

Aphrodite had to struggle again with the impulse to laugh. "Very well," she said, "I will set you another task. This one will indeed test your cleverness"— Aphrodite's eyes flicked to the weapons covered by the blanket—"and your courage too."

She paused, her brows raised as if she were challenging Psyche to protest, but Psyche said nothing. She simply stared back at Aphrodite with her mouth set hard.

"There is a river that flows from the southwest to the northeast across the western edge of the valley of Olympus," Aphrodite continued. "On the north bank of the river, many leagues to the west of the city, there are wild beasts called the sheep of the burning fleece. Bring me back that leather bag full of their wool."

Psyche's heart sank. She had known Aphrodite had intended that she fail to gather the seeds. She had not been surprised when the Olympian had claimed her use of magic was cheating and negated the completion of the task, but she had been beguiled by Aphrodite's tenderness to the children into believing she would be treated fairly. This, however, she sensed, was no test; it was a trap.

"No," she said, "not unless—"

"You refuse?"

Psyche saw the flicker in Aphrodite's eyes and said. "I am willing to fetch the wool, but first I must see Teras."

"There is no such being as Teras," Aphrodite said icily.

"Very well," Psyche snapped, "Eros. I wish to be certain he knows I was here—that I came all this way to see him—"

Psyche's voice caught as she suddenly wondered why she could not simply walk past Aphrodite, find Teras's room, and look at him. She would see soon enough whether he was so ill that speaking to her would harm him. Her eyes blazed and she stepped toward Aphrodite, who gave back a step, but laughed.

"If you intend to knock me down and force your way into Eros's presence," she said, "I warn you to think twice. You will do him irreparable harm, and if you make one bruise on me, Eros will never forgive you. He may love you, but he has been my friend for eons." Then she shrugged. "You are not important enough to lie about, and you are a fool to think I would try. The children have seen you. How could I silence them? I will make no bargains with you. Do as I bid you, or go."

"Go where?" Psyche put a hand on the table, fighting to keep from trembling with defeat.

"Wherever you like. I could not care less."

No, Psyche thought, she would not yield so easily. She drew herself up. "Sooner or later, no matter what trials you set me, I will see Ter—Eros. Whatever hurt I did him, he will soon understand that I meant him no harm—as I would understand if he hurt me. He does love you, Lady Aphrodite, but he loves me, too. I do not wish to carry such bitterness and spite in my heart that I will speak ill of you to one who loves you and would be hurt by my words, even if he knew them to be true. Will you not at least promise that you will tell him the truth when I return?" Psyche still stood tall, but her eyes were full of tears. "I will swear not to disturb him if you think it would hurt him to see me. I just want to look at him . . ."

"Look at who, Eros?"

"No!" Psyche exclaimed, and hid her face in her hands.

"But that is who you would see," Aphrodite pointed out, her voice softer, almost sympathetic. "He could not wear the cloud of blackness even if he wished. You burned that spell away. Think about it, Psyche. It is Eros you would see. But yes, I will promise even more than you ask. If you return and you still wish it, you will see Eros, and if he is willing, speak to him."

"Thank you," Psyche said, responding more to the kinder voice than to the promise. "Thank you." She hesitated; then, moved by an impulse she did not understand but could not restrain, she went on in a rush. "I am torn apart, lady. I love Teras, but I do not know if I could bear it that Teras, whom I love, should wear Eros's face. I do not even like Eros."

Something in her voice or expression apparently struck Aphrodite as exquisitely funny. The Olympian burst out laughing and laughed and laughed. When she had gasped herself into silence, to Psyche's surprise, there were tears in her eyes, and not tears of laughter.

"I wish you had been born an Olympian," she said.

It was like a slap in the face. Because she was a native, she was not good enough for Eros. Angered, Psyche turned away, about to take up her pack and leave without another word, but common sense prevailed. She turned back and said coldly, "If I am to make another long journey, I must have supplies. Is there a place in Olympus where I will be permitted to wash my traveling clothes and sell this gown to buy some food?"

Aphrodite shook her head. "This is a test, not a sentence of execution. My servants will see to your clothing and provide any supplies for your journey. I would suggest that you remain here until morning. You may ask the children for anything you need or desire."

She went to the open arch and clapped her hands. In a few moments, a young girl, about nine, came in, bowed to Aphrodite, and asked, "How may I serve you, Lady?"

"For today by serving Lady Psyche, who will be our guest."

Aphrodite nodded and walked out. The girl smiled at Psyche and said, "I am Lysis. We do not often have guests—at least, not lady guests—so if I forget something, please just remind me. You will want to see your

chamber first, I imagine, and then perhaps you would
like a bath?"

"A bath," Psyche breathed. "How wonderful."

Wonderful it had been. When Psyche started off the
next morning, just as dawn was tinting the eastern sky
with pink, she was still utterly confused. Harsh as
Aphrodite's manner and words had been, the treatment
provided by her household had been just the opposite.
Not that Psyche had been able to think about it while
she was enjoying it. The exhaustion of her journey
topped by the violent emotions engendered by reaching
her goal and the confrontation with Aphrodite had
overwhelmed her as soon as she sank into the hot water
of the luxurious bath. She had barely been able to crawl
out and stagger to an adjoining chamber, where she fell
into the bed and quickly went to sleep.

She had not thought once then, or even when she was
wakened by Lysis to eat a lavish meal, to ask that her
traveling garb be cleaned and some supplies be packed.
Oddly, despite the hours she had slept, she had almost
fallen asleep over her dinner and had to be helped back
to bed. When she was wakened by Lysis in the gray
light before dawn the next day, she had realized the
food had been drugged and thought it a mean spiteful-
ness, an excuse to send her off in her filthy clothes with
an empty pack to make her way as best she could.

Far from it. Her leather tunic and leggings had been
brushed spotless and rubbed soft, and there was a new
loop sewn on her belt which held a small ax. Everything
in her pouch had been replaced or renewed: fresh
thongs, a roll of cord, a large pad of well-oiled tinder,
a new and finer firestriker, several long, sharp pins,
some hard wooden pegs, other items she did not bother

to examine. And her pack was bulging with perfect trail food of every kind.

A huge breakfast was provided, but Lysis, having served, stood at her elbow when she began to eat, shifting from foot to foot, so clearly tense and eager for her to finish that she might as well have shouted, "Get out." Psyche realized she was no longer welcome and at once stood up to leave. Lysis fairly glowed with gratitude at her understanding, but it was soon clear that she was not meant to be deprived of her breakfast. Before she got through the door, Lysis was beside her with all the remaining delicacies packed into a large napkin. She urged Psyche to take the food, and a small leather bottle of wine, with such insistence that Psyche did so without protest, accounting it another puzzle of Aphrodite's behavior that she was unlikely to fathom.

She bent her mind, as she strode along, to considering what she had found in her pouch and pack. If anything were missing, she might still be able to try to sell her dress and buy it before she left the city. But she could not think of a thing—except, perhaps, a boat in which to cross the river. She laughed at the thought, and then stopped dead for a moment. How would Aphrodite, or even her servants, know what was needed for a journey in the wilderness?

From what Teras had told her, she knew a great deal about Aphrodite and the way she lived. Journeys in the wilderness were no part of that delicate Olympian's experience. And the arrows—Psyche looked down at the quiver hanging at her hip—yes, the arrows were all newly fletched. She took a deep breath and began to walk again, feeling light as a feather. The perfect selection of supplies, the newly fletched arrows—Teras, not Aphrodite, had overseen the preparations for her journey.

As soon as she was out of the city, Psyche found a

place by the side of the road and ate most of the breakfast she had missed. She drank only a little of the wine, thinking she would keep the rest to warm her in the evening, and she took out a new leather thong, smiling at it and thinking of Teras's care, as she fastened the bottle to her belt. By the time the sun had come up over the mountains, the road had again changed from polished stone to smooth earth. She walked on, warm and content.

Although she could not be sure why Teras would take such care for her and still allow Aphrodite to send her away without speaking to her, she guessed he could not yet stand against Aphrodite's will. She felt a twinge of disappointment in her lover, but she was so glad that he was strong enough to do anything and that he *did* know she had come to Olympus that she put aside that small dissatisfaction. It was not unreasonable, she told herself, that he would doubt her and himself and trust only Aphrodite after she had nearly killed him.

The smooth earth of the road turned into a rutted track and then petered out into grazing land by noon. Psyche found a convenient flat rock, slipped her pack from her shoulders, and opened it. She smiled, a little mistily, at the careful layering, a layering very familiar to her after the many times she had unpacked a noon meal and then a supper when she and Teras were in the forest together.

The little sadness at his obedience to Aphrodite returned to trouble her, and to divert herself, she studied the land around her while she ate. The fields were empty, the grass not yet lush enough to make it worthwhile to drive a herd this far. But in the distance, back toward the city, she saw a single figure moving. A shepherd checking on the growth of the grass? A hunter making for the woods? Psyche watched idly—he was something to look at while she ate—and then turned to look north, dismissing him from her mind as she wondered whether she should continue west or turn north immediately.

She decided to go north even though she knew she could travel farther and more quickly over the grazing fields. The ground rose to the north, and she might be able to catch sight of the river. Possibly she could find a tree on the high ground and be able to see how the river ran. Sometimes a river would make a great loop and much time and energy could be saved by cutting across. In addition, although Aphrodite had said the sheep she sought were many leagues to the west, she might pass a good place to cross the river if she could not see it. It was not an irrevocable decision; if she found the terrain too rough, she might turn west again.

She walked sturdily, looking back after a while to be sure the land was still dropping behind her. Although on a steep hill her thighs would tell her she was climbing, on a gentle rise it was harder to judge. To her surprise, she saw a figure also coming north behind her. She could not be sure it was the same person, but she had not passed a living soul once she was beyond the ploughed fields and did not at all like the fact that the man had changed direction from west to north just as she had. That made her suspicious that he was not an accidental follower, but actually a pursuer. She turned somewhat west again and walked a little faster.

As she came to the crest of the hill, Psyche hunkered down so that she was less visible to anyone following her and looked back. At first she was relieved, thinking she had been mistaken and the follower had only gone her way for a time and had now struck out on a different path. Then she saw him emerge from behind a tree and take almost the same line she had up the hill. She swallowed hard. She had understood from Teras that the valley of Olympus was safe from thieves and outlaws. If that man was following her, it was on Aphrodite's orders. Quietly she loosened her bow from her pack, took the bowstring from her pouch and strung it, then drew out an arrow. If he came near enough to hurt her, she would shoot him.

She did not draw the bow, but held it loosely in her hand so that her pursuer would see it if he came close. Then she stared northward, but the hill was not high enough to give her a clear view. Farther north the land seemed to rise again and to be wooded, and she could not detect any sparkle of silver that might hint of a river. Since the ridge ran to the west Psyche followed it, hoping she would find a tree large enough to allow her to see over the next wooded ridge. From time to time she looked back; if she waited long enough, her pursuer always appeared—but, she soon realized, he was coming no closer.

That gave her food for thought. She had first believed that Aphrodite had sent someone to kill her so that she could tell Eros that his beloved had died. After a time, she realized that was ridiculous. Angry as Eros might be with her, he would never forgive Aphrodite for sending her on a mission on which she died—and Aphrodite could not be unaware of the depth of his feelings. Teras had grieved himself thin when she was late returning from Iolkas. But if the man was not sent to harm her, could he have been sent to protect her? No, that was equally silly. What protection could he give at that distance? But if she could see him, he could see her. Psyche uttered an annoyed little snort. Doubtless he had been sent to watch her.

The ridge bent southward—that was easy to tell because the sun began to dazzle the corner of her eye instead of warming her back. Psyche paused and turned to look northwest but could not see past the next ridge. She started down the hill, noting that the open area was not as smoothly grazed as on the side facing the valley of Olympus. There was more brush, some thickets a man's height or taller. An idea concerning the thickets stirred in her brain, and she turned to look behind again. This time she could not see her follower.

Hastily, she ran some distance down the north side of the ridge, moving quickly between the patches of brush and pausing beside one to rest when she needed to stop. By the time she was at the bottom, the sun was down behind the crest. The sky was still light, but it could not be long before evening and she had not seen her follower in some time.

Perhaps she had been mistaken and the man had business of his own. Nonetheless, she kept a sharp eye out for a site that could implement her plan. It was nearly dark before she found what she wanted—a dense thicket barely within sight of a large tree. She was so tired that she almost gave up the idea, but she set her teeth and began to bend aside the outer branches of a thick patch of brush. When she had eased herself inside, she used her new ax to cut away an area large enough to lie down in. Wrapping her cloak around the cut branches, she left a "sleeping body" lying in the space and wormed her way out of the thicket.

Psyche found the tree before it was too dark to see it. She had little difficulty climbing because she had chosen a conifer with low-growing, regularly spaced branches; finding a place in which to be safe and comfortable was not so simple. She was too tired to do more than sip from her bottle of wine and eat a piece of bread when she had finally jammed her pack firmly between two branches, and found two more that would support her safely and allow her to lean against a third and the trunk for support. When she had eaten, she wrapped herself in her blanket and tried to watch the thicket.

If the man had been following her, he did not appear

before it grew too dark to see a shadow moving. Psyche leaned sideways, passed her arms around a nearby limb to steady herself, pillowed her cheek against a wadded up bit of blanket, closed her eyes to rest—and did not open them again until the persistent flicker of light beyond her eyelids teased her awake.

For a moment she stared without comprehension at the rough bark and twigs tipped with long green needles that her eyes opened on. Then an attempt to lift her head made her groan aloud. Her neck, her arms and shoulders—and as she twitched involuntarily in reaction to the initial twinge—every muscle in her back and thighs had stiffened like stone set in mortar. The involuntary twitch also brought about a sense of insecurity which caused an equally involuntary tightening of her arms around the branch against which she was resting. That wrung another groan from her, but the feel of the bark against her arms and the slight movement of the branch also brought an instant recollection of where she was and why she was up a tree.

Suppressing another groan, Psyche lifted her head and looked toward the brush where she had left her cloak. She could not see into the "nest" she had made, however, and could detect no outward signs of disturbance from her current perch, so she dismissed the problem of the man who had followed her in favor of flexing and twisting her muscles in an attempt to make them fit for climbing down the tree. When a combination of an urgent need to relieve herself and some reduction in stiffness caused her to glance down to choose a way, she gasped in horror. A man was sitting at the base of the tree looking up at her.

CHAPTER 20

Psyche's first reaction was to fumble in her belt for her knife, but her hand stopped before it found the hilt. Clearly there was no need to protect herself. If he had wanted to harm her, he could have climbed up and slit her throat any time during the night. Then she started to reach out for the bow and quiver she had cached on another, lower limb, but she aborted that movement too. She could not possibly murder the man just for sitting below the tree she had climbed. She had been at his mercy all night and he had done her no hurt. Even as a threat, stringing the bow and drawing an arrow were useless. He might move away, but she could not send an arrow far enough to prevent him from following her.

Frustrated, and with a growing need to relieve her bladder and bowels, Psyche stared down at the man who stared back up, smiling. She had a peculiar feeling that she had seen him somewhere before.

"Do not be afraid to come down," he said at last. "I swear I will do you no harm—I will swear not to touch you at all, if you wish—and I will catch you if you fall."

Psyche's lips parted, but between surprise at the familiarity of the voice, which reinforced her feeling that she knew him, and indignation at the idea that she could not climb down without falling, all she got out was, "Why should I trust you? You have already forsworn yourself. There is no way you could catch me if I should fall without touching me."

"Very well," the man said, with a brisk shrug and an amused chuckle. "Then I will let you fall."

"Atomos!" Psyche exclaimed, the teasing humor recalling the suitor who had said she weighed too much to buy by the pound. "What are you doing here?"

"Following you," he answered promptly, adding, "Why do you not come down? If you remember me, you cannot be afraid of me."

"That is a stupid thing to say," Psyche retorted, but with a smile. "I remember one conversation with you under my father's eye and with all his liegemen present. That is scarcely a guarantee for your behavior when we are alone."

He laughed aloud. "True enough. However, since you cannot perch in that tree forever, you might just as well come down in time to share my breakfast. I will gladly withdraw a suitable distance so that I cannot seize you, but I thought you would rather have me close enough to catch you if you fall."

"You just said you were going to *let* me fall," Psyche remarked, prying her pack free from the branches into which she had forced it and pulling it toward her.

"Only in jest," he replied, his smile gone. "I do not believe I could bear to see you hurt, even against my own oath."

Psyche, who had just lifted the pack to her lap, froze. For those last few words, Atomos's voice seemed different—even more familiar, perhaps more musical, but somehow distorted so she could not pin down why she felt she knew it. Then he laughed and offered to toss up a rope that she could tie to the trunk and cling to as she came down. In that case, he pointed out, he could withdraw to a distance so she need not fear him. The voice was only Atomos's without any disturbing echoes of another.

"Oh, I do not fear you," she said. "After all, you could have climbed up any time during the night if you wished to take me prisoner or do me harm. If I were afraid, I would string my bow and shoot you. Instead I will consign my supplies and weapons to your keeping. Catch this." And she dropped her pack.

Since there was nothing breakable in it, Psyche did not care whether he caught it or not. She heard it crashing through the branches and a surprised oath from Atomos as she twisted around and reached up to take hold of a limb above and behind her. Her arms and back protested, but not nearly so much as they had when she first moved, and she was able to raise one foot to the branch on which she was sitting and pull herself upright. The week and more that she had spent making her way to Olympus had hardened her; she had always been strong; now she was tough as well.

Below Atomos was silent, uttering no cries of alarm, no cautions or warnings. Psyche paused, biting her lip. That was Teras's way too. But there was no Teras . . . no dearly beloved monster . . . only Eros. She looked down hastily to see where her pack had fallen and her eyes found Atomos. She was rather surprised to see an expression of real anxiety on his face. It gave her a little fillip of pleasure that he should care about her and yet let her act without giving advice, but it annoyed her too. Then she reminded herself that Atomos could not know of her adventures since he had seen her, an idle lady in her father's court.

In fact she made it safely to the ground without great difficulty and hurried away without a word to attend to her most pressing needs. When she returned she found that Atomos had cleared a patch of ground and started a fire. A pot holding coarse-ground meal and water sat on a tripod above the flames, not yet boiling, but with a faint vapor rising from it. On a large stone near the fire were a small crock, which Psyche was sure contained honey, and a wrapped packet, almost certainly of raisins or dates.

"You do not stint yourself," she said, smiling.

"I am an old, experienced hunter," he replied. "And usually this breakfast is my first meal after a long chase with no other meal to follow until dark."

Psyche sat down on the blanket she had dropped when she ran off into the brush, which Atomos had folded neatly and set at a comfortable speaking distance from his own. Just beyond the blanket was her pack—with her cloak folded neatly on top. She smiled as she reached for it and pulled it around her. So he had seen through her little device. He certainly was an excellent tracker, to have discerned that the cloak-wrapped body was a fake and then followed her trail in the dark—an experienced hunter, indeed.

Hunter? The word echoed in Psyche's mind as she watched Atomos lean forward to stir the porridge. What could he have been hunting in the ploughed fields and grazing land of Olympus? What was a native hunter from Cellae doing in Olympus at all? Then she recalled with a sinking heart that Atomos was a special devotee of Aphrodite, that he had broken off his courtship of her when her father had told him the temple of Aphrodite was closed to worshippers and that he could not offer sacrifice there for help in his suit. Had that suit ever been real? Or had he been sent by Aphrodite as a spy? Psyche stood up abruptly and began to roll her blanket.

"What are you doing?" Atomos asked.

"Leaving," Psyche said.

"Why?"

"Because you are Aphrodite's servant. You came to my father's court to spy on us, and you have come now to make it impossible for me to fulfill Aphrodite's task."

"No," he said, eyes wide open, startled.

"Yes," she hissed. "You liar, oh yes! I do not think she can claim you gave me any help by sleeping by the foot of my tree because I was asleep when you came and could not send you away. But with one spoon of that porridge you are mixing, she will have a new excuse to keep me from my Teras."

"Nonsense," he said, also standing up.

Psyche made no reply, merely strapping her blanket to her pack and pushing her cloak aside so she could slide her arms through the straps. She glanced briefly at the sun to orient herself and took a step toward the north.

"Psyche, wait!" Atomos cried, blocking her path. "It is not true!"

"What is not true?" she asked with cold fury, "That you are Aphrodite's servant and are doing her bidding?"

"No, that she will claim my accompanying you violates the task she has set. How can she? She . . . she agreed that I should follow you, yes, but to protect you. And she did not say you must go alone. If you fear she will blame you for accepting help, I will not help you gather the burning wool, that you will do by yourself."

Psyche drew back a step, rigid with rage. "She did not say I must not use magic to complete my first task either, but she used that as an excuse to forbid me to see Teras. Oh, no, you fooled me once—that was a shameful thing for you to do, but not very shameful perhaps because you did not have to lie much. I was overused to suitors and did not sense your falseness."

"There was no falseness," Atomos cried. "Not about my feeling for you."

"Liar!" Psyche breathed, and as his lips parted on another protest, her voice overrode his. "But if you fool me again—that is a shame on me for vanity and stupidity. Go back to your mistress and say I did not fall into her trap. I will find the sheep and fetch the wool, and I *will* see and speak to Teras."

She turned to go around him, but he stepped in front of her again. "I never fooled you, never!" he exclaimed passionately. "When I saw you, I was amazed at your beauty and I said so, but when you told me what beauty was worth, you ravished my soul. I admit I am Aphrodite's servant, but I swear I love you, have loved you ever since I first met you. I would never do anything to hurt you."

"Love me, do you?" Psyche's brows lifted in disbelief while her anger built to bursting. "Then go back to Aphrodite and speak the truth," she snarled. "Tell her that I have rejected your help and protection, that I will go alone and come back alone to Olympus to claim my reward."

As she spoke the last word, she jumped closer, pushed him hard so that he staggered out of her way, leapt past him, and ran as fast as she could. She heard him cry out, but no footsteps pounded behind her, and when, a long while later, pain lanced through her side, she slowed to a walk and glanced over her shoulder. He was not close enough to see. Psyche walked more slowly, drawing deep breaths, but she did not think she had escaped him. He would surely follow. Aphrodite had faithful servants.

Now Psyche began to doubt her wisdom in pushing him away and running off. It would not stop him from tracking her and probably had made him angry. Doubtless that would make him more willing to lie and say she had accepted his help. Her word against his, which would Aphrodite take? More important, which would Eros take?

Disgusted with herself for losing her temper and wondering whether she should let Atomos catch up, she slowed further and began to glance around rather than just looking at where she was putting her feet. She had come down to the bottom of the ridge she had climbed and about halfway up the one she had seen the previous afternoon. The countryside was much rougher here, with more brush and trees, and the grass tangled and growing in coarse tussocks.

Just ahead was a fallen tree. Psyche slid her pack off her shoulders, propped it against the trunk, and sat down to get something to eat. She did not hurry, munching on the waybread and dried apples and sipping at the wine in the flask while she watched the back trail for Atomos. She tried to plan what to say to him but could not imagine any way to convince him to disobey his mistress.

Only he had not appeared when she was finished eating, and Psyche began to wonder whether she had misjudged him—and Aphrodite. Perhaps his arrival was only a test and she had passed it? Psyche was a little surprised that her spirits did not rise more at the hope that she was rid of him. He was almost as much fun to talk to as Teras and had almost the same kind of sense of humor. Psyche sighed.

She had enjoyed their conversation . . . before she'd realized that Aphrodite had sent him. She looked around at the empty landscape and sighed again. The truth was that she was lonely. Tears blurred her eyes. She wanted Teras. She shuddered. There was no Teras, only Eros . . . Eros of the beautiful face and hard, cold heart. Did she want Eros? But they were the same—or were they? With his beauty hidden, had Eros felt a need to be more the kind of person she would like? Nonsense! He could have maintained such a pretense for a few hours, a few days, not for the length of time they had been together. If Eros was the being in the black cloud, then it was Eros she loved.

Nonetheless, Psyche found her eyes wandering back along the way she had come as she put away what she had not eaten and closed her pack again. There was still no sign of Atomos. She drew a deep breath, swung her pack to her shoulders, and set out northward again. Soon the trees grew closer and closer and she knew she would see nothing if she turned to look back.

It was less easy to keep her direction with the sun hidden by the trees, but the growth was not so thick that glances of light did not penetrate. Between the angle at which the shadows fell and the growth of moss on trunk and rock, she was reasonably sure she was headed in the right direction. Because she found it a relief to concentrate on the mechanics of her travel, she felt immediately the change in the demands on her muscles when she had topped the hill she was climbing and started to go down.

She trudged on, a little more carefully after she came to a steep slope where her feet slid and she almost fell. Oddly, it was harder work to go downhill on the sharp grade than it had been to climb the hill, and she stopped more often to rest. At the third pause Psyche decided she might as well eat a midday meal. The forest was silent in her immediate vicinity as usual, but in the distance there was sound, and as she stood perfectly still, for the moment too sad and discouraged even to take off her pack or find a seat, she realized the sound was the rushing of water. The river!

The oppression on her spirit flew away. It was as if reaching her first goal had made the purpose of struggling toward that goal worthwhile again. With renewed energy and considerably greater speed, she hurried downward, barely stopping herself from falling in at the end because the trees grew thickly right down to the bank, which had been cut away steeply under the roots.

Psyche chose a nest of intertwined roots right over the water in which to sit down and unpack her food. As she ate, with better appetite than she had had that morning, she looked upriver and down, faced with the same problem she had had on her way to Olympus—how to get across the water. She was not nearly so worried now as she had been then. For one thing, she was hardened to travel; for another, she had an ax. At worst, she could cut and tie several logs together on which to rest her pack and help support her so she could wade and swim to the opposite bank.

Not just here, however, she decided, as she finished the wine and lay flat on the roots to rinse out the bottle. Right here the current was too violent, even as close to the bank as she was, and the opposite bank was too steep. Psyche sat up and looked upstream. Aphrodite had said the sheep were many leagues to the west. She could well afford to walk along the river and try to find a better spot to cross.

She reached out to draw her pack to her when she heard an odd sound. Her hand checked for a heartbeat; it was not a footstep, more a creaking of wood, as if someone had leaned against a young tree. Psyche's eyes brightened and her lips curved a little, but she did not look upward into the forest; she finished pulling her pack closer, replaced the piece of cheese she had not finished and the now-empty bottle (no need to carry water when she would stay near the river for the rest of her journey), and closed the pack. Then she rose and started westward, her eyes bent on the rather treacherous terrain of the bank.

Psyche saw enough to keep her from stumbling, but

that was all, because her mind was very busy. It seemed that Atomos had followed her, after all, and that he had decided not to accost her again. That was well and good if he would admit that he had traveled separately from her and given her no help or advice. But if he were going to pander to Aphrodite's whim and say she had accepted assistance from him no matter what she did, why not accept his offer?

Aphrodite had said she had failed the test of patience, but had mostly used the excuse that Teras was not well enough to keep her from seeing him. Teras—no, Eros. She would have to grow accustomed to using his real name. For a while Psyche's mind was diverted from whether to acknowledge Atomos's presence to the frightening problem of whether Teras and Eros truly were the same person. She walked on almost unseeing, longing for Teras and battling the doubts and fears seared into her by the meeting with Eros when he cursed her father. At last she thrust those disturbing thoughts from her mind to reconsider whether she dared quibble about the terms of this new task.

It was true that Aphrodite had not said she must go alone; this was to be a test of her cleverness and courage. Courage might mean she must face the dangers and problems all on her own, but cleverness might mean that she would be judged stupid if she rejected the help of a man who admitted Aphrodite had sent him to protect her. Psyche bit her lip. That meant that whatever she did, Aphrodite could claim that she had failed.

Psyche hesitated and half turned to call out to Atomos, then shook her head sharply and began to walk forward again. She was only finding excuses to accept his company. He was a pleasant companion, and she was so very tired of being alone. However, there was another reason to ignore him. He had said he loved her. If that were true, it would be cruel to laugh and joke with him and possibly bind him closer when she cared only for Teras . . . Eros. Did she care for Eros? She tossed her head. That Atomos loved her was almost certainly a lie. Surely it was Aphrodite he loved and served. But if he loved Aphrodite, then he would say whatever Aphrodite wanted him to say, so why should she not make this journey easier and pleasanter by making it with him?

Psyche's thoughts went round and round while her feet found a way along the bank of the river, until at last a message her eyes had been receiving for some time drew her out of her self-absorption. Ahead the light was much brighter. As soon as the thought penetrated, she took in what she had been seeing. Beyond her a large tree had fallen, taking with it many of the smaller trees and opening an area into a meadow where the sun glinted blindingly into her eyes.

The low angle of the light told her most of the day had passed and the knowledge made her aware of the strong ache in her shoulders—the generously filled pack was heavier than she had carried in many days—and the tiredness in her legs. Well, at least she had become aware of her fatigue in an ideal place to camp. She could just settle herself in the curve between the roots of the tree and the trunk. Water was right at hand, and the dead branches would be perfect fuel for a fire.

When she dropped her pack against the tree trunk, Psyche thought she heard a snort. She looked first at the trees where Atomos might emerge, but with the westering sun shining in among them she could see a fair way into the woods and there was no sign of him. Either he was farther back or hiding, and he certainly had not made the sound she'd heard. Then she looked all around the clearing, but nothing moved in it. A second survey showed a slightly disturbing sight. On the other side of the fallen tree, the bank had broken away so that it sloped gently to the river. In that slope the grass was trampled and torn and the earth was disturbed. Psyche leaned across the roots to look more carefully and thought she could discern hoofprints.

Likely, she thought, this was a watering place for deer. Well, they would do her no harm, she told herself, surprised by the uneasiness that the idea generated. Was it some half-buried memory of a warning that such a watering place might be dangerous? Sighing, she reached for her pack, but when she started to lift it, it seemed like the burden of Sisyphus. What danger could deer be to her? She had her javelins; she would have the tree at her back and a fire. She was simply too tired to look for another camping place, which would probably be less suitable.

Still, she was uneasy enough to be reluctant to unpack everything, which might have to be abandoned if danger did threaten. For the moment she merely unstrapped a blanket and sat down on it, leaning back against the trunk, which shifted very slightly with an odd little grunt. Psyche jumped to her feet, pulling a javelin free of the straps that held it, but no further sound followed and nothing at all moved in the clearing. She stood indecisively, too uncertain to begin preparations for camping, but too aware of the ache in her shoulders and legs, and too sad and discouraged to wish to go on.

Finally Psyche decided to rest for a while; if no threat showed itself, she would start cutting wood for a fire. She sat down slowly, putting her weight on the tree trunk with care not to tip it. The sound was not repeated. She listened hard, but the clearing was quiet, holding only the common sounds of spring: insects buzzed somewhere in a monotonous manner, leaves and grass rustled in a faint breeze. Idly, Psyche watched the trees on the side of the clearing she had entered, but

no tall, dark-haired man stepped into the open, and the
sunlight, glancing off the moving leaves, dazzled her
tired eyes.

An enormous squealing and squalling jerked Psyche
awake. Gasping with fear and shock, she leapt to her
feet, clutching at the javelin, which had been lying
across her lap. She was at first too dazed to do more
than wonder why it was so dark and stare wildly
around, whimpering softly when she could see nothing
to account for the noise. A heartbeat later she realized
the sound was coming from behind her. She whirled
about and cried out more loudly at the sight of a large
boar confronting a mountain cat on the slope to the
watering place. Both were already bleeding, the boar
bearing deep scratches along his shoulder where the big
cat had missed his strike or been thrown off, and the cat
with a gouge in his chest where the boar's tusk had dug
deep and torn down.

The second cry was a mistake. Her first had been
swallowed up in the squalling of the beasts; the louder
cry drew momentarily the attention of the mountain
cat. The boar, more stubborn and fixed of purpose,
charged the moment the big cat's head turned. Both
startled and alerted by the movement, the cat jumped
forward, reaching out for a grip with its jaws and striking out with a paw instead of leaping out of the way.

Both beasts suffered. The boar's tusk caught the fore-
foot of the cat above the pads and ripped it apart; the
impact held the boar's head up for just long enough for
the cat to catch the top of the skull in its jaws, crushing
the eyes and tearing the flesh away. The sight and the
screaming of both animals was so terrible that Psyche
stood frozen until at last the boar was toppled to its side
and the mountain cat's teeth fastened in its throat.

The near silence freed Psyche from her paralysis. Thinking the cat fully occupied with its kill, she snatched at her pack and blanket and began a hasty retreat. Her movements were jerky with fear and she could not lift her pack and blanket in her left hand alone—her right still clutched the javelin—so she dragged them.

The sound made the cat raise its head; her retreat was an irresistible attraction to it. Snarling a challenge, the beast rose, tried to put the damaged paw to the ground, and squalled with rage and pain. Psyche whirled back to face it, screamed with terror as she saw it leap over the dead boar to the tree trunk, and cast her javelin as it leapt again, toward her.

She dodged sideways, wrenching at a second javelin, knowing she could not possibly free it and throw or even jab in time; she heard the cat squall again and turned to face it. Three arrows seemed to have grown out of the creature's head and body in the few moments in which she had been trying to free her javelin, which was finally loose in her hand. Momentum carried the dead cat forward; desperate determination, lagging behind what her senses perceived but her mind had not absorbed, led Psyche to jab at it with her weapon even as it fell. A shocked cry and a bright blade, which beat the javelin aside, drew a shriek from Psyche.

She dropped the weapon, crying, "Did I hurt you?"

He caught her to him, crying, "Did I hurt you?"

"The cat," she sobbed, "I was trying to hold off the cat. I didn't see you."

"It's all right, love," he said, stroking her hair. And after a moment he chuckled and added, "I didn't think you would be so annoyed with me for killing the mountain cat that you would try to spit me."

The chuckle made her conscious that she was clinging to him, and she drew herself away, shaking her head and finding a tremulous smile. "Even I cannot be so unreasonable as to prefer death to accepting your help." They stood staring at each other for a moment, then Psyche took another step backward and said, "Thank you."

Atomos walked to the cat and heaved it over, squatting down beside it. "I do not know that thanks are needed," he said. "Your javelin was well cast. I think it was dying when my arrows hit." He began to wrench out the missiles.

Psyche shuddered. "If so, it was pure luck, and it might well have lived long enough to tear me apart." She drew a shaken breath and looked around fearfully. "We had better go."

"No, why should we?" He smiled at her. "They are lone hunters. No other will be close, and the smell of blood will keep away the boars, if any should be near. This is a very good place to camp. I was envying you your snug retreat before the boar came out from under the tree and the mountain cat leapt upon it."

"Under the tree?" she breathed, and shivered again, remembering the grunt she had heard when her weight had moved the tree trunk. "I can hardly believe I didn't notice it."

"Neither did I," he replied, "until it moved. It had a lair in a hollow up at the other end where the branches divide." He smiled up at her then stood up. "Now we will have boar steak for dinner if you will make a fire while I butcher it."

Psyche nodded, but for a moment stood still, watching Atomos move to the boar. Any number of emotions pulled her this way and that. She needed to burst into tears of relief and exhaustion; she wanted to laugh with joy at having so sturdy and practical a companion; she thought her shaking knees would pitch her face down on the ground if she tried to walk a single step, and she felt it impossible to force her trembling arms to lift an ax; but most of all, her stomach clenched and gurgled at the thought of a sizzling boar steak. Although she knew she had eaten an excellent meal in Aphrodite's house, she had not the faintest memory of it and it seemed to her that she had not really eaten since she had cast the counterspell and nearly killed Teras . . . Eros. Eros.

During her brief delay, Atomos had climbed over the fallen tree and drawn his knife. Psyche saw him pull the boar's foreleg aside and push the knife through the thinner hide at the neck. She remembered suddenly a time when Teras had been interrupted and the darkness had withdrawn from a kill he had begun to skin, that the cuts were made the same way. Psyche shook herself and walked around the cat toward the branches. Naturally they were the same; doubtless all hunters made the same kind of cuts to begin skinning. Yet it seemed that she had seen Damianos start his skinning differently. She shrugged and pulled her ax from her belt. Maybe the styles were local, Damianos's that of Iolkas, and Ter—Eros's and Atomos's that of Olympus.

She made quick work of cutting several medium-sized branches from the trunk, finding her strength had returned as fear and shock diminished. Still she dragged them to the place where she had been sitting so she could rest against the largest part of the trunk. There she broke off all the twigs. Using the trunk as a base, she hacked the side branches into usable lengths. By the time she had torn away a circle of grass and started the fire in the center, Atomos had brought over a dozen neat strips of meat. Psyche laid thicker branches on the flames and went to the edge of the woods to cut green branches for skewers. When she returned with the pointed sticks, Atomos stood up from his butchering.

"I have enough for tonight and to eat cold for tomor-

ow afternoon. I will also trim a haunch to be partly
oasted. That will keep for one more day, I think. We
ould smoke more if we remained here for another day
r two—"

"No," Psyche said. "I mean, you may remain as long
s you like, of course, but I must go on. I must get back
o Teras—Eros—as soon as I can. I know Aphrodite
oves Ter—Eros, but she is a great lady and has busi-
ess of her own. Perhaps she cannot watch over him
losely enough. I am sure if I could nurse him he would
ecover more quickly."

"I assure you no one and no business is as dear to
Aphrodite as Eros," Atomos said, lips twisted wryly.
"She will be as attentive as even you could wish." He
hrugged. "Eros is an Olympian, as is Aphrodite. They
nderstand each other. Are you sure you understand
hem?"

"I understand Teras," Psyche said. "If Eros and
Teras are the same person, and I know they are because
myself broke the spell of darkness—and Eros was the
eing inside—then Eros and I think alike, whether that
s Olympian thinking or native thinking." She shook
er head. "Perhaps it would be better for you to remain
ere and let me go on alone."

"You know I will not do that." Atomos smiled. "I
m not *that* fond of smoked boar, and though it may
vell be that the mountain cat would have died before it
eached you, you still could have been hurt by the beast.
tell you, I was sent to protect you."

"I do not trust Aphrodite," Psyche said flatly.
Nonetheless, it is plainly too late for me to worry
bout whether she will use your protection to try to
eep me from my love." She sighed. "Love. That is
nother problem. You say you love me. If that is true,
am very sorry for it, but I cannot return that love. I
m bound to Ter—Eros—"

"Bound to him?" Atomos repeated, an odd tone in his voice.

"I love Teras," Psyche cried, her eyes filling with tears. "I do not know Eros. The only time I saw him, he was as cruel as he was beautiful. Teras was never cruel. I love Teras—" She sobbed softly, wrapping her arms around herself as if she were suddenly cold.

Atomos watched her, his head cocked to the side, then smiled slowly. "You do not fear that Aphrodite will turn you away. You fear that Eros will not forgive you." Suddenly he closed his mouth hard, his lips thinned; then he added quickly, "So much the better for me. If Eros cast off his kindness and understanding with the spell that hid his beauty, you will turn to me in the end and I will have you, Psyche."

"So you might!" she snapped. "But the more fool you would be to take the leavings of a heart already given. You are a good man, a fine man. Seek out a woman who will give you all her love. I love the being in the black cloud, man or monster, whatever his name is. If he casts me off, I might accept second best to assuage my loneliness, my need for sharing. But it would only be second best to me. Why should you accept second best?"

"Because half of your loaf, your second best, is ten times the worth of what any other woman has to offer to me."

Psyche blinked with surprise as he laughed lightly and turned back to carve out the haunch they would sear for the day after tomorrow. His answer to her was so strange for a man whose love had been rejected, so lighthearted, and with a trace of smugness in the voice and in the half-smile with which the words had been uttered. Why, it was as if he were glad she'd said she would always love Teras, even if she were forced to give up hope of living with him.

Then, as she knelt down to add more branches to the fire, to spit the slices of meat and set them so they would cook without burning through the spit too quickly, she shook her head at herself. How stupid she was. Of course Atomos was glad. He was a good, kind person—and he loved Aphrodite and served her. He did not really want Psyche to love him for the same reasons she did not want him to love her.

CHAPTER 21

In the days that followed, after they crossed the river in a small, round boat that Atomos unearthed from a cache of leaves and branches and as they worked their way upstream, Psyche grew more and more puzzled by her companion's behavior. His concern for her clearly went far beyond Aphrodite's order to protect her from harm. Not only did he do his very best to ease her journey and provide all the comfort that could be obtained in the wilderness, but his manner was . . . loving. When he took her hand to help her over an obstacle, his fingers would linger, as would his arm around her when he drew a blanket over her shoulders or pulled her cloak close to ward off the evening chill.

That seemed to Psyche an expression of desire, yet when she pulled her hand out of his or slipped from his embrace and reminded him that she loved another, she could swear he was not hurt or displeased. Usually he turned his face away, but there was something in his gait if they were walking, in the set of his shoulders, in the tilt of his head that bespoke satisfaction rather than discouragement.

Psyche kept telling herself that Aphrodite must have told him to woo her, to wean her from loving Eros, and that Atomos was trying to obey but was still glad not to be successful. She found that answer unsatisfying, however, for she remained certain the looks, the little gestures that hinted of desire, were genuine.

At first she argued that if his desire was pretense, she would have detected some false note, that as the days passed, he would have been driven to some more overt display to satisfy Aphrodite's command. Then she began to fear that she was willfully missing signs of falsity because she wanted those lingering touches, the occasional looks of longing, to be real. She was afraid that she was finding as much pleasure in Atomos's company as she would have found in Teras's.

Most frightening of all, she realized she was beginning to confuse the two. Their hunting styles, the quickness with which they could pick a path through the brush, recognize a bird call, the manner in which they went about making camp, gathering brush, choosing firewood, were very similar. Well, of course they were, Psyche reasoned. An experienced hunter is an experienced hunter. It was only natural that both Teras and Atomos should behave in similar ways.

Soon she had to admit it was more than that; their senses of humor were very much alike, too. And when she was looking away and Atomos laughed, her breath caught in her throat and her head snapped around so fast her neck hurt—because she had thought it was Teras laughing. There was no simple explanation for that—except coincidence. Coincidences did happen, but Psyche wished this one had not happened. She was beginning to see Atomos's face inside the blackness that came to her mind when she thought of Teras. Never Eros. She never saw Eros.

For several days after the attack of the mountain cat, Psyche had allowed Atomos to set the pace, almost forgetting in the pleasure of easy companionship that her journey had a purpose. Once she became aware of her growing confusion between Teras and Atomos, she began to insist on traveling farther and farther each day, eager to complete her mission and be free of Atomos's company so she might concentrate on learning to know Eros. She did not need to explain herself; at first the longer days of travel were a natural result of her waking earlier and earlier.

Atomos asked concerned questions about her inability to sleep, and she put him off with merry answers. Could she admit that in her dreams she embraced her beloved Teras in the beloved dark—only to find Atomos in her arms? Could she admit that her guilt over the pleasure it gave her made her afraid to sleep again?

At last, too aware of Atomos's presence, too unwilling to share again the intimacy of a campsite, a meal, his amusing conversation, she refused to stop when Atomos pointed out a perfect campsite; and when he remarked sharply that he was tired and it would soon be too dark to see, she shrugged.

"I do not care," Psyche said, surreptitiously resting her pack against a tree and tightening her knees against the trembling of fatigue. "I am not tired. I will go on."

"Why?" Atomos asked, exasperated. And when she did not answer, but just turned and started off again, he called after her, "Go on, then, but you will go alone. I *am* tired, and here I stay."

Choking back hysterical laughter at finally having rid herself of him when she wanted only to be with him, Psyche managed to keep up a brisk pace in a relatively straight line until she thought she was beyond his detection. Then she stumbled on, indifferent to where she was going, thinking only that she had been wrong. Atomos did not love her, but he had very nearly succeeded in the task Aphrodite had laid upon him and weaned her from Eros. Later, half blind with fatigue, she had fallen and just lay there, content to be at rest. In the blackness of the night, the blackness in her heart, a hand touched her face, a strong arm lifted her.

"Teras!" she cried.

"No, it is Atomos," a male voice, soft and beautiful, replied.

Psyche began to weep uncontrollably because she was so sure it was Teras's hand she felt in hers. And Atomos held her tight against him and stroked her gently—but it was Teras who had always done that. You stupid slut, she told herself, pulling away. You are just giving the name most familiar to you to a body and gestures that have become familiar. Likely you will find Teras strange when you are reunited with him because you have been long apart. And then she wiped away a new rush of tears and sighed. She would never be reunited with Teras, and Eros *was* a stranger.

The natural punishment for such stubborn stupidity was cold, dry food, no comforting brush-filled bed, and a terrified refusal even to lean against Atomos for warmth. In the morning, however, Psyche had reason to be glad of her foolishness. Not more than half a stadium farther, the bank of the river along which they had been traveling flattened into a marshy area where it met another smaller stream. Turning northward along the marsh to find a place to cross, they found Psyche's goal, the sheep of the flaming fleece.

On the other side of the tributary stream, a hillside rose out of the marshy land, not forested, but grassy. Psyche almost laughed over a flicker of doubt, which had assailed her from time to time, over not being able to recognize the animals Aphrodite meant. It was immediately apparent there could be no mistake! The "sheep" stood out on the green hillside like beacons. Their fleece, even at this distance, was glowingly brilliant in flickering shades of red and orange and yellow.

Psyche was reluctant to turn her back on her goal, but an attempt to cross against Atomos's advice—watched from a safe distance by a sardonically grinning Atomos with arms folded over his chest—soon convinced her she would accomplish nothing but miring herself if she persisted. Not much farther north, just as Atomos had promised, the banks of the stream were dry. Psyche could see that the water was not very deep, perhaps no more than ankle-high, although it was as much as an arrow's flight wide.

Another short walk brought them to an excellent crossing spot. Here the banks were higher but not so high as to make descending them difficult, and although the stream was deeper, it was narrower, less than a stone's throw wide. Psyche began to make her way down the bank, but Atomos caught her arm.

"Let us find a campsite," he said. "Then—"

"Why bother with a campsite?" Psyche asked impatiently. "I would like to cross, see if I can catch one of those sheep and get enough wool—"

"Catch one of those sheep?" Atomos echoed, his face and voice displaying horror. "We must look for a campsite on this side of the stream because it is the only way I know to keep those 'sheep' from catching *us*. They hate water and will not cross the stream."

"But I must catch one if I am to get enough fleece to fill my bag," Psyche said, frowning.

"You cannot catch one. Those creatures make the mountain cat you killed seem like a house cat. Psyche—" he caught her shoulders and shook her gently "—I am not jesting. I am *not* trying to prevent you from completing the task Aphrodite set you. I am merely trying to keep my skin—and yours—whole. This time I will not let you go your own way. I swear I will tie you up if you will not promise not to try to catch one of those creatures."

She saw how serious he was, that he looked truly frightened and worried. In addition, she was quite sure that Aphrodite would not have set her too simple a task. She had thought at first that the journey was to be the test of her courage and cleverness—after all, how difficult could it be to catch a sheep and cut or comb out enough fleece to fill a relatively small bag? But Atomos had come to make the journey easy—or to seduce her into unfaithfulness; no, she would not think about that—so the difficulty must be something other than the journey.

Having seen the open countryside, Psyche now realized it would not be so easy to catch one of the sheep, but it might well be true that, in addition, the creatures were dangerous. Still . . .

"But I saw them grazing on the hillside," Psyche protested.

"You've seen pigs grazing on acorns, too," Atomos pointed out. "Would you walk uninvited into a herd of pigs?"

"Could I be invited?" Psyche asked eagerly. "Is there a shepherd I could approach?"

"And what would you offer this shepherd?" Atomos snapped.

"Whatever I offered would be none of your affair," she retorted sharply, "but I can assure you it would be nothing I would be ashamed to tell Ter—Eros."

"You think Eros would not be jealous?"

"He will have no reason," Psyche replied shortly, but her eyes dropped and she repeated, *"Is* there a shepherd?"

Atomos sighed. "Do not be ridiculous. They are monsters, I tell you. No one can approach them."

"Then why did you ask what I would offer the shepherd?" Psyche snapped, her eyes hard with suspicion.

"Because *I* am jealous," Atomos snapped back.

Psyche opened her mouth to remind him that she had repeatedly warned him she loved another man and had begged him to go away. Instead she sighed again and said, "I must approach one, at least. I must get some of the fleece."

Atomos unclenched his teeth and smiled. "You will have to find another way to do that. No, it is useless to discuss it. I will not let you go near those sheep alone. For now, let us make camp and rid ourselves of our packs so that we will have more freedom of movement. Then we can walk downstream again and look for the beasts and work out some plan."

Psyche hesitated, then shrugged. Atomos was right about being rid of the packs. Chasing an agile creature like a wild sheep while burdened with a heavy pack was a sure way to fail to catch it. She also realized that this time he would not yield to her and let her cross the stream. Since she suspected he might know more about the creatures than she did, she felt it would be foolish to ignore his advice—until she was sure the advice was designed to make her fail. One day's delay was not serious, and that should be long enough for her to discover whether he was telling the truth or trying, what he had specifically denied, to hinder her from completing her task.

It was not difficult to find a campsite. Not far from where they had stopped to talk, a huge tree cast sufficient shade to have discouraged the growth of saplings and heavy brush. After extracting a promise from her that she would not try to approach the sheep, Atomos went back deeper into the woods to hunt and collect firewood. Psyche took a javelin in hand and went down to the stream to rinse and refill the water bottles. That done, she intended to search for edible plants, but the sheep and the problem of collecting their wool filled her mind.

When she stood she was frowning, recalling that Atomos had said they would go together and try to devise a plan to get the fleece. But she could not allow Atomos to help her. She might be able to make a case for his accompanying her and protecting her; he had said that Aphrodite had sent him for that purpose. However, she could not pretend that she had not understood that gathering the fleece was her task. That much she must do alone, and without the help of magic, either.

Setting the water bottles safely on the bank in the shade of a large boulder, she set out downstream at a quick pace. She soon noted that the higher land on the opposite side was grazed clean, but brush and brambles grew along the bank close to the water. Thinking that she might be able to shoot one of the creatures who came down to drink, she walked more slowly, watching for a path through the brush that would mark a watering place. Although she passed several spots where the bank was very low, almost flat against the water, there was no indication that any animal had pushed through the brush to drink. However, here and there in the brambles Psyche saw flecks of color.

Farther down, where the stream was quite shallow but before the ground became truly marshy, lilies grew thickly on both banks. For the moment Psyche dismissed the sheep of the burning fleece from her mind and happily dug lily bulbs to lend a fresh garnish to the next meal. She thought idly as she brushed dirt from the bulbs that a little later in the year she could have gathered berries from the brambles. Her mind checked on the thought. Humans were not alone in their taste for brambleberries; all animals loved them, goats especially, even dogs, cows and sheep . . . sheep! The flecks of color caught in the brambles might well be bits of fleece.

Gathering up her bulbs, Psyche hurried back upstream to where the brambles grew thickest and stared across. Yes, here and there were flecks of orange on the thorny green-leafed stems. But were those flecks fleece, or merely a few of last year's brown leaves turned orange by the sunlight? She peered and peered, pushing her way through the brush on her side of the stream and standing tiptoe to stare across, but she could not satisfy herself about what she was seeing. She edged closer to the water, closer, staring hard first at one spot of color and then at another—and her foot suddenly slipped and she was in the stream.

The cold shocked her into stillness and then into a consideration of what she had promised Atomos. She had said she would not try to approach the sheep. She knew Atomos assumed that meant she would not cross the stream, but what if there were no sheep across the stream?

Psyche got back on the bank and stared around at the grazed-over land. There were no sheep. There had been no sheep even at her farthest stop downstream. Then crossing the stream to determine whether the color in the brambles was fleece would not be approaching the sheep. And what if Atomos's purpose in saying the sheep were so terrible was to keep her from fulfilling her task? She had no proof one way or the other of *his* truthfulness.

She laid down her bulbs, removed her boots, and stepped into the water. Wading carefully over the water-smoothed pebbles and rocks, she reached the far shore without getting wet above her knees, and climbed out. She paused only to put her boots back on, then edged her way into the bushes toward a fleck of color. It was fleece! She picked up that fleck and moved carefully to the next little wisp, grateful for her leather traveling clothes, which protected her from the thorns.

Psyche had no idea how long she had been sidling along, weaving and bending to avoid the worst of the stickers, and plucking here a thread and there a whole patch of wool from the thorns. She had a handful of fleece and was pleased with her acquisition, but she knew it would take far too long to collect a bagful of the stuff in this manner. Her eyes were fixed on the next patch of color, her mind busy with the problem of how to get the sheep through the brambles so they would leave more wool there, when a thin sound, a cross between a baa and a hiss, made her turn hastily.

Beyond the brambles was a lamb. It was utterly adorable, watching her with the slightly demented look all young creatures have. Psyche smiled. What a dear little thing! She did remember her promise to Atomos, but she had not tried to approach the sheep. An adorable little lamb had approached her. Cooing softly, Psyche surreptitiously stripped a few leaves from the bushes and held out her hand, palm up and open, to show the leaves. The lamb did not run, so Psyche took one slow step toward the creature. What harm could a dear little lamb do her, she thought.

The lamb, equally tentatively, took a step toward her. That seemed a trifle odd; most lambs or kids either stood their ground or backed away unless they already knew humans, but since the creature was so bold, Psyche took another step. The lamb raised its head. This close, the fleece truly looked as though it were blazing. Even as she had the thought, Psyche became aware that the hand extended toward the lamb felt hot. Could it truly be afire? Momentarily forgetting everything beyond her curiosity, Psyche leaned forward.

On the instant, the lamb lashed out with a foreleg that ended not in a hoof but in claws that rivaled the panther's and opened a mouth lined with teeth that would have put an adult wolf to shame. Psyche was so shocked that she only jerked back, but her movement seemed to drive the lamb into a frenzy. It pressed into the brambles baa-hissing at the top of its lungs, so she was forced to thrust out with the javelin to hold it at bay. The point could no more than have pricked it, but it screamed like a stuck pig and went on screaming, all the time lunging forward, snapping and clawing, as Psyche continued to back away as fast as she could.

Since she dared not turn her head away from the "dear little lamb," which was threatening to lunge at her and tear her apart the moment it could avoid the point of her javelin, Psyche had no idea how close she was to the river. It was not really difficult to hold off the lamb, but she already heard the louder and deeper bellows of the adult animals coming to succor an infant of the herd. A single quick glance showed her a score or more of the creatures rushing toward her out of what must have been a fold in the ground.

She pressed backward faster, then gasped with terror as she was caught by a particularly sturdy bush and held fast. With no choice, Psyche struck harder and faster, stabbing the lamb deeply enough to draw blood. Hurt, the creature recoiled, pausing in its efforts to savage her, and she was able to tear herself free of the bush and step sideways and backward again. Even then she knew it was too late. Adult sheep were pushing through the brambles, bellowing and hissing with rage. A sharp thrust at first one, then another, prevented them from coming at her for another moment, and she took two more steps backward. Then two lunged at her at the same time and Psyche jumped back—only to find that there was no ground behind her.

Psyche was mute with terror as she fell—right into the stream—sending up a huge gush of water. She struggled backward frantically, backstroking with her arms and scrabbling with her feet, splashing more water, as she tried to put some distance between her and her pursuers. She expected any moment one would leap on her and savage her. But though they hissed and bellowed, none attacked, and Psyche thought she heard among the sounds of rage some high cries of pain and fear. Desperately she struggled to a sitting position, pulling herself farther into the stream as she did, but no longer splashing. On the bank the sheep milled, baa-hissing, but none would step into the water and Psyche saw on some of them dark spots and splotches. Had the water quenched the burning?

As the question rose into her mind, Psyche called herself an idiot for allowing such an idea to divert her from escaping. But when she got to her feet, she realized the question was pertinent. If the water had quenched the wool and the cries she had heard were of pain and fear, she had already escaped. Her panic subsided as she remembered what Atomos had told her; the sheep would not come into the stream after her.

In reaction, spite and rage shook her. She thought of stooping and sending showers of water at them. Then she felt ashamed. The poor creatures were only acting according to their nature. There was no reason to inflict pain on them or drive them away. As long as she was in the stream or on the other side, they could not hurt her. She had no right to be angry at them. She had not been angry at the panther that had attacked her. Psyche uttered a shaken little laugh. The panther looked what he was; he did not appear deceptively sweet and cuddly.

All reason to the contrary, Psyche found she could not turn her back on the burning sheep and simply wade across. Since she did not want to fall in again—she had been remarkably lucky not to have hurt herself badly on the rocks in the shallow water—she started toward the opposite bank at a diagonal that permitted her to keep the sheep as well as her goal in sight. When she moved, new bellows of rage arose and the animals went forward, too, pacing her. Afraid that what she was doing would make one or more so angry that it would forget how unpleasant water was, Psyche stopped. In looking back and forth to check what the creatures were doing, she caught sight of the brambles through which the sheep had come—and they were thick with fleece.

Psyche laughed with relief and revelation, which called forth more bellows of rage and a few rushes forward and back, which left more fleece on the bushes and brambles. She took a step and several animals, ignoring the sharp twigs and thorns, pushed ahead, as if she would be forced to come ashore and they intended to intercept her. Psyche laughed again. All she needed to do was to keep them interested and angry and she could have ten bags of burning fleece.

First she waded a little farther out in the stream to allow a safe distance for the pain of the wetting to cure rage if any sheep were infuriated enough to charge, then she began to walk upstream toward the campsite. By now she was badly chilled from her immersion and she had to move quickly and beat her arms around herself to generate warmth because she was soaked and freezing, but since the gestures seemed to keep the sheep angry and draw them after her, she was satisfied. As she approached an area where woods encroached on the open land, however, the sheep shied away from the shadows cast by taller trees and seemed ready to abandon the chase.

Psyche was tired herself, but she was sure Atomos would be back in camp by now and furious at her absence. Recalling the bulbs she had dug, she decided to use them as an excuse. She hurried across to the safe bank and ran all the way back—actually it was no great distance; wading in the stream over the uncertain footing had made it seem much farther. Nonetheless, she was winded when she found her cache. Then she plodded back the much longer distance to where she had left the water bottles. She was very weary by the time she trudged back to the camp.

"Where have you been?" Atomos roared, as soon as he saw her.

Psyche's first reaction to the angry question was relief. Apparently the distance and the woods had masked the noise of her confrontation with the monster sheep. "Downstream, nearly to the marsh," she replied mildly, swallowing her guilt over the lies she was implying and some she might have to tell. "You knew I meant to glean. There was not much, but I dug some lily bulbs for our meal. And . . . ah . . . I fell into the stream and lost the javelin I took with me."

"Fell into the stream? How?"

Psyche would have told Teras the truth, endured his scolding, and teased him into laughter over the "dear little lamb." It caused her nearly physical pain to shrug and utter a false laugh. But she dared not tell Atomos—she dared not. At all costs she must keep him from going downstream and seeing the fleece on the bramblebushes. Even if he only insisted on accompanying her while she gathered it, that would certainly violate the terms of the task Aphrodite had laid upon her. What if he went and gathered it for her? Psyche was still not in the least sure of his purpose. She had the means now to gather that fleece by herself and she would be far better off, she decided, if he knew nothing about it.

"By carelessness," she said. "I was right at the edge of the stream and stepped backward—and fell in. I was lucky not to crack my head on a rock. You needn't tell me how stupid I was. I assure you I will be more careful in the future."

"Are you hurt?" he asked anxiously.

Psyche felt guilty again over what she felt was true caring and at how easily his anxiety had diverted him from asking more embarrassing questions. However, she was too close to her goal to let her feeling for Atomos interfere. She shook her head, saying, "Oh, a bruise here and there. But I am freezing. I must take off these clothes and let them dry."

On the words, she put down her burdens, took her blanket from her pack, and went back into the woods a little way to undress, returning wrapped in her cloak and the blanket. By the time she returned, Atomos had a small fire going near which Psyche hung her under-clothing. Then she sat down wearily and removed her boots, which she stood by the fire to dry. As she placed them there, she felt a pulse of satisfaction. There could be no question about Atomos accompanying her down-stream to look for the sheep until she could wear the boots again. Dry garments could be cobbled together, but not dry boots.

In fact, the combination of her past sleepless nights and the exhaustion following her adventure saved her from needing to make any excuses at all. She ate her meal, complaining about her bruises—she had begun to feel them as soon as she began to warm up—and then fell asleep. By the time she woke, in the dusk of early evening, it was too late to do any exploring and she accepted Atomos's statement to that effect with such meek alacrity that he at once became suspicious and warned her against going off alone.

She laughed and pointed to her still-wet boots, saying she wasn't going anywhere until they dried. But she realized that knowing her task was almost complete had betrayed her into an unnatural compliance. It was not safe to talk to Atomos; he knew her too well and she wanted far too much to trust him. Suppressing another impulse to confess what she planned, Psyche instead complained that she was still weary and aching and would soon go to sleep.

Her complaint called forth such attentive tenderness from Atomos that she was hard put, particularly as the increasing darkness hid him from her, to refrain from moving over to him and snuggling down in his arms. In self-defense, she claimed to be hungry again so that he came into the light of the fire to broil more of his catch. When she could see him and not just hear his voice, he did not seem quite so much like Teras.

After eating, Psyche claimed that the undergarments she had dried were dirty and irritating, which permitted her to unpack in order to take out clean underclothes and stockings—and the bag she needed to fill with wool. She looked at it, shrugged, and deliberately left it out before she dressed herself again in her traveling clothes, which Atomos had dried in the sun and by the fire. These were also stiff, but Psyche said she had nothing else suitable and the well-tanned leather would soon soften.

Then she turned the talk to how they might obtain fleece from the sheep. To her surprise, Atomos contributed a number of practical ideas to the discussion with enthusiasm—with so much enthusiasm that Psyche felt a false note and her suspicions were again aroused. Unfortunately, the notion that his suggestions were only a device to interfere with her success gave her more pleasure than pain. All she could do when that shameful realization came to her was to claim to be too tired to talk longer, and lie down to sleep.

In fact, she was not in the least sleepy, although she took care to breathe slowly and even snort a little now and again after she had turned this way and that until she could see a reasonably bright star in a clear patch between the branches of the tree. For a time she kept her eyes closed and listened to Atomos breathing. She knew he was not asleep any more than she, and she thought sadly of the misfortune that had prevented him from coming as a suitor before her father had offended Aphrodite. She had liked him from the first, she thought. She could have been happy with him if she had never met Teras.

Her head moved impatiently as she tried to bury that dangerous thought and she deliberately turned her mind to how she could collect the wool caught in the brambles. All the grazing animals she knew settled into what shelter they could find at night to protect themselves from the hunters of the dark. She could only hope that the monstrous creatures that wore the burning fleece also did so, that despite their terrible armament, they were not themselves predators. The well-grazed land they inhabited seemed to imply that was true.

She thought about where to cross the stream and the advantage of starting to collect the wool as far from what seemed to be the natural range of the sheep versus the disadvantage that if she crossed too close to the campsite Atomos might hear her. She thought about whether it would be better to collect where most of the wool had been torn free, which was nearest where she had encountered the creatures, or farther away, where they would be least likely to sense her. She thought about everything she possibly could—except Atomos— even counting slowly to one hundred again and again, and still the star she watched would not move, the moon would not rise, and Atomos was not asleep.

At long last, when she thought she would go mad from the strain of keeping her breathing quiet and steady and listening for Atomos's breathing without thinking about him . . . much . . . the breaths that were not hers took on a different rhythm. Holding to the hope that he was dozing on the edge of sleep, Psyche was able to maintain her pretense of that state, and before she lost all patience, the star she had been watching had moved enough to be obscured behind a thick branch. There had been a silvery cast to the highest leaves for some time, which meant that the moon was up.

Very softly, with long pauses between movements, Psyche rose, reached out for her boots, picked up the bag for the fleece and the javelin she had left lying loose near it, and stole from camp. She had decided on a compromise and crossed the stream at the point she thought was about midway between the forested area the sheep avoided and the place where she had come upon the lamb. She went very slowly, setting her teeth against the cold bite of the water and feeling her way, concerned only that she not step on a stone that would shift or splash.

Psyche moved equally slowly when she reached the opposite bank, carefully bending each branch of the brush aside rather than pushing her way through by force. She made only one sound before she began gathering her prize: she gasped with relief and pleasure when she saw that the burning fleece glowed in the moonlight. Its color was muted to silver and pale gold, but it could not be mistaken for anything else.

Her ears straining so hard for baaing or hissing that she thought they would surely grow to twice their size, Psyche picked and pushed flock after flock of the wool into the bag. As the bag grew fuller, she grew less cautious in her movements. Ignoring the prick and scratch of the thorns, she thrust her way through the briars to reach particularly large patches of fleece or areas in which it was thickly caught. Once she set her foot arwy and uttered a half-stifled cry. She stiffened into immobility, listening even more intently, but heard no sound that she could associate with the sheep and began to pick with even more frantic haste.

Once more she paused, when she thought she heard a faint cry, but it might have been an owl and it was not repeated. More important, nothing moved on the open hillsides, which were well silvered with moonlight. Psyche picked and stuffed until it grew difficult to cram any more fleece into the bag. Then she pressed her gleanings down, which she had done before, but this time she could pack the wool no tighter and she drew the neck of the bag tight with its draw-cords, tied it firmly, and slung it over her shoulder.

Until that moment she had felt little beyond the driving need to fulfill her task, intensified by her growing guilt. Now that her quest was finished, it all seemed too easy. Suddenly, she was frightened. Surely the sheep were lying in wait for her; she pulled her javelin out of her belt and started to push frantically through the brambles and brush. Naturally the javelin tangled in the thin branches and she jerked it loose repeatedly, forgetting to watch for the edge of the bank until she nearly fell into the stream again.

Gaining the safety of the water only woke new fears. Surely she would turn her foot on a stone, break her leg, hit her head, and drown. But instead of extra caution, Psyche found her fears generated haste. She had to struggle with herself not to run in the water, which surely would have brought her to disaster.

Safe on the opposite bank, she began to run back to camp but almost immediately stopped short, aware of a thrashing in the brush ahead and to the left, between her and the bank of the stream. Between her and the camp, too. Psyche shuddered with terror. Was the beast coming from the camp? Had it hurt Atomos?

"Atomos!" Psyche shrieked.

"Here!" he bellowed in return.

His voice came from where the sound of breaking brush had come and that noise became louder. Still in the grip of unreasoning fear, Psyche imagined that he was fighting something dreadful. Hefting her javelin, she ran toward the sound, saw a huge shadow, and thrust.

"Psyche!" Atomos roared. He wrenched the javelin from her grasp and threw it on the ground. "That is the second time you have tried to kill me—"

"No!" she cried, clutching at him. "I would never hurt you, never!"

She lifted her face and found his lips. A raw flame raced from her mouth across her breasts down her belly. His mouth was what she knew and loved; the way his body fitted into hers was part of her, what she had known from her first experience of a man in precoupling play. He took fire with her; his hands touched her, and she knew that touching too.

"No," she cried again, and pushed him away.

"Psyche," he murmured, his hand outstretched, but making no attempt to grasp her, "it is too late to say 'no.' You cannot pretend that you do not want me."

"I want Teras," she said, her breath coming hard and fast as she backed away. "I am afraid of Eros. You have been kind to me, and between my loneliness and my fear I have painted your face into my Teras's blackness—"

He uttered a gasp and Psyche hesitated, then went on. "I am sorry if I have hurt you, Atomos. I warned you that if you really cared for me and did not merely woo me on Aphrodite's order that you would be hurt." Her voice shook on the last words, but she steadied it. "There was hunger in that kiss, but that hunger is for Teras, not for Atomos."

"You are a fool," he replied, but strangely, he sounded smug and self-satisfied. His voice held not the smallest harshness of pain. Then he said—rather anxiously, she thought—"Eros is an Olympian. You will be happier with me, a native like yourself."

Tears filled Psyche's eyes. "Teras was also an Olympian. If Eros and Teras are the same, then I can be happier with no one than with Eros, and he deserves the chance to show that exposing the beauty of his face has not stripped away the sweetness that was hidden in the black cloud."

"But—"

"Enough!" Psyche snapped. "It is too dangerous for us both to remain together longer. I will take my pack from the camp and find somewhere else to sleep. I cannot prevent you from following me, but I can and will prevent you from coming close enough for me to see or hear. Farewell, Atomos."

CHAPTER 22

Those were brave and honest words, and they were the last that Psyche uttered. Although he had been thrilled both by her response to Atomos and her rejection of him, Eros was quite exasperated by Psyche's determination to separate. He had followed her back to the camp still pleading for her to change her mind, not about admitting that she loved Atomos—Eros was a little ashamed of adding deliberate temptation to the trial he had set poor Psyche—but about returning to Olympus alone. In a way, he understood and even honored her decision not to expose either herself or "Atomos" to further temptation, but it was also foolhardy.

The wilderness they had traveled, as she well knew, was not totally benign. She should have been reasonable and made some compromise, or at least accepted the fact that if he followed far enough behind her to be out of sight and hearing, he would not be close enough should danger threaten her. Instead of discussing the matter, she had silently gathered her belongings and set off downstream, pausing only to throw rocks at him when he persisted in following her. She'd hit him twice, hard enough to make him angry and tempt him to catch up with her and shake some sense into her. But he thought better of that. He knew Psyche. She would try to hold him off with the javelin, and one of them was likely to take greater hurt than a minor bruise.

He compromised by lengthening the distance between them, trying to make her understand that he only wished to be near enough to protect her, not near enough to importune her, but she would not yield even that much. And when he saw her weaving from side to side with weariness, yet still struggling onward, he realized she would continue walking as long as he continued to follow. Then he gave up; he was only driving her farther and farther from the campsite, where he had stupidly left his pack and where he had to return.

Furious with himself and with Psyche, Eros at last yelled at her that he was going back and if she were not an idiot, she would come back too. When he arrived, he dropped down onto a pallet, threw more wood on the fire, and glowered at it. He was not really worried about her safety in this area. He had seen no signs of any predators when he was hunting the previous day, and the sheep on the other side of the stream guaranteed no predators from that area either.

Half his rage, Eros knew, was owing to guilt—and fear. Psyche was honest herself and would not be pleased with his deception. He knew he should drop his disguise, go after her again, and confess, but a tiny dissatisfaction fed his bad temper. He knew it was unreasonable, but he had wanted her to pierce his disguise as Atomos and recognize him. So he sat and stared into the flames, smiling one moment over Psyche's steadfastness and frowning the next over her blindness and stubbornness—waiting for her to grow frightened and return, proud when she did not, and so weary at last that he lay down on the pallet he had gathered for her, on which he thought he could detect her scent, and slept.

Desperation—for that kiss she and Atomos had shared had shaken her far more than she would admit—had made Psyche's decision adamant. She drove herself on and on out of disgust and terror, although each wavering step made her wonder whether she would be able to stay on her feet if Atomos persisted in following. When at last he had angrily told her he would follow no farther, she dropped by the first tree with low branches, a tree she knew she could climb quickly if she were threatened, and lay still, too tired at first even to unfasten her blanket and draw it around her. After a while the trembling in her limbs eased and she pulled off her wet boots, drew on dry stockings, and huddled into the blanket. At least the sack full of fleece made a comfortable pillow.

Slowly warmth returned to her body, but nothing could warm her heart. Tears ran down her cheeks and soaked into the bag of fleece. It was a terrible thing to know oneself for a whore. She had lied to Atomos and lied to herself for days. Teras was only a vague memory of joy and pleasure; Eros was a future terror; Atomos was the man for whom she yearned. Psyche shuddered.

How could it be? Could she be such a lecherous slut as to be incapable of faithfulness, to be inflamed to lust by whatever man was close by? How could any woman be so light-minded? It was less than two moons since she had last lain in Teras's arms. She could hear his voice, feel the touch of his hands, the taste of his mouth . . . or was it Atomos's voice, hands, lips that she recalled? What was wrong with her that she could be so easily beguiled, that she could so completely forget everything about the being in whom she had delighted for almost two years? How was it possible that she could not recall one single jest or gesture that was purely Teras's, not echoed by Atomos? What kind of an idiot—

At that point, Psyche's thoughts stuck. She was *not* an idiot and never had been. She was not even a fool. Had she been a fool, she would have been enchanted by her own beauty. She would have been happy to act like a graven image, satisfied with an admiration that cared nothing if she were as hollow as an artwork cast in brass. She would never have seen the dangers inherent in her abnormal beauty, never have warned her father. Iolkas might now be ruined by war or destroyed. No, she was not a fool.

Nor, Psyche thought—tears drying and lips thinned as an idea came to her mind, one too strange to be entertained, for a native, but perhaps not so impossible for an Olympian—was she particularly lustful. Until Teras had taught her the joys of the body, she had found the kisses and touches of the men she could not avoid rather unpleasant—and a few even repulsive. That thought brought the realization that she *could* tell one man's kiss and touch from another's. She remembered that even when accosted in the dark, she had known which of her suitors had caught her into an unwelcome embrace and pressed his lips to her hand or cheek or mouth.

Was it not strange, then, that she could not tell Atomos from Teras? She had kissed and caressed Teras, talked with him and laughed with him for almost two years; Atomos she had talked with once, briefly . . . and even that once, so long ago in her father's house, his jests, his tones of voice—had they not been near those of the monster? Teras had worn a black cloud to hide his features. Was it utterly impossible that he should wear a different disguise? Suddenly she thought of the way he—whoever he was—had gasped when she said she'd seen Atomos's face in Teras's blackness. Was that because her guess had been too close to the truth?

No, that could not be. She had burned away the blackness and seen Eros lying in her bed. But if Eros had worn one false seeming, why not two false seemings? But why the pretense at all?

The one true note in everything Atomos had done was saying he wished to protect her from harm. Would not Eros wish to protect her if he loved her? She had wondered why, if he were well enough to prepare her clothing and weapons, Eros had permitted Aphrodite to send her on so dangerous a journey. Gritting her teeth, Psyche pushed herself upright. Because, of course, he intended to accompany her and see that she was safe!

But why? To punish her for hurting him, for dispelling his disguise? She did not doubt that she had really hurt him, that he had nearly died from her meddling— the children's words had proved that. But what sort of punishment inflicted only pleasure? She *liked* hunting; she *liked* camping out. Until she had begun to fear that she was growing too fond of Atomos, she had been enjoying herself enormously.

The juxtaposition of those two ideas was a new revelation. Psyche's teeth ground together again, this time so hard that she could hear the grating noise and hurriedly relaxed her jaw before she broke something. That idiot! That consummate idiot had dreamed up this entire plot to test her devotion. She reached out and snatched a javelin from her pack. This time she *would* kill him!

Psyche was so furious that she had risen to her knees, only to find her body trembling so much with fatigue that she knew she could not walk. Even the small check was sufficient to make her realize how ridiculous she was. Atomos/Teras/Eros, she could hurt none of them. Beat them over the head with a distaff, yes! If only she had a distaff! But try to kill any . . . all . . . Her mind whirled as she realized that that was what she had done, nearly killed him.

She knew she had only wanted to clear away the darkness, to look on the monster she loved, no matter how horrible, so she could prove she loved him, the monster, that she did not fear him or pretend love because she was a prisoner. But how could he—whichever he was—know that? She had told Aphrodite, but how did she know Aphrodite had told him? But she did know. Only Eros could have provided the travel gear she had taken from Aphrodite's house, and that loving gesture doubtless came from a man who hoped she meant no ill.

Psyche's teeth gritted still again. They had planned this together, Eros and Aphrodite, to make her appear ridiculous, because she was not an Olympian. Because . . . No, that was only false pride speaking. No matter what she said, how could Teras/Eros/Atomos *know* she had not tried to kill him? He had a right to test her, and she had no right to be angry. Had she not asked Teras a hundred times, if not a thousand, how she could prove her love? But, right or no right, Psyche was thoroughly annoyed.

The testing was over. She had proved herself. She had passed every test . . . well, almost. There was the small problem of her attraction to Atomos. Suddenly Psyche uttered a smothered giggle. No wonder Atomos felt smug instead of hurt when she rejected his avowals and reiterated her love for Teras. Atomos *was* Teras, so it was doubly noble of her to have resisted him. Psyche sighed and closed her eyes.

She did not really sleep. A delighted contemplation

of her reunion with her naughty lover kept her at least minimally alert for the coming of first light. However, for the first time in many, many days, she was completely at peace. All the tension—some of which she had not even been aware, but which robbed her of much of the benefit of sleep—drained from her muscles, and she truly rested well and deeply. When the color beyond her eyelids lightened from utter black to a grayness, she opened her eyes and smiled at the false dawn.

Although she had not been consciously thinking, Psyche had resolved other problems while she rested. She had decided she was tired of living alone. She was tired of being treated like a blot on the landscape, a shame to be hidden, because she was native and not Olympian.

While she believed the monster was hiding his one bit of joy from a cruel Aphrodite, Psyche had been willing to endure the isolation for his sake. But to spend so many bored, miserable, lonely hours to pander to pampered Eros? No. Eros had his proof that she was faithful and loving, not a fool, not a lecher. She had confronted Aphrodite. She would no longer consent to be imprisoned in the lodge. Much as she loved the lodge, she intended to be free to come to Olympus anytime she liked and remain as long as she liked.

This time Psyche had no trouble at all getting to her feet. She did not mind the dampness of her boots. She slung her pack and her bag of fleece over her shoulders as if they were thistledown, and she set off to retrace her steps to the old campsite as if she were walking on air.

What had seemed hours of struggle and many leagues while she was trying to escape Atomos resolved into a couple of stadia and, perhaps, a quarter of a candlemark of walking time—and that only because the last half of the journey to the camp she crept slowly and quietly, hoping to catch Atomos/Teras/Eros still sleeping. In that she was successful, and for a moment she stood at the edge of the woods and watched him tenderly. He was sunk into that first depth of sleep that told her he had sat listening and watching for her almost all night. Then, her eyes alight with mischief and satisfaction, she advanced silently on her prey.

With great care she loosed the bag of fleece from her shoulder, lifted it high, and dropped it on Atomos's head. "There is the fulfillment of my task," she snarled, and in the same instant she kicked him, quite hard, in the behind. Atomos jerked upright, gasping with shock.

"Monster!" Psyche stamped her foot, suddenly furious at the sight of Atomos and full of a sense of injury she knew was unjustified. "I know you now! I never saw your face, but I know the touch of your hands and lips better than the touch of my own. Whatever face you wear, you are my monster."

He sat gaping at her, eyes blinking as he tried to come fully awake.

"Are you not ashamed of yourself?" she asked, submerging in the memory of her recent unhappiness her knowledge of the physical injury she had done him.

"No," he said, grinning. "Not at all. For I have won such a prize as is worth any price."

"Including that of an underhanded trick that caused me great misery? Do you not understand that for days I have been thinking myself the lowest kind of whore because I could desire Atomos when I loved Teras?"

He shook his head, still smiling. "Did I charm you? You hid it well." Then the merriment died out of his face. "You are true as steel and as pure as gold, Psyche. You are my soul. When I am apart from you, I am truly a monster."

"Not a monster. The only monster I ever knew was a better person than I, far better. But that trick you played is worthy of Eros. Are you also Eros?"

He lowered his eyes. "Do not think so ill of Eros. When you are with Eros, Psyche, he, too, will have a soul."

"Will you stop talking as if I were an avatar of the Mother!" Psyche snapped. "You cannot divert me by flattery from the disgusting thing you did. Games! Olympian games played on a poor, stupid native."

Eros was shaking his head, saying, "No. No."

Psyche ignored the protest. "Now show me your reality," she cried. "Bestial or beautiful, I do not care, so long as it is the truth."

He bent his head, shivering as he dissolved the spell, and then looked up. "I am Eros. This is the truth."

There was a long pause while Psyche studied him and then averted her eyes. "You are shockingly beautiful," she said, her voice disapproving. "It is almost painful to look at you."

"I don't like it any better than you do," Eros snapped.

"I didn't say I didn't like it," Psyche soothed, seeing the hurt in his face. But she found a kind of twisted amusement in his echo of her recoil and could not help adding, "It's rather a shock when your mouth moves, though. Like a marble mask in action. I almost expect it to crack."

"You don't find me attractive?" Eros asked, his voice uncertain, his exquisite features reflecting every emotion—first relief, then indignation, and finally an anxious doubt.

Psyche sighed. "If I close my eyes and listen to your voice, you are my own dear Teras again and I love you with all my heart." She paused, sighed again, and gazed at him soulfully. "And if I could put your head on a shelf on the wall as an ornament, I would admire it with all my heart—"

"Put my head on a shelf for an ornament?" Eros echoed indignantly.

"Well, what else is so much beauty good for?" she asked.

"Nothing," he said, looking away. "Nothing at all, except to cause pain and more pain. Do you understand now why Teras said it was not good to look upon him? You loved Teras, believing him ugly beyond bearing. I know that. Do you love me? Can you love me?"

Psyche sank down beside him and took his hands in hers. She had been half jesting. In trying to absorb the shock of his beauty, she had forgotten how much her own had hurt her.

"I do not know," she admitted. "But I have already loved a monster in a black cloud and a very ordinary native man because both were kind and merry of heart and cared for me—I mean for what I am, not for the mask of my face. Will you be kind and caring and laugh with me?"

He looked at her sidelong from under his long lashes and said mournfully, "I care so much I cannot live without you. My kindness and indifference to your appearance you must judge for yourself. But I cannot be merry of heart—not when I know you want to put my head on a shelf."

Psyche had raised her hand to his cheek in a gesture of comfort. That hand, cupping his face tenderly, had tensed a trifle by the time he stopped speaking, but she did not jerk it away. She used it to lift his head a little, so she could look earnestly into his eyes.

"But I will place your head in the very best position," she said cajolingly. "And dust it frequently, I promise."

Upon which they both burst out laughing and Psyche flung herself into his arms, crying, "Ter—At—oh, curse you, Eros. I must learn a new name and my tongue will be tripping and stumbling the whole way home."

"Beloved, beloved," he breathed, clutching her tight, "I do not care what name you call me."

Their lips came together, and it was the same mouth, which wakened the same fire in her. "Need we hurry back?" she murmured after a moment, her lips against his, her eyes closed, feeling with joy the back of his neck, the shape of his shoulders—a shape she knew so well.

For answer, he undid her cloak and dropped it beside the blanket he had cast off when he sat up. Then he began to undo the tie of her tunic. She returned the compliment, opening her eyes to stare at the strong, white column of his neck, closing them again to feel the little V where his collarbones joined. Teras's collarbones—Eros's collarbones.

They took off their clothing, slowly at first, savoring their new/old knowledge of one another, and then hurrying when the cold air of early morning nipped at their increasingly naked bodies. Then they huddled together under blanket and cloak on the pallet of brush and grass that Eros had gathered for Psyche the night before, warming each other, soon shivering with joy and eagerness instead of with cold.

Eager as she was, Psyche could not yet bring herself to join their bodies. Although the hungry mouth between her legs gaped and she could feel Eros, hard and hot, against her closed thighs, she could not yet open them and grasp the pleasure she craved. Her heart had to understand what her mind knew, that Teras and Eros were one, or within herself she would always be soiled, a mindless, soulless, thing who needed a man and took the nearest one.

She closed her eyes and stroked Eros's body, feeling each curve, each muscle, caressing his buttocks and the hot shaft that jumped and quivered with her touch. She opened her eyes and lifted her head as she touched him so that she could see the effect of her caresses mirrored on that perfect countenance. Again and again she looked, then closed her eyes and felt blindly with hands and lips, listened to the voice she knew so well sighing praises and joy, moaning softly with passion. Slowly she melded together what she heard with her ears, felt with her hands, and saw with her eyes, bonding forever the being she knew as Teras with the face of Eros.

"Psyche," he pleaded, brokenly, "let me—"

"Yes," she whispered, at last drawing him into her, "my Teras, my Eros, my beloved."

He gasped as his shaft was sheathed, stiffened, and cried out in protest when she gave him no time to master the violent thrill of pleasure that pulsed through him as he was swallowed by that moist and hungry mouth. He tried to hold her still, but she writhed against him, desiring only to bring immediate fruition to the agony of pleasure for which she had waited too long. He cried out again, despairing, as the convulsions of his climax wrenched him, but she did not hear, did not care. She was singing her own bursting joy.

Without a word exchanged, both slept, plunging into the depths so far and so fully that when they woke hours later they were still entwined—and stiff and sore with lying so still for so long. There was a lot of laughter as they disentangled themselves, washed, and ate. Later they made love again, playfully, leisurely, and with the rich satisfaction of those who know well what will give the greatest pleasure to the other. Psyche had only to close her eyes for memory to instruct her on how to bring Eros to a peak of pleasure, calm him again, and build his passion still higher. And that second loving confirmed her acceptance of him as the body and the mind that she had long known and loved without seeing.

Unfortunately, when her eyes were open, Psyche still

felt a sense of shock whenever she saw Eros's face, and she could not always completely control her expression. The widened eyes, parted lips, and sharply indrawn breath were particularly apparent in the quiet camp when Eros returned from hunting in the late afternoon with a brace of birds at his belt. The sun had been full on his face when he stepped into the clearing, and Psyche looked up at the sound of moving brush. Her gasp was so loud, he heard it across the campsite.

"If you really cannot bear my face," he said, "I could be Atomos again—or wear a veil."

Psyche laughed. "Oh, no. I will become accustomed soon enough. It would have been the same, you know, if you had been a monster, all warts and with a single eye and snaggle teeth. I would have been startled each time I saw you for a few days, and then I would not have noticed." She pursed her lips thoughtfully. "I *think* I prefer you as you are."

To her surprise, he did not laugh but looked troubled. "You know what beauty is worth," he said slowly, "and you know I know. You will not be jealous of me."

Psyche cocked her head. "No more than you will be of me," she said tartly. "I hope you did not believe that I would go meekly back to the lodge and remain a prisoner there forever. I understand that you have no home of your own, Eros, and that you cannot impose a common native on Aphrodite—"

"No. Psyche—"

She overrode his voice. "I understand, I say. I will be content to stay at the shop, out of her way, and you can visit me when Aphrodite is willing. I acknowledge her power and her right to being first with you, but I will no longer endure the isolation in which I have lived to pacify her."

"Psyche, Psyche, do not blame Aphrodite for my own foolishness, my own greediness." Eros knelt beside her, put one hand on her shoulder and lifted her face with the other. "She is my friend, my benefactor. You do not know how long we have been together—and still she is *not* first with me. She cannot bring meaning or desire to my life. Only you, my soul, can do that. But fair is fair. It is not her fault that I kept you in the lodge."

"Nothing is ever Aphrodite's fault," Psyche said flatly.

Eros laughed. "Oh, yes it is. She is the most mischievous little devil and loves to create trouble and then leave me to sort it out for her. But she did not turn the lodge into your prison, I did."

"Are you telling me you could have brought me to Olympus when you took me from the altar?"

"No, I first took you to the lodge and wore the black cloud because of my promise to Aphrodite to punish you for refusing to worship her and because I did not want you to see me as Eros. You cannot blame Aphrodite for that, nor for her judgment against you and your father. I explained long ago the need of the great mages for the offerings of their worshippers. If the priests and priestesses are defied, the sacrifices would soon stop."

"Yes, I understand that. I think it unfair, but I agree also it is better than having the great mages living among us and bedeviling us far worse."

Eros looked indignant. "Aphrodite is the least exigient, demands the least from her worshippers, but you must admit that you and your father went too far."

"I am not quarreling with Aphrodite's right, I tell you. Aphrodite's quarrel with my father is settled. He is the most devout of her worshippers, and all of Iolkas bows down to the priestess of her temple. This has nothing to do with me. No one in Iolkas will know that I am no longer the prisoner of a monster. I will never return there—"

"You do not still long for your home, Psyche?"

"I never did long for it, only to rid myself of the guilt of hearing in my mind my mother and sisters wail for me. They do so no longer, and I certainly do not wail for them. However, I would like very much to have friends. I have been told all the folk of Olympus are beautiful. I will live at the shop, or if that is impossible, find another place. Perhaps in Olympus I will be ordinary enough—"

Eros laughed heartily. "No, love. I am afraid you will set on edge the teeth of any woman who cares about beauty—and who except you and Aphrodite do not? They will not permit their men to visit you and will not come themselves out of envy. So you will have to swallow your stiff native pride and come to live with me in Aphrodite's house. *There* you will be quite ordinary."

"That is not very funny," Psyche said. "If you think you can force me to stay only in the lodge by insisting I live in Olympus in the one place I am sure I am not welcome—"

"Why should you think you would not be welcome in Aphrodite's house? I assure you she will not be jealous of your beauty."

"Of course not. She is far more beautiful than I. You jackass! She is jealous of you."

"Of me?" Eros shook his head, his mouth turned down as if he tasted or smelled something foul. "No. Aphrodite does not desire me, nor do I desire her. We are old friends only. I swear to you, she does not care whom I take into my bed."

"I daresay she does not," Psyche replied, sighing. "But there is more between us than coupling, Eros. When you were Teras, we worked together and laughed together. I expect the same of Eros, and I do not think Aphrodite will welcome a rival for your attention living in her home."

He took Psyche into his arms. "You will not be rivals," he murmured, holding her against him. "You will be friends. Aphrodite is lonely too. She has me, but I am a man and there are many things I do not understand. You are a woman and can give her much that I cannot."

CHAPTER 23

Psyche did not contest Eros's statement that Aphrodite would be her friend, although she did not believe it. However, on the slow journey back to Olympus—neither was in any hurry to interrupt the idyll in which they were living—her confidence in her hold on Eros grew. And as Psyche became more secure, more certain of the depth of his need for her, which seemed, strangely, even greater than Teras's need had been, her concern about Aphrodite diminished.

After a week of sharing the Olympian's house, that concern increased again—not because Psyche feared that Aphrodite could affect her relationship with Eros, but because she saw that he had spoken the truth. Although her life was full of lovers, Aphrodite was lonely. Psyche tried once or twice to extend a friendly gesture but was rebuffed. Strangely, Aphrodite's withdrawal seemed not one of hatred or contempt. Had she been native rather than Olympian, Psyche would have judged Aphrodite's emotion to be fear.

First Psyche resolved to let well enough alone. Aphrodite did not seem to seek to make trouble for her, nor was she ever discourteous when they met by accident, even when Eros was not present. And Psyche was busy with her own concerns: her shop, her small spells to enhance her lotions and potions—oddly, her well never seemed empty or aching now—her duties as householder of the lodge to which Eros took her by translocation whenever she wished to be there, and, contrary to what Eros had told her, many new acquaintances. None could be called friends, but having Eros, Psyche did not seek that. They were interesting people to whom she could speak and who regarded her—for the most part—with either casual approval or indifference.

Thus Psyche did her best to ignore the problem of Aphrodite, avoiding her when she could and leaving it to Eros to apportion his time between them. She never felt jealous or neglected, but she knew Eros was disappointed by the coldness between her and Aphrodite, and one day when she came upon Aphrodite sitting alone by the fountain in the room painted as a garden, on an impulse, instead of turning away, she went boldly up to her.

"Lady," she said, "why will you not allow me to be your friend? For Eros's sake, cannot you look upon me kindly? I hope you are not jealous of me. I am not jealous of you."

Aphrodite smiled, but her blue eyes were sad, lending for a moment an odd look of maturity to her almost childlike face. "No, I am not jealous. Eros is a better friend to me now than he has ever been. He is awake, alive. He not only listens to me but hears, and you have not turned him into a pious prude. He truly enjoys our little games—"

"Then why do you close me out? I am very ready to love you. Can you not love me?"

"I dare not," Aphrodite replied. "Before Eros touched my heart, no one could hurt me. Now what hurts him hurts me. I cannot allow you to wound me too. It is enough that Eros is my only friend, and you will kill him."

"Kill him?" Psyche echoed and then asked, "How?" her voice cracking in the sudden dryness of her mouth and throat. "He is sure of me now, happy. I know he is. Do you foresee some change in me—"

"Of course I do. You are native—"

Psyche took a step forward, her eyes blazing with fury. "That does not make me foul or bestial—"

"No, of course it does not," Aphrodite said, her eyes steady on Psyche's. "It makes you short-lived. You have heard me wish you were an Olympian and you have been angry, thinking I believed you lesser, but it was not that. The years of an Olympian are very long. I am ten times your age and still little more than a girl, and I will live, oh, I do not know how much longer. Eros is much older than I." She shifted her gaze and stared blankly into nothing for a moment, then sighed. "But when you die, he will die too."

"No!" Psyche exclaimed. "Why should he? He will cling all the closer to you. We both know that I will grow old. We have talked about it. Eros swears he will love me just as much when I am old and ugly." Her voice trembled; she was not as sure of that as she should have been. "He is perfectly cheerful about it," she assured Aphrodite.

"Of course he is perfectly cheerful," Aphrodite snarled. "He intends to stick a knife in his throat the moment your spirit flies, so he can go with you to the Mother."

"Stick a knife in his throat?" Psyche echoed faintly. "No. No. Why should he do such a thing? He has you. There will be other women—"

"There will be no other woman. Eros has gone that route many times and found it led nowhere he wanted to be. He is *old,* I tell you. He came with Kronos from our homeland before ever I was born. In all those years, he never found a lover who would live with him in peace—only you. He is tired of living . . . But I am not, and when he dies I will be alone . . . all alone, as I was before I took him in. Do you still wonder why I do not love you?"

Psyche stared down at her, half horrified, half pleased about what she had said, and thoroughly exasperated too. "But Aphrodite, what do you want me to do? I will gladly beg Eros or even command him not to harm himself if I should die, but I doubt he will obey. Be reasonable, do. I cannot help dying. I do not want to die . . ."

"You do not need to die," Aphrodite said softly. "All you need is courage. In the underworld is a shrine of the Mother of which Persephone is priestess. On my word, Persephone will take you there. If the Mother chooses, you can have an Olympian's length of life. She has granted that to others, to Hecate and to Heracles and to Semele—"

"And if She does not choose?"

"You will die, there at the altar. It has befallen others who were rejected." Aphrodite shrugged. "That is why I have not spoken of this before."

Psyche stood looking at the goddess. Was this some last, desperate effort of Aphrodite's to be rid of her? No, for it could accomplish nothing, except to tear Eros from her sooner. Now that she thought about it, Psyche realized what Aphrodite had said about Eros's plan to die with her must be the truth. He had said again and again that she was his soul and he could not be parted from her. Nor did she relish the long, slow decline to her own death. For all she had said about the uselessness of beauty, Psyche thought ruefully, she was not so indifferent to growing old and ugly as she should be.

She could wait. She had many years before she

needed to worry about any decline. Even as the thought came to her, Psyche knew she could not. The Gifts of the Mother, no matter how perilous, must be taken when and as offered; they were not subject to bargain or compromise. And Psyche grew surer by the moment that she had not come into the chamber of her own will and that, likely, Aphrodite had not spoken of her own will. The Olympian looked strange—older—and she was uncharacteristically still and silent.

If this was the Mother's doing, then Psyche knew she had no choice. In the past, the Mother's urgings had brought her only good, but this—was this the calling in of many favors? Was she to be a sacrifice? Psyche shivered, knowing that the Mother was not some great mage who under his or her power was only human. A mage could be fooled or bribed; the Mother could only be obeyed or defied. And yet there was a small chance, Psyche thought, that she was reading too much into some ploy of Aphrodite's.

"Lady Aphrodite," she said, "if I succeed in this last task you have set me, will you then welcome me as a friend, as an equal?"

Aphrodite rose from her chair and held out her hand. "I have long known you for my equal or my better, Psyche. I fear you because you, like Eros, could bind my heart and hurt me. How could I let myself love you and then watch you fade and die? I do not seek such pain. I still think Eros is a fool to love you. But if you come from the Mother renewed and accepted, I will welcome you back to my house with open arms and into my heart with no reservations."

"Then I will go to the underworld," Psyche said slowly.

* * *

Psyche had not yet decided, even when she stood in the great hall of Plutos, clenching her teeth to keep them from chattering with fear, whether she was truly following the inspiration of the Mother or simply leaping after the lure of immortality dangled before her. Had Aphrodite sent her to Persephone to make her whole or to be rid of her?

Certainly the Olympian had done everything she could to ease Psyche's way to Plutos. She had sent Eros on an errand to a native temple and had arranged with Hermes to have Psyche transported. Now Psyche realized, feeling even more frightened, she had been so locked into her own doubts and reasonings that she did not even know whether her return had been arranged.

Her gaze fixed on Persephone, who had been so gentle to her less Gifted mother in the field behind the lodge. There was nothing gentle in her now. She might have been modeled by stone-working Hades from the same rock that made up the white pillars of the hall, and locked within that rigid exterior was a bubbling, seething cauldron of power that she somehow kept leashed. If the queen of the Dead knew anything about Aphrodite's intentions, no sign of that knowledge appeared in her exquisite face—and Psyche was not about to ask her any questions.

She listened to Psyche's request—made in Aphrodite's name—and glanced at her husband. Inside, Psyche shivered harder. His black eyes were bottomless pools that took in light and returned nothing; his face might have been carved from the gray stone of the cavern. Yet Persephone showed no fear and felt none. Psyche set her teeth harder. What had she to fear who held within her a volcano of earth-power, blood-power?

"You are the priestess," Hades said, in response to

his wife's look. His voice was like stone grating on stone.

Persephone nodded at him and turned to Psyche. As she met the gaze of those clear, gold eyes, behind which flickered just a little red from the tongues of power that lashed out from their confinement, Psyche shuddered visibly. If the Mother offered her the power that manifested itself as that red-brown roiling violence, the cap would seal her well. And even if the Mother could tear off that cap or break it, Psyche knew she could not accept such power. It would sear away her gentle, shimmering mist, and she would be so changed as not to be Psyche anymore. Was that what Aphrodite desired? Would Eros be repelled and reject a being that held so much violence?

If she saw her petitioner's doubts, Persephone ignored them. All she said was, "We must go at once. You cannot remain here long because you must not eat or drink in Plutos. You must be blindfolded, too. To see too much here might also bind you to the underworld, and that would not suit you or Aphrodite, whom Hades and I always wish to please."

Were those last words an answer to the questions she had not asked, Psyche wondered. It was enough to keep her from backing away as Persephone rose from her throne and came toward her. And, actually, she was not sorry to submit to having her eyes bound. The great cavern in which the twin thrones of Hades and Persephone stood was terrifying to her. Immensely high, and dimly lit by flaring torches, here the only bright spots were Persephone herself, the two great thrones, gilded and bejeweled, and on either side beyond the thrones, giant gates of gleaming brass. Psyche did not want to see herself go beyond those gates. Although she knew she could not be more in the underworld than she already was, she felt that when those gates closed on her, it would be forever.

It was already too late, she told herself, and with grim determination she went where she was led. A small relief was granted in that she heard no clang of metal, and when, in her judgment, she had been led far beyond the distance that would take her through the gates, she was warned she must climb up.

That was a welcome warning, and she grasped eagerly at a rope guide that was presented to her hand. She started to climb wide steps and had just begun to wonder why the dead needed a rope to guide them when a rushing sound she had been hearing changed to the howling of a thousand thousand souls in torment. Psyche froze and heard within that sound an echo of Eros's voice calling her name. She cried out in answer and would have turned back then, but Persephone's strong hand fastened on her shoulder and urged her up.

"In Plutos," Persephone said, "you do not look back. You *never* look back. The crying is the wind, only the wind."

And, indeed, so strong a gale swept over the top of the stairs Psyche climbed that, unprepared, she might have been whirled away, except for strong hands that clamped on her arms and drew her up and thrust her forward into the teeth of the gale—and out into the sunshine. She knew she felt the sun, for it warmed her—it had been cold and still in the cavern until the gale caught her—and she smelled growing things, and a faint breeze lifted her hair.

The warmth did not touch her inner being. The assurance she had gained from Persephone's seemingly casual remark that Aphrodite did not desire Psyche to be caught in the underworld had vanished with that half-heard crying of her name in Eros's voice. Surely that was only in her mind. Eros could not be in

Plutos—or could he? Once he had heard her cry for help all the way from Iolkas to Olympus and had come for her. In the darkness behind her blindfolded eyes, Psyche wondered, am I, all unaware, crying so loud for help?

They walked, Psyche was sure, along a smooth, graveled path for a while and then there were more steps, not many this time, and the warmth of the sun vanished. In another moment, the blindfold was removed.

She was in the shrine of a temple, such a temple as Psyche had never seen, all of white marble, polished until it shone softly and was smoother than the finest woven silk. The altar and the Goddess were bedecked with gold and jewels enough to blind one, even in the subdued light. But Psyche hardly saw them. She saw the face of the Mother. Such a face! Not beautiful at all! Not beautiful, and yet it held enormous beauty. Strong. Enduring.

"Mother," Psyche said, forgetting Persephone, forgetting all her fear, "I have come partly because I am a vain and fearful mortal and partly because two beings that I love will be hurt by that mortality. I do not know what is best for all of us. I have been very happy of late, and I would like that happiness to continue, but if the face I see shows what You are, then I am content to leave to You what is best. Only, I am frail and mortal. I am not strong, like Your favorite daughter, Persephone. Be gentle with me?"

She raised her hands, not like a priestess invoking, but like a child begging to be lifted into a parent's arms. That grace was not accorded her, but from the Mother's outstretched hand poured a shimmering splendor, an opalescent mist that touched her, caressed her, as a mother might stroke the hair and face and body of a beloved child. Psyche had no sense of drawing in, of the "gathering of power" that was forbidden to her people. Nonetheless, power filled her, not only the well within, but her flesh and bones and blood. She knew she would always be full, always, no matter how much she used—so long as that usage did not offend the Mother.

She looked eagerly up toward that powerful face, hoping that more would be granted her—not more power; she would never have need, she thought, of half of what had been so freely given—but of some understanding, some deep comprehension of what was, is, and needs to be. Behind her there was a bawling, a roaring. For an instant she strove to shut it out, but one voice—ah, that voice would call her back, not only from the grave, but from eternal bliss.

Psyche whipped around, crying, "Eros!"

She could have sworn that as she turned away from immortal enlightenment she heard a deep, but female, chuckle. It was something about which she would puzzle and chuckle herself for the rest of her very, very long life. At the moment, however, Persephone's shriek of "Hades!" and the sight of her slender Eros grappling with the stone giant that was the king of the Dead was far more compelling.

As one, Psyche and Persephone leapt out of the temple and down the steps, crying in chorus, "Stop that!"

Hades's arms fell away and Eros rushed to gather Psyche to him, crying, "My soul, my soul, suddenly you were gone. I could not feel you within me. I could see you, but I could not feel you. Where were you?"

Psyche's head turned toward the shrine, and then she looked back at Eros and smiled. "With the Mother, I think." She kissed him, wondering where she would be now and if she still would be Psyche if he had not called her, but all she said was, "How did you know I was here?"

"Aphrodite called me back. She was half mad with

grief and fear, regretting what she had done. Still, I think if I had not been so frantic to come here and get you, I would have killed her. She had a spell all ready to give me and sent me after you, but when I arrived, Hades would not tell me where he had hidden you—"

"I told you I had *not* hidden her," Hades said indignantly. "I told you that several times, very loudly."

Persephone cocked her head, and giggled. "I think you did not use your full powers, my love. I know you can be very persuasive."

Hades cast a glance at her that flicked up her body like a single bright flame. White teeth shone behind his neat black beard. "Perhaps I am more persuasive to those who are stricken by my charms," he retorted, with an answering chuckle. Then he shrugged, winced, and rubbed his shoulder where Eros had hit him in their struggle. "Eros seems immune. He would not listen to a word I said, and then he heard Psyche's voice, and before I could lay a hand on him, he was away and up the stair." He shrugged again and grinned. "He runs much faster than I do."

"You are growing a little thickabout, my love," Persephone said, reproachfully.

"Because I cannot pry you away from the table," Hades retorted. "I do not understand how you can still walk."

Psyche was staring from one to the other. Was this the awesome queen of the Dead? The stone-hard king of Plutos? Had the Mother worked some magic, or was it only the ending of her own fear that changed models of terror into charming people who loved each other? Then Hades turned his eyes to her, those deep black pools, but he did not look hard and gray; he looked kind.

"Do you have your answer, Psyche?"

"Indeed, Hades, I do. Thank you for keeping Eros

from drawing me away from the Mother too soon."
She turned to Persephone. "And thank you for allowing me to come here."

Smiling, Persephone embraced her and shook her
head. "She loves you," she said. "You needed no inter-
vention of any priestess. You could have drawn Her to
any shrine, or to anyplace from which you called Her."

"Perhaps," Psyche agreed, "but that does not make
your kindness less."

Her eyes flashed around the fertile valley below the
temple, took in the men and women working the rich
crop, the herds dappling the hillsides. She remembered
the blindfold and that Persephone had forgotten it in
her anxiety over the fighting men. With a smile, she
drew Eros closer.

"I have been very frightened," she said to Persephone, "by your awesome majesty and Hades's iron
command of his dark and gloomy world. I admit you
have been kind to me, but this is a dreadful place." She
smiled around at the peaceful, sunlit scene. "Just dreadful!"

Eros grinned also. "Yes, I can fully understand your
reluctance to have visitors. No one would be able to
understand how you endured life in so horrible a
place."

"You have not seen half the beauty of my realm,"
Hades said eagerly. "Under the earth are such glories—
and good hunting, too."

"Good hunting?" Eros repeated, smiling with obvious interest at Hades.

"No," Psyche said. "This is no time for hunting.
Have you forgotten Aphrodite?"

Eros shrugged and sighed. "My soul and my conscience. Thank you, Hades. I hope you will invite me
again, but we must return. My friend is grieving for us,
and Aphrodite should never grieve."

To that Hades and Persephone agreed at once, and they all walked together down the smooth, sunlit path, through the wide mouth of a cave, braced against the howling wind that rushed in and buffeted them until they got down the stair and entered the huge cavern that was Hades' throne room.

When she reached the foot of the dais, Psyche realized that an opalescent drop within her had grown very large. She knew immediately that it was a translocation spell and that Aphrodite had spoken the exact truth. She had arranged for Hermes to give her the return spell; if the Mother gave enough power, Psyche could use it and would be welcomed in every way. Holding Eros, she invoked it. A shining veil enveloped them and parted to show the fountain in the garden room—she felt not the smallest chill, not the slightest weakness; in fact, the shimmering splendor within her was no less.

"Beloveds, oh my beloveds, you are come back to me," Aphrodite cried, jumping up from her chair, and her voice mingled with the happy cries of the children she had gathered around her in her need for comfort.

Both Psyche and Eros embraced her, and she kissed both and then stood holding a hand of each, laughing like bells pealing. "So we are bound together," she said, "love and beauty and the soul."

"And none of us will ever be alone or lack a friend ever again," Psyche murmured, at last as sure of Aphrodite as she was of Eros.